Gift of the Shaper

"An exceptional series opener ..."

–Kirkus Reviews

"...a rollicking good read that is for the fantasy fiction lover in all of us. ... packed full of adventure, action, suspense, and horror. ...akin to the classics of fantasy fiction from Tolkien and modern-day George RR Martin.

–Seattle Book Review

"The Highglade series is nothing short of pure wonder. This is what fantasy should be. D.L. Jennings has created a rich, layered world that readers will love to get lost in. A must read for any fan of fantasy."

–Luke Newman, Amazon bestseller, and author of "the LEGENDARY series."

Awaken the Three

"*Awaken the Three* is an epic fantasy tale of creation and destruction, of gods and mortals...high drama and suspense."

–Foreword Reviews

"*Awaken the Three* is a stand-alone, action-filled mytho-fantasy epic, and those who sense and savor its deftly woven story strands will doubtless rush to read the earlier book in the Highglade series and excitedly await the next installment.

–Feathered Quill Book Reviews

Days of the Dark

DAYS OF THE DARK

BOOK THREE OF THE HIGHGLADE SERIES

D.L. JENNINGS

Days of the Dark: Book Three of the Highglade Series

© 2024 by D. L. Jennings

Editors: David Remy, Mary Ward Menke
Cover Illustration: Panjooolart
Cover and Interior Design: Emma Elzinga

Indigo River Publishing
3 West Garden Street, Ste. 718
Pensacola, FL 32502

www.indigoriverpublishing.com

Ordering Information:

Quantity Sales: Special discounts are available on quantity purchases by corporations, associations, and others. For details, contact the publisher at the address above.

Orders by US trade bookstores and wholesalers: Please contact the publisher at the address above.

Printed in the United States of America

Library of Congress Control Number: 2023923809

Hardcover ISBN: 978-1-954676-76-3
Paperback ISBN: 978-1-954676-75-6
eBook ISBN: 978-1-954676-77-0

First Edition

With Indigo River Publishing, you can always expect great books, strong voices, and meaningful messages. Most importantly, you'll always find . . . *words worth reading.*

For Mom.
I'll always remember you as strong.

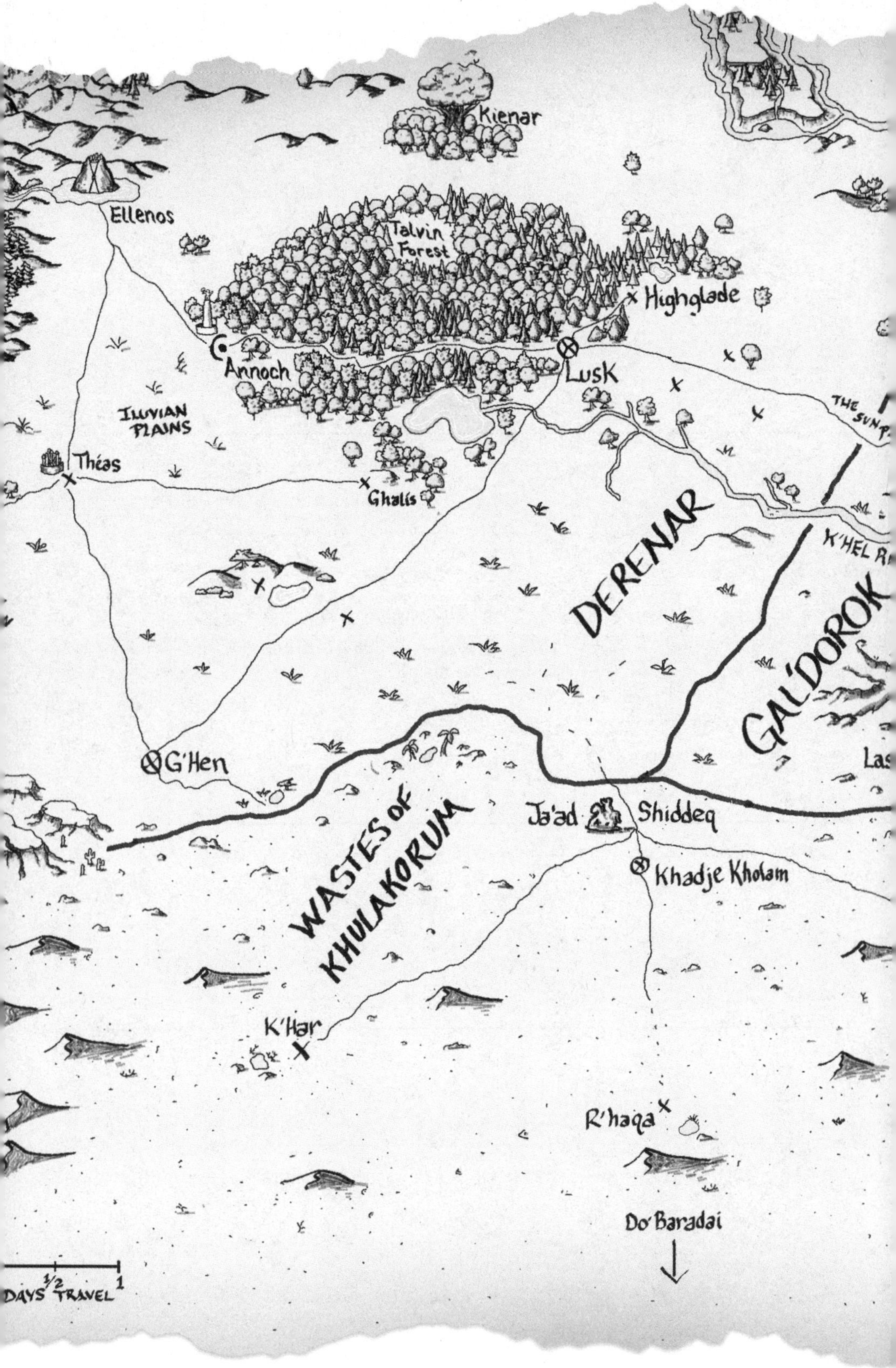

Kienar

Ellenos

Talvin
Forest

Highglade

Annoch

Lusk

ILUVIAN
PLAINS

THE SUN T...

Théas

Ghalis

DERENAR

K'HEL R...

GALÚDOROK

G'Hen

WASTES of
KHULAKORUM

Ja'ad   Shiddeq

Las...

Khadje Kholam

K'Hₐʳ

R'haqa

Do Baradai

½   1
DAYS TRAVEL

N
W E
S

GAL'BEHEM

Khala Valur

Ghal Thurai

Haidan'Shar

TASHKAR SEA

Menat

THE SPEARS

© Capital City
⊗ Major City
X Village

0   ½   1
DAYS' TRAVEL

HALMES '19

Contents

Ten thousand tons of earth pulsed with power and blood.

Few things in this world are more painful than birth. Whether it be the old devoured by the new, or simply a passing of power, there is one thing all births have in common: every one comes at a price. Some are paid swiftly, some over time, but all of them come due—and all of them bring pain.

Far beneath the surface, where Ghal Thurái once stood, a new power grew. It was not new in the sense of taking a first breath, or seeing the sun for the first time; it was new in the way that two rivers merge to form one: through violent clashing of tides blending together to form a stronger current.

. . . Yet even the strongest current is at the mercy of stone.

This current, however, was formed by stone.

This current embraced it.

This current grew.

And soon it would rival the gods.

Prologue

MIERA'S BREATHS CAME IN GASPS, quick and short. She was dying, and there was no way out—she had made sure of that herself when she'd sealed off the Otherworld. Another burst of the Breaker's power surged through her body. Her vision went white as she dropped to her knees, putting out a hand to keep from collapsing. The warm taste of copper filled her mouth.

It was never supposed to be this way.

She blinked away the pain as she retched. The ground below her, soaked with blood and spit, only seemed to confirm what she already knew: this was the end. She felt it as it came: the emptiness, the darkness, the pain. She let it come, greeting it with the weariness of a thousand lifetimes.

...But before the shadows could swallow her, something reached out.

Hope. Like the faintest glimmer of a distant star—a glimmer that took the form of an idea. She choked on fresh blood as she laughed at its absurdity. The possibility of succeeding was so remote that it was almost not even worth trying—but there was so much more at stake than just failure. She knew right then that she would not give up—could not give up.

No. This, she must do.

She braced herself. The pain came again, along with the sickening fear that she might be wrong. She closed her eyes as fresh pain flooded her body. It was too much to bear.

It came again, and she felt her fire going out. She tried to cry out as she felt herself being torn apart, but she was too weak for even that. The next one would kill her; of that she was certain. She readied herself. Sickness rose in her throat with her fear and her doubt. And as the power of the Breaker ripped through her once again, the light inside the Shaper went out. The only thing to leave her lips was a breath—her final, dying breath . . .

. . . and on that breath rode the hopes of the Athrani.

Chapter 1

Ghal Thurái

It awoke. All was darkness, yet the creature knew there was so much more to it. Strange sensations clawed their way into his mind like rats: indiscriminate, frenzied, sharp. The smell of soil and the feel of blood, the hunger that came with it. These things the creature knew, but he did not know why he knew them; he had lain there, dormant beneath the earth for a long, long time. Or, at least . . . part of him had.

There was another part—small, fragile—that knew things, too; a part that understood why things were the way they were, a part that understood the wills of men and their curious lust for power, though their lives were fleeting and small. It understood death. What it did not understand, however, was how it had come to be.

Three parts of a new whole were united as one, through blood and stone, death and rebirth. They—he—moved toward the surface, toward the light. The earth split, making way for the hands that reached upward, pulling a gargantuan body up from the ground. The face that breached the surface was wracked with anger, its eyes tempered with confusion.

All around him was death; the only thing he knew was that he had caused it. He felt no remorse, though, just as one does not mourn the passing of flies, or lament the turning of leaves. These things were all necessary, inevitable.

He was inevitable.

✦ ✦ ✦

Beneath the ruins of Ghal Thurái, the chovathi stirred. They were waking from their slumber of rebirth, of death and new life. They began to crawl toward the surface, bigger, stronger, new. Hundreds, thousands, coming to life and to conquer.

The time had come at last.

He looked toward the heavens . . . and laughed.

Chapter 2

Wastes of Khulakorum

Sera

A COFFIN WAS NEVER SO HEAVY.

Seralith Edos groaned under the weight, cursing the fact that the man who'd raised her had never prepared her for this moment. He had done everything else for her: fed her, clothed her, given her a place at the forefront of the Valurian army, even positioned her to inherit a kingdom—yet he had never once brought up how to deal with his own death. She didn't know whether to mourn him or simply offer her respects. Would she succeed him? Should she step aside, and let one of the captains lead? Somehow the currency in which the man had dealt had never found itself on Sera's table. It angered her with every heavy step: death had come for him, and she was not yet ready to pay its toll.

Up ahead, she spied what would be his final resting place.

"There," she said, nodding. "By the alcove."

The men with her shuffled after her, following her lead toward the shores of the Tashkar sea.

✦ ✦ ✦

The journey from the east had been long, and had not been without its difficulties; transporting a body had been the easy part—it was traversing a desert that had proven hard—so, after a trek such as theirs, Sera welcomed the sweat that now beaded on her brow.

"Do it here," she said, "while we still have the light."

The six of them set the coffin down to the sound of waves. Behind them, the peaks of the Spears obscured the fading rays of the sun.

Their Khôl escorts nodded and set to work constructing a barge of lumber and fuel that would serve as the base for the pyre. The fact that Djozen Yelto was willing to part with such a scarce resource as wood at Sera's request was encouraging. The Wastes of Khulakorum provided few things, and lumber was at the bottom of the list. It was a good sign that the Djozen—de facto leader of the Tribes of the Sun beyond the Wastes—was willing to indulge her such a luxury.

+ + +

When they were finished building, Sera helped them load the casket onto the pile of wood. It seemed heavier now, though it all could have been in her mind. They pushed it off with a collective heave, and the whole thing began the slow journey out with the tide.

Stepping back, Sera felt a hand on her shoulder. It was Cavan Hullis, one of the Thurians that had been with her in Kienar. The captain's long, blond hair framed a chiseled jaw that made his blue eyes look like frost on a mountain peak.

"I didn't know him well," he said with a tight smile, "but his reputation was unsurpassed." He turned and crossed his arms across his chest, looking out across the sea. "He was brilliant, you know. Only ever thought of what it took to achieve victory. Nothing else seemed to matter."

She laughed, but there was no joy behind it. Captain Hullis's words were meant to comfort her, she knew, but they only succeeded in making it worse.

I had mattered to him, she thought. *Somehow. For some reason. I mattered.*

She had mattered enough to keep him from victory, too, she knew. The man had once abandoned an entire army for her when he thought that she'd been killed, lying there in a pool of her own blood beneath the branches of Kienar. He had never even told her why—and for some reason, she never thought to ask.

Sera watched as the casket floated out to sea, cloaked in the dark of the desert dusk. Hullis, the surest marksman out of all of them, set afire the tip of an arrow. He nocked it, aimed, and released. The shot was true, and the flame began to spread—haltingly at first, like the fire too doubted his death. Soon, though, that doubt—and the casket—would be nothing

5

more than ash.

A warrior's death deserved a warrior's burial, Sera knew, and there was none deserving of such a burial more than General Aldis Tennech, the Dagger of Derenar. The greatest leader that the Dorokian army had ever known. The only father she'd ever known.

Sera watched the flames as they burned. She was lost in their brilliance, as well as in the questions they brought: who would lead the army now to take Khala Val'ur? Could it be her? Was she ready? Was the Holder of the Dead to be trusted, or did the fallen god seek more than just a way to get back into the Otherworld?

All of those questions and more weighed heavily on Sera's mind. They were as heavy as Tennech's coffin had been, but their weight was somehow different. Challenging. Inviting.

She turned to the west and watched the setting sun that loomed low behind the mountaintops of the Spears, over the Wastes of Khulakorum. If anyone was suited to lead, she reasoned, it was her. Holder of the Dead be damned.

Chapter 3

Théas

Alysana

ALYSANA PULLED AT HER DRESS, hoping that the dagger concealed beneath it was hidden well enough. She'd had no other options, though: either she could come in unarmed, or she could be uncomfortable. She'd opted to go with the latter, but regretted not slipping an extra two or three daggers into her long black boots as well. G'henni men were easily distracted by such things.

"This way, my lady," grinned the large, dark-skinned man as he held the door open for her. He probably didn't think she saw the glance that he gave the rest of her too, but Alysana noticed a lot of things about the personal lackey of Ghaja Rus that would surprise even him.

"Thank you, Yuta," she said. "Always the gentleman." She rolled her eyes hard as she slipped past him.

After the slave auction, both Ghaja Rus and Yuta had taken a keen fascination with Alysana. They'd said it was because she was a fellow G'henni, but Alysana knew the real reason why—after all, one doesn't spend over a decade as a serving girl in an Annochian inn without realizing the true measure of one's attractiveness. The constant propositions from men, some even in front of their own wives, were enough to confirm the words of every other man who came through the Driving Steed: Alysana was beautiful. So it was no surprise that Yuta had agreed to give her a "personal tour" of the merchandise.

The darkness of the Théan night had just begun to settle in, and the two of them were walking over the cobbled stone that led from the common square in the City of a Thousand Towers. Alysana didn't like being here more than she had to—and right now, she had to.

"Where did you say they were being held?" she asked, trying to phrase the question as innocently and delicately as she could.

"In a cell further down, below the city," Yuta replied. "Though I don't know why a lady such as yourself would want to visit such a pigsty.

Nothing but vermin and waste down there." The clank of a metal lock echoed through the halls of the subterranean passage as Yuta pulled the barred iron door open. "But what the lady wants, the lady gets. This way," he said with a bow.

Alysana felt his eyes on her as she passed.

The two of them entered a cold interior with walls of crushed rock and burnt lime. Yuta had a torch in his hand ready to go, and he lit it as they entered, pulling the door shut behind him and relocking it. He jingled the keys on his key ring and smiled at Alysana. "Don't worry," he said. "Old Yuta will keep you safe."

Alysana forced a smile at his joke, running her finger over the outline of the dagger beneath her dress. "That puts my heart at ease, Yuta, thank you."

At this time of night, the prisoners were mostly asleep, and the silence of the underground passage was as thick and heavy as the walls that surrounded them. Alysana followed Yuta as he led them deeper in, talking to her in a friendly tone that Alysana found more patronizing than polite. He was droning on about the construction of the cells and how secure they were when they rounded the corner.

There were the prisoners. Probably twenty or so, by her count—but she was only interested in one. She looked at the iron bars of the cage, then over to Yuta.

"Aren't you afraid they'll break out?" Alysana asked with wide eyes, doing her best frightened maiden impression.

"Not at all," he said. "The iron on these doors is as thick as an Athrani whore's thighs, and the only way they would get out is with these." He flashed a grin as he patted the key ring.

Alysana turned her eyes, still wide with affected fright, back to the prisoners in their cages. "You are so brave," she said. It was revolting to her to have to say the words out loud, but the act had worked surprisingly well thus far. Now she just had one more thing to do and she would be done. It was risky, but she had a backup plan. "Do you think I could see one of them up close?"

Yuta paused, considering. He looked past her to the heavy iron bars that held the slaves, then back to her. "I suppose. But only as close as from the outside of the cell," he said. "Ghaja Rus would have my hide if one of them were to escape."

"Escape?" Alysana yelped. "Breaker above," she swore, "why would you want to let them escape?"

Her words carried well inside the echo-laden underground, bouncing off the smooth walls of the tunnel and catching the ears of the sleeping prisoners. Yuta looked at her, horrified, and motioned for her to be quiet.

"We are not supposed to be down here, my lady," he said in a desperate whisper.

Alysana ignored him for the faces of the men imprisoned within: some young, some old—yet each and every one lined with a cynical hardness that came from the life of being a slave. It did not take long to find exactly what she was looking for—the reason she had come down to this stinking prison and put on a performance for this wretched man. A wretched man who worked for an even more wretched man . . . a problem for another time, she knew.

Now, however, there was a solution to the problem for which she had come.

"I promise not to tell," she said sweetly, reaching down for the end of her dress. She began to pull it up, slowly, and watched Yuta's eyes as they traced her figure and her long, dark legs. "After all, you have been so accommodating."

"Well," he began, fidgeting. "I suppose—"

He never got to finish his sentence, but Alysana thought that she knew how it ended anyway. The gurgling sound he made as he slumped to the floor clutching his throat was the most pleasant thing he had done all night.

She had been right: her dagger was very well-concealed. She could feel the eyes of the prisoners on her as she put it away and knelt down to remove the key ring off Yuta's still-warm corpse. She stood up, moving the keys around and trying to figure out which one went to the cells. She stopped when she came to a simple iron key that looked like it had seen the most use and decided that was it. Walking over to the least-populated cell, she put the key in the lock and turned it. Click.

She looked at the men inside and gave them a cold, hard stare. "Any one of you thinking of trying anything, know that I am better with daggers than I am with keys. Understand?"

She saw several nods.

"Good. Now who else wants to escape?"

Chapter 4

Haidan Shar

Duna

FOOTSTEPS ECHOED THROUGH THE THRONE room of Haidan Shar as Duna walked through doors heavy enough to keep out an army. Inside, it was as cold as she remembered, and she found herself wishing she were anywhere else.

A solid mass of polished granite stood before her, the first throne that Haidan Shar had ever known. Illuminated by the skylight above, it looked the same as when it was first occupied by her father all those years ago.

"Remind me again why I'm here, Captain," she said over her shoulder to the brown-eyed Sharian behind her.

"I'm afraid it's a simple matter of ascendancy, Majesty," Captain Jahaz said. The word made Duna cringe. *Majesty*. In a matter of weeks she had gone from second-in-command of the Fist of Ghal Thurái to general of the armies of Gal'dorok—and now she found herself leading a kingdom. "Your place is on the throne, now."

Right. The real reason she was here: Lena. While the former Queen had always been headstrong and reckless, Duna had never expected that to bring about her younger sister's end; she had always been too strong for that. Lena was like a lightning storm: always striking too fast for anyone to react, and, by the time the damage was done, she had already moved on.

Only that had not happened this time. This time, Queen Lena's recklessness had gotten her killed—along with most of the Sharian army, whose funeral pyres still smoldered above the ruins of Ghal Thurái. The mountain-city had collapsed on top of them, ensuring that anyone caught beneath it had perished—Queen Lena included. With her death, the rule of Haidan Shar fell to their father's only surviving heir.

"Then at least tell me what comes next," Duna said with a sigh, unclasping her sheath and dropping it to the floor beneath her. She approached the throne.

"Well," Jahaz said, "there will be a coronation ceremony with all eleven captains attending—"

"I don't want any more fanfare," Duna interrupted, waving him off. She approached the throne and reached out to trace the gilded stone, unchanged since she was a girl. It was hers now.

"Noted. I am sure that we, ah, could find a way around it . . ."

"Gods, please," Duna said as she positioned herself on the throne.

She leaned back and pressed the heels of her palms into her eyes. She was so tired; they all were. The survivors had marched home over the last few days and fatigue was clawing at all of them.

"Your Grace," said Jahaz from behind her, his voice noticeably quieter. "May I speak freely?"

Duna's hands dropped back to her side and looked up at the captain. "Always," she said. Her head still swam.

The Sharian captain cleared his throat. "My people—your people," he corrected, "are used to Queen Lena's style of leadership. She was very hands-on, very insistent. Deliberate. Unwavering." He paused, as if searching for the right words. "I do not believe that you are the same type of leader. And I do not believe that to be a bad thing."

Duna took a breath and looked around.

She hadn't been here since she was a young woman—a girl really—before she and her sister had fought over Lena's suitor, Allyn. Duna had suspected that the man was only using her sister for political gain, and when she presented Lena with incontrovertible proof that he was, Lena had lost her mind. Having the man killed was something that Duna never regretted—she only regretted the fallout that came with it.

"I am not my sister," Duna finally said after a long silence. She looked back at Jahaz. "The rebuilding of our cities that must take place after the heavy losses we've taken will be slow. It will be painful. It will be something that Lena would not have been able to do." She paused. "For the sake of Haidan Shar, and all the armies of Gal'dorok, be glad that Queen

Lena is dead."

Decades old feelings burst forth like sudden light flooding a room, and Duna knew that her words were much more than just spite from being banished from the kingdom that was rightfully hers. She was always the rightful heir. She was the one fit for the throne. She was queen now, and she would be the one to bring them to glory.

And back to Ghal Thurái.

"Now send in Cortus Venn," she said. "We have an army to build."

Chapter 5

Khel-hârad,
Land of the Dead

Thornton

LIKE A SEARING HEADACHE, THE essence of the Breaker of the Dawn now burned in Thornton in a way that only Khyth power could. Born a Khyth through his mother, Thornton had inherited the power to move and reshape matter—"Breaking"—a power that originated from the Breaker himself. Yet the power Thornton once knew was but a drop of water in the vast ocean now roiling inside of him. It was a power that had helped shape the world and was undoubtedly enough to destroy it. Thornton could barely fathom it. He felt like a dam holding back a deluge.

Yet there was a part of him that was fighting back, resisting. How had the healer in Théas put it? Two halves of a whole? Like oil poured over water, there was a second power inside him that simply refused to acquiesce. His insides churned, and part of him feared what it might mean if they stopped. He could almost feel a smile from the ancient god hiding somewhere inside his mind.

"Are you alright?"

The words startled Thornton, as did the hand on his shoulder. He turned around to see the Traveler, the god who had brought him here to the Land of the Dead . . . or at least that's who he was now. Back in Théas, he had been the young man that Thornton knew as Rathma, with his fiery red hair and eyes and wind-whipped skin. But much like how the Breaker of the Dawn now inhabited Thornton, the Traveler now inhabited Rathma. Somehow Rathma had not been so lucky, though: his consciousness had been tossed overboard in a god-driven mutiny. Both men now had gods inside of them; one of them still maintained control . . . for now.

"I . . . I'm fine," Thornton said. He didn't mean it, but the Traveler didn't have to know that. The fact remained that Thornton wasn't sure how much to trust this god anyway. He had brought him into Khelhârad, yes, but he had concealed his reason for doing so. "We need to do what we came here to do."

The Traveler nodded. "Then you should start by picking that up."

The god was looking at Thornton's hammer, the Hammer of the Worldforge. Used along with the Anvil of the Worldforge in the creation of the world itself, the hammer had been previously used to seal the Otherworld—and had also just been used to break it back open. The Traveler had done so in order to free the Breaker and, ultimately, to defeat him, siphoning his power and essence into Thornton.

Something shifted inside Thornton as his unwilling passenger struggled against Thornton's nature. Maybe the hammer would quell it.

Thornton walked over and wrapped his fingers around the worn, wooden handle he'd known since boyhood. He felt the cool embrace that comes with welcoming an old friend . . . but he also felt something recoil inside of him, like a hand jerking away upon touching an open flame.

The Hammer of the Worldforge had been the instrument of the Breaker's undoing, forged before time by the Shaper of Ages herself and used to make the chains that bound the ancient god for millennia; it was what the Shaper had used to seal him in the Otherworld and what Thornton had used to subdue him. Thornton did not have to ask why he resisted it so fervently.

"I can feel him," Thornton began, "the Breaker, moving around inside. Struggling." He looked at the Traveler, whose red eyes were calm and still. "I'm afraid of what might happen if he wins."

The Traveler frowned. "That makes two of us."

"But I'm more afraid of what he did to Miera. To the Shaper."

The red-haired god let out a sigh. "Are you sure I cannot talk you out of going?" he asked.

Thornton didn't bother with a reply; he simply shook his head.

The Traveler looked uncomfortable at this decision. "Then there is something you must know: the reason we fought him here. Why we had to fight him here." Thornton turned around to face him. "He does not have power in this realm. It's how you and I were able to defeat him. He is much, much stronger than I am—stronger than any of the gods." He paused, searching for the right words. "If he yet stirs inside you, and you enter the Otherworld . . ."

Thornton finished the thought. "He'll regain his strength." It was a statement of fact, not a question.

The Traveler nodded gravely. "More so than you can imagine. If he was able to defeat the Shaper . . ." His voice trailed off.

The dark presence in Thornton shifted again. It felt like goading. Laughter.

"You can still come with me," the Traveler said.

Thornton looked at him, puzzled. "You're not coming?"

"I . . . can't," he answered.

"Why not?" Thornton asked.

The Traveler gave him a weak smile. "I was banished. I couldn't go back even if I tried." He looked around at the vast expanse of Khel-hârad, with its burning deserts and teeming jungles, its endless sky and boundless oceans, and sighed. "Although it is not bad here." Thornton had to agree. Of all the places to spend an eternity, this one was surely high up on the list. "But," the Traveler continued, "as much as I would love to stay, the fact is that there are other things in motion that require my . . . intervention."

"What do you mean?"

"My brother, the Holder of the Dead. I felt his spirit leave this place for the realm of the living," he said. "And I would guess that he does not mean to bring peace with him."

"And you mean to stop him," Thornton said, again as a statement of fact.

"I do." The Traveler nodded. "But he is stronger than I am. I cannot do it alone."

Thornton looked again at the crack in the Otherworld from his vantage point in the Land of the Dead. He felt the thrashing force within him, the Breaker of the Dawn. He thought of Miera, his beloved friend, who now embodied the goddess the Shaper of Ages. Who knows what cruelties she had endured at the hand of D'kane? He clenched his fist. Going after her might mean victory for the Breaker—but not going after her would mean essentially the same. She had sealed herself in the Otherworld with the Breaker to try and imprison him, but in doing so had doomed herself. The Breaker did not take to imprisonment well.

"I suppose," the Traveler went on with a furrowed brow, "that there are worse things than succumbing to the will of a god. Think of it like . . . falling asleep. Forever."

Thornton blinked. "Is that supposed to encourage me?"

"No," the Traveler said. "It's supposed to tell you not to lose. Now," he said, placing his hands on Thornton's shoulders and turning him to the ethereal crack between realms, "I believe you have a goddess to find."

Thornton stared at the shimmering break in reality that looked like translucent ice coming to a thaw. He thought wryly that he was getting good at traversing realms.

"I do," Thornton said without looking back. He moved toward the Otherworld. "And if I make it back, maybe you'll have help against your brother."

He heard a mirthless chuckle from the Traveler.

Thornton approached the ripples in the light. He stepped through, held his breath, and was gone.

Chapter 6

Théas

Kethras

KETHRAS WATCHED THE YOUNG KHYTH woman as she walked, hood down, exposing the red hair that stood in contrast to the muted gray of her body. The streets of Théas were lightly populated this early in the morning, and the light that fell around them let him appreciate how truly remarkable this woman was. When they had first met, Elyasha had been fleeing from her former master, D'kane, a ruthless Khyth whose ambitions had led him to the very gates of the Otherworld to challenge the Breaker himself—and when she had tried to stop D'kane with the help of her brother Thornton, the raw power that she managed to channel had almost torn her apart. Now, that power showed on her body in the cracked, charred skin that was the result of her Breaking. It had changed her—inside and out.

As if feeling his eyes on her, Elyasha stopped and looked back at him.

"What is it?" she asked, her swirling, green eyes a storm.

Even in the daylight, Kethras did not need his heat vision to tell him that Elyasha was pulsing with power. It was in her eyes and in her veins; it looked like fire flowing over a burning log.

"You are . . . different," he said.

Elyasha gave him a look that he did not fully understand, but it was one that he had seen before. He thought it meant "I agree with you," but in a condescending way. Human expressions were still difficult for him.

"You're just now noticing?" she replied. Even among her people, red hair and green eyes were somewhat rare, but now that she had gone through the Breaking, she was different from almost everyone else in the world.

"It is more than that," Kethras deflected. "Something inside you has . . . changed. Can you not feel it?"

Elyasha reflected for a moment. She cocked her head to one side and furrowed her brows. "I suppose," she said after a silence, and shrugged.

"A lot has happened since leaving the Otherworld. Finding out that I'm Khyth through my mother and Athrani through my father was surprising, yes, but it's nothing I can't handle now that I've had time to process it." She turned around and started walking again, back to the inn where they were to meet Alysana.

She was certainly taking it all in stride.

It worried him.

+ + +

Alysana had still not returned by the time dusk began to fall, but Kethras knew that she wasn't far. She had left the healer, Silus, quickly after the ritual to invoke the Traveler had been complete, citing "something that needs to be resolved." He was unsure of how long this "something" would take, but Alysana was a competent woman, and he knew she was able to handle herself. All that was left for them to do was wait, and then the three of them would make their way back to their respective cities.

. . . Or would they? Kethras glanced over at Elyasha.

"Yasha," he asked, getting her attention. She'd been sitting cross-legged on her bed with her eyes closed. He'd seen her do it before and thought it was some form of meditation.

"Yes?" she asked without opening her eyes.

"What will you do now?" he asked. "Where will you go?"

Elyasha shifted as if the thought was weighing her down. She opened her eyes. "I don't know," she answered. She was quiet for a moment, then looked up at Kethras. "I can't go back to Khala Val'ur, and I doubt that Ellenos would take me."

"Well," he said with a grin, "you could always come with me, back to Kienar."

Elyasha laughed, the first time she had done so since Ellenos—before she had found out that Thornton was her brother . . . and that her father was dead.

"I don't think so," she said as she shook her head. "I have to live indoors, not under a bunch of trees."

"Suit yourself," Kethras replied. "Although I'll never understand how you humans do it." He looked up at the roof over their heads. It bothered him that he could not see the sky.

"Maybe I could live here," she wondered aloud. "The people don't seem to mind me being Khyth." She paused, frowning. "But I do miss the mountains."

Just then, a familiar scent hit Kethras's nostrils. He smelled it before he heard the accompanying footsteps. He stood up and narrowed his eyes. Elyasha glanced from him to the door.

"What is it?"

Before he could answer, the door to their room creaked open. In stepped Alysana, clutching the dagger that had once belonged to Kethras's sister, Ynara. Streaked across the blade and covering her hands was the source of the scent that Kethras had smelled.

Blood. Human blood.

Elyasha's eyes were as wide as the river K'hel. "What. Did. You. Do?" she asked, punctuating each word with blinks of disbelief.

"What I had to," Alysana answered, wiping off the bloody dagger.

More surprising than the blood on her hands, however, was the man who stepped into the room behind her, dark of hair and skin, the archetypical G'henni. He looked to be about twenty years her senior and wore little more than tattered rags. He reeked of filth and steel.

"Kethras, Elyasha," Alysana said, closing the door behind her. "I would like you to meet my father, Yozna."

With a deep G'henni accent and a smile, the man said, "Pleased to meet you."

Chapter 7

South, Beyond the Wastes

Asha

THE JOURNEY FROM KHADJE KHOLAM to Do'baradai was not meant to be done alone, yet Asha Imha-khet had no choice. Necessity was what had forced her to take this body, too—something she had not done in a long, long time.

Necessity . . . Desperation? Recklessness?

Regardless of what she called it, it was what compelled her forward. She must reach Do'baradai. She must find the first Vessel of the Holder— and she must destroy it.

Her vision blurred by thirst, she looked out across the Wastes. Somewhere out there was the power that slept beneath the ancient city. She wasn't sure if this mortal body of hers would make it intact.*

Regardless, she kept coming back to the same conclusion: she had no choice.

✦ ✦ ✦

The god called the Holder of the Dead was not always known to her as that: once, he had been called Ahmaan Ka, and he had loved her—at least that's what he had told her—yet love does not do the things that he did to her. Love does not bring about the hurt and consequences that all three of them had suffered. No, love had nothing to do with how the Holder treated her. Yet, despite all that, she had still raised their child— the one that he'd planted in her by force.

Asha Imha-khet had in fact given birth to two sons: one son fathered by the Traveler and the other by the Holder. The first son had gone on to father the line of those called Farsteppers: men who could move seamlessly from one point in space to the other, doing so as easily as one steps through a door. The second son had taken after her, giving birth to the Wolfwalkers who could shed their human forms for lupine ones. Both sons had spread their seed among the dwellers of the desert, a loose group of people known as the Tribes of the Sun, and had ensured that the population of the Wastes of Khulakorum was one filled with warriors and pride. Though united in blood by their mother, the two groups could not have been more different: the Farsteppers were known to their enemies and allies alike as deadly and swift and only fought when provoked; the Wolfwalkers, on the other hand, were warlike and fierce, forming loose bands of tribes who waged war on a whim. For those reasons, the two peoples never truly mixed—until Djozen Yelto and the Holder of the Dead forced their hand.

Now, fleeing the city of Khadje Kholam, where Farstepper had stood by Wolfwalker in defiance of the Djozen, Asha Imha-khet was nearing the forgotten city of Do'baradai in hopes of retrieving the original Vessel of the Holder of the Dead—and putting a stop to him once and for all.

+ + +

It was nearing three days since Asha had left the city, just as many since she'd had water, and it was taking its toll on her. She traveled at night when it was cool, but the dry air of the desert did her no favors, even in the dark. Even though she spent much of the journey as a wolf—it pleased her to find that she retained her power to do so even in this borrowed body—she knew that wolves needed water to survive too. If she didn't come across some water soon, she was afraid of what might happen. Her spirit was immortal, yes, but this body was not . . . and she needed it alive.

Coming over the crest of a dune, Asha's heartbeat quickened. It was nearly dawn, and the first rays of sunlight had just crested the horizon to the east, spilling oranges and yellows onto a vast array of tents and torches. It had been many years since she had seen the roaming tribal city of R'haqa, and the sight of it now was almost too much for her to bear. Her head was already pounding by now, its way of telling her that she needed water. She was so thirsty.

Dizziness swept over her, but so did the hope that she would find the help that she so desperately needed this far from Khadje Kholam. She had made it: the first step in a long journey to the city of Do'baradai; she just needed to make it a bit further, and she would be safe. Her eyelids felt so heavy, though. And so did her legs.

So thirsty.

Just a bit further . . .

The thought echoed in her mind as her eyes rolled back in her head. She felt her legs give out beneath her as the sand came up to greet her, the last thing she felt before her vision went dark.

Chapter 8

Khadje Kholam

Sera

KHADJE KHOLAM WAS A WRECK of bodies and blood. Djozen Yelto's forces had fought to the bone defending the walls of the fortress, and most of the survivors were still in a daze. They had never seen a battle as fierce as the one that had almost destroyed them, tribes of Wolfwalkers and warriors alike throwing themselves against the palace gates. Walking around the recovering forces, Sera thought of her own youth in Khala Val'ur, city of the Khyth, where General Tennech had raised her as his own.

When she was still just a girl, Sera's mother had taken her away from their home in the Athrani city of Ellenos and entrusted her into the hands of smugglers—smugglers who ultimately delivered her to Tennech. Fortunately for Sera, Tennech had taken pity on her and kept her safe. Although she was an Athrani in the heart of her enemy's city, everyone knew that she belonged to Tennech and was not to be harmed. And, so, he had brought her up in the ways of the Khyth and the ways of the warrior elite, making sure that she had access to the best training that Gal'dorok had to offer. More than a few times, that training saved her life.

+ + +

"How many times do I have to tell you, Sera?" Tennech barked.

Lily was still getting used to the name that the young captain had chosen for her, but it was crucial she use it and remember it; if her true identity came out, there would be dire consequences for her—and for her mother.

"Bend at the knees! You're far too stiff. And loosen your grip." Her teacher tapped her knees and wrists with the flat of his sword. "Feel the weight of the weapon being taken by your shoulder, an extension of your body. A good warrior is never what?"

"An arm's length away from their weapon," Lily recited. She and the captain had been training for a few hours now, and it was starting to wear on her.

"Why?"

"Because a warrior without a weapon is useless. Understood, Captain Tennech," she said, trying not to sound as exhausted as she felt.

"You know," he said, lowering his sword, "I think you'd benefit from some riding practice. It might help with your balance and fluidity—two crucial parts of swordplay."

Lily thought of their long trip from Ellenos and groaned. She hated riding horses: the smell, the soreness from riding, their unpredictable personalities. The horse she rode in on, Ruen, was wild and young, and she found it an unbridled challenge to get him to listen to her commands as a rider.

"If you say so," she said. She knew by now not to contradict him.

"If you say so, Captain," Tennech corrected, leveling his sword at her again. "Now, let's do it again."

✦ ✦ ✦

Lily's whole body was sore, but at least her training was done for the day. Now was the time to rest and reflect.

Tennech, a brilliant swordsman, was an even better teacher. He knew the value of communicating things in a way that people could understand. Lily had once overheard his superiors talking about "fast-tracking him to general," whatever that meant. She had just taken it for idle banter, soldiers whiling away the boredom that resulted from a longstanding but fragile peace with the Athrani. When she was not busy training in whatever it was that Tennech thought would be valuable to her, Lily tried to familiarize herself with the city of Khala Val'ur as much as she could. She was getting good at being invisible beneath the walls of the Sunken City, and oftentimes that invisibility led to useful information—useful, and sometimes puzzling. She had no idea what the leadership of Khala

Val'ur was thinking when they appointed an Athrani envoy, Yetz, to a lofty position in the Hand of the Black Dawn, but Lily had made it her goal to figure him out.

She had opted for a route back home that just so happened to pass by an area Yetz frequented. As she rounded the corner, she saw him there, seated, speaking in hushed tones with another man, whose robes Lily recognized as those of a Master Khyth. He looked quite young for the role.

"Exactly what are you saying, Yetz? That you understand the secrets of the Otherworld?" asked the Master Khyth.

"In some regards," Yetz answered. "I understand how a spirit can pass into a new body if the conditions are right. And I certainly understand how, if one were to choose a Vessel that is loyal, one would be able to one influence the very will of the gods of creation."

The Master Khyth stood up. "That certainly sounds like something to consider, then." He gave Yetz a tight smile. "I knew it was a good idea to bring you in. You might turn out to be useful after all."

Yetz bowed his head. "You are too kind, D'kane."

"I've never been accused of that before," said the Master Khyth. "But I want to be with you when you present your idea to the council. I imagine they will be most pleased."

Lily saw him start to leave and disappeared around the corner before either man could see her.

Starting the long walk back to the quarters that she shared with the rest of the lower-ranking cadets, she thought about what she had just overheard. Vessels? The Otherworld? Controlling a god? The ideas sounded lofty—and dangerous. She would have to keep an eye on the one called D'kane: he might turn out to be a valuable ally . . . or a formidable foe.

Chapter 9

Théas

Alysana

"YOU ARE JUST AS MY daughter described," Yozna exclaimed with a gleeful clap of his hands. "I practically ran here when she told me that a Kienari was traveling with her. I just had to see it for myself." Her father looked at Kethras like a child watching a street performer, with awe and fascination. "And the tail!" he said, pointing. "You didn't mention the tail!"

Alysana laughed. It was good to see him like this. "If I had known it would make you this happy to see him, I would have brought him with me to break you out," she said.

Kethras didn't seem bothered—in fact, it almost looked like he was enjoying it. Alysana knew that most reactions to seeing him were fear, confusion, or both; amusement had not been on the list. She turned her attention to Yasha, who was clearly on a different side of the emotional spectrum altogether.

"Would you mind telling us what's going on?" she asked. Her arms were crossed and she was glancing back and forth between Alysana and Yozna.

"Of course," Alysana said. She peeked out into the hall one more time, making sure that they had not been followed. They had left in a hurry—and the waves of chaos from the freed slaves would soon be making their way through the city—but she had not been careless. She closed and locked the door, turning to address the others.

"I apologize for not telling you where I was going or what I was doing, but I couldn't risk anything going wrong."

Yasha, arms still crossed, asked "Then I assume it worked?"

Alysana nodded and ushered them further inside the darkened room with two oil lamps providing meager light. Yasha took a seat on the bed and Kethras stood beside her.

"Before the ritual to summon the Traveler," Alysana began, "Rathma told me that he had befriended a man in jail when he was captured. He said that man was the only one who would talk to him, and mentioned that he was G'henni."

Yasha had her hands folded in her lap, her gray apprentice robes looking black in the dim light. "And you figured that he was your father?"

Alysana shook her head. "Not at first." She turned to her father, and a smile spread across her face. "It was only when he mentioned that the man had given up everything to save his daughters many years ago . . ." She choked back tears as she embraced her father. His embrace was life itself, and Alysana loved it. "It fit the description of someone I knew, and there was no question as to what I should do."

She had never dreamed that she would see her father again, especially after she'd received word that he was dead. It turned out to be misinformation on the part of Ghaja Rus and his men, but Alysana had never been happier than when she found out the truth.

"So what, exactly," Kethras began, "did you do?"

"It is a short list," Alysana replied, turning back to face him, "but thievery and murder are at the top." Yasha gasped and covered her mouth. "And Ghaja Rus will not be pleased."

The words, and the realization of what they meant weighed heavily in the room. Her companions knew the story well of how she and Mordha were saved from Rus when she was just a child.

Kethras gave her a worried look. "So, the blood on your hands—" he started to say.

"Rus's bodyguard, Yuta," Alysana answered. "It is much harder to get to Rus than it is to get to his men."

The Kienari grunted. "Perhaps that will not matter. He will come looking for you."

Elyasha, behind them, was already gathering her belongings. "Well, I'm not waiting around to find out if he does. If you and Kethras are both worried, I'm worried." She stopped, looking up from stuffing her pack. "You are worried, aren't you?"

Alysana had kept herself cautiously optimistic until the very moment she laid eyes on her father again in the prison below the world. Now that she had freed him, she would take no further chances. "You are right," she said, moving to gather her things. "We should leave Théas. It is no longer safe, and we have done everything here that we need to . . ." She trailed off, and her eyes went to the door. Ghaja Rus was still out there. "Almost everything," she added bitterly.

She felt a hand on her shoulder. Turning to see the smiling face of her father, though, the bitterness descended. She smiled back. Perhaps the opportunity to tie up that loose end would present itself some day, but she had the most important thing in the world right now: hope. In the chaos of the prison break, she realized, they would most likely be able to leave unhindered.

"I may be able to be of some assistance," Yozna said. The years had taken the sharpness from his voice and softened it into a deep, gentle rumble.

"I am listening," Alysana said.

"Well," her father replied as a smile formed on his lips, "how would you like to once again see the land of your birth?"

Chapter 10

Khala Val'ur

Yetz

THE CRACKLING FIRE FILLED THE room with light and sound, yet Yetz felt none of it; his mind was elsewhere. He didn't know when it would happen, but he knew it was coming. He licked his dry lips in anticipation.

He wrung his hands.

He waited. It was not in his nature to wait.

There were only two things that waited: hunter and prey. He was wise enough to know which one he was in this scenario.

"High Khyth," came the muffled voice from beyond the great door. It was lined with nervousness. Fear.

Ah. There it is. "What is it?" he asked, knowing the answer full well.

"Our scouts from the east bring news. It's—" he choked. "It's the chovathi. And there is something with them. Something big."

Yetz frowned and stood up. It was time. He'd been preparing for this moment for years, and it felt all too surreal to be enacting the plan.

"Send word to the remaining Master Khyth in the city. Pull all troops from their garrison and have them line the mountain walls of the outer ring. They will be our first line of defense, and the Khyth will be our last." He turned around, then stopped, adding, "And send a message to Haidan Shar—we are going to need reinforcements."

The words hung in the air as the guard outside seemed to be processing them.

Yetz spoke again. "Did you hear me?"

"Y-yes, High Khyth," he stammered.

"Good. Then go—and bring fire."

"Fire?" asked the guard. There was another pause for thought. "Fire won't stop the chovathi."

"No," Yetz replied. "It won't. But it will slow them down."

If he could have seen through the walls, he was sure that he would have seen the color drain from the face of his most trusted guards, hand-picked men who feared only two things: Yetz, and death—and in exactly that order.

"F-Fire," the guard repeated. "Yes, High Khyth."

The next sounds to reach Yetz's ears was that of retreating footsteps as the guard went to carry out the commands. There would be nervousness and fear, he knew, as word was spread. These things were expected; the chovathi had never been aggressive. They had been content to stay in their underground dwellings for as long as anyone alive had ever known. Even the stories about them now were just faded memories, hearkening back to a time when the creatures were first driven from their ancestral home of Ghal Thurái. Even that seemed like an eternity ago. Now that Ghal Thurái lay in ruins from a seemingly pyrrhic victory by the chovathi, though, no one knew what to expect.

No one, that is, save Yetz.

Reaching out with his power of Breaking to suffocate the flames, the Athrani-turned-Khyth looked down at his hands. They had changed greatly since he had first come to the city under the guise of a peace treaty. Once, through these hands, the gift of the Shaper had flowed—a gift which contained a spark of the power of creation, of manifestation and form. He flexed his fingers, which had long forgotten what it was like to touch the power of his goddess. Fingers which now knew nothing but the power of the Breaker.

He clenched his fists, then let his hands drop to his side in futility. What use was his power now—the power of Breaking—against an army bred by death? Everything he would throw at them would be met with ferocity and pain.

. . . And more chovathi.

He looked around the room. What he wouldn't give to conjure flame from nothing, like he had done when he was a boy, before he'd set his plan in motion—a plan that had brought nothing but pain and sacrifice with it. He had left his whole life behind in the walls of the First City. A wife. A daughter.

A daughter. The faintest hint of a smile tugged at the corners of his mouth.

At least Cora had been kind enough to let him raise her here, even if it had been in secret. Watching Lily grow and mature to become the woman that she was had been the greatest joy of Yetz's life. It had almost seemed worth sacrificing everything that he knew in order to do so. It hurt him that he could never tell her the truth, but the only way to keep her here was if her mother had been the one to tell her that she must never come looking. It had worked, for better or for worse.

It had all been part of a plan that was set in motion so long ago that he'd almost forgotten his reluctance when the High Keeper had first brought it up. It had seemed like folly, this lofty, impossible goal; how would he, emissary of the Athrani, possibly be able to convince these Khyth—enemies of theirs since the beginning—that he was one of them? That his goals aligned with theirs?

Yetz winced at the recollection. The answer, of course, had been the Breaking—and it almost did just that to him. He reached down to trace the scars where the ancient ritual had left its mark. That day, all the power of the Otherworld had come flooding through him, forcing out the power of Shaping in order to make room for Breaking. Like water and oil, the two powers of the opposing gods could never coexist together in one Vessel.

. . . Never, that is, but for one glaring exception.

"High Khyth."

The words brought Yetz's mind reeling back to the present. He dropped his hands to his sides again. "Report."

"Our army is positioning themselves as we speak, and the remaining Master Khyth have gathered in the mouth of the city."

"Good," he said, standing up and making his way to the entrance. He paused before breaking the threshold, and looked back at his study. All these years he had lost here—years at first of duty, then eventually expectation— spent, like so many embers in the fire. "I will address them."

He reached out and felt the cold metal of the door. After the briefest hesitation, he pushed it open and stepped out into the blackened heart of Khala Val'ur. Above him, blazing and bright, was the fi-re that had burned for far longer than he'd been alive. He looked up at it now as it shed its light on the Sunken City, a symbol of the Khyth's fierce independence and pride: they needed nothing but themselves to survive—not even the light of the sun. How haughty and shortsighted that notion seemed now, in the face of this threat.

Before him was the sprawling city of the Khyth, with its eternal and unmoving shadows cast by a fixed source of light. Closing his eyes, Yetz tried to recall the rolling hills of Ellenos, so lush and green, and the way they caught the light of the sun when it rose. He let the images fill him in ways that power never could. For the briefest, fleeting moment, it felt like he was back there. It was faint, but welcome.

He opened his eyes to the flat and disappointing reality of the last bastion of the Khyth. Their time had come, and his with it. He had known it before he'd set the first domino in motion.

Now it was simply time to watch them fall.

"Close the door behind me," he said to the guard as he walked away. "I won't be returning."

"You won't be returning . . . today?" the guard asked, sounding confused.

Yetz stopped, and turned. He rarely looked his guards in the eye, knowing it frightened them. Today, he would make an exception.

"When was the last time the gates of Khala Val'ur were breached?"

"N-never, High Khyth Yetz."

"Never. And do you know why that is?"

The guard's eyes darted about nervously. "Because . . . because no army has ever tried."

Yetz turned on his heels and left the guard to ponder his own answer. After a few steps, not breaking stride, he called over his shoulder to the guard. "Today, an army will try—and the only thing that might be able to stop them is the Breaker Himself."

The words tasted bittersweet to Yetz even as he spoke them. The Breaker wouldn't help them here. He was needed elsewhere, in another form.

No other walk to the mouth of the Sunken City would ever be as dolorous and slow as the walk of a man meeting fate. Today, Yetz was such a man.

The darkness of Khala Val'ur had never seemed so utterly bleak.

Chapter 11

The Otherworld

Thornton

IT WAS AS IF HE'D never left.

The surging power and unearthly feel of the Otherworld struck Thornton immediately, as did his recollection of the last time he'd been there. It felt like an eternity ago—it could have been, in this place—but the memories were still fresh, and they stung like an open wound. He knew that he'd left Miera here, and he knew that this was where D'kane had killed his father. The anger and the hurt that he'd felt the day he found out were twin daggers in his back, being driven further in with every step. He would have to bury his thoughts even deeper, though, if he were to have any hope of finding Miera.

. . . Hope. Something he'd had very little of these days.

The old energies of the realm of creation swirled around him. As they did, he realized that it felt different than the last time he'd been here, when he had first learned that he was Khyth. It was stronger somehow, fiercer, like the opening of a furnace door that let the flames claw the air. He was thinking the power was calling to him more strongly than it did last time, too, when it dawned on him: it wasn't calling to him.

He could feel the power of the Breaker of the Dawn inside of him, a harmony to the melody that the Otherworld was singing. It made him wish that he was anywhere else, but still he pressed on, deeper into the heart of the realm. If he was going to find his friend, he could waste no more time on idle thoughts.

You will never find her, the voice inside him taunted. It was the Breaker's voice, haunting and hollow, reeking of malice and pride. *We killed her. She is no more.*

Shut up! Thornton shot back. It seemed to jostle the old god, who was clearly not used to insolence, and Thornton felt the heat of rage swelling inside of him.

This is a fool's errand, boy, he mocked. *Your Shaper is gone.*

Thornton gritted his teeth and tried to suppress the voice again. Pressing forward was his only option, and he could feel the Breaker growing stronger inside him with every passing moment. He was a fire, and this place was fuel.

It was all Thornton could do to try to see a way that this ended without him being burned alive.

+ + +

His eyes were closed in concentration—he wasn't worried about running into anything, as there essentially was nothing to run into—and the blocking out of one sensation made him focus on the others more fully. It was only then that he could realize that the Otherworld was not at all like Khel-hârad, despite both of them being realms of the gods. Each had its own feel, and the Land of the Dead, he recalled, had felt like trying to walk on the bottom of a lake: slow and heavy.

The Otherworld, though, was very . . -. different. The primordial energies that were contained here—the very seat of all creation—made Thornton feel empowered and light. Every step he took, despite the mental pull that the Breaker exerted on him, was light and easy. In fact, it almost felt . . .

. . . like he . . . was . . .

. . . flying!

Thornton looked down at what passed for the ground in the Otherworld, a churning mass of gray clouds, and realized they were far, far below him. The lightness all over his body was in stark contrast to the weight he had previously felt in Khel-hârad. It was as if he had gone from being thousands of times heavier to thousands of times lighter. He was flying without even realizing it. There were no clouds here, though, no birds to contend with; the sky of the Otherworld currently had one occupant, and Thornton was it.

The vastness of the realm spread out before him in a way that it never had before. When he had seen the Otherworld before, it had been entirely from the ground; now from his vantage point in the sky, he realized that there was much more to the ethereal realm than he had imagined. Behind him was the entrance to Khel-hârad, where he had just come from, and the tear in the realms manifested itself as an enormous fissure, a sky-crawling chasm that extended upward into eternity. Before him, Thornton could see vast stretches of land that might have been plains had they existed in a grass-rich land like Derenar. There were rivers of pure light that wove their way across the land; there were roads, valleys, hills, even a . . . castle?

He spotted the white monstrosity far off in the distance. He wasn't even sure that's what he was seeing, and he had to blink his eyes a few times just to make sure. When he focused again, there was no mistaking it: it was a castle made of the whitest brick that he had ever seen.

She is not there, came the voice again. *She is not in this realm. We have destroyed her, and we will destroy you too. Your existence will be snuffed out like a candle in a storm.*

Thornton had stopped listening to the voice by now. It gnawed behind his eyes, and he knew it was speaking, but he did his best to ignore it. It was like plunging a gloved hand into the coals of the forge: he could feel the warmth and knew the danger behind it—knew that there was only a thin layer separating fire from flesh—but he also knew this was one threat he could not pull away from. He had to hold his hand in the fire as long as was necessary to find Miera.

He was beginning to wonder just how long that was . . . and how long the glove would last.

+ + +

When Thornton landed, he found that he had traversed in hours a distance that might have taken him weeks had he walked it instead. The Otherworld, he was beginning to find out, was more vast than he had ever imagined—and more diverse than he'd realized. The part of the Otherworld that he had entered had been drab and sparse, looking like an overcast sky in all directions. Here, however, it was clear as day and was more like a grassland or a prairie. Behind him was the drab and colorless land he'd just come from, which seemed to him to be a sort of entryway into the real Otherworld.

The castle he had seen from the distance was now in full view in front of him, spanning the visible horizon. It was bigger than anything that he could even conceive of back in Derenar. He began to walk toward it when he heard something. He looked around but didn't immediately see anyone. He thought for a moment that his sanity was starting to slip as a result of the Breaker's influence—but then something caught his eye. He squinted, not sure of what he was seeing.

It started out as a ripple, almost undetectable: a spherical pocket of air no larger than a fist. It hung there, pulsing, waiting almost like it was . . . searching—and then, without warning, it exploded, doubling in size, expanding rapidly and violently as it consumed the air around it. It grew larger and larger, doubling and doubling again, twisting and spinning as it went, a vast, roiling vortex that nearly took up the entire sky.

The world darkened.

A sound like a falling tree pierced the air.

And then, just like that, all was still. It had only been seconds, but now the gigantic sphere was all that Thornton could see. It loomed above like a small moon, its perfectly smooth edge barely making contact with the ground—then, from the middle of the sphere, a light shone; it was like looking at a light beneath the ocean. It shimmered and pulsed, and began to move away from the center, toward the earth below. As it did, the sphere began to fade away. When the light touched the ground, the sphere had gone completely. The light pulsed for a moment, and then it too disappeared—revealing, in its place, a lone figure.

. . . A figure that was looking right at Thornton.

"It's not often we get visitors here." The voice was deep, and strangely human.

Thornton was gawking and didn't try to hide it. "H-How do you know I'm a visitor?" he managed to ask.

The man laughed. "I am the Herald," he answered. He had smooth, silver skin, blazing white eyes, and a gray, hooded robe. "I have been here since the Shaper of Ages brought this realm into existence, and I know each and every god by name—and you, little human, are no god." His eyes narrowed, as if to say, *Or are you?*

"I'm doing the work of one," he countered, "looking for the Shaper of Ages. I was here when she sealed this place off, and I've come to take her from it now that the Breaker has been set free."

The Herald gave him a mirthless laugh. "I'm afraid I cannot help you," he said. "The Shaper is no longer here."

"What?" Thornton cried. He felt the laughter from inside him, the satisfaction of the Breaker. "Where is she?"

"I cannot say," the Herald replied. He paused, cocking his head as if seeing something for the first time. He moved closer, his sleek silver form mere inches away from Thornton. "Yet her blood runs through your veins," he said, sounding puzzled.

Thornton, unsure of how to respond, simply nodded.

"And the blood of the Breaker does as well," the Herald added. "How—?"

The abrupt end to his question made Thornton think he was going to say more. but he simply stood there, a puzzled look on his face.

The Herald reached out, and to Thornton's surprise, touched his face.

Thornton pulled back, confused. "What are you doing?"

"You are male," the man said, his voice a mix of puzzlement and disappointment.

"Yes," Thornton replied, growing increasingly impatient.

"I thought for a moment . . ." he said, trailing off. "No. You are certainly not the one of whom the prophecy speaks."

"Prophecy?" Thornton repeated, confused. He knew as much about prophecy as he did about farming—next to nothing. "What prophecy?"

The Herald looked him up and down again, more slowly this time as if making sure that he was right. "The stories speak of a Great Uniter," he began, looking up pensively, "who will come when the Breaker is freed, and the Three are awakened. Raised in the shadow of enemies and wielding a weapon of the gods, the Uniter shall act as the bond between Breaking and Shaping, making whole that which was broken in ages past." He looked again at Thornton. "Only then shall the world truly know peace."

Thornton reached behind his back and felt the wooden handle of the object that had brought him boundless joy and endless frustration. "I wield a weapon of the gods: the Hammer of the Worldforge."

"So I see," said the Herald. "But I say it again: you are not the one of whom the prophecy speaks."

More curious than let down, Thornton asked, "How can you be so sure?"

"Because," the Herald smiled, "the Great Uniter is a woman."

Chapter 12

Haidan Shar

Duna

DUNA RUBBED HER LOWER BACK, which was already sore from spending less than an hour on that damnable granite beast of a throne. She opened the double doors to her study where a small fire was still going and decided that the throne would have to be strictly symbolic in the future; she had no intention of making any important decisions from atop the lofty seat. Instead, she decided that the warm, inviting study filled with books and maps would be where all important meetings would take place. She was queen, after all. She should be able to make that decision.

She crossed her arms and looked around the room. The study was smaller, yes, but it was certainly more comfortable. The bookshelves that made up most of the walls were lined with tomes of knowledge of all sorts, and the ceiling was high enough for a gwarái to stand in. Blue curtains with white trim—the colors of Haidan Shar—were tied together over a large bay window, letting the noonday sun come in and illuminate the room. Duna walked over and took a seat on the bench beneath it, sinking into the plush white cushion and looking through the window to what had just become her kingdom. The study's window, situated on the third story of the castle and facing east, looked out over the bay of the Tashkar Sea, allowing her to appreciate the luster of the Gem of the East.

"Well, you've wasted no time admiring your kingdom," came a voice from behind her.

Duna turned to see the onetime commander of the Lonely Guard of Lash'Kargá, Cortus Venn, striding into the room like he owned the place. If he were so inclined, Duna reflected, he probably could. The burly man wore his brown hair tied up, making the beard that reached his mid-chest all the more conspicuous, and the sunlight that poured into the room blanched his already marble-white skin. He wasn't wearing his armor but carried himself like he was.

Beside him was the young Stoneborn armiger, Benj, who had been at his side since the battle of Ghal Thurái. Venn had obviously taken a liking to him, probably due to their shared nature.

"Good to see you again, young armiger," she said with a smile. Benj beamed back. "I see the commander has taken you under his wing."

Benj nodded. "No disrespect to Captain Jahaz, Commander Venn is a lot nicer."

Duna laughed. "I have no doubt about that. The captain is certainly not known for his pleasantries."

The sound of wood scraping against the floor made her turn. Duna shook her head as she watched Venn drag an ornate wooden chair across the room and set it close to the fire.

"I would tell you to make yourself at home, Commander, but you have clearly wasted no time in doing that."

"Never been friends with a king before," he said. Catching himself, he added over his shoulder, "or a queen." Hands folded behind his head and facing the fire again, he grunted. "Could get used to it."

"Well," Duna said as she looked back out the window, "enjoy it while you can. We aren't staying here long."

"I know," grumbled Venn. He poked at the fire a bit with a tool he'd found hanging beside the mantle. "I was just hoping you wouldn't say it."

The waves were calm below, and the crescent shape of the city along the bay—of which the castle was the center—made it look like Haidan Shar was a hand trying to clasp the sea. To think that only two generations ago it had been a simple fishing village was enough to make Duna appreciate that hardiness and determination of her people. They had managed to build themselves a great city using their newfound wealth in a manner that was both sensible and efficient. They had come from nothing and had a great deal to show for it—but there had never been any real threat to any of it either. Duna realized darkly that that was no longer the case.

The fire popped and crackled with Venn's attention, and Duna decided she wanted some part of it too. She stood up and walked over to the great brick fireplace that centered the room so well. Making herself comfortable in a second wooden chair, she joined him in repose.

"Well, I didn't want any of this," she said to the fire. "Yet here we are."

Venn grunted in agreement beside her. He stood up to put back the poker and sat down again. "Back when I was just a lieutenant, I would have told you the same thing. I never wanted to be stationed in Lash'Kargá, let alone one day command the guard there." He looked at her. With a chuckle and a shake of his head he said, "You know they call it 'Death's Edge,' right? It's no wonder no one wants to go."

Duna laughed, grateful that Venn had been sent to support her and her army. He was indispensable in battle, that was sure—but more importantly, he was a force to be reckoned with in conversation as well.

"You mean to tell me you didn't volunteer to go there and take command?" she asked, genuinely curious. "I would figure that men would be lining up to take command of the Lonely Guard."

"You would think that," he said, uncrossing and recrossing his legs. "But you'd be wrong. It's a respected position, yes, but there's also a reason they don't just call it 'the Guard.' You have to really want to be there, and there is nothing to do but train, fight . . . and die."

Venn went silent. He stared hard at the fire as if he were reliving some of those moments in his mind, clashing over and over with the Tribes of the Sun, invaders from beyond the Wastes, savage and battle born. Duna had never met one in person, but she had heard stories. Some of those stories, in fact, said that there were more things to fear in the night than just swords and spears. Wolves, for one . . .

"But," Venn said, breaking out of his trance, "when I found myself there, I knew it was where I was meant to be." He turned to her and gave a weak smile. "It was also when I found out that I was Stoneborn."

If Duna hadn't been paying attention before, she certainly was now.

"Now that is a surprise. I would have thought they'd have sent you there because you were Stoneborn."

Venn shook his head. "No one knew," he said. "Not even me. It's a condition so rare that it can skip entire generations." He paused, pursing his lips, as if pondering whether or not to go on. He looked at Benj out of the corner of his eye, then back to the fire. "Every Stoneborn," he started, "dies twice."

Duna was staring intently now, barely even able to hear the crackling of the fire beside them.

"The first death is one that all men know," Venn continued, holding up one finger. "We are born and we bleed, just like everyone else. We feel pain, we feel loss, and we know what it is to die. Then, and only then, can we begin our transformation into Stoneborn.

"The second death," he said, holding up as many fingers, "comes when we have fulfilled our purpose. What our purpose is," he said with a shrug, "is anyone's guess. It's a question that no amount of reflection or self-examination can answer."

"That seems . . . inconvenient," Duna said.

"Agreed. Which is why, despite the fact that no one knows which god was responsible for bringing about the first Stoneborn, we can all agree on one thing: he—or she—was cruel."

"Cruel?" Duna echoed. "Why?"

Venn looked at her for a moment, considering. He turned to look at a weapon mounted above the fireplace and said, "Benj, fetch that sword for Queen Duna."

The boy, who had been poking and prodding at various items in the room, eagerly agreed. He practically sprinted over to the fireplace, reached up, and grabbed the worn handle of a longsword that, despite its apparent age, still held an edge. He walked over to Duna and knelt down.

"Here you are, Your Majesty," Benj said, holding out the sword, handle first.

Duna took it. She could feel the tremendous weight behind it. It was definitely a two-handed weapon—or a one-handed weapon for a chovathi.

"Now," Venn said as he stood up, "chop off my head."

54

"What?!" Duna nearly shouted. "No."

"Trust me."

"Venn . . ."

"Listen, just trust me."

Duna sighed. She grasped the sword in both hands, raised it up, and pointed it at him. His gaze was unwavering, and not at all the look of a man who was staring at his own death.

She cocked back in preparation to swing. "You had better not ruin this rug," she said. "It's from Théas."

Venn smirked. "Quit stalling," he said, "and swing."

With that, she put her whole body behind a blow that would have been good enough to cleave Gal'behem in two. The sword cut through the air, its edge headed straight for Venn's neck. It connected—and Duna felt her arms go numb. She wasn't sure exactly how hard she hit him, but the stinging in her hands told her that she'd connected with a wall of solid granite. The sword clanged to the ground; her grip didn't stand a chance.

"Imagine waking up every morning," Venn said, "knowing that you can't be killed."

Duna was bent over in pain, cursing under her breath.

"Until one day," he went on, "something changes. You don't know how or why, but it's like standing up too fast after laying down: you feel everything come rushing back . . . And you know that it is your day to die."

The agony in her arms had mostly subsided, and Duna was once again able to stand upright, albeit with a fair amount of effort. She hung onto her wrist in pain.

Venn turned to Benj, with the slightest hint of sadness in his eyes. "I'm sorry you had to hear that, my boy. Most of us go our whole lives without having to know of the cruelty that the gods delivered to us."

Benj stood up tall. "I don't mind," he said. "I'm proud to be a Stoneborn."

"Good lad," Venn said, and gave him a reassuring pat on the cheek.

"I suppose it is a little cruel," Duna said after some thought. "But how is it different from what any of us go through? At least you know when you're going to die."

Venn smiled his weak smile again. "Guess how old I am."

Duna stood up and looked the man up and down. "Thirty-four," she said.

"Put a 'one' in front of that and you're surprisingly close," he replied.

Duna mouthed the whole number, to which Venn simply nodded. She sat down in shock. Benj, wide-eyed, shouted, "You're over a hundred?"

Venn nodded silently. "That is why it is cruel," he said. "Immortality: a gift I neither sought nor desire. I have far outlived my usefulness." He sighed. "I await my second death like winter longs for spring."

The weight of all of it was only beginning to sink in. "I'm sorry, I . . . I didn't know."

He waved it off.

Duna thought for a moment about something he had said earlier. "Back in Ghal Thurái," she said, "you told me that the only way to stop the chovathi is through more Stoneborn."

The commander nodded gravely. "It is," he said. "And I couldn't ask you to do it without telling you the price."

Duna stood up and made her way to the window again. She leaned out over the wooden frame and watched the sea. The tide was starting to recede, and she could see a multitude of rocks above the waterline that had been below it only moments before.

Time, like the tide, was an inevitability. Perhaps this was as well.

She sighed. "Then tell me what I have to do," she said.

+ + +

Nighttime in the Gem of the East had brought with it the first calm that Duna could remember since Ghal Thurái, as she traded the warmth of her study for the open air and lapping waves of the edge of the Tashkar

56

Sea. It was a fair trade, she thought, as her bare feet sunk into the wet sand of the shore.

It would not last long, however.

"Majesty," came a voice behind her. It was Eowyn, her lead scout.

Duna sighed. Still facing the sea, she asked, "What is it?"

"A message from Khala Val'ur brings word: the chovathi are headed west. The Valurians have called for aid."

"Valurians?" she repeated, turning to look back at him. "Why are the chovathi not heading east toward us?"

"The message did not say," he began nervously, "but there are whispers that they are after the Anvil of the Worldforge."

Duna scoffed and shook her head. "No. That makes no sense. They have no use for the Anvil."

Instead of Eowen's voice, though, the one that answered her came from further back in the darkness.

"Perhaps not," it said, "but it does serve as one of two possible ways into the Otherworld. The second, of course, being through Kienar."

Low and smooth, the voice sounded familiar, with a quality to it that Duna couldn't quite place, like the owner were speaking from the bottom of a well.

"Who's there?" Duna asked, eyes searching the darkness. Soft footsteps crunched in the sand just beyond her vision. She drew her sword as they approached. "Show yourself."

What she saw next made her drop her sword.

Despite the moonless night, Duna could clearly make out the face of the man who had once been responsible for nearly wiping all the chovathi off the face of the earth; the same man who had been the first to lead the combined armies of Gal'dorok toward a single, united goal; and the man who, by all accounts, had recently lay dead beneath the skies of Khulakorum.

Disbelief came in and covered her like a sea swell.

"General Tennech," she said as she bowed her head and dropped to a knee in the wet sand.

Apparently the Dagger of Derenar did nothing easily—up to and including death.

Chapter 13

R'haqa, the Roaming City

Asha

ASHA AWOKE TO A POUNDING head and the taste of water on her lips. Her eyes were closed, but her body's instinct to thirstily gulp down the cool liquid offering was so strong that she hardly even realized she was doing it.

"There you are. Drink up," said a man's voice. "You're lucky I found you when I did. You could have been out there for days."

She could feel that she was lying on a cot, and that there was a sheet covering her. She ventured to open one eye, a difficult task in her weakened state. They were inside a spacious tent, sparsely decorated, but well suited for the nomadic lifestyle that the R'haqans were known for. Lucky indeed; the Roaming City could have been on the other side of the Wastes instead of here, where she needed it. Kneeling beside her and holding the animal-skin flask that she drank from was a bearded man with kind eyes and graying hair. He wore the simple garb of a goatherd: a white kaftan that covered him from shoulders to ankles, and a light brown shawl draped over top.

"Thank you," Asha said, and immediately clasped her hands over her mouth. The voice that came forth from her was not her own, and she realized that it belonged to Kuu, the true owner of the body she now possessed. It had never occurred to her that her voice would be different, despite knowing full well that she was merely a guest in the body of the Vessel. This was the first time she had spoken since taking control. It would take some getting used to.

"Think nothing of it," the man said, waving it off. He offered her the flask, which she gladly took. "How are you called?"

Asha took the opportunity for a long drink, realizing that her answer might be complicated.

"I am . . ." she began, hesitant. "I am called Asha," she finally answered. It had been her name for millennia, she reasoned; no sense in renaming a forest just because some trees may have changed. She was still Asha. She was still the Ghost of the Morning.

"Asha," the man echoed. He gave her a long, silent look. "Like the goddess?"

She nodded.

"That is a strange name for a young man."

Asha shrugged, smiling. "It is my name."

"Well, Asha, you should be more careful when you travel—especially alone," he replied. "The Wastes are unforgiving, and I have seen them lay claim to many a traveler." The goatherd stood up, making his way across the tent to the entrance. "I am Ulten, and my home is yours," he said, opening the flap that had been keeping out the heat of the day. Sunlight spilled in and illuminated the dark tent. "Where are you going? Surely you did not come all this way just for R'haqa."

Asha had finished what water was left in the animal-skin flask and placed it on the cot. "I am bound for Do'baradai," she answered, choking down the last of the liquid.

The old man had been securing the tent flaps to keep them open when he paused and looked back at her. "Nothing good awaits you in Do'baradai," he said. "Why would you go there?"

Eyeing the goatherd, Asha decided that he looked like someone that she could trust. He had saved her life, after all, and he had offered her water and shelter—two things in short supply out among the Wastes. "Because I share more than just my name with the Ghost of the Morning," she said, "and the Holder of the Dead must be stopped." She added, more to herself than to Ulten, "At any cost."

Silence unfolded before her like a shadow, and Ulten did nothing to banish it. His sun-drenched outline was all that Asha could see in the sunlight, eyes hidden in the darkness of his face. She couldn't be sure if he was skeptical or alarmed. His body language gave nothing away.

She began to think that she had been too hasty in trusting this man when, finally, he spoke.

"Ten years ago," he began, walking over to her cot and taking a seat beside her, "the man who calls himself Djozen Yelto came to R'haqa. His riding party was large when he first arrived, and they were well-provisioned for a trip across the sands."

Now that he was closer, Asha could see his eyes again. They were stern and unmoving, and looking right into hers.

"But when he returned," he went on, "there were only five riders. Do you know who they were?"

Asha blinked and gave him a mirthless smile. "The Djozen, his Priests of the Holder," she answered, "and a prisoner: me."

Ulten studied her face, taking in her features and her reply. "Yet you wore a different form that day."

"I did."

"Why do you not wear it now?" the goatherd asked.

It was certainly a fair question and one that deserved an answer. Asha knew that she could trust this man, but she wasn't yet sure how far. He didn't need to know that she was bound to the Wolfblade, which Yelto controlled. He also didn't need to know that what she sought in Do'baradai was more than just the Vessel of the Holder.

"One does what one must sometimes," she said at last.

Ulten grunted a laugh. "Well, if you are truly the Ghost incarnate, you already know the dangers of Do'baradai—and what it asks of those who enter its gates."

"I knew them then, and I know them now," she said.

Bowing his head, Ulten kneeled beside the cot that Asha was seated upon. "Then I am at your service, my lord," he said. Looking up at her from the corner of his eye, he added, "My . . . lady?"

"Asha is fine," she smiled. "And thank you. Please, stand up. I'm not royalty."

Ulten did as he was asked, but still looked at her with reverence. "Perhaps not, but you are still a goddess," he protested, dusting off his kaftan.

"By circumstance, not birth," she replied. "And if I could change that, too, I would."

Ulten considered her for a long, silent while.

"Then," he began slowly, "you will find what you are looking for in the shadows of Do'baradai."

Chapter 14

Derenar, North of G'hen

Elyasha

KETHRAS WAS RIGHT: SOMETHING WAS off, but Yasha couldn't put her finger on it. They had been traveling the road from Théas to G'hen for what seemed like days and, while she had a great deal of riding experience from growing up under Aldis Tennech in Khala Val'ur, Yasha had never gone on as many long-distance rides as she found herself on lately. It was starting to wear on her.

Even worse than the fatigue of travel, though, was something that had come after she'd woken up at Silus the Healer's. It was a feeling of intrusion, like the one that sometimes comes in dreams where you know someone is watching but can't tell who. At first, she thought it was a side effect of the Breaking, but of all the other Khyth of the Breaking that she knew, none of them had said anything about this feeling. It made her uneasy, like a fog that she was trying to cut through to see. A few times in the past couple of days, she swore that she had seen someone out of the corner of her eye—but when she turned to see what it might be, there was nothing there. Maybe it was all in her head. Maybe she was being paranoid.

Or maybe, even worse, she was right.

" . . . Yasha, did you hear me?"

Kethras's voice. Her attention snapped back to the real world, to the sound of hoofbeats on a dirt road. They were riding the horses that Ellenos and the Athrani Legion had provided them. They were of excellent stock, but their presence was a reminder of Endar's attempted betrayal, and Yasha would sooner forget all about the whole thing if she could.

"Ah, sorry," she admitted. "I think I drifted off again."

Kethras gave her a patient look from beside her mount. "Yozna was just asking if any of us had ever been to G'hen."

Yasha looked over at the smiling G'henni whose gaunt figure and sagging skin told the story of a man who once ate very well. She had no idea how long he'd been held in prison as a slave in Théas, but it had not been too long as to extinguish the joy of knowing his daughter was alive and well.

"I have not," she said to Yozna, who was riding a flea-bitten gray horse that carried his weight with ease. "But Alysana has told me it's quite nice."

"Oh, it is," he said with a nod. "Or at least it was when I left. I have not been back in quite some time."

"Nor have I," Alysana said. "I never had any reason to when I received word that you were dead," she said, turning in the saddle of her dark bay horse to look at her father.

"Unfounded rumors," said Yozna with a grunt and a wave of his hand, and the two of them laughed. "You know," the elder G'henni went on, "I have always wondered how your sister Mordha is doing. Tell me, how is she?"

Alysana beamed. "You would be proud. She is second in command of the guard of Annoch under the Farstepper Jinda Yhun."

Yozna nearly fell off his horse. "Second in command!" he marveled. "When she left to accompany you to Annoch, she couldn't even lift a sword."

"She can do much more than that now, Father. In fact, she taught me almost everything I know about fighting."

"Is that right?" Yozna asked with a touch of reproach. "Like how you handled Yuta back there in the jail?"

There was a brief silence as Alysana looked on, troubled. "I am . . . sorry you had to see that," she said. "But sometimes to save a life, you have to take one in exchange. And besides," she said, turning in her saddle to face him again, "he deserved it."

Yozna took a breath, exhaling slowly through his nostrils. "I do not care for violence," he said as he looked at his daughter, "and never would have raised you to either. Where did you learn such things? Was that Mordha's doing as well?"

"No—" she began, but the rest of her words were cut off by a growl from the Kienari.

"I am afraid," Kethras said, "that it is a Kienari's."

Yozna blinked at Kethras. He then looked to his daughter in confusion. "I do not understand."

Alysana looked at him as if mentally weighing her options. She hesitated, then spoke. "When Ghaja Rus's men took us from G'hen, did he tell you where he was taking us?"

"Ghaja Rus?" Yozna echoed incredulously.

"Did he tell you?" Alysana nearly shouted.

"Well, no . . ."

"Annoch, Father," Alysana bitterly. "But that is also where he left us, intent on selling us as slaves."

"Slaves?" Yozna looked like a bird who just had its feathers ruffled. "I knew of no such thing! Ghaja Rus—"

"Does not deserve to breathe," Alysana shouted. She gripped the reins on her horse so tight that Yasha could hear the leather creaking in her hands. There was fire in her eyes, and she directed it right at her father. "I might have been better off dead over what he and his men had in store for us! Do you know what happens to young G'henni girls who get sold into slavery? Do you?" She left no room for an answer. "Half of them do not even make it to where they are going!"

"I did not sell you into slavery!" Yozna shouted back. His face was stone as he looked at his daughter, jaw clenched.

Yasha looked back and forth between the two of them. She knew she should say something; the silence and tension were wound tight enough to snap. "How . . . how much further until we stop?" she asked.

"Until we are sure that we are not being followed," was Alysana's swift reply.

Yasha suppressed a groan. "How long will that be?"

"You will know," Alysana said through her teeth, "when we have stopped."

At this rate, Yasha thought that might be never. She rubbed her lower back hoping to relieve some of the pain that was already starting to radiate through her, but it was like trying to stop a windstorm by using a knife. She knew that it was just the beginning of the soreness too—tomorrow would bring a whole new level of pain. She closed her eyes to try and take her mind off it, and the world faded away as she blocked it all out: the pain, the fatigue, the tension.

The darkness was welcome . . . yet inside it, she still had a feeling like she was being watched.

And she would have been fine with it had it not begun, just then, to speak to her.

Chapter 15

Khadje Kholam

Sera

THE VOICE OF THE HOLDER of the Dead echoed through the halls of Djozen Yelto's chambers.

"Ah, Sera," he said. "Do come in." The words were as cold as the stone that comprised the walls.

Two big Khôl guards stepped away, allowing her passage into the lavishly decorated throne room. It reminded her of the opulence of Ghal Thurái in that it was meant to impress, even intimidate any visitors lucky enough to have an audience with a god—but like a gold tooth over a rotting molar, all the jewels in the world could not cover up the scent of decay.

This place reeked of death.

"Holder," Sera said, kneeling and bowing her head. A lifetime of working under Tennech for D'kane and Yetz had prepared her well for dealing with malignant power. "How may I serve?"

The god had taken the body of a male half-eye, whose blue left eye was flushed with a ring of gold that proclaimed his half-human heritage. Sera had no doubt that the half-eye would have been treated poorly in life, but she wasn't sure that this existence was any better. Used as a puppet by a god; the thought made her shiver.

"The Djozen has told me of your bloodline," the Holder said. Of course. The line that Tennech had fed Yelto about Sera being able to bear the next Shaper of Ages. No surprise that it had reached the ears of the Holder.

"Did he?" Sera looked up and scanned the room for the Djozen, intending to stare daggers at the fat man. She was almost disappointed to find him absent.

"He did. And I believe it will be useful," he said. "I have always known that the way to the Otherworld was opened with a key, but its whereabouts have always eluded me . . . until now." His unblinking eyes bored into her, making Sera shiver. "They call you 'Seed,' do they not?"

The words caught her off guard. "No. Well, yes. The Ghost did."

"The Ghost," repeated the Holder. "She always did have a knack for speaking out of turn. Did she tell you why you are called this?"

Sera shook her head.

The Holder of the Dead stood up from his gaudy throne and walked toward her, descending the steps in quick strides that nonetheless looked smooth and calm. "Come with me," he said as he walked toward the exit. The two guards standing outside snapped to attention as he passed, followed closely by Sera who was now wondering just where this was all going.

The Holder walked with his hands behind his back, right hand on his left wrist, as he led them out of the palace. As they passed, Yelto's Khôl guards all paused to render salutes. "When the Shaper of Ages forged the world," he said, not looking back, "she did so crudely, deliberately. There was no graceful crafting or loving touch—only violence and strength, the twin hands that helped shape you, pulling you from the womb, screaming and bloody." He glanced back at Sera. "Fitting, I suppose." Sera could never tell if he was smiling.

"Hands like hers only understand brute force," he went on. "You think it coincidence that she chose a hammer as her instrument of creation?" Sera was silent, and the Holder gave a mirthless chuckle. "Of course not. It embodies everything wrong about her: a tool of creation capable of endless destruction."

The air outside the palace was cool as they made their way toward the wall that surrounded the city-within-a-city of the Djozen's palace. Nestled in the bosom of Khadje Kholam, it was the beating heart of the Tribes of the Sun, a loosely connected people whom Yelto had sought to conquer. Now, with the help of a god, he seemed to have done just that.

"What the Shaper fails to understand," the Holder said as they exited the well-guarded compound, "is that creation and destruction do not always have to be so . . . forceful. They can be slow, elegant. Gradual."

He looked at her in a lidless stare caught between madness and calm. "Guided. She does not seem to grasp the careful precision necessary for something to truly grow."

They passed through the crowded inner city that was busy despite the hour. Most of the populace was still reeling from the battle between the soldiers of the city and the allies of the Wolfwalkers, but that was not overly evident here. Sera noticed a few people staring at them, but the faceless Lord of the Dead did not seem to pay them any mind. He kept his stride, toward the outskirts of the city, chasing the sun as it sank.

When they had reached the edge of the city, the Holder came to a stop.

"You and I have met before," he said, eyes fixed on a sky the color of molten steel.

Sera wasn't sure if he meant the man whose body he now inhabited, or if he meant himself, Ahmaan Ka, Holder of the Dead. "When?" she asked, unsure of how else to phrase it.

The god turned his skeletal face to hers. "You know when."

And, strangely enough, he was right; she knew in that moment exactly when they had met before. "Kienar," she replied.

"You never should have left the forest that day," he said. "Your wounds were too severe. You died back there, on that battlefield."

The words were jarring, but she knew they were right. She remembered what it had felt like to have the candle of her life snuffed out, slipping into the cold and the dark.

"But . . . h-how?" She stammered. "How am I alive now?"

"A simple bargain," he replied, "between myself and Aldis Tennech." His name still had weight, even here, even now. "An agreement that would see your life returned to you, among other things." He looked back at the horizon. "That was when the seed was first planted."

"I don't understand," Sera said.

"There are some . . . changes . . . that must take place," the Holder replied. He produced a small, silver blade from beneath his dark cowl that

Sera had somehow failed to notice. On its handle in gold was the likeness of a wolf. "Changes that *have* taken place."

Changes? What was he . . .

"The first one occurred at the moment of your death, when your spirit left the mortal realm for mine. The second, when you spilled blood in the name of vengeance. The third," he said, with a chuckle under his breath, "now."

The blade of the Holder began to emit an eerie dark light, and Sera felt something shift inside of her, like a key sliding into a lock. She looked at the Holder in a panic.

"What . . . what are you doing?" she asked. She grabbed at her sides as a sharp pain flitted through her body.

"You will see," the Holder said. "Be not afraid; I need you. Rest assured that I will not destroy that which I require to carry out my plans."

Sera could feel something cold inside her, like an emptiness forming in her chest. It held there, pulsing like a heartbeat, growing, hungering. Waiting. She put her hand over her heart, thinking that it couldn't get any worse—only to find out how wrong she could be. The pain spread like waves of frost, chilling her blood and numbing her fingers. Her vision began to darken. She dropped to a knee, barely cognizant of the world around her.

"It will only hurt for a bit," said the blurry form of the Holder as he drew closer, blade in hand. "When it is over, you will be transformed. But you will see that not all creation has to be sudden; sometimes it can grow from a seed planted long, long ago."

The Holder took the handle, which was glowing with a sickening blackness, and pressed it against her chest. Instantly, a feeling of white hot pain shot through her as the chill in her chest went straight for the blade; it felt like her body was being ripped apart at the seams. Her hands were shaking, and she could feel beads of sweat forming on her forehead.

"What," she groaned through clenched teeth, "is happening?"

The Holder removed the blade—and instant that he did, the

pain subsided.

He tucked it back into his robes as he looked at her, his unblinking eyes reflecting the terror in her own. Then, for the first time since she had been in his presence, Sera realized something: he was smiling.

She looked down to her chest, where the Holder had pressed in the blade, and saw that the likeness of a wolf had been burned into her skin, swollen, red, and freshly bleeding. Looking back up at the Holder, she found herself wishing that she had died there on the floor of the forest of Kienar—at least then Tennech might still be alive.

Chapter 16

Haidan Shar

Duna

THE LAST SCOUTING REPORT THAT Duna had heard was that Aldis Tennech had fled south for Khadje Kholam, where he was killed in a battle for the city by something called a Wolfwalker—yet here he was, standing before her as if nothing had changed, as though he still commanded the armies that were now hers. Yet something *had* changed.

"Please, Duna, stand up," Tennech said as he offered his hand. "I am a general no longer."

Speechless, she took his hand and stood, trying to figure out just what was happening. Her mind reeled.

"I know what you're asking yourself," he said as he took a deep breath of the salty sea air. "And the answer is no, your scouting reports were not wrong—about me or the chovathi."

Words did not avail her. She just gaped, and blinked.

He pointed to his neck. "Right here," he said, indicating a thick scar that marbled its way across his throat. "That's where the Wolfwalker sunk his teeth—tore it open as easily as a man breathes. I bled out right there on the desert floor."

"Then . . ." she stammered, still gathering her words. "How?" She indicated him with her hands.

Tennech looked at her grimly. "I made a deal," he answered, "with the Holder of the Dead."

Duna had heard the name from the tales that her mother told her as a child, but knew next to nothing about the so-called Lord of the Dead. Apparently he was not just a god who made corpses . . . he was also a god who made deals.

"What kind of a deal?"

Tennech looked at her for a long, silent moment. He crossed his arms and looked away. "I told him he would have a leader for his army."

"You what?" Duna nearly shouted.

"I know," he replied. "But you have to understand the position I was in. Desperation," he said as he faced her again, and Duna could see it reflected in his eyes. "I didn't even think about it when he made the offer."

"But a deal with the Holder?" she asked. "You know that whatever he has planned can't be good."

"I do," he said as he looked her in the eyes. "Which is why I've come to you. I may have a way to stop him and get what you want at the same time."

Chapter 17

G'hen

Alysana

ALTHOUGH THE LANDSCAPE WAS FAMILIAR, the land of Alysana's birth looked completely different to her now. It had been far too long since she'd seen the rolling hills and fields of wheat that served as the city's lifeblood: farming. Her own father had once owned a sizable amount of land here too.

Once.

"As good as it is to be back," Yozna said as they rode in, "I can't help but feel like a stranger."

They had followed the road down from Théas that had taken them in to the northern entrance of the city which, despite its size, had no city guard to keep the peace. That was much to Yozna's apparent relief, as he was looking around like he was expecting to be scooped up by the Théan guard.

"Why do you say that?" Alysana asked. She had undone her ever-present braids during the ride and was finishing tying her hair up behind her.

"When I sold off my land to get you the help that you needed," he said as he looked around, "they told me that it was the only way. But now that I'm back, I can't help but feel that, well—they were lying."

The four of them left the tree-lined road behind them and came to a stop at the edge of a freshly plowed field. Alysana dismounted and took in the sights and smells of the land around her: the sturdy trees, the sharp smell of tilled earth, the pale golden wheat fields. They were just as she remembered—only now, everything seemed smaller. . . . Smaller, that is, except for the group of people that was moving towards them. That was most certainly getting larger.

"Is someone expecting you?" Alysana asked with a sidelong glance at her father.

Yozna wrung his hands. "I was hoping not, but it appears that hope was misplaced."

"Should we worry?" Kethras asked. He already looked fidgety; Alysana knew he didn't like being around humans. The thought of him—a towering, deadly hunter—being afraid of a few villagers made her laugh to herself.

"Worry? About them?" she asked, looking back from the crowd to the tall Kienari. "Only about if they will worship you as a god."

Kethras frowned. "In that case I would rather not be seen," he said, and began walking to the trees behind them. Alysana watched him go, knowing he would be listening.

"He's got the right idea," said Elyasha as she pulled up her hood. "I tend to stand out a bit."

"You'll be fine," Alysana said immediately. "You are with me." With a nod to the forest, she added, "And him."

Elyasha gave her a look of uncertainty but kept her hood up. "If you say so."

✦ ✦ ✦

There were about a half-dozen faces in the crowd that Alysana recognized from her youth, all of them touched by time. She realized then just how long she'd been away as one of the men toward the front of the crowd caught her eye. His hair was matted and gray, and the beard on his face had only traces of the once deep black that it used to be. Time had certainly taken its toll on him; he was no longer the man that used to bounce her on his knee when she was a child. Yes, indeed: her uncle had aged.

"Something the matter?" he asked Yozna. "No warm embrace for your own brother?"

Yozna put on a smile that looked more like a grimace. "Hello, Ezna. It has been . . . some time." The two men did little beyond acknowledging each other in an awkward, forced reunion.

Ezna turned his eyes to Alysana and appeared to have the same realization that she did: time had continued its march and had left many casualties in its wake. "And is this little Alysana, all grown up?"

He seemed different from the man she knew—her uncle, who used to be so warm and approachable. This man had an air of contempt about him. And, judging by her father's reaction, she wasn't the only one who noticed.

"Uncle Ezna," she said, giving him a smile with only the corners of her mouth. "What brings you and this welcome party out to meet us? Surely this is not the typical greeting you give all travelers."

"It is not," he answered, and the affected friendliness had gone out of his voice. "But it is a greeting for a thief."

Alysana looked from Ezna to her father as confusion took over. "Thief? Father, what does he mean?"

Yozna was staring cold daggers at his brother, crossing his arms in defiance. "He is a fool, Alysana. He thinks that the land was not mine to sell."

"And I am right!" countered Ezna. A few men behind him shifted nervously as though they were waiting for something to happen. "I am firstborn. The land should have always gone to me."

"You keep saying that," Yozna replied. "But you forget: it was my father's land, *half-brother*. You have no claim to anything but your own poverty."

The confusion in Alysana's head made no sign of slowing. *Half-brother?*

Ezna waved it off. "A technicality. One that I am sure will be overlooked at your trial."

"Trial!" Yozna shouted. "What nonsense are you spouting?"

The two men were nearly at each other's throats.

"I have every right to demand a trial," Ezna said, poking his finger into Yozna's chest. "Whether or not you come peacefully—now that is up to you."

A bald, burly man with a pair of irons made his way up from the back of the crowd, approaching Yozna. He looked despondent as he placed his hand on Yozna's shoulder. "You know he is right, Yozna. I am sorry."

Yozna looked how Alysana felt: confused and outraged. She had only just gotten her father back, and she wasn't about to watch him be thrown back in prison—or worse. "I am clearly too young to have gotten a sense of G'henni justice," she began, placing her hand on her hip and casually drawing attention to the dagger that hung from her waist, "but my father is not going anywhere."

Her uncle turned to her in surprise as if he'd forgotten she was there. "That is not for you to decide, little one."

The words snapped something inside of her. She found herself holding her drawn dagger.

"Do not talk down to me, Uncle," she warned. "You may have known me when I was a child, but I am a woman now, and I assure you," she said as she narrowed her eyes, "I have spilled blood for less."

The jaws of Ezna and Yozna both fell open. To Alysana's surprise, it was her father who urged her back.

"Please, daughter," he said, placing his hands on the arm that held her dagger. "Ezna is right. It is not your decision—nor is it mine. If he wants justice, then that is what he will get. Although," he said, looking back at his brother, "I do not believe I will receive what can be called 'justice.'"

Ezna glowered. "Say what you will, but you had no right to leave me with nothing."

"You seem to be doing just fine," Yozna said, nodding at the fine clothes he was wearing.

"Only because Ghaja Rus—" Ezna caught himself before he finished the sentence as his eyes went to Alysana. But there was no stopping her now. She lunged at her uncle and grabbed him by the collar of his shirt.

"Because Ghaja Rus *what*?" she asked through her teeth. A part of her was cognizant of the fact that she was holding a knife to her uncle's throat, but another part of her didn't care. "That man nearly cost me my life and my innocence; how dare you even speak his name!"

Alysana was barely aware of the rumblings from the men around them, but she didn't care. Hearing Rus's name, even after all this time, brought something to the surface that she'd thought she had long since buried. She'd never even considered it before, but her uncle had just let slip his involvement with the monster who tried to sell her into slavery . . . Or may have been the very one to initiate it in the first place.

"L-let me go," her uncle stammered. "Or you'll both be on trial."

Alysana shoved him back in disgust. "Damn your trials," she spat, "and damn you, Uncle. How could you act this way toward your own blood?"

"My own blood," Ezna repeated mockingly. "My own blood took everything I had and sold it."

"For me, Uncle!" Alysana shouted. "He did for me—so that I could live. And you would put a price on that?"

Ezna thought about it, but not for long. "I would."

She shook her head. "Then you have truly changed from the man I once knew."

The G'henni air was still as the two of them glared at each other. The crowd that Ezna had brought with him—so sure of themselves at the start—began to waver in their certainty.

When Ezna spoke, though, he had every ounce of that certainty behind him. "Take him to a holding cell until the witness arrives," he said.

Alysana shot him a look that would have made the Breaker Himself hesitate. "If any of you so much as lay a hand on him . . ." she began.

"Don't listen to her," Ezna retorted.

Turning her head to the forest but keeping her eyes on them, she gave a loud, shrill whistle. She smiled as the men before her looked around, confused about what she was doing . . . but then from the forest came a growl so great that even Alysana's hair stood on end. Her smile deepened. " . . . I will tell my Kienari where you sleep."

The crowd scattered before her like shadows in sunlight, each of them making their way to their homes—all of them, that is, but Uncle Ezna. He stood before her defiant as always.

"I will have justice," he said as he looked at his brother. "And your

Kienari doesn't scare me."

When a second growl came from the forest, Ezna seemed to reconsider his words. Before he could say anything, though, Yozna interjected.

"I'd rather be held here than in Théas," her father said. "And I would much rather go peacefully than with a fight. I will go with you. Just leave my daughter out of it."

Alysana couldn't believe her ears. "Have you lost your mind?" she asked, turning to him with wide eyes.

"No, dearest one," he said with a fleeting smile. "Just everything else."

Ezna grabbed him by the arm and carted him off toward the center of the city, following the frightened men from the crowd. Alysana could only watch as he was dragged away, losing him for the second time in her life.

Watching the two of them disappear into the land of her birth, Alysana realized that she felt like more of a stranger among her own people than she did when she first came to Annoch. That was when she realized: this was not her home—Annoch was her home; this was just a piece of land that she happened to be born on. "I should never have come here," she said after some silence.

"Then leave," Elyasha said from behind her.

"Would that I could, but I must see this through."

Elyasha shrugged. She paused, as if listening to something. After a silence, she nodded. "Miera is right."

Now all of them were looking at the red-haired Khyth, who seemed to not think that the non-sequitur was all that strange.

"Right . . . about what?" Alysana asked, wondering just what was going on behind those swirling green eyes.

Cocking her head like she had asked the color of clouds, Elyasha blinked a few times like the answer should have been obvious. "Kienar," she answered. "Weren't you listening?"

Alysana could do nothing but stare.

"Yasha," Kethras began, "are you trying to say that Miera is here?

Right now?"

Elyasha furrowed her brow. She scanned the faces of her friends, then turned her head to a point in space where nothing was—nothing, that is, that anyone else could see. Then, much to everyone's surprise, she burst into laughter. "She says I'm not crazy, but I'm not sure if I believe her."

"That depends," Kethras said. "What else is she saying?"

Elyasha's smile faded from her face as she looked up at the son of the forest.

"That Kienar is in danger . . . and so is Thornton."

Chapter 18

Haidan Shar

Duna

THE MORNING AIR WAS FILLED with the beating of waves and wings. Duna, eyes closed, drank it in. She had nearly forgotten what life was like here on the edge of the sea, and she now found herself regretting ever having left. She knew that it had been her sister's fault that she'd been forced into exile, but there was still a part of her that blamed herself.

The distant cries of the gulls seemed to agree. The sounds almost made her forget where she was until she opened her eyes to the reality that came with it.

The throne room of Haidan Shar, cold and rigid, was the physical manifestation of discomfort, and—as much as she hated doing so—she knew that she had to appear like the queen that she was. Seated upon the granite throne, she was accomplishing just that. It was a good thing, too: she needed to command authority for some of the things that she was going to talk about.

✦ ✦ ✦

"Proceed," came a voice from the guard outside the throne room. The sound was followed by the groaning of metal as the doors were pulled open, and the sight of Eowen, stoic and formal, walking toward the throne. His footsteps as he approached masked the sounds of the Tashkar Sea.

"Your majesty," he said in an official tone. He knelt down, and Duna immediately waved it off. After he had risen, he said, "Your audience has arrived."

"Good," she replied. "Send them in."

Eowen started to bow, stopped himself, and retreated back past the open doors of the throne room, disappearing around the corner. When he reappeared, there were more than a dozen men following him. Duna gave a smile as they entered.

"Welcome," she said as formally as possible. "Thank you for coming." She realized too late that the summons of a queen was not something one refused; she was still getting used to being royalty. Straightening her back, she did her best to exude command; she thought she was doing a good job. "Before we begin," she said, folding her hands and knowing that the next words out of her mouth usually had the opposite effect intended. "I need everyone to remain calm. I have recently uncovered some news that is both shocking and unbelievable—yet beneficial to our cause."

There were looks of curiosity on the faces of the men before her, and several glances exchanged between them. These were some of her most trusted captains and advisors—Captains Jahaz and Zheyo, her messenger Eowen, and Cortus Venn—along with some that she did not know so well, yet trusted anyway. It was due to that trust that they were all gathered right now.

"I know you would not believe me without seeing it for yourself, so I will show you. General," she said, her words echoing loudly. "Please come forth."

The small assembly began to murmur with disbelief as loud footsteps made their way into the throne room, and none other than Aldis Tennech strode into their midst, decidedly alive and well. The crowd parted when he approached the throne, walking up the stone steps to stand beside Duna.

"I know you are probably wondering some of the same things I did when I saw him," Duna said. "And those answers will come in time. For now, however, I want to focus on the road ahead— and the enemies that await us at the end of it. General," she said, turning her head and looking at him, "the floor is yours."

"Thank you, Majesty," he said to her with a slight nod of his head. Turning to address the crowd, he spoke with all the weight of a man who once commanded armies. "Everyone in this room knows how dangerous the chovathi can be. But I am here to tell you that we have only seen a shadow of what they are capable of. The destruction of Ghal Thurái at their hands is nothing short of a tragedy, but it will pale in comparison to what they will accomplish if we do not stop them. I have seen visions of what will happen if they are left unchecked, and I assure you of this: not even the gods are safe."

The throne room exploded into a furor. There were shouts of, "What does that mean?" "Who gave you this vision?" and "What can we do in light of that?"

Tennech merely held up his hands for silence. When only the cries of the gulls outside could be heard, he spoke again.

"Each of you in this room is a warrior," he said. "And each of you knows the nature of battle: the mercilessness, the savagery; the way it surges and swells like the sea. No man can predict how a battle will go—believe me, I've tried." The tension in the room seemed to lessen with those words, and there was even a nervous chuckle or two from the crowd. "But one thing I can tell you is this," he went on. "Every battle ever fought was for a reason, trivial or not—and before us lies a battle that is unsurpassed in importance."

The walls of the chamber gave his words a boldness that only stone and emptiness could, and the men seemed to be reflecting on their meaning.

Following a brief silence, Captain Jahaz spoke up. "All this talk of battles, General" he said, "and none of direction. You say that we are bound for war, yet you still have not told us why."

Before Tennech could answer, though, Cortus Venn did it for him. "Is not the razing of Ghal Thurái enough?" he asked, stepping forward. "They spilled the blood of your brothers—maybe not your people, but your brothers—and some of those men that lie dead beneath those rocks were friends of mine. I'd wager that every man in this room could say the same."

Jahaz looked at him but did not reply. Duna knew that he was right.

"If paying back death with death is not enough for you to go to war," Tennech said, "preventing more deaths should certainly be. I know of what is to come—of the machinations of the chovathi—and I know that their plans to eliminate all human life does not stop there. They intend to march to the Otherworld and supplant the Breaker Himself. They plan to cleanse this world and start anew . . . with the chovathi themselves as the authors of the next."

Cortus Venn eyed the general. "And what would you have us do about it?"

Tennech looked at him. "We march to where it all started," he said, adding with a smile, "and make sure they don't."

Chapter 19

The Otherworld

Thornton

THIS DEEP INSIDE THE OTHERWORLD, Thornton could feel the power where creation took its first breath. He had followed the Herald inside the castle, and it had felt like piercing a thick veil of fog.

He felt the churning of the Breaker inside him, and it seemed to shift in reaction to it.

"What is this place?" Thornton asked. "Why is it here?"

The Herald stopped and looked back at him, his face still bearing that apathetic look that somehow seemed disparaging. "This place—this whole structure—is the Hall of Creation," he answered. "It's where everything began, all of it," he said, gesturing around. He paused, turning fully to face Thornton now. "It was where the decision to bind the Breaker was made too."

Thornton felt the churning more strongly than ever. The power in this place was almost palpable, it—

He stopped. About thirty feet away from him were two figures facing each other. He rubbed his eyes to make sure he wasn't seeing things, because these were figures that he recognized.

Here, in the heart of the Otherworld, were Miera and Ynara.

. . . Only it wasn't Miera and Ynara—not exactly. These figures were more like ghosts or shadows, translucent and fleeting, but looking very much alive and animated. Their gray outlines made them look like living smoke that cut through the air with deliberate, defined motion.

Thornton walked closer and realized that no sounds were coming from the figures—and as he looked again at the figure of Ynara, he realized that it wasn't her, either. It was a taller version of her, somehow older and more pronounced. He realized immediately that it must have been the previous Binder of Worlds, Ynara's mother.

"What are they?" he asked. He walked up to them and reached out his hand, placing the back of his fingers on Miera's cheek as she spoke. He pulled them back quickly when, instead of passing through it like smoke, he felt the warmth of flesh.

"Echoes," said the Herald. "Their power still resonates here, like scars on the face of time."

The two of them seemed to be having a heated argument, with Miera gesturing wildly and the Binder with her arms crossed, frowning. The Binder pointed to herself. This made Miera stop and look into the eyes of the Binder. Thornton didn't need to hear them to know what Miera was saying; it was written on her face and on her lips when she spoke the word.

No.

She said it again, and a third time, shaking her head and gesturing with her arms.

The Binder looked distraught at this but spoke a few words that appeared to soften Miera's vehemence. Then Miera, the Shaper of Ages, took a long and mournful breath. Her eyes looked pleadingly at the Binder. Between her furrowed brows and the pain that marred her face, Thornton could almost hear the next words she spoke.

Is there no other way?

The Binder shook her head and Miera looked away at something that Thornton couldn't see. She turned back and spoke again.

In a jolt of panic, Thornton whirled around to look at the Herald. "What is she saying?"

"I'm afraid I can't say," he answered, fingers splayed.

"Can't? Or won't?"

The Herald smiled and, to Thornton's surprise, there was pain behind it. Regret.

"Both, I'm afraid."

At this, Thornton was perplexed. He looked back to where, seconds before, the two ghostly figures had been. They were gone, and the Hall of Creation was as silent as ever.

"Did you do this?" he asked the Herald, but the silvery being was already shaking his head.

"I can no more control what occurs in this world any more than you can control what occurs in yours. What I can tell you is this: whatever you saw was meant for your eyes because you saw it; if it was meant for your ears, you would have heard it; and if it was meant for your understanding, you would have known it."

Thornton narrowed his eyes and felt an incredible urge to swing at the Herald, but he wasn't sure how good of an idea it was. He clenched and unclenched his fist.

"If it wasn't meant for my ears," he began slowly, "then whose was it meant for?"

The Herald brightened at this question. "Now that I can tell you," he said, and he held up one silver finger. "The Great Uniter." Almost as an afterthought, he held it up a second, saying, "And whatever living creature now embodies the spirit of the Shaper of Ages."

Chapter 20

Derenar

Kunas

MADDENING: THAT WAS THE ONLY way that Kunas could describe the cacophony of sensations and thoughts that he was experiencing, through his blood bond with the chovathi matriarch, Zhala. The candle of his life had been snuffed out by the collapse of Ghal Thurái, yet Zhala had brought him back—saved him—and molded him into something different. Something new. Something powerful.

Go, my child, she said. She was still there with him, just like before. She spoke to him in thought, but not always in words. Her will was his, and he did not hear her as much as he understood her. He was hers. *We will reclaim that which is ours—that which we have waited for all these centuries past.*

Yes, he replied, and he felt the desire to please her, the urge to follow her commands... but also the draw of power that was promised. It pulled at him more strongly than anything ever had, stronger than hunger or thirst, stronger than the need to draw breath or the urge to sleep. He couldn't see Khala Val'ur, but he knew exactly where it was.

He turned to the west and started walking.

His brothers and sisters followed.

Chapter 21

Khadje Kholam

Sera

THE LIGHT IN THE ROOM felt as heavy as a blanket. Sera rubbed her eyes and sat up in bed. Something had changed. She thought back to what the Holder had said, how he had called her the Seed.

If I'm the seed, she thought to herself, *I wonder what it is he expects me to grow into.*

She couldn't even begin to imagine. One thing, at least, was clear to her: she knew she would not like the answer.

She swung her feet off the bed and onto the stone floor to get dressed.

✦ ✦ ✦

Walking down the hall toward Yelto's chambers, she felt something inside her, something flickering, burning, like the hint of newborn flame. Before she could give it any more attention, though, she heard the sharp whispers of one of the Priests of the Holder coming from the throne room. She heard the words "Kienar" and "Otherworld;" the rest was too garbled to make out.

Striding into the room, she saw three priests kneeling before the throne—atop which sat the Holder. The Lord of the Dead looked up at her as she came in.

"There you are," he said in his hollow, unearthly tone. "We have matters to discuss. Join us," he said, motioning by the throne.

She approached the throne and knelt, once again noting the absence of Djozen Yelto. Come to think of it, she had not seen him in quite some time . . . and the dagger that he always wore around his neck was now in the possession of the Holder . . .

"Would you say that Tennech did a good job raising you?"

The words caught her entirely off guard. Not only did she never mention Tennech to the Holder, but she knew that he had never even met the man. He'd died before he had the chance.

98

"How . . . how did you . . .?" she stammered.

Her bewilderment must have been amusing to the Holder, who let out a deep chuckle. "Lilyana Coros," he said, invoking the name that she was born with but had shed when she fled her home of Ellenos. "There are many things about your past of which I am aware. Some that even you do not know." Sera's eyes narrowed. "The circumstances of your birth, for example . . ." He paused, his lidless eyes boring into her own. " . . . And that of your younger sister."

Her head jolted backward in shock. If the death of Aldis Tennech had been a rainstorm, this revelation was a hurricane. "My . . ." she stammered, "what?"

The Holder's amusement only grew. "Of course there was no way for you to know," he said, leaning forward in the gaudy throne. "With you being raised in Khala Val'ur, and your mother, well . . ."

Sera stood up. "What about my mother?" she demanded. The fire that had been smoldering inside her was now a roaring blaze. "Tell me what you know."

The Holder did not so much as flinch. "Sit back down, child. Surely you do not think that information such as that would be given away for free."

Sera felt a hand on her shoulder as she was forced roughly to the ground by one of the priests behind her. She shrugged it off, maintaining eye contact with the Holder the entire time. She had dealt with pow-er-hungry madmen before, but admittedly, this was her first time dealing with a power-hungry madman who also happened to be a god. *God or not*, she thought darkly, *everyone can be made to talk.* "Of course not," she said with a forced smile.

"I knew you were smarter than that. The price," he said as he locked eyes with her, "will be paid beneath the branches of Kienar." Turning to the one who had forced Sera to the ground, "What of the chovathi, Priest?"

Chovathi? Sera thought. *That was the last word I expected to hear down here.*

"Our scouts report them marching above ground, in the daylight no less. They have grown bold and strong, and appear to have a singular goal in mind."

The Holder pressed his index fingers together in a steeple. "Good," he said, leaning forward. "The seeds of chaos have been sown. They will have a head start, but I do not expect the battle to be quick. The Binder will make sure of that. How go the preparations for the journey?"

"Complete, Master," the priest answered with a bow of his head. "We are ready to depart on your command."

"Good." The Holder stood up and stepped down from his throne, approaching Sera. He paused for a moment and laughed to himself, a private joke that made his eyes flicker with malevolence. "How appropriate it is that the Seed will return to the forest. When it is done, you will have the answers you seek . . . although you may not like them when they come."

Sera took a deep breath. She knew she had no choice in the matter. The Holder controlled her fate, the mortal coil that bound her to this world. If he were to sever it . . .

Well, she preferred not to think of it.

"I suppose that remains to be seen," she said after a silence.

"Indeed it does. Gather the gwarái and the two Thurians. You will begin immediate preparations to lead my army to Kienar." He turned to one of the priests and motioned for him to follow. "Come, Priest, we have wasted too much time here."

Sera watched him as he headed toward the exit of the throne room., thinking that she had spent more time than she cared to with Captains Hullis and Dhrostain, but they were at least agreeable. The gwarái, on the other hand . . .

"Oh, and Sera," the Holder said, stopping short as he reached the doors. He turned, his gold-on-blue left eye twinkled with power and acerbity. "We are going to need a general."

Chapter 22

Wastes of Khulakorum

Asha

ASHA AND ULTEN HAD BEEN traveling for nearly a day, yet the sands beyond the Wastes still seemed to go on forever. The sun beat down on them angrily, and Asha began to question her decision to make the journey.

"How can you live out here?" she asked Ulten, mopping her forehead with a piece of cloth from the kaftan he had given her.

Ulten chuckled. "This desert life is not for everyone," he said. "But the strength of R'haqa is that it is never in the same place. We go where there is food and, more importantly, where there is water. And, speaking of." He reached for the skin on his belt and offered it to her.

Asha gladly accepted it, and drank.

The trek was supposed to only last a few days, but Ulten had packed like it would last a month. The two camels he brought—gifts from the Hedjetten who had given them gladly when he learned of Asha's true identity—were loaded down with dried meats, water flasks, and the thick, sturdy cloth that they would use as a makeshift shelter. The R'haqans were masters of nomadism and it showed in the man's preparation.

"But why move at all?" she asked. "Why not stay put when you find a place that could sustain you?"

"Look around you," he said, gesturing at the sky. "The world is not the same today as it was the day before, and it will be different tomorrow from how it is today." He pointed to a number of circling buzzards in the far-off distance. "Those birds will not be here in a few days. The animal they are feeding on will also be gone, food for the creatures that sleep beneath the sands. The water in the area may have dried up, which caused the poor creature to die in the first place. So it is with us," he said as he looked at her again. "We go where there is food and water, but even those will not last forever."

They had traveled through the late evening and into the night, stopping to put up a tent around dawn. The heat was uncomfortable, but not to the point where Asha couldn't sleep. She found herself waking up every few hours with a parched tongue, thanking the Shaper that Ulten had brought as much water as he did. The insulation of the animal-skin flasks did a good job of keeping the water cool. She must have been drinking particularly loudly, and was surprised by Ulten's voice from the other side of the shelter.

"More precious than gold, it is," he said as he held a flask of water in his hand gently as if he were weighing it. "Yet not as precious as what awaits."

Asha gave him a sidelong glance. Exactly how much did this goatherd know? And how did he know it? She took another drink. "How long have you lived in the shadow of Do'baradai?" she asked him.

He smiled. "Every R'haqan grows up hearing about the Two Brothers," he replied. "Both the gods that the city is named after, and the city itself."

"Then you know what lies in its depths?"

"The true Vessel of the Holder."

"And you still wish to accompany me there?"

"I do."

"Why?"

Ulten was smiling at her, but the warmth of it had faded. He let it slip from his face until his expression was as dry as the night around them. "It is not entirely selfless," he said.

"Tell me," Asha urged. Until he said it out loud, she could only guess at his motives for coming along on something so dangerous.

"I know about the Wolfblade," he said. "But I also know of another weapon—a weapon made in secret—an instrument of which even the Holder of the Dead does not know."

Asha's eyes grew wide. *Who was this man?* "I know of no such weapon," she said.

"You wouldn't. And there is a good reason for your ignorance. If it were to fall in the wrong hands . . ." His words trailed off.

"And whose hands are the right ones?"

Ulten smiled again, the warmth returning to his face. "A mortal's," he replied. "Or one intent on becoming one again. That is the only one who shall find *Burqhan'alakh* . . . the godkiller."

Chapter 23

Haidan Shar

Duna

THE THRONE ROOM OF HAIDAN Shar was empty now, save for Duna, Venn, and the resurrected Aldis Tennech. Filling the air was the sound of Venn's footsteps and the crashing of waves below as the Commander of the Lonely Guard paced back and forth. He had been at it long enough that Duna was worried he might wear a hole through the stone.

Before she could ask him to stop, the general broke the silence.

"That was quite a speech you gave back there," Tennech said. "It was just what the men needed to hear."

Venn stopped pacing. He turned his head and looked at Tennech. "It was no speech, General, and they weren't just words. I say what's on my mind and in my heart." He paused as he gathered himself up. "I like to think it's one of the reasons my men still keep me around."

Tennech, eyes fixed ahead, was peering through one of the many windows that lined the room, providing a perfect portal to the Tashkar Sea. He was leaning with his hands braced against the stone window sill, and Duna thought she heard a laugh.

"I imagine that Stoneborn blood coursing through your veins helps too."

Venn's smirk turned into a smile. "I suppose it does come in handy every now and again."

Tennech, seemingly having drunk his fill of the view, turned to give Venn a smile of his own. He crossed his arms and leaned his back against the wall. "Well it's a good thing we have you then. Duna tells me you know how to make more Stoneborn."

The look that Venn gave Duna could have frozen the Tashkar clean. Duna, unapologetic, simply shrugged and flashed him a look that said, *Well, it's true.*

Venn sighed. "I do," he said, putting a finger to his temple. "And I might be the only mortal who does."

Tennech raised his eyebrows at this. "Is that so?"

With a shrug he said, "It was a secret that was supposed to die with me." He sighed and resumed his pacing. "I've kept it for generations, General. Do you know what that's like?"

Duna knew that he did not expect an answer, and the general didn't give one.

"I've spent years with this curse, this burden of knowledge," Venn continued, "hoping—praying—that the next sunrise I see will be my last." He stopped short of the closed throne room doors, and the next words he spoke seemed to be directed at them, rather than Duna or Tennech. "But now it appears that all this accursed waiting has served a purpose."

"I would think so, Commander," Tennech said as he traced the scar on his throat. "You are not the only one with unfinished business in the world."

A rumbling sound began to emanate from the Commander, whose shoulders began convulsing—as Duna suddenly realized that the man was laughing.

Venn, doubled over, gave a laugh that shook the very foundation of Haidan Shar. He stood up, turned back around, and looked at both of them, grinning wider than the river K'Hel.

"You know," he said wiping a tear from his eye, "it's been a long time since I've had a laugh like that, let alone someone else to sympathize with."

He crossed the room to where Tennech was standing and reached up to clasp him by the shoulder. When he spoke next, he did so in a near-whisper, looking him in the eye.

"Few people understand what it's like to be what we are, General: alive at the mercy of someone else. Unnatural. Undying."

Tennech nodded but did not speak.

"I know it," Venn went on. "She knows it," he said with a nod to Duna, "and I hope you know it too." He held up a finger. "Whatever your plan is, General," he said, as he placed the tip of his finger on Tennech's chest, "if it involves making more Stoneborn, I hope you've had a good, long look in there to consider the price."

Tennech gave Venn a long, solemn look. "Believe me, Commander," he began, "I have. But the difference between you and me is this: your condition has thus far prevented you from ever entering Khel-hârad—mine did not. When I died, my spirit departed the land of the living for the one of the dead. I saw the beginning and the end, the darkness and the light; I have seen what once was, and what is to come. I saw the visions of eternity that only the dead may know, and I assure you of this, my Stoneborn friend: there is no price too great to pay in order to stop these chovathi who now march to Kienar."

Duna felt her chest tighten as the old general's words sent a shiver through her. She caught Venn's eye as he broke eye contact with Tennech. Sensing that he was waiting for her approval, she gave him a hesitant nod.

"Then I'm going to need two dozen swords, two dozen scabbards," Venn replied, "and two dozen men and women who are not afraid to die."

Chapter 24

G'hen

Alysana

THE FACT THAT THE HOLDING cells were dark was nothing new, but the fact that they were G'henni certainly was—and it was more than a little disconcerting. Alysana had finally managed to make her way past the guards—bribing the ones that she could and sneaking past the rest—and she now found herself standing inside the room where a single, solitary prisoner waited. It all seemed so familiar, yet this time something had changed.

She closed the door behind her with a clank that rang throughout. A voice followed soon after.

"So. Have you come to bring me to justice?"

Above her was a torch which Alysana took and put to flame. When it was lit, she walked down the short hallway that led out to the cells. Coming around the corner, she could see the shape of her father, head bowed and looking at the floor of his cell in dismay. He hadn't even bothered looking up.

"No, Father. I have not," she said. As she placed the torch in a holder on the wall, the prison sang with light.

Yozna raised his head. "Alysana," he said with a weak smile, "you are a sight for sore eyes." His short, dark hair was unkempt, looking like he'd been nervously running his hands thought it for the past few hours. "I am sorry that you keep finding me behind bars," he said, "but I am not sorry that you keep finding me."

When the words left his mouth, so did his smile. Alysana could see the exhaustion behind his eyes.

"Father," she said in a near-whisper. "Your heart is too kind. I keep finding you behind bars because you lack the sense to stay out of them."

At this, Yozna cracked a real smile. "I suppose you are right, my daughter—and Mordha would certainly agree."

The thought of her sister brought warmth to an otherwise cold and lonely room.

Looking around for someplace to sit, Alysana saw nothing but the weathered brick and fading mortar of the walls. Not a chair or a bench in sight, save for the one Yozna sat upon—and she had no intention of joining him inside the cell.

Of course G'henni would not make a holding cell that was comfortable, she thought. Knowing that she had some things to say, and not seeing anywhere comfortable to say them from, she took a seat right where she was, sitting cross-legged on the floor.

"I think Mordha would agree too," Alysana replied, staring into the eyes of her father. "She always told me that you were too well-intentioned for your own good."

The two of them shared a laugh that lit up the room more than any torch ever could.

"Your sister really is something," Yozna said. "You know that, right?"

Alysana nodded. "I do. I could not have asked for a better friend and protector." She leaned in and placed a hand on one of the bars of Yozna's cell. "I really hope you will come see her after this, Father. She would be overjoyed to know that you are still alive."

Yozna sighed. "I am not so sure about that."

"What?" Alysana asked. She blinked a few times. "Why would you say that?"

He fumbled with his hands and his words. "Well . . . I am afraid that . . . your sister and I, well . . . we did not always see eye to eye." Yozna stood up in the cell and turned away, clasping his hands behind his back, and looking up at the ceiling. "And there is much that you do not know."

Alysana waited in silence for her father to continue, the flickering flame of the torch the only sound in the room.

Yozna took a breath.

"You were so young back then, and your health so fragile," he said. "I, of course, wanted to take you to Ellenos myself. Your sister, though," he said as he shook a finger, "was having none of it. She was—she *is*— a fighter. She is stubborn. Relentless. Passionate." He paused to put a hand on one of the bars, and Alysana could see him rubbing his eyes with the other. "I forbade her to go, told her that I must be the one to take you. One of us had to remain here to look after the farm, after all, and I knew that she would be infinitely more useful here than I would have been." He turned back around to look at Alysana, a bitter smile on his lips. "But she disagreed, your sister. She would not tolerate 'abandoning you,' as she put it."

"But..." Alysana began. There were so many questions on her tongue, and she struggled with which one to spit out first. Her father must have been able to hear some of them rolling around.

"How is it that I remained in G'hen while your sister went with you?" he asked on her behalf.

She nodded.

"The answer is simple . . . yet . . . needlessly complex as well." He turned away again. "Of course, if I had known that your sister was going to leave like that in the middle of the night, I would have taken a different path. But the fact remains that she went behind my back—and yours too. I had no choice to do what I did."

"To do . . ." Alysana began. "I don't understand, Father; what did you do?"

The clank of the prison door filled the room as a pair of heavy footsteps made their way inside the room.

"He made a bargain," came a voice from the entryway. "And I made a fortune."

Alysana rose quicker than her pulse. She had not expected to hear the voice which made the bile rise in her throat, the one voice that could make her hot with hate, yet cold with fear all at once.

"After all," it went on, "who knew that the slave trade would come to be so lucrative?"

Yes: one voice alone could make her this enraged, and it was doing so now.

"Rus," she spat. The word itself was hate. She didn't have to say it—didn't want to say it—but it flew off her tongue regardless.

. . . And suddenly, without even realizing it, she was clutching her dagger.

She saw herself lunge for him, the fat G'henni, whose throat was an easy target even in the dark.

She saw herself plunge the dagger into his neck as his eyes flew open in fear.

She saw herself stand over his body as hot liquid red spilled forth.

She saw the life slowly drain from his eyes.

She saw his death.

Yet . . .

"These days," said the well-dressed G'henni, "I go by 'Magistrate Rus.'"

. . . Seeing the death of one's worst enemy and actually carrying out the task are two separate things, indeed.

"And you, my dear," Rus grinned, "have some explaining to do."

Chapter 25

Wastes of Khulakorum

Asha

THE UNFORGIVING HEAT OF THE Wastes beat down on them like a whip. Their only solace would come with the occasional breeze blowing through, but even that brought its own special torture. It was truly a double-edged sword, and Asha wasn't sure which edge was worse: being hot, or being pelted with sand.

She wiped the sweat from her forehead and bemoaned the mortal body to which she was now tethered. She almost considered asking Ulten if they could stop . . . yet the call of Do'baradai was growing ever stronger.

Even if she were to ask, she already knew the answer.

Pulling her shemagh tighter across her face, she braced for another breeze.

✦ ✦ ✦

It had been two days since they had seen another living creature. This deep in the heart of the Wastes, nothing truly lived. Asha eyed their packs again and, for the first time, wondered if their supplies would even last them one way—let alone the journey back.

"I know what you are thinking," Ulten said, his words slightly muffled by the shemagh that was wrapped around his own face. "And the answer is no, there is not enough for a return trip."

Asha was speechless for a moment as she was sure she misheard him. Finally she found her voice.

"I'm sorry," she said. "Did you—"

"Yes," Ulten replied, cutting her off. "Not enough for a return trip."

Asha reeled around to look at him, disbelief flooding through her. "And why would you do a thing like that?"

"Because I was instructed to."

"By whom?"

"Him," he said, pointing ahead of them.

Turning back and straining her eyes to see past the swirling sands ahead, she did not have to recognize the figure before them to know who it was. She had not felt his presence in quite some time; in fact, she could not reliably remember the last time that he had been close to her—yet even though the two of them now wore different flesh, their spirits knew each other.

Pulling on the reins of her mount and urging him to a stop, she swung her legs to the side and dropped to the ground.

"There was a time when I thought that I might not see you again."

He was just a shadow, now, obscured by the light wall of dust and sand that blew between them, choking out the sun. He was walking toward her, features becoming clearer through the haze, and Asha's jaw dropped when he came into view. Even if Asha hadn't known that it was him by the call of his spirit, she knew who was standing before her now.

"My Asha," he said. It was him; there was no mistaking it. "I can still see you behind those eyes."

"Lash'kun," she replied, in a voice barely above a whisper. "I heard your voice in my head for a thousand nights, and dreamt of you for a thousand more. Is it truly you?"

"It is, my love," he said as he approached. "And I am sorry I could not come sooner."

The two of them were standing only a few feet apart now. The eternity that had once separated them, the worlds that stood in their way— gone, like water in the desert. It didn't seem real. In fact, Asha wasn't sure that it was. Without thinking, she reached out to touch him, hoping that at least one of her senses would not betray her—but she caught herself before she did. "I'm . . . I'm sorry," she said with a touch of embarrassment. "All those years in Yelto's prison and I've forgotten my manners. May I?"

Without hesitation, the Traveler took her hand and placed it on his cheek. She could feel his muscles tense beneath her hand as he smiled.

It was him, her Lash'kun.

It was *him*!

Suddenly the heat of the desert seemed like nothing compared to the warmth that now spread through her body. She leaned in to kiss him, and he kissed her back. Eternity was meaningless to the two of them; their lips were made for each other. Decades—centuries—of passion was captured in a moment, and Asha let it wash over her. She was finally back with the one that she loved. She let his soft lips caress her own, as their bodies did the same.

"I see you and I feel you," she said, looking up at him with wonder, "but still I do not believe it. Your Vessel . . ." She said haltingly. "I thought Ahmaan had it destroyed."

The Traveler nodded. "He did."

"Then . . . how?"

The Traveler shrugged, still not letting her go. "One of my descendants," he smiled. "One of *our* descendants."

Asha's eyes left Lash'kun and shifted into the distance, toward the city called the Two Brothers. "Then it all truly has come full circle," she said.

"Almost," said the Traveler, turning his gaze to match hers. "There still remains one loose end."

Asha felt its pull before she could see it. She knew what was there waiting for her. She knew the dangers. She knew the cost—but the rough fingers interlaced with her own told her that she wouldn't have to face it alone.

Chapter 26

G'hen

Elyasha

As Yasha paced around the room, she could feel Miera pacing around her mind . . . and the feeling was undeniably odd.

Sometimes the Shaper would appear beside her, a ghostly image of the blonde woman whom Yasha recognized as the very same one who had sealed the Otherworld; other times she existed entirely in Yasha's mind, a mental manifestation of frustration and power. The former was almost comforting; the latter was like a dull, thudding headache.

This was one of those thudding times.

I wish she would quit stomping around in there, Yasha thought.

. . . And suddenly, as if on cue: silence. It felt like a cooling balm on a sunburn. It was rapturous.

Oh. Sorry, Miera said, her words clear and crisp inside Yasha's mind, almost clearer than her own thoughts.

"It's fine," Yasha said out loud, and then stopped. *Wait. Can you hear me?*

Yasha had never known what it felt like to hear someone blink until that moment.

How is that even a question? Miera replied.

I don't know! Yasha shot back. *I've never had someone in my head before. I wasn't sure how it all*—she mentally waved her hands around vaguely—*worked!*

Well I can hear your thoughts and then some, Miera answered. *At least your surface thoughts, your inner monologue—which you have an abundance of, by the way.*

Yasha frowned inwardly.

But your deeper thoughts, Miera went on, *I don't so much as hear them as I feel them. It's like the difference between thinking about moving your arm, and actually moving your arm, if that makes sense.*

Yasha nodded, noting that it was likely superfluous.

I don't know what "superfluous" means, Miera thought, *but I get your meaning.*

There would be no secrets kept from Miera, Yasha realized, as she suddenly found herself desperately trying to not think about the things that she didn't want Miera to know that she thought about—and then, by reflex, thinking about exactly those things.

Ahh! Miera mentally shouted. The feeling was worse than when Miera was stomping around inside her head. *Why would you even wonder that about Dailus?*

I don't know!

Well, stop!

You're not helping! Yasha nearly shrieked.

Suddenly the form of Miera appeared beside her, doubled over.

"If it's okay with you," she said, "I'll just stay out here while you're awake."

Yasha nodded vigorously, happy to be rid of her mental passenger—along with all the untimely and bizarre thoughts that had flooded her mind despite hardly ever showing up in the normal course of most of her days. "Dreams I can deal with. That," she said, pointing at Yasha, "I can't."

"It's fine," Yasha said, gathering herself. "People already gawk at me for how I look. I'm alright with them thinking that I'm talking to myself too."

As Yasha stared at the incorporeal form of her friend, Miera, the Shaper of Ages, she noticed a flickering that reminded her of a candle flame dancing in a light breeze. She had a lot of questions, and she wasn't sure where to start; that particular one seemed as fine a jumping-off point as any.

"So, what . . . happened?" She asked. "How are you even here right now?"

The ghostly form of Miera turned to her and seemed to fade even more, as if concentrating on more than one thing took not just mental energy but spiritual as well.

"It's . . ." Miera started. "Complicated."

Yasha walked over to the single bed that occupied the room, and sat down. She looked up at Miera expectantly. "I think we both have some time on our hands," she said with a smile. She patted the spot beside her on the bed, and immediately felt foolish for offering a spirit a place to sit.

Miera graciously shrugged it off with a laugh and, like Yasha had seen her do in the Otherworld, simply lifted herself off the ground and sat, cross-legged, in the middle of the air.

With a breath followed by a pause, Miera began: "Not long after I finished sealing off the Otherworld did it begin to sink in that I had not just prevented D'kane from escaping," she said. Her form solidified for a moment as if to emphasize the words. "I had also trapped myself inside there, with him.

"He was furious. Merciless." The pain in Miera's eyes was punctuated by her opacity. Her flickering form was as solid as Yasha had ever seen it. "And I was no match for him, nor the power he wields."

Her form began to fade again, resuming its intermittent flicker.

"What did you do?" Yasha asked softly.

"The only thing I could," she said with a shrug. "I let him defeat me."

"You—wait, what?"

Miera shrugged. "D'kane carries inside him the power of the gods of creation, as well as the ambition and drive to use it. I didn't stand a chance."

Yasha's jaw hung open as she blinked her silent questions at Miera.

"I had to. It was the only way I could get out. At that very moment, when D'kane's full power coursed through me, the Shaper of Ages ceased to exist—not just me, but all of them, stretching back to the beginning of time. Gone, in the blink of an eye. Destroyed." As she said the words, though, a smirk worked its way onto her face.

"Alright, what is that look for?" Yasha asked, suspicious. "Is something funny?"

Miera nodded. "I know something that D'kane doesn't."

"Are you going to tell me, or do I have to guess?"

Miera gave her a look that said her sarcasm was understood. "The only way for a god to die is when it happens here, outside of the Otherworld, in the mortal realm."

Yasha cocked her head as she let the thought twirl around inside her head. "So you're saying . . . he thinks he's beaten you. That he's destroyed you."

Miera nodded, and her smile widened. "Not only that," she said, "but when he leaves the Otherworld, we can do to him what he did to the Binder of Worlds—and what he tried to do to the Shaper of Ages."

Miera's form once again solidified, and Yasha had to take a step back from the sheer power that had just manifest itself in the room.

"There is a way to destroy the Breaker, Yasha—and we can do it once and for all."

Yasha looked at her and nodded. "Tell me what I have to do."

Chapter 27

Do'baradai

Asha

The sands of time, eternal falling, flit through countless hourglasses in a dance to remind us all of one thing: we are but mortal.

— Inscription on the tomb of Hedjetten Hota

THE CITY OF THE TWO Brothers stood silent and tall above the deepest parts of the Wastes of Khulakorum, its ancient pillars and looming walls rising high enough to meet the sky. Though the identity of its architects had long been buried with the centuries, their legacy lived on in the ambitious design: wall after reinforced wall formed a perimeter around a city whose chief defense was the nigh-impassibility of the desert that led into it. Any army attempting to invade would have to cross endless burning seas of sand in the most inhospitable part of the Wastes. That was, no doubt, the reason that the number of invasions Do'baradai had suffered remained steadfastly at zero.

"She's just like I remember," the Traveler said. His voice was lined with a pain that Asha recognized as the kind that comes with reopening an old wound; he had slept beneath these walls, trapped in exile, for longer than she cared to think about. And now he faced them again—willingly—knowing that even greater pain lay ahead.

Ulten had already dismounted behind them and was speaking soft words of reassurance to his camel. Asha decided that now was as good a time as any to dismount as well, and let her feet slide from the stirrups of her sturdy desert Vessel.

Once on the ground, she knelt down to sort through the contents of her pack, not really sure how much of it she would actually need. "It's been much longer for you than it's been for me," she said, looking up, "but Do'baradai has remained unchanged through the ages." Her eyes went over the solid stone of the walls, placed there in ages past by the strength of men and gods, and understood why. "Perhaps it's time that we change that," she sneered.

+ + +

The three of them approached the outer gates and Asha felt the old, familiar, creeping cold. She knew right then that her fears were real. She turned to Lash'kun, beside her, and the look on his face told her that she was not alone in the thought.

"His influence still lingers," said the Traveler. "I can feel it."

Asha looked to the gates of the great, ancient city. "It's somewhere in there," she said. "His Vessel. The key to ending this all."

Lash'kun nodded. "Finding it will not be easy, but it will be far easier than getting to it." Squinting as he scanned the perimeter, he must have found what he was looking for. With a mirthless chuckle, he said, pointing, "Even after all these years, they still man the walls."

Asha looked to where he was indicating and was surprised to find that he was right: on either side on top of the gargantuan gate was a Priest of the Holder, standing in silent watch over the city where the Lord of the Dead's Vessel was buried. She wasn't sure how much power they would have here—far away from the living spirit of Ahmaan Ka, which now inhabited a new body in Khadje Kholam—but something told her that the uncomfortable cold she'd felt earlier might hold a hint.

"What should we do?" Asha asked, suddenly feeling the urge to duck down or find cover.

The Traveler looked down at her, and his form seemed to flicker like the flame of a candle in a breeze. He smirked and gave Asha a wink. Then, as quickly as someone snuffs a candle, he disappeared, with nothing but the dull thud of rushing air to announce his exit. He was gone, a pair of boot prints in the sand the only evidence that he had existed at all.

A distant scream from the tower made Asha jerk her head over in surprise. She squinted, able to make out three figures: the first was standing on top of the left gate; the second atop the right; and the third one was plummeting, shrieking, down the length of the near-thousand-foot drop that made up the outer wall of Do'baradai. Following another distant thud, a second scream could be heard. Finally, after both screams had ceased, a third thud sounded—and the Traveler reappeared beside her.

"We walk right in."

Chapter 28

Haidan Shar

Duna

GATHERED BY THE SHORE OF the Tashkar sea were Duna, General Tennech, Cortus Venn, and about two dozen men and women who looked more nervous than a Khyth in an Athrani bathhouse. Absent was Venn's newest protege, Benj, but Duna assumed what was about to happen was not meant for young eyes.

Venn was looking the men up and down, stuck between inspection and hesitation, and Duna wasn't sure how much of the former played into the latter. Occasionally the Stoneborn commander of the Lonely Guard would glance back at her in a way that almost seemed to ask the question, *Are you sure?*

Every single time, Duna would meet his gaze with steely resolve.

Yes.

Finally, after what seemed like an eternity in the early morning light, Venn gave a nod. "We are ready," he declared.

Duna held back the urge to say, "Finally."

"What now?" asked Tennech from beside her.

"Now we can begin the burial rites," he said as he swept his gaze over the men one more time. "Each of them, before they can become Stoneborn, has to die."

Duna noticed on the faces of the men gathered before her a flutter of realized terror as Venn's words carried. Though he had surely not meant for them to ring out like they did, his booming voice and the calmness of the sea ensured that every last man knew what lay ahead. That, Duna was sure, was by design.

"Normally," Venn began in an official tone, "Stoneborn are born in battle; that is to say, no one is ever made a Stoneborn—at least not intentionally." He was walking toward the front of the loose formation of men who were facing out toward the sea. When he made it to the front, he paused, back still toward them. "But today, that will change. Today," he said as he turned his head just enough to give them a sidelong glance, "they will be born out of necessity."

As he spoke, Duna heard the sound of a wagon approaching. She turned to watch it roll in and saw that it was stacked high with a large number of wooden boxes.

Odd, she thought. *That looks like a lot of supplies for a simple ceremony.*

Then, as it got closer, she realized they weren't boxes—they were coffins.

"Death is the heart of the Stoneborn," Venn said. "The coffin serves as both symbol and catalyst for your transformation. Without it, the ritual will fail—and you must trust me when I say: you do not want the ritual to fail." He was looking each man in the eye as he spoke, marble skin shining softly in the morning sun. "But fear not," he said as a prideful grin worked its way across his lips, "you have me."

He gave a nod at the two burly men, who began to unload the cargo. Venn turned to address the small crowd of men gathered before him.

"The fact remains," Venn continued, his voice carrying easily over the calm sea air, "that I gave each of you the chance to back out when I first approached you. I extend to you that same offer now."

As the two men finished unloading the coffins from the wagon, the lapping waves of the Tashkar Sea's low tide were the only sounds as the Stoneborn paused for dissension. He let the silence linger as if testing the resolve of the men once again—or just letting it sink in that what they were volunteering for was indeed mortally perilous. "There will be no more chances after this one," he said finally. "The executioner's axe will be swung. There is no turning back."

It was all rather mysterious, Duna noted, supposing it was happening this way at Venn's request. She wondered at the last time this particular ritual had been performed, remembering his words earlier that he was probably "the only mortal" who knew how to perform it. A grisly afterthought came that perhaps it was how he came to be Stoneborn in the first place.

Days of the Dark

The thought must have shown on her face as Tennech, beside her, leaned over and whispered, "I hope he knows what he's doing."

"Me too, General. I admit I am a little nervous about the whole thing."

Venn was making his way through the silent crowd toward where the coffins had been unloaded. Duna counted: there was one for every person gathered on the shore.

"Last chance," Venn said as he walked past the coffins and looked up toward the Keep of Haidan Shar.

One candidate that Duna had been watching, a handsome young man with tender eyes and wispy blond locks, seemed to finally make up his mind that he wasn't cut out for this. His shoulders sagged and he took a step out of the formation. He slunk away, making barely more than a sound as he trudged through the sand of the shore. Venn must have heard him break ranks because he turned his head—very slightly—in acknowledgement of the man's exit.

Duna was surprised that Venn held his tongue; her former commander, Caladan Durakas, would have had a deserter like that flogged before he took a second step. In fact, Durakas's cruel tendencies were so deeply ingrained in her that she realized she had been bracing herself for the man to be cut down even as he continued to walk away. When she looked back to Venn, though, she felt her entire body relax as a new realization worked its way through her. Looking at him now, she saw in him the polar opposite of the heart that once beat in the last commander of the Thurian army. Venn was a leader, yes, but with an entirely different style than Durakas—and, as the commander of the Lonely Guard of Lash'Kargá, one whose successes and failures came at even higher costs.

She saw in him compassion; she saw strength; she saw a genuine desire for no other mortal men to suffer the same fate that he had been forced to endure.

She turned to Tennech and, in acknowledgment of the general's earlier comment, said, "I take it back, General. I am no longer nervous."

Tennech didn't hide his smile. "Venn's reputation precedes him,

Your Majesty. I didn't want to take anything away from him by reassuring you of his qualifications or telling you that I believe that he is the right man for the job." He looked at her, still beaming. "I wanted you to see it for yourself."

Duna, looking back at Cortus Venn, simply nodded.

I have, she thought to herself. *And he will be the reason for our victory.*

Chapter 29

G'hen

D. L. Jennings

Alysana

A G'HENNI COURTROOM IS NOT A thing that most outsiders see the inside of, and Alysana was now wishing that she *were* an outsider; she certainly felt like one. The city of her birth had been nothing more than that in name as, in the last few days, her entire world had been turned upside-down with revelations and discoveries that she now preferred to have never learned. G'hen was no longer her home, and she had never felt it more strongly than now.

For her entire life, Alysana had thought that Ghaja Rus had been the sole source of her psychological scars that came in the form of a near abduction of her and her sister, Mordha. Now she was learning that not only did Ghaja Rus have help, but her own father was the one who provided it. The knowledge had soured on her tongue.

She was seated in the back of the small courtroom, with nothing more than benches carved from mahogany and a raised platform in the middle upon which the accused would stand. All of it was arranged in a circle around the platform, representing the fact that everyone in the room had an equal voice that would be considered in both the sentencing and the conviction.

In G'henni justice there were no judges—only the people.

She looked across the room where Ghaja Rus sat, and she scowled. He was a G'henni by birth, which meant that he had a voice in this trial as well. She did not have to guess which way he would lean.

The grand wooden door to the courtroom creaked open, and in strode her uncle, Ezna.

"Thank you all for coming," he said as he made his way, slowly and dramatically, to the center of the room. "You all know that I have called this trial, and I have made my position clear in not only the last few days, but in the last few years after the offense occurred. It has only been until now that I am able to face my brother with these accusations, and finally

133

bring to light the gross injustices that have been perpetrated upon me and my—" he cleared his throat "—family."

Alysana rolled her eyes.

Having reached the center where the accused would stand, Ezna came to a halt, as if he meant to heighten the dramatic intensity that he was working so hard to build. He looked around the room at the faces of the men and women gathered inside—all of them G'henni, as the law demanded—and paused when he met the eyes of Ghaja Rus. Alysana's own eyes narrowed as the two men seemed to share a glance. Ezna's eyes continued to scan the room until he came, at last, to her. He stopped, gazing intently. Venomously.

"But I do have to extend my sincerest thanks to my niece, Alysana, without whom this trial would not have been possible." His lips curled up in a mocking smile. "Thank you, dear niece, for bringing my brother back home to me."

Alysana resisted the urge to shout back at him; she would save it for the trial. She knew that right now was no place for an uncontrolled emotional outburst—no matter how warranted it may have been. She simply narrowed her eyes at him and clenched her jaw in an act of self-restraint that, surprisingly, seemed to have more of an effect on Ezna than she had intended. The smile on his lips faded momentarily as if he was questioning its use and possibly even his ability to handle Alysana's presence. He tore his eyes away and sent them darting around the room as if looking for reassurance; he must have found it in the eyes of Ghaja Rus—the fat and self-assured slaver roosting in the rear of the courtroom—because the smile returned to his face once more.

"So, without further ado, I would like to formally request that we bring forth the prisoner, Yozna, to be tried in this matter."

The silence in the room signified the lack of objection from those gathered, and one of the guards in the room nodded and slipped out the door that led to Yozna's cell. After a long, quiet moment, there was a chaotic commotion that came from the direction of the cells. A panicked cry of confusion rang out, followed by unintelligible shouts that came from what Alysana assumed were the guards.

The guard who had left came crashing back into the room, wide eyed and breathing heavily.

"I-I . . ." he stammered. "He . . ."

"What!" demanded Ezna. "Spit it out!"

"Yozna," the guard said between breaths. "The prisoner. He's . . . he's dead."

The gasp that filled the room echoed the sentiment in Aysana's own heart as she could scarcely believe the words. She could only stare at the guard who had uttered them, unable to blink so much as breathe, trying her best to sort through the cacophony of thoughts that were clamoring in her head.

It was only when she looked to her uncle, and then to Ghaja Rus, that all other thoughts halted, save one: they both looked as shocked as she felt.

Chapter 30

The Otherworld

D. C. Jennings

Thornton

THORNTON HAD BEEN WANDERING AIMLESSLY now for hours—although, he had to admit, it was difficult for him to keep track of time in this place. He wasn't sure what he was looking for, exactly, either. Another god, perhaps? A human who had somehow wandered through? A way back home? Whatever the answer, and for whatever reason, he was compelled to keep looking.

The inside of the great castle that the Herald had referred to as "the Hall of Creation" was large—somehow larger, Thornton thought, than it had seemed on the outside. For a place that was designed by and made for gods, the Hall had a surprisingly . . . human quality to it. There were carefully carved statues of men and women placed throughout, and lining the walkway were great white columns decorated in silver, platinum, and gold. The ceilings were impossibly high, adding to the feeling of the castle's greatness. Every time he looked up, Thornton expected to see sky. The floors were mostly bare, and made from the most beautiful marble that Thornton had ever laid eyes on.

The walls, however, put all the rest to shame.

Every inch of space that Thornton had seen on his long walk through the Hall had been decorated with carvings or drawings, the complexity and style of which varied immensely. Some were simple colored lines that depicted a moment in time; others looked to be burned into the walls with hot iron or flames; still others looked to be inlaid with gold. All of them, however, hummed with an energy that Thornton knew was but a fragment of the power of creation.

+ + +

Coming back to the place where he had seen the figures of the Shaper and the Binder speaking before, Thornton was surprised to see a ghostly figure standing there that, if he didn't know better, almost seemed to be waiting for him. It was a woman, whose protruding midsection told Thornton that she was pregnant—very pregnant.

She was standing there, frozen, mid-stride. Worry was etched on her face as she seemed to be looking off at something. Thornton walked closer.

When he did, darkness consumed him.

✦ ✦ ✦

"Something is wrong, Revered Mother, I can feel it."

The young woman wore a maternity gown of silk that looked like it had been purchased just yesterday for the occasion.

"You've come this far, Cora," the older woman replied. She was wearing stately robes and a blindfold over her eyes. "Let me feel." She reached out a hand; Cora, seeing this, took her hand and placed it on her belly. "Thank you, my dear." Keeping her hand there for a moment, a smile finally came to her face. "The baby is healthy and fine." She stood up, adding, "Strong, too, from the feel of it."

"I hope you're right," Cora said. She patted her belly nervously.

"I raised you, didn't I?" the old woman asked with a smile. "Of course I'm right." Cora smiled, and the old woman put her hand out. "Now let's keep moving. Delivery is never easy, and we all want you to be comfortable." Tilting her head up to the sky she added softly, "This one is special."

The two of them continued down the Ellenian road, toward the blue-hued Temple of the Shaper that loomed above all other buildings in the city.

✦ ✦ ✦

The faces of the Athrani inside were a mixture of nervousness and joy. This was no ordinary birth, and Cora was no ordinary mother.

"Today is the day, so I hear." Stepping out into the grand entryway to greet them was none other than the seemingly ageless High Keeper of Ellenos, flanked by two young women in serving gowns.

"Ah, Sh'thanna," answered the old woman, still being led by Cora. "The gods will deliver unto us a child this day, the holiest of days."

Sh'thanna smiled. "They seldom make their minds and wills known to us," she said, "but we can be thankful for this gift. Please, Cora," she said, extending her arm toward a room to the right. "Your birthing suite has been carefully arranged for you."

As she said these words, the two women who had been standing behind her stepped forth.

The old woman turned toward the High Keeper and gave a low and reverent bow. "If the High Keeper wills it," she said, "I would like to be present for the birth."

"Of course, Revered Mother," answered Sh'thanna. "And you know you do not have to ask."

The old woman tilted her head to the side. "Tradition is tradition," she said with a smile.

Cora looked up at the High Keeper with a hint of confusion in her eyes. A smile tugged at the corner of her lips. "I still don't understand what all the fuss is about," she said. "An orphan from the streets of Ellenos giving birth in the Temple of the Shaper? What is the world coming to?"

The High Keeper looked at Cora for a moment, a placating smile dancing across her face. She looked to the Revered Mother and blinked a few times, as if asking for permission to speak.

"I gather by the silence that the High Keeper is looking at me," the old woman said with a smile, much to the giggling delight of those in attendance. "But I suppose we can tell her. There's no harm in it. We've kept it secret her whole life, and . . ." she said, trailing off. A worried, mournful look flashed briefly across her face. "Well . . ."

The High Keeper nodded knowingly. "Coraline, daughter of Eidaline," she said, looking the young woman in the eye. "Yours is no ordinary child, just as you are no ordinary woman."

Cora furrowed her brow. "What . . . what do you mean?"

The High Keeper shifted uncomfortably. "What you have said is true, Cora: you are an orphan—but that is not all you are. I am sorry that we have had to keep it a secret this long, but the knowledge of what you are, of who you are, had to be kept safe—even from you. But now that the time of your child's birth draws near, we have no reason to keep it from you any longer. Now, come," she said, placing a hand on her back and extending the other in invitation to enter the birthing suite. "You'll want to be comfortable when you hear this."

Cora blinked a few times and managed to eke out a few words. "Yes. Right. Comfortable."

✦ ✦ ✦

The birthing suite took advantage of the large, open windows carved into the side of the Temple of the Shaper, allowing sunlight to flood in and illuminate the room. It was sparsely decorated save for a few essentials: clean cloths, medical instruments, and a large bed in the center with plush pillows and fresh sheets. The room was warm, thanks to the sunlight, and quiet.

Cora stepped inside and looked around. With a glance back at the Revered Mother, she said, "This is the nicest room I've ever been in."

"I wish I could see it, my dear," she said, putting her fingers gently on the wall beside her. She nodded approvingly. "Sharian marble, just like I asked. Only the best for you." She took her hand away and turned toward Cora. "Now, my dear, lay down," she said with a shooing motion. "We want you comfortable—and not just for the birth."

Cora acquiesced and walked to the bed. She reached out and pressed her hand into the mattress. "It certainly feels comfortable. Thank you," she said, and climbed on with the help of the midwives beside her.

The High Keeper strode in behind them and looked around.

"A beautiful day for a beautiful thing," she remarked. The Revered Mother beside her gave a hum of agreement. "Now, Cora, I . . ."

The words of the High Keeper trailed off as the room was plunged into darkness. Every eye went to the windows, wide open and unobstructed—yet somehow the sunlight was blocked from coming in.

"What . . . what is—" Cora began to say, but her words turned into a shriek as she suddenly grabbed her side. "Ahhhhh!"

The Revered Mother rushed to her side in an instant. "Midwives, to me," she said. "She is coming." The two of them set about their practiced routines. One of them made sure that Cora was comfortable, while the other one positioned herself near her feet, spreading the cloths below and bringing over the tray of instruments that had been placed beside the bed.

"No," Cora gasped. Her eyes were wide, and she looked straight at the Revered Mother. "Something is wrong."

"My dear," said the Revered Mother, placing a hand on Cora, "you are safe. You are in the care of the best midwives in Derenar, under the watchful eye of the spirit of the Shaper Herself."

The words gave no comfort to Cora, who was frantic from the pain that she was feeling. She looked fearfully at the Revered Mother, then to the High Keeper, who stood, arms crossed, watching the scene unfold.

"There is nothing to fear," said Sh'thanna. "The Shaper knows what She is doing. This was all set in motion long before any of us were born, and will continue after we are gone. This," she said, raising her hands and eyes, "is destiny."

+ + +

The air was pierced with a shrill cry as Cora once again felt the throes of some invisible pain coursing through her. "Something is wrong!" she repeated.

She had been in labor for just over an hour already, but nothing about the birth seemed right.

"Make sure she is taken care of," said the Revered Mother, and the two midwives did as they were told. The one closest to Cora's head dipped a cloth in a bucket of water nearby and dabbed it on her forehead. "We do not want Her born into chaos."

Cora continued to scream, but managed to turn her head just enough to look at the High Keeper. "Please," she said, "do something."

The High Keeper gave her a look of pity. "We are doing what we can, young one. And we have done what we can to protect you all these years. Though the ignorance has protected you, it is also the cause of your pain. But I can assure you: neither will last long."

Cora grunted in pain as she gritted her teeth. Her face contorted as her eyes went from panicked to pleading. "Why . . . is the baby . . . coming . . . so fast?"

The Revered Mother put her hands on Cora's belly—and pulled back almost immediately. "She is right: something is wrong."

"I see it!" shouted the midwife at Cora's feet. "It's . . . it's crowning already. This is—"

"Not supposed to happen," said the Revered Mother. She had stood up and faced the windows, frowning at the darkening room. "Is this your will?" she asked of the air.

Everyone was silent as they watched the old woman move a hand, slowly, to her blindfold and pull it down. "So be it," she called out again. She turned around.

The midwives gasped as orange light began to pour out from the Revered Mother—right where her eyes should have been. The light radiated outward, quickly enveloping her as she walked toward Cora.

"The head is out!" cried the lower midwife. "Push!"

Cora's forehead was matted in sweat; her grunts of pain were sharp and prolonged. She looked up nervously at the Revered Mother, who reached out to her and put her hand on her forehead. The orange light filled Cora's eyes, and she looked at the old woman in fear and confusion.

"Push!" the midwife shouted again, and Cora's wailing shook the room. "Push! You're nearly there!" With the baby's head out, the shoulders began to emerge as the child's body rotated. "I've got it," the midwife said, placing a hand to cradle the head.

Cora grunted as she pushed, and the child continued to come out, much to the shock and confusion of everyone else in the room.

"Impossible," said Sh'thanna.

The Revered Mother stood up, and the light began to fade. She placed the blindfold back over her eyes.

The midwives continued to help Cora, but gave no indication that anything was wrong.

"The child," the old woman said softly, "is not what we thought. Not what we hoped."

The High Keeper placed a hand on the old woman's shoulder and turned, facing away from Cora. "You and I both know that Cora's spirit should have passed to the child's the moment she emerged from the womb. This child is not the Shaper." She paused. "What happened? What went wrong?"

The Revered Mother took a breath. "I did everything in my power. The spirit of the Shaper of Ages still lives—I can feel her now, waiting to pass into Her next Vessel," she said, glancing back at Cora. "But the child born this day is devoid of spirit—empty. She should not *be*."

The High Keeper considered this carefully. "What do we do?"

"What the Shaper wills: we wait, and we obey."

"And of Cora?"

The old woman paused in thought. "She will continue to do what she does, and be what she is. It is not our place to say why the Shaper chooses the ones that she does, but when Cora's next daughter is born, we must pray that the Vessel is suitable." She added gravely, "That may very well be the last hope of the Athrani."

When the two women turned back to Cora, the midwives had already finished swaddling the newborn. Cora, with her sweat-matted hair and tear-stained cheeks, radiated joy as she held her child.

"Congratulations are in order, my dear," said the Revered Mother as she put on a smile, taking her place beside Cora. Tilting her ear toward the crying baby, still so new to the world, she asked, "What will you call her?"

"I was thinking of naming her something in the old tongue," she said looking up, "in Old Athrani."

"A lovely thought," said the High Keeper. "The Old Ones often gave names to their children that reflect the nature of their birth or their hopes for what they will become."

"I like that idea," Cora said. "And it might sound silly, but I think the old words have some power to them."

"That isn't silly at all, child—it's true," said the Revered Mother. "There is a reason that our ancestors carved runes into the Anvil of the Worldforge in Annoch. The very same power that shaped the world is present in them and continues to be present every time we invoke the name of the gods." Warmly, she regarded the child, who had since ceased crying. "So, what words of power will you give to this little one?"

"It's not what I give to her," Cora said, looking down at her newborn. The light that filled her eyes showed that, for the first time, she had found some semblance of peace. "It's what she gives to us." Looking at the woman who had raised her, she said, "Hope, Revered Mother. She gives us hope."

Both the High Keeper and Revered Mother nodded solemnly, like Cora had just stumbled on some ancient truth that only they two knew.

"'She Gives Us Hope,'" the old woman repeated as a smile graced her lips. "A beautiful phrase, Cora—and just as beautiful in the old tongue." She turned toward the High Keeper. "Sh'thanna, you have always had a better handle on Old Athrani than I have. Would you like to do the honors?"

Sh'thanna nodded. "Thank you, Revered Mother, I would."

The High Keeper walked over to them, gliding across the floor like a leaf on the breeze, coming to a stop by the bedside where mother and daughter lay. She stretched out a hand and brought her palm within inches from the child's forehead, closing her eyes to speak the words of the tongue of their ancestors.

"To the one who gives us hope," she said, and pressed the palm to her head. "Li'lyan'a!"

The Temple of the Shaper shuddered . . . and a world that was dark became light.

Chapter 31

Khadje Kholam

Sera

SERA OPENED HER EYES AND sat up in bed. Her room was still dark, with the light of dawn only just beginning to peek through her window. She listened to the silence, gazed at the dark . . . and a shadow shifted.

Without a thought, Sera's dagger was in her hand. She leapt from her bed, holding the blade in front of her, bending at the knees, ready to strike. Squinting, she wished that her eyes would adjust to the darkness more quickly—when a voice came from the dark corner of her room.

"The Holder wishes to deliver to you a message."

Sera tightened her grip on the dagger. She hated their voices, the Priests of the Holder, and she hated their master even more. Taking a breath, she reluctantly let her guard drop.

"Very well," she replied, dropping the dagger back on the nightstand. "What is it?"

The robed figure was standing in the middle of her room, draped in shadow and blue. He took a step forward from the darkness, his fleshless face bathed dimly in the light of the dawn.

"He wishes for you to see, with your own eyes, the army that you will command," he said with another step toward her. "The army," he continued with a slow, consuming reverence, "that shall be the undoing of the gods."

Despite the dryness in her throat, Sera swallowed and kept her poise. Being commanded by the Holder of the Dead, she determined, was equal parts terrifying and aggravating: she was afraid of what the god of death could do, yes, but she was also annoyed by how much power he held—power over her, which extended somehow beyond even death.

She wondered, briefly, if oblivion was a preferable alternative. Deciding against it, she asked, "Where must I go?"

"Ja'ad Shiddeq."

"Ja . . . ad . . . Shi-deq," she repeated, balking at the unfamiliar words.

"I do not know of such a place."

The Priest scoffed. "You will know it soon enough," he said with an air of indignation. "It is a half-day's ride north." He turned and began to exit the room.

Sera called after him. "I will need my captains," she said.

The skeletal priest stopped fast in his tracks. He paused and tilted his head upward, as if listening a conversation only he could hear.

"Very well," he said; he continued walking.

Just as he reached the door to her chambers, though, he stopped. Turning his head to Sera, leering with his lidless eyes, he went on, "Your usefulness will be weighed in blood, Seed." Sera tried to control the shiver that danced down her spine, but to no avail.

He turned and left without another word.

Maybe having Hullis and Dhrostain along will help ease my mind, Sera thought as she made another attempt to contain her revulsion; this time she succeeded.

It was indeed a strange comfort to have the two captains there with her, even if their allegiance was pledged to Tennech and not to her. Despite that fact, though, even after witnessing his death at the hands— or, rather, the jaws— of the Wolfwalker, Sivulu, neither of the captains had abandoned their pledge.

Sera closed the door to her chambers and began the walk out from Yelto's inner sanctum.

Like a blacksmith with a piece of battered steel, Sera was about to put their pledge to the fire. She would find out how strongly it was forged, and what it was made of—and whether it would harden and grow, or be broken and consumed by the flames.

+ + +

"Captains," Sera said after a series of knocks, "may I come in?" There was a brief silence followed by a commotion, and unintelligible whispers of panic. "Captains?" Sera repeated. Her hand was on the knocker but moved toward the handle.

"Just a moment," came the voice of Dhrostain, low and gruff.

Sera thought she heard bottles clanking, and, confusingly, a bell.

"Just let her in," Hullis whispered harshly behind the door. "They'll have to go out that way anyway."

Sera heard Dhrostain's voice but couldn't make out his words.

"It wouldn't be a problem," Hullis replied to the unheard protestation, his voice well above a whisper now, "if they'd left before the sun, like I told you they should."

"Well, it's your fault for not getting us the room with windows."

Sera leaned in closer to the door. "I will not ask again," she said.

The commotion stopped, along with the voices inside. Sera saw the door crack open. Much to her surprise, though, she was not greeted with the face of either Hullis or Dhrostain—instead, she saw a scantily-clad serving girl slip through the small opening in the door.

"Excuse me, Lady Edos," said the serving girl as she did her best to hide her face. She was wearing loose, flowing pants whose transparency hid nothing from the imagination, and a top which covered her breasts in name alone. Sera watched with a raised eyebrow as the girl scurried down the hall and out of sight, clearly able to see that she wasn't wearing undergarments.

Sera turned back as another identically-dressed servant exited the room, carrying a bucket of fresh milk. "Excuse me," the girl echoed.

When a third was hot on her heels, Sera pushed the door open impatiently where four more were crowding the entrance.

"Exc—" they began.

"You're excused," Sera growled. "Out."

The girls moved as if their silken clothing was on fire. Bringing up the rear was, Sera realized, the source of the bell noise that she thought she was hearing.

"The women, I can understand," Sera said as she walked in and shut the door. The distant bleating of a goat being led away almost drowned out her words. "The rest, I simply don't want to."

Hullis was fidgeting with his visor. He was inexplicably dressed in full battle regalia—including the helmet.

Dhrostain was standing with his back to her, donning a cloth tunic over his head. "Probably for the best," he said. "I doubt you Valurians would understand."

"Valurian?" Sera asked incredulously. She allowed herself a welcome chuckle. "I think that's the first time in my life anyone has called me anything but Athrani."

"My point stands either way," Dhrostain said as he faced her. Both of his eyes were swollen and black, and the grin on his face outshone both of them. "You come to Ghal Thurái, and we'll show you a good time."

"To be honest, Captain," Sera began as she looked around. There was a large wooden barrel in the middle of the room with a single spigot attached to it, about ten wooden mugs, a step stool, and a set of throwing knives. "I don't think I want any part of your version of a good time."

Dhrostain shrugged. "Your loss." He walked over to the mugs, inspecting each of them. Finding one of them still containing liquid, he finished it in a single gulp, wiped off his beard, and belched. "But if you didn't come here for a good time, I assume you're here to tell us we're finally leaving this sweltering hellhole."

"Something like that," Sera said, still eyeing the fully-armored Hullis. "The Holder has put me in charge of his army. We're to go someplace called . . ." she scrunched up her face to try and remember the name that the Priest had given her. "Jod-she-deck."

Dhrostain chuckled.

"Is something funny?"

"Aye," said the short, bearded man. "Your pronunciation is off. You've got the right sounds in there, but Khôl is an unforgiving language: you have to have the right tone and cadence. Otherwise," he said as a sneer formed on his face, "instead of saying 'the rider who throws a spear at the heavens,' you'll end up saying something that would even make a serving girl with a goat blush."

Sera narrowed her eyes at the captain. "So what did I say?"

Dhrostain looked at her a moment as he apparently tried to read her expression. She was doing her best to be as straight-faced as possible, as if the entire pot of a game of liar's dice was on the line, and she had the winning hand.

Whether Dhrostain could read her or if he simply didn't care, he flashed her a grin. "'Ride me with your spear and you'll see the heavens.'"

Sera tried to keep her serious demeanor, but the fact was that the crude, flippant captain from Ghal Thurái had been the perfect antithesis to the Priest of the Holder—and the Holder himself.

She couldn't help herself. She sputtered a laugh that made Dhrostain's grin grow wider, turning into a laugh of his own.

Hullis laughed nervously.

At that point there was no stopping it, and Sera found herself in the throes of a laugh that she swore she hadn't felt since Ellenos. In fact, she wasn't even sure that she'd laughed that hard then, either. It felt like there had been a spring inside her—having been wound tighter and tighter and tighter—that was finally allowed release.

Dhrostain was already howling with laughter that Sera was certain was influenced by whatever was in that mug he'd just polished off. Hullis had flipped the visor of his helmet up and was laughing through the single opening in his armor. Even if that view wasn't enough to make her laugh harder, she would have done it anyway. She doubled over and grabbed her knees as the relief surged through her. She treasured it, she savored it—because in the back of her mind, a distant memory reminded her of the last time that she should have held onto a moment like this.

For a brief moment in time, there was no Holder. There was no Breaker or Shaper, no chovathi, no Khala Val'ur, no Khadje Kholam. There was only her, and the two men with whom she'd traveled half the continent.

If anyone could appreciate the value of hanging onto a moment like this, it was the woman once known as Lilyana Coros.

. . . And, buried somewhere deep inside her mind, a seed began to bloom.

Chapter 32

Do'baradai

Asha

GAZING UP AT THE GREAT gates of Do'baradai, Asha admired the minds that had built such a defensible city—but lamented the fact that it was so terribly underutilized. *A city this size could shelter thousands,* she thought to herself, *but I wouldn't guess there were more than a few hundred here now.* As her eyes drifted back to the spot where Ulten and their camels waited, though, a grim afterthought entered her mind: *Every soul inside those walls serves the Holder.*

The thought did little to convince her that they had made the right decision in coming to the city. Then again, she knew that they had not had a choice—and the Traveler had reminded her of that fact.

Lash'kun Yho, in his never-ending desire to control as many variables as he could, had gone ahead to get a better lay of the land. There had not been much of a discussion about it, and Asha was more or less fine with that fact—she just wished that she was left with better partners in conversation while he was gone; after nearly a decade of being alone in a cell, she was left to desire more than just camels, and the voices in her head.

Behind her, Ulten was taking advantage of the natural shade that the towering walls provided, letting the camels rest in the shadows of Do'baradai. He had his back against his own camel, legs splayed out in front of him, looking very much like a man who had rested like this for most of his life. Asha almost hated to wake him up.

As she approached him, though, the sound of light snoring told her that the nomad perhaps needed the rest just as much as the camels did.

The dry heat of the Wastes was not nearly as savage in the shade—it might have even been called bearable—and a light breeze dancing over the sands was the only other sound besides Ulten's snoring. Taking a seat on the ground beside her own camel, Asha decided to wait until Lash'kun returned from his scouting to wake up the sleeping goatherd.

Leaning her back against the sturdy beast, she closed her eyes to join Ulten in a rest.

+ + +

Asha awoke with a slow satisfaction and the benefits of a much-needed rest. That, however, was quickly washed away by the realization that she had dozed more deeply than she had intended. She blinked her eyes a few times to fight off the bleariness, and her heart nearly leapt from her chest when she saw that the shadows of the tower were not the only shadows surrounding them.

The whole city was dark.

She looked up to the sky, and a heaviness spread throughout her body as she gazed into the darkness. The fear blanketed her more deeply than the stars above: it was night, and Lash'kun had still not returned.

She leapt to her feet. "Ulten," she said, trying to steady the panic in her voice. "Ulten, wake up."

The soft snoring stopped and the goatherd opened one eye. "Eh?" he managed.

"Wake up," she repeated. "He's still not back."

Ulten rubbed the sleep from his eyes, looking to be as tired as Asha had felt. "How . . . how long did we . . . ?" he started to ask.

"I don't know. Hours."

Ulten was quiet as he stood and looked up at the stars. He squinted and mumbled something under his breath like he was doing calculations.

"It is one hour past midnight," he announced. Turning to Asha, he said, "He should definitely be back."

Asha frowned at the words. They did not come as a surprise, but the fact that Ulten was saying them and not her meant that her fear was not unfounded.

"What should we do?"

Ulten turned to her and, for a while, said nothing. He looked up at the stars again, as if asking them for guidance. Apparently finding the answer he sought, he looked back to Asha.

"We do what we came to do."

Asha did not like that answer, but she knew that it was the right one.

She looked inside, past the walls of Do'baradai, to the stairs of the structure from which the city took its name. The tower of the Two Brothers: a sky-scraping monstrosity of limestone and granite, an eternal reminder to the world that not all things forgotten in slumber are lost.

Now three things awaited them in Do'baradai: the Vessel of the Holder, the weapon called the godkiller, and—perhaps most important-ly—the Traveler himself, Lash'kun Yho.

Chapter 33

G'hen

Alysana

THE COURTROOM WAS CHAOS.

"How could this happen? He was supposed to be under guard!"

"He was under guard!"

"Then why is he dead in his cell instead of out here on trial?"

There was more shouting in the last few minutes than Alysana had heard in the last few years. At least it was controlled chaos.

She remembered the feeling that was starting to creep through her: it was the same feeling that she'd had when she heard the rumor of her father's death all those years ago. She had taken the time to mourn him and come to grips with her loss. She had let herself cry, and be comforted by her sister Mordha. The two of them had been without a father then—and it was happening all over again now.

This time, it was real. The only thing that would make it any more real would be if Alysana saw her father's body with her own eyes. Part of her wanted nothing to do with that—unfortunately, a much larger part of her knew that she would have to see it. She had to be sure.

It had hurt to lose him, but it hurt even more when she realized that the years she'd spent mourning him could have been spent growing up with him instead. She had been raised by the gates of Annoch, whose cold steel walls were no match for a father's warmth. There was a mix of bitterness and regret growing inside her and she knew that the only way to stop it from consuming her would be to see Yozna with her own eyes.

Amid the arguing, Alysana began to make her way to the door that led to the holding cell. As she did so, the shouting began to die down. With every step she took, the room seemed to grow quieter. It was as if, in the chaos of trying to place blame, no one had stopped to consider the actual cost. The shouting turned instead to whispers.

She couldn't hear the words, but Alysana was sure that she knew what they were anyway. She was too old to be considered an orphan, but she found herself transported back to her childhood when she had been one in everything but fact.

"Where do you think you're going?"

The words, while unexpected, were not what made Alysana flinch; it was the way that they had been uttered—and the man who had uttered them.

Rus.

"I'm going to see my father."

She had not turned to address him and felt no need to do so. She imagined that fact was making Ghaja Rus flustered, and the thought brought the faintest of smiles to her face.

"No one said you could leave."

She kept walking as if the words had never met the world. Staring down the guard in front of her, Alysana mustered every ounce of self control that she had to keep from shaking. Whether it was from rage or grief—or both—she wasn't sure, but it was all she could do to maintain her composure. The guard must have sensed it because he shifted his eyes nervously from floor to courtroom to ceiling—everywhere, in fact, but Alysana's eyes.

"No one . . . said . . . you could leave!"

If the courtroom had been silent before, it was a tomb now as Ghaja Rus's words rumbled through the air like a stampede. It was enough to make Alysana pause in her tracks and turn.

"Then stop me."

She didn't even give the guard the chance, stepping past him before Rus could bark anymore.

+ + +

The hallway leading to the holding cell was silent but for the distant rumbling of arguing G'henni behind her and, walking further in, Alysana got the feeling that she was headed for her own execution. It was a sense of dread that she couldn't quite place: she knew what awaited her further in, and that knowledge both compelled her and held her. She didn't want to find the body of her father, but she had to.

The darkness of the prison was strangely welcoming to her, like it was somehow trying to help her by concealing its mysteries. Her footsteps echoed off the silent stones as she drew nearer, yet each one was heavier in her own head than it was in the prison; she wondered what she was going to find, and if it would make a difference when she did.

Yet no matter how much mental preparation, introspection, and mourning she had done, none of it could never have prepared her for what she saw—or rather, *whom* she saw—when she rounded the corner.

"You would be surprised how quickly word can travel about a G'henni masterminding a prison break. It spreads far and wide, and somehow managed to make it into the ears of the captain of the guard of Annoch." If Alysana had her dagger drawn, she would have dropped it. She settled for her jaw instead. "Close your mouth, sister. You have no use for catching flies."

Even though it had not been long since leaving Mordha behind in Annoch, it had seemed like an eternity since Alysana had last seen her—and to see her here, in this context, in the land where the two of them were born, was almost too much for her to bear. It took everything in her to even remain standing, let alone close her mouth.

Alysana tried to find her voice.

"Is this—is this a dream?" she managed. The words were barely above a whisper.

"I am afraid it is not," Mordha answered, moving gracefully toward her and out of the cell where she'd been standing. Even in full armor, Mordha was a wonder of movement and beauty. "But if it is, it is surely a nightmare."

Alysana found it impossible to voice any more words. Everything unraveling around her was simply too much for her to bear: the now-realized death of her father, the return of her sister, the betrayal of her uncle, and the reappearance of Ghaja Rus. It was all too much. She closed her eyes and began to weep.

It was not surprising that she felt Mordha's arms around her in comfort—in fact, she had felt them thousands upon thousands of times throughout her life. The thing that surprised her was how strong she was now. Strong, and warm. And . . . breathing hard.

Alysana opened her eyes and looked at her sister. She glanced, for the first time, into the cell where her father's body lay. The body was slumped over, lifeless, surrounded by a pool of blood.

"What exactly are you doing here?" she asked.

"Only what is needed." The embrace continued, but now it felt less like comfort and more like prevention. "You know that I love you, right?"

Alysana went from nervous to scared. She looked her sister in the eye, though, and saw nothing but the same compassion that she had grown up with her entire life. She swallowed her fear and nodded.

"Good," Mordha answered, turning her head to the darkened corner of the cell. "Give me the dagger and get us out of here."

Alysana turned her gaze to where Mordha was looking, realizing that there was another person in the cell with them. She saw the red eyes before she saw the rest of the man, but it was enough to know exactly who it was.

"With pleasure," Jinda said as he walked toward them, holding out a dagger hilt-first. Alysana could see that it was well-crafted and expensive, lined with jewels and gold—and monogrammed with the unmistakable seal of the magistrate of Théas, Ghaja Rus.

Mordha kissed her sister on the forehead and let go of her. She strode over to Jinda and took the dagger, then walked into the cell where the body of Yozna lay in repose. Placing the dagger beside the body, she walked back out to Jinda. The captain of the guard of Annoch nodded at her and took her hand.

"Please, Alysana, trust me and know that this must happen."

Then, in the blink of an eye, they disappeared.

✦ ✦ ✦

Alysana was left alone in the horrid, cold place, suddenly feeling lonelier than she'd ever felt before. The awful realization began to sink in that her father was growing colder; Mordha had not even bothered with a goodbye. She fought the urge to collapse and somehow managed to stay on her feet, wrestling internally with the thought of whether or not to take one last look at the man who was responsible for her being here—in more ways than just one.

Finally, she decided that she would give her father a proper, private goodbye before the official—very public—ceremony. She gathered her strength and stepped into the cell with him.

Each step was heavy, like she was treading through quicksand. She both did and did not want to cover the remaining distance between her and her father—who now in death seemed even more imposing than he had ever seemed in life.

In fact, he looked even larger.

As Alysana drew nearer, her brow furrowed in confusion. The body was face down in a pool of blood, but its posture was not what confused Alysana—it was its shape. When she had last seen her father, his large frame had seemed weak, almost frail. This man—this body before her— was rounder, more filled out. She had a thought that she nearly dismissed but, on instinct, reached for the hair on his head and pulled it up. What she saw was even more surprising than if she had stared into the dead eyes of her father.

Only—this was not her father.

This was someone else entirely—someone she knew.

Oh, gods, Mordha. What in the world have you done?

Chapter 34

Khala Val'ur

Yetz

YETZ BREATHED IN THE CRISPNESS of the Valurian air, embracing the calm before the inevitable storm. His old bones ached as he neared the top. He didn't like to use his cane, but he knew that he would need it if he had any hope of reaching the surface.

No wonder it's been years since I've been up here, he thought bitterly. It had been a struggle to come this far, and Yetz almost wished he would never have to do it again. A voice in the back of his mind told him that, if he waited any longer, his wish would be granted.

Clearing the last steps to the mouth of the Sunken City, Yetz saw a half dozen of his Master Khyth gathered outside in a semicircle, facing toward the path that led out of the city. The light from the rising sun above made their shadows stretch behind them to the west in apparent greeting to the High Khyth's ascent. They all faced away from him, robes haloed by the yellowish-orange of morning.

Before stepping out, Yetz paused to take in the sight and a breath. Standing at the edge of shadow, it sunk in just how long it had actually been since he'd seen the real sun—the real sky—and felt its warmth on his skin; it paled in comparison to the light of their flame, or the warmth of a fire.

. . . Fire.

Yetz's eyes moved from the semicircle of Khyth to the massive brazier that had been set by his men, burning away in the center of this last line of defense. Since the Khyth could not make fire themselves like the Athrani could, they had to make sure that they had some on hand in order to use it against the chovathi. If that spark were to die . . .

"High Khyth Yetz," came a voice from one of his men. It was Tirius, a young Master Khyth in whom Yetz saw a bit of himself: he was intelligent and brave, yet lacked the ambition that would make him both an asset and a threat. Yetz was fine with that.

"Master Tirius," Yetz replied, walking down the steps of the mouth. He had to squint as he stepped out into the light—he'd forgotten just how bright it was in the daytime! It had truly been too long. "I see that you and the other Master Khyth received my message."

"We did," Tirius said with a slight bow of his head. "And we are ready to serve."

Yetz looked at the faces of the others gathered before him. They were Master Khyth, yes, but they all seemed so young. D'kane had been the most senior of them before his . . . regrettable . . . absence. After D'kane, of course, had been Kunas.

Seniority in the ranks of Master Khyth, it would seem, did not bode well.

"And serve you shall," Yetz replied with a point of his cane. He paused, taking the time to look at each of them individually. After he had finished, he turned his back and faced the mouth of the Sunken City. "I will tell you now something that you may have already guessed but should never be repeated." He looked at the black rock that made up the interior of the mouth, so strong and hardy. It had been the reason the Khyth had chosen this place to begin with. It suited their ideals of strength and independence. These walls needed nothing more than themselves to hold up an entire mountain. So it was with the Khyth—and the centuries of their seclusion had proven that fact time and again. "The warriors that now line the mountain paths and guard the entrance to our city," he said, words echoing off the case walls, "are nothing more than fodder for the chovathi. They will fight valiantly, I am sure, but I know of only one man who has fought against chovathi and lived," he said, looking over his shoulder at them. "And what I would not give to have General Tennech here with us today."

Tirius looked a little nervous, as did some of the older Khyth.

"Then what are we to do?" asked Kostas, a tall, thin master Khyth with sunken eyes. "Surely a handful of us are just as useless."

Yetz gave him a tight-lipped smile. "That brazier," he said, pointing with his cane at the roiling flames, "will be our weapon; these rocks," he said as he spread his arms, "our strength."

Kostas returned Yetz's smile, just as disingenuous. "I pledged to follow you to death, High Khyth. Today, it appears I will fulfill my oath."

"Never underestimate the power of the Breaker," Yetz replied, and stepped forward into the light.

✦ ✦ ✦

Kunas

THE SCENT OF MAN WAS strong in the air, and Kunas could feel the excitement in the chovathi around him as they drew closer to Khala Val'ur, the land that was promised. Ever since Zhala had shown him visions of their conquests, it had been his singular goal to make them manifest. She had shown him a future written and ruled by chovathi, built upon the pillars of the corpses of man. Closing in on the mountains of Gal'behem, he could nearly taste the blood they would spill.

"Onward!" he shouted, taking to the four-legged stride that lent him swiftness and power.

The footfalls of thousands of his brothers and sisters shook the earth as they lumbered across the rocky land of Gal'dorok. He had never made this journey before, although he did make its corollary when he was sent from Khala Val'ur to Ghal Thurái as barely more than a Khyth apprentice fresh off his Breaking. That life, now, seemed like an eternity ago as he charged across the land in his new, more powerful form—a form that Zhala had seen fit to gift him after his loyal service at Ghal Thurái, where the armies of men met their end.

Today would be no different. Any mortal flesh that stood in their way would be met by the fury of chovathi teeth and claws. Kunas's thirst grew at the thought.

Flanking him on both sides and keeping pace with him effortlessly were his lieutenants, Khaz and Yet'nal. The perfect example of chovathi specimens, the two warriors were as large as they were fearsome, and their claws rent the ground with each thunderous stride they took. Khaz, his powerful forelimbs striking the ground in wicked syncopation with his legs, looked more like a force of nature.

"Khaz smell fear," said the hulking chovathi. "Want kill."

Kunas smiled to himself at the words from his lieutenant—not only because of their message, but because of how they were being delivered: Khaz was unique among all chovathi, as he alone had developed the ability to speak. That fact was not lost on Kunas—nor their matriarch, Zhala—and choosing him to help lead the army had been easier than blinking an eye.

"You will have that chance," Kunas replied over his shoulder. "Zhala wills it."

Kunas could not so much as see Khaz's smile as he could feel it. It pleased him to know that his lieutenants were just as eager to spill blood as he was—and, in doing so, to carry out their matriarch's wishes. Zhala, far away as she was, still made her desires known to them—known to all chovathi — by the invisible bond that flowed through all those who drew breath.

+ + +

The chovathi horde had covered most of the distance between Ghal Thurái and Khala Val'ur when the mountains began to come into view.

Although this body was new to him, there was a dim part of Kunas that was impressed that he could smell the humans before he could see them. He was not used to the power that came with Zhala's gift.

His lieutenants at his heels, the chovathi army surged forward in pursuit of the Sunken City, the first mark on their map of conquest de-creed by Zhala. It was just like he'd seen it in his visions: chovathi spring-ing forth, first from Ghal Thurái and then from Khala Val'ur, followed soon after by every city once ruled by mankind, captured once again by the strength of the chovathi, and shaped to their own desires.

Ghal Thurái had already fallen to their might; now, the last bastion of Khyth lay before them like the soft underbelly of a serpent. All they had to do was lay waste to the soldiers that waited for them in the crags of Gal'behem.

Then, after them, the Khyth.

The army slowed as the peaks of the Great Serpent loomed near and, with an unspoken command, the whole of the chovathi army came to a halt.

Kunas could hear their hard breathing behind him.

He stood up on his hind legs to face them, towering over his brethren, as he looked out over the sea of white.

"Brothers and sisters," he shouted, "the road to conquest is long, but it all begins with a single step." He bared his fangs in a smile. "Today, we make that first step into the Sunken City of Khala Val'ur."

His army shook the earth as they pounded their fists on the ground, the chovathi signal of approval. When the rumbling stopped, Kunas gestured for Khaz to stand. The lieutenant, large even by chovathi standards, barely came up to his shoulders. Kunas motioned for him to address the troops.

Khaz cocked his head, seeming not to understand at first, when light seemed to come on in his head. He turned, looking out over the gathered horde, and a low growl emanated from his throat. He raised his hands to his side. "Chovathi strong," he said, clenching his fists, and the earth shook again as his warriors agreed. "Chovathi hungry." The shaking continued. "Chovathi feared!"

The rumbling at the last comment was so strong that Kunas was afraid they would split the earth open if they continued. Before they could, though, it died off. . . and, looking back at Khaz, Kunas knew just why. The lieutenant was standing with his arms outstretched, palms facing the sky, as if he bore some great weight or responsibility. His chest swelled; Kunas could see that he was breathing in.

"Chovathi . . . conquer!" Khaz roared, shaking the earth all by himself. His brothers and sisters joined him in a roar so mighty that Kunas knew even the gods would feel it.

Turning to the mountains that surrounded Khala Val'ur, Kunas thought he saw them shaking, too. It might have been his imagination . . . then again, it might not. If Yetz and his Khyth knew what was coming for them, perhaps they would have brought down the mountains on themselves to save themselves the suffering.

Only a few short miles separated them now. Kunas grinned wickedly in anticipation as he eyed the peaks.

The sun was beginning to set on the age of man, with the dawn of the chovathi drawing nigh.

Chapter 35

Do'baradai

D. C. Jennings

Asha

BENEATH THE DARKNESS OF DO'BARADAI, Asha and Ulten were no more than shades moving in the night, two dots in a sprawling desert landscape. The only problem, Asha knew, was that anyone watching them was also similarly obscured.

As the two of them moved inside, trying their best to remain concealed against the walls of the city, Asha was certain that they were being watched. Try as she might, though, she simply could not see well in the dark. She didn't like it.

Coming to a stop, she put out her hand for Ulten to do the same.

"What are you doing?" he asked.

Asha turned to the goatherd who had been walking behind her, "I have an idea."

"I'm listening."

"Don't listen," she said. " . . . Watch."

With that, she closed her eyes and reached inside, grasping the ancient power which stood in waiting like a man on the edge of a dream. It felt like dipping her hands into a stream, warm and rushing, and trying to grab a hold of the bottom.

"What . . . are—" Ulten began, his words trailing off into the night.

Asha could feel her body changing, becoming stronger, more adapted to the desert and the dark. She had knelt down to begin the transformation, and she was glad that she had, She would have doubled over in pain if she was not already there.

The snapping and reforming of bones in her body reminded her that everything came with a price, and the ability to see in the dark was no exception. She felt her teeth sharpen and grow, filling her mouth with the ferocious canines that served only one purpose that Asha knew; her hands and feet thickened and changed as well, turning into massive paws that lent themselves perfectly to treading softly over any surface; and,

171

finally, her eyes became mirrors for the light—dim as it was—and gave her exactly what she was hoping for.

She realized, though, that she had never tried to talk while in this form. The tissue in her throat felt different from when she was in human form, and she found herself desperately hoping that she would still be able to manipulate it.

"I needed my eyes," she said, and was surprised by how the words sounded: a low growl that sounded more threatening than informative, but intelligible nonetheless. Rough words were better than no words, she reasoned.

Ulten stood, frozen. His mouth twitched a little, but no sound came out.

"R'haqan," Asha said, invoking the name of his people. "You are still needed. Come back to me."

A wave of recognition began to slowly work its way across the goat-herd's face as his wide eyes began darting around, as if to reconcile his physical presence in the world.

"I . . . I am here," he said haltingly. "I just . . . I do not have a good history with wolves."

"You have a good history with this one," Asha replied, trying to give a calming edge to her words that she found increasingly difficult to do. Everything about her lupine body was fearsome and strong; trying to be gentle was like using a greatsword to carve her name on a piece of tree bark: it required immense concentration and force of will.

It must have worked. Ulten gave her the slightest hint of a smile and said, "Thank you."

Asha bowed her head to him in return. "I am simply adapting to the task at hand. Do not thank me until after we have made it back here safely. Now," she said, turning her eyes toward the tower of the Two Brothers, "let me see what I can see."

This was her first time being back inside the walls of Do'baradai in over a decade, so looking around felt like going over the fading paint of her memory with a brand new brush. Everywhere she looked, an old memory became brilliant and new again, fresh in her mind as if she had never left. The city itself was massive, well-built, and laid out in a practical manner. She looked up and down the rows of buildings that were protected by the mighty walls that stood so eerily empty these days. Climbing onto a nearby hut for a better vantage point, she remained low to the ground, continuing her search. There had been Priests of the Holder manning the walls outside, but so far she had not been able to see any others.

The hackles on her neck began to rise before she even saw them. She *felt* them.

She had her eyes fixed on the tower of the Two Brothers when she caught her first glimpse of them.

There were only a handful to begin with, and she wasn't even certain what she was seeing at first, but soon after they began streaming forth from the tower like ants from a colony: dozens—perhaps even hundreds—of Priests of the Holder. They spilled out onto the massive steps that led down from the tower, two priests stopping on either side of the ancient stairway, lining it like unlit candles in a dark hall.

There they stood, in the soundless Baradian night, dotting the steps of the tower. Asha could hear her heartbeat in her head as she realized she was holding her breath. She exhaled slowly and strained her eyes to see inside the tower, past the twin iron doors that now stood open, perhaps for the first time in years.

A shadow moved in the doorway. Stepping forward, it began to take shape as Asha struggled to make out what it was. She froze. Marched out at spearpoint by a Priest of the Holder, laden with chains and disappointment, was the Traveler.

Emerging behind him, though, was a figure whose mere outline made the blood run cold in Asha's veins. A dark hood concealed his face, but Asha knew exactly who it was—there could be no doubt.

"I know you're out there, Asha. Won't you come in? We have so many things to discuss."

She bared her teeth and growled.

It was him.

+ + +

There he was, in the flesh: the Holder of the Dead. It was not *his* flesh, Asha knew, but it was his own nonetheless. Whoever he was using as a Vessel most likely had no choice in the matter: when a god has need of a thing, he—or she—simply takes it.

From behind her, Ulten asked, "Is that who I think it is?" The goatherd's words were quiet, despite the fact that there was still a great distance between the two of them and the Lord of the Dead.

"It is, and it concerns me greatly that he would deign to be here himself," Asha growled in her lupine voice. "He must have guessed at our endgame."

She heard Ulten shifting about behind her, taking a knee, and bringing himself down to her level; though Asha's lupine form was large, the fact that she stood on four legs gave her a height disadvantage. "What do we do?" he whispered.

Asha took a moment to think. The Holder knew she was there—he could probably feel her presence—but he had no idea as to where.

. . . Or, if anyone else was with her.

She looked back at Ulten, who was staring straight ahead, eyes locked on the Traveler and the Holder. In that moment, Asha realized, Ulten became much more than a humble goatherd: He was a man who was prepared to defy the will of a god merely by being at her side. He had shown her loyalty and compassion, demonstrated competency and resourcefulness.

She hoped that all those things would be enough. "I will go see what he wants."

Ulten gave her a look of shocked disbelief. "What? No, you cannot!"

Asha shook her head. "I can, and I must, even if it means putting my

---

D. L. Jennings

own life in jeopardy."

"But—"

"I cannot—*will* not—let him hurt Lash'kun Yho."

Ulten looked flustered, as if trying to find the words to an argument that could somehow make her stay. Asha was determined not let him find them if they even existed at all.

"Listen to me, Ulten: this is our only hope. The Holder doesn't know I have help, so you can still get in and retrieve the godkiller." She continued softly, "You just won't have the help of myself or the Traveler."

She looked at the goatherd, steadfast and silent. "Do you understand?"

He swallowed. "Yes."

The two of them looked back to where the Holder was standing, atop the great stone steps that led inside the tower of the Two Brothers. Asha knew all too well that the steel doors were the only way in and out—and that the tower led to the crypts below, where the Holder's prime Vessel lay.

Among other things, came the afterthought.

"Then I will make myself known to him and hear what he has to say. You, on the other hand, must remain concealed. Secret. Hidden." She looked back at the goatherd, who nodded. "To say that this will be dangerous is an understatement," she went on, "but I believe in you. I believe that your heart is in the right place, and I believe your mind is as sharp as any blade you'll find inside those walls."

Ulten bowed his head at the compliment, and Asha could sense an influx of blood to the dark man's face.

"You are too kind, Asha," he said, head hovering inches above the ground. "I am but an old man who tends his flock."

Asha nudged the R'haqan's face upward with her snout. Were she in human form, she would have lifted his chin with her hands, but the simple act seemed to have caught the man's attention all the same. "No, Ulten, you are much more than that," she said, eyes fixed on his. "You are a guide in the desert, a light in the dark; you gave shade from the sun, and

175

water for my thirst. You are bold and caring, asking naught in return—but most importantly, now, you are hope."

Ulten's blushing continued, accompanied by a smile both wide and contagious. "It is my hope that I can do what you need," he said, dusting off his hands and standing.

"What I need is to get beyond those doors," Asha said as she looked up again to the base of the tower. "And for you to follow behind me——safely and at a distance."

"But after you go inside," Ulten began, "what will happen?"

Asha paused, eyes fixed on the road ahead. "I can't say for certain, but the answer lies within. We were always meant to end up here, beneath the shadows of Do'baradai . . . I just never thought the time would come so soon."

"Are you sure that this is the way?"

"The Holder has forced my hand by taking Lash'kun Yho as his prisoner. I have no choice. This is the *only* way."

Ulten sighed. "Then I will assist you as best I can. I just hope these old hands of mine will be of some use."

Asha snorted a breathy laugh that came out through her nose. "I am sure they will," she said as she began to move, heading for the base of the great steps. Suddenly, though, a thought came to her and she stopped, looking back at Ulten one last time before she went on. "I do not think it a coincidence that our paths have crossed, Ulten—once, ten years ago, and once again when you aided me outside R'haqa."

Behind her, in the tower of the Two Brothers, Asha knew what awaited. Perhaps the dread significance of the moment gave her pause, but it mattered little to her now. She was here, and she was determined—and when a goddess has need of a thing, she takes it.

"If things go our way," she went on, "and I hope with every sliver of my being that they do, then our paths shall cross again a third time." Curling her lips into a lupine grin, she added, "I have always had a fondness for threes."

Asha turned her eyes once again to the tower, and with the resolve that comes with a thousand years of waiting, set one foot in front of the other to meet fate.

Chapter 36

The Otherworld

Thornton

THORNTON HAD BEEN IN THE Otherworld and its sister realm, Khel-hârad, for so long that he had almost forgotten what dreaming felt like—after all, there was no need for sleep here—so, finding himself finally caught up in one at long last, he embraced it. It was comforting. Clean. He let himself be taken in.

The transient, shifting images and shapes, the faded whispers and subtle sounds, the feeling that something more was waiting, just beyond the façade—all of it resonated right down to his core. He moved around weightlessly through the formless ether, letting his thoughts flow through him, into him, out of him. It reminded him of something—something he couldn't quite put his finger on. It was beautiful.

What is this place? he thought with bliss.

The Otherworld, came the unbidden response.

Of course. Yes.

Yes, it was.

. . . But . . .

. . . was it?

He tried to collect his cloudy thoughts. The Otherworld, playground of the gods. Last he remembered, that's where he was.

. . . Right?

The teardrop of doubt made him question his memories. Why would he, a blacksmith from the small village of Highglade, be in the Otherworld? He should be forging chains or horseshoes, not walking in the halls of creation. Maybe this all just was some strange dream, some fanciful imagining brought on by too many stories and ales.

Before long he would wake up in the room that he and his father shared, and . . .

. . . and . . .

His thoughts jostled like a cart hitting a bump.

His father.

Images and feelings awakened one by one, like crickets in the night. He felt the sting of his father's absence, although he wasn't sure why. He knew that he was gone, but he wasn't sure of the reason. Had he left? Was he coming back? Where was he?

Was he . . . dead?

Dead. Another bump . . . and a black, eerie silence closed in around him. There was only Thornton, and the echo of that terrible word.

Dead. It resonated like ripples in a pond.

The dream was slowly turning into a nightmare.

✦ ✦ ✦

Thornton found himself floating in a sea of thoughts and images, caught up in a relentless, conspiring tide. He felt himself being pulled— but toward what, he couldn't say. As if in response, two figures shifted into view—blurry, indistinct shapes that Thornton somehow knew. The tide brought him closer. The figures came into focus.

It was him: it was Olson.

Father! Thornton screamed, but the scream came out as nothing more than a muted cry in the ether. He tried again. *Father!*

No sound. All he could do was watch and be pulled. Dragged closer, he watched the blurriness of the shapes melt away into sharp, distinct features. It was his father, that much was certain—and with him . . . was that . . . D'kane? The two men were struggling, without any clear indication as to who was winning: Olson on the ground with Thornton's hammer in his hand, the figure of the Khyth over top of him. It was like watching water try to put out a fire: a flurry of smoke and struggle, a burst of flame and light. Back and forth, back and forth, with no way of knowing who was in control.

. . . Until . . .

There was a blur of movement as the two men struggled. A surge of power. A recess like an outgoing tide. A moment of calm. Then, in vivid and awful detail, Thornton watched as D'kane overtook his father and thrust a knife into his chest in a violent and powerful stroke.

FATHER!

Thornton knew then that he was now witnessing the very moment of his father's death as he saw the light leave Olson's eyes. Even though he hadn't been there when it had happened, Thornton knew that, somehow, he was witnessing it right now. This was how his father had died. This dream was real. He needed to wake up—now.

Panic drenched in fear came and passed as Thornton waited expectantly for the dream to end. Usually in moments like these where he had become aware of the fact that he was in a dream at all, he would jolt awake like one does after being hit in the face with cold water. He could feel his heart beating in his head, and he felt like it was going to explode when he realized he wasn't waking up. In fact, it felt like the opposite: he was somehow falling deeper into slumber . . . or whatever it is this was.

The feeling of dread and oppression was not receding—it was growing.

It was in that moment where Thornton had the very distinct feeling that he was standing in a room where the walls were closing in. He could sense them all around him, wolves hidden in the forest, just out of sight but not out of mind. A terrible feeling manifested in the back of his subconscious that slowly worked its way to the rest of his being.

Thornton felt the ground beneath his feet tremble as his reality began to feel smaller, more constricting. He couldn't see the walls closing in, but he could feel them. He knew they were coming. It was like the difference between watching a rock drop in a pond, and hearing its splash: one was an action; the other was the result of that action. Just because Thornton could not see the walls closing in did not mean that they wouldn't soon crush him.

He was trapped. Threatened. Suffocated. He felt his fear bubbling up and, for the briefest of moments, thought that he could feel the walls shudder to a stop. The instant that he shifted his attention back to the walls, though, they began to move again.

A pin prick of panic.

A stop to the walls.

Thornton paused to consider.

It's the fear, he found himself saying. *The fear is stopping the walls from closing in.* He felt like he had just discovered that heat on wood makes fire. Feeling the walls beginning to close again, he reached inside himself. He backed himself up against the sharpness of the fear . . . and he fell.

It was like plunging into a hive of bees: swarming and chaotic, dark and pulsing, a writhing, angry mass with no solid center. It was his fear, he knew, and he embraced it. He let it cover him, reaching his arms in deeper and deeper, and surrendering to it. He let it wash over him and cover him completely. He couldn't breathe, but he didn't need to.

The walls had stopped. He had done it.

Beneath the mask of his fear, he felt the suffocation of the walls relent. He wasn't sure how he was doing it, but he did know that it was happening. It was like looking at the world from inside a dark cloud, filtering everything through a blackened lens. It was perfect.

For a moment he thought he felt the trembling of the walls again, but could tell right away that it was different. It was a quaking that felt fluid, dynamic . . . organic.

It felt like . . . laughter.

Laughter?

But . . . whose?

The answer was a terror that surrounded him in a way that the invisible walls never could.

Thank you for doing the work for me, came the voice, deep and piercing. He knew whose voice it was, and the realization made the writhing fear around him darken and set.

I was wondering how long it would take for you to give yourself up. I was not yet strong enough to overtake you myself, even though you were kind—or stupid—enough to bring me back to the source of my power. I thought that it would have been much harder!

Thornton cursed at himself and felt his anger churning inside him. Alysana had been right about him that day in Théas: he was a fool.

All I had to do was use your father's death to make you latch onto your fear and let it enfold you.

Thornton felt a chill run through him as he realize that the Breaker had orchestrated this whole thing—from passing from D'kane into him, dragging him into the Otherworld, and now locking him in a prison inside his own mind . . . and of Thornton's own design. Without meaning to, he had wrapped himself in a cloak of his own terror, and formed a new set of walls to hold him in.

I can feel your anger and fear, but there is no need to worry: yours is not the first Vessel that I have found myself in command of—nor will you be the last. At that moment, Thornton felt the power of the Hammer of the Worldforge begin to pulse madly, like a heartbeat wracked with terror and shock. *You will, however, be the most important.*

Through his prison, Thornton saw the sky glow blue with the power of the hammer. It was a cool, comforting power that enveloped the sky.

Long have you been my oppressor, Hammer, the Breaker went on, his voice crawling through Thornton's mind. *You were nearly the instrument of my undoing.*

Thornton winced as streaks of orange forked across the sky like lightning, and he knew that it was the influence of the ancient god.

But now you will be much more than that.

The orange streaks multiplied, flashing and crashing in a tumultuous frenzy that threatened to envelop the sky.

"Stop!" Thornton cried, but he felt his words drop dead at the impenetrable walls of his prison. The blue power of the hammer pulsed—but it felt more like a weakened heartbeat than the primordial power of creation.

That which is broken always seeks to be remade whole, quoted the Breaker as the orange light became increasingly more violent and pronounced.

The sky above Thornton now flashed with a white light so bright that it could well have consumed the whole of creation. It pulsed—momentarily—and receded. It took a moment for Thornton to process the change that had taken place above him as he knew that he was watching two titanic powers struggle for dominance—but the moment that the white light faded, Thornton's heart sank. The entire sky was now overcast in a burning, wicked orange that made even the fiercest of fires look dim.

And the power that was once fractured has been returned to its rightful place.

The world around Thornton pulsed, shuddered, and collapsed as blackness rushed in to replace the power that once surrounded him.

Nothing was left now but silence, stillness—and fear.

Chapter 37

Ja'ad Shiddeq

Sera

SERALITH EDOS RODE ACROSS THE desert, and the Thurian captains followed.

They had made it past the outskirts of Khadje Kholam and into the open desert where nothing seemed to exist but sand and time. The expanse of the Wastes that opened up before them was beyond anything that Sera had encountered before, and riding into it beneath the noonday sun made her realize just how vast and empty it truly was: the rolling dunes, the sparse vegetation, the wind-worn rocky outcroppings that jutted toward the sky—all these things spoke of death, yet it all seemed to be so defiantly alive.

The captains— both of them—were seasoned warriors and riders, and the way they handled their mounts made it look effortless. It made Sera envious of how well they took to it. Despite the best efforts of Aldis Tennech, she never did seem to blossom into the horse master that he'd wished for her to become. Perhaps it would do her some good to keep them around.

They were, at the very least, entertaining, and almost made her forget the looming shadow in the back of her mind—the Priest of the Holder— still somewhere out there waiting for them. Sera shivered despite the heat; she was not looking forward to their reunion.

Riding just ahead of the two captains from Ghal Thurái, Sera didn't have to turn her head far to speak.

"While I'm happy to be leaving Khadje Kholam behind," she began, "I can't help but think that we are just moving out of the flames and into the furnace."

Dhrostain, riding behind her, seemed to have formed his own opinion about the place as well. "You know . . . in all my time with the Lonely Guard," he said through the woven cloth of his shemagh, "one thing I never questioned was why someone would flee this place for the north.

I mean, look at it. The Wastes," he said with a sweeping gesture. "At least they got the name right."

Sera laughed. The captain, along with his countryman, Hullis, was dressed more like a rider than a warrior for their journey across the desert. The two of them had stashed their heavier armor in saddlebags so that all they wore now was light leather beneath a kaftan of pale brown. This garb, Sera noted, allowed them a greater degree of freedom of movement—and Dhrostain was taking advantage of it. He waved his arms around wildly to punctuate his words.

"What did anyone ever see here," he nearly shouted, "that made them say, 'You know what? Let's live here. This is great'?"

Sera chuckled. The man had a point.

"In fact," he went on, "I'm not entirely convinced that anyone lives here on their own accord. They all probably owe someone money, and they're hiding out here until the debt clears."

"All of tens of thousands of them?" Sera asked, amused.

"The whole lot of them," Dhrostain retorted. "It's the only explanation."

Hullis chuckled. "I think you may be on to something," he said. Sera couldn't see it through his shemagh, but she was certain that he wore a smile on his lips. "I'll bet there is a bounty hunter in the north who is just waiting for his chance to come down here and collect." The sarcasm was thicker than the head on a Thurian stout.

✦ ✦ ✦

After another hour of riding, Khadje Kholam had long disappeared behind them, not even a dot on the horizon as they charged forth toward the northern desert. If they were to keep on their current course, they would eventually reach the border—a ride of at least two days. Even the mere thought of Derenar, with its lush vegetation and green grass, was enough to put Sera's mind at ease. It was like a cooling salve on a fresh burn: not enough to cure, but at least it would ease the pain.

The Priest had told Sera that he would find them, but she was beginning to have her doubts. It was a big desert, after all, and they were only three riders.

How would he—

She didn't even have time to finish the thought. Coming into view in the distance, seated atop a great black mare, was the robed figure of a lone rider. Sera didn't have to guess who it was; even from this far out, the bleach-white skull of the Priest was apparent.

"There he is," she said with an upward nod. "Up ahead." She tapped her heels into the ribcage of her mount, sending him from a trot into a canter. "Let's see what he wants."

She heard the hoofbeats of the riders behind her as they followed.

The priest, facing away from them, made no indication that he heard them approaching, as he appeared to be fixated on a point in the distance. As Sera got closer, though, there was no mistaking that he had heard them.

"Beyond those dunes," the priest said in his grating, skeletal rasp, "waits the greatest army ever assembled."

Sera said nothing as she rode up beside him, squinting as she looked out to where the priest was indicating, trying to see for herself just what he was talking about. She saw nothing, thinking to herself that the soldiers were too far away for her to see, or that he was speaking metaphorically. After a few moments of scanning the horizon for any sign of this so-called great army, she gave up.

"I see nothing."

The Priest, beside her, gave a laugh that sounded more menacing than mirthful—which she was sure was the case. "That is because there is nothing to see," he replied, still not taking his eyes off the desert beyond.

Sera looked back, puzzled, to Hullis and Dhrostain, who appeared to share in her confusion.

"Then . . . how . . ." Sera began. "You said that it is the greatest army ever assembled."

The Priest, for the first time since they had ridden up, took his eyes off the horizon. He craned his head toward Sera in a sidelong glance that made the hairs on her neck stand up. "Until you have been enlightened by the Holder," he croaked, "you cannot truly understand the relationship of time and inevitability. I speak of something which, to the Holder and to me, has already occurred; your feeble grasp of concepts like present and future is both bothersome and risible."

Dhrostain, who had been scanning the horizon for this army as well, dropped the hand that had been shading his eyes. He growled, and pointed it at the living skeleton. "Now just hold on, you skinless sack of—"

"Dhrostain," Sera said as she held up her hand for silence. She turned her attention back to the Priest. "The man who raised me had no patience for riddles," Sera said, "and neither do I. Speak plainly."

In reply, the Priest simply spurred his mount forward, riding down the dune toward Ja'ad Shiddeq. "Your army awaits, Seed, like the Holder has promised," he said as he rode ahead. "The only obstacle is that it has not yet been made."

Chapter 38

G'hen

Kethras

THE WORDS "KIENAR IS IN danger" had been on Kethras's mind all day. It was such a foreign concept to him for the entirety of his existence that he almost didn't believe it. There had, of course, been the recent invasion by the Khyth, but even that was not a direct threat to the forest—they were merely after the passage into the Otherworld. He had lost his mother in that invasion, yes . . . but the forest still lived on. This time, judging by both Elyasha's words and tone, it was much more than that. This time it was different. He felt something that he had not felt in a long time: fear.

Upon hearing the news that the forest of his birth and life was in danger, he had retreated from the brick and stone of the cities of man and made his way into the one place he truly felt calm. The forest that surrounded the city of G'hen was small, but it would suffice. He closed his eyes and breathed deep. He let the world speak to him. The forest spoke back.

His nostrils were filled with the familiar scent of earth, and he could almost feel the churning below him of the thousand-year process of turning dead things into life. It was all part of a vast macrocosm that looped and twisted, breathed and trembled, grew and shrank.

He was one with the forest, with the darkness . . . and from that darkness came a light.

Confusion jostled him like a strong wind; this deep in meditation, he was in control of what he saw. He had been doing it for hundreds of years now at this point and was as well-versed in introspective meditation as he was in archery or hunting; it was second nature to him. Everything inside the fortress of his mind was something that he himself permitted or summoned.

Except for this.

What was . . . *this?*

He turned his attention to it like turning his eyes to the sun. It was an anomaly in the empty desert of his mind, a single star in a black void. And it was growing.

No, he thought, *it's not growing. It's . . . coming closer.*

His curiosity now shifted to alarm. What was this intruder; this unwelcome, unbidden interloper who dared interject itself inside his thoughts? It crept toward him, a point of light blossoming into a globe, a globe bursting into a figure.

Alarm shifted to anger. He directed his thoughts at the figure. *This place is my own. None are permitted entry save me!*

In the recesses of his mind, Kethras was god and king. This thing—whatever it was—would pay for its incursion. To his surprise, the figure spoke.

I have respected that rule for as long as I can remember; I hope, given that fact, that you can forgive me this intrusion.

The presence was sadness and bitterness wrapped in a blanket of joy, for the power he felt was his mother—but the voice was his sister.

Ynara, he thought. The inner tranquility that he had worked so hard to cultivate had been stirred up like a glass of water, tumultuous, fazed. He did not try to calm himself.

Yes, Brother, and I am sorry to come to you like this, but I had nowhere else to turn. Her form hovered mere feet from Kethras, her meditative pose reflecting his own. *Our sister has returned, just as we had always feared.*

The thoughts battered Kethras like icy raindrops that penetrated his skin. His mind reeled.

Zhala? he replied. *She has broken free? How?*

I do not know, and it is of no consequence now—all that I know is that she is here.

Kethras could now feel Ynara's thoughts when he closed his eyes. It was the strength of their bloodline, passed down from their mother, to be able to empathize with one another, even across worlds. He felt the fear in his sister, heard the gnashing of chovathi teeth, smelled the blood they had spilled. Zhala's nebulous white form appeared in his mind's eye as Ynara let her emotions pour out. All but detached from his corporeal form, Kethras was only vaguely aware of the frown that formed on his face as his thoughts embodied it.

Why must it be like this? he thought. Waves of regret and sorrow crashed around him, adding to the swirling emotions that penetrated the space. He knew the path ahead and knew its consequences, yet was as helpless to stop it as a tree stopping its own growth. He would continue like branches to the sun, knowing that the further he stretched, the closer he came to the end.

You know why, Ynara answered sadly. *You have known since you were young, since the day you first opened your eyes beneath the branches of Naknamu. You have known since before the loss of our mother, and before I took up the mantle of Binder. You know, Kethras—and I do too.*

Hearing it from his sister didn't make it any easier, but she was right. It was a strange comfort to hear her words, like the recitation of a familiar song, tracing the notes and phrases over and over in a mournful, bitter dirge. He knew this stanza, and the chorus that came after it; it was one he had sung since birth. The words may have changed, but the song remained the same.

I know, he relented. *Just . . . let me have my moment.* As if in response, he felt Ynara's presence wane. She did not retreat completely, but her light did dim. *The pieces are already in motion?* he asked, knowing the answer.

He felt, instead of heard, Ynara's reply: *Yes.*

And the Breaker?

He is where he needs to be, was her reply.

Then I'm sure you know the Shaper is here too.

Of course, came the reply, and he could feel her smiling behind the words.

Kethras let that smile warm up the freezing sorrow, and wrapped himself in it like a blanket. As master of this kingdom, he would not let his subjects rule him—he would rule them. He scattered the seeds of joy in Ynara's words and let them grow. After all, why shouldn't he? Sadness and regret were but bricks laid on the path of existence—they were not the path itself. It was only right to walk in the shade of joy when the path became too rough.

Then I will do what I must, he answered.

I know you will, came Ynara's response. This time, however, the warmth was gone. It was more like a statement of fact than reassurance. *You always do,* she said as she began to retreat from Kethras's mind. Like the sun moving toward the horizon, the rays of her presence waned and Kethras felt her leaving.

Then he felt her stop—hesitate—and turn toward him.

Kethras, she said, and he knew right then that it was not Ynara speaking—it was his mother. He felt the weight of her presence more greatly than he ever had in life. She was his protector now; she was the forest. She was the Binder of Worlds. *I love you always and forever.*

He didn't have to say it back to her but he did anyway. *I know you do, and I'm so lucky. I love you too.*

He felt her presence leave his mind, and the absence was heavier than any responsibility that he had ever had to carry. He had already lost her once, and now he was experiencing it all over again. The grief was almost too much to bear. He let his coat of joy fall to the ground as he felt himself crumple upon the bricks of bitterness, reluctance, and loss.

This path would be the hardest to tread.

Throughout his life he had known his sibling by many names—"Sister," "Ynara," "Binder of Worlds"—but none of them carried the sting and weight of the one that he loathed the most.

The Last Kienari.

He forced his eyes open to get away from the awful feeling. Standing before him, looking as grave as he felt, was Elyasha.

Chapter 39

Haidan Shar

Duna

THE SHARIAN AIR FELT HEAVIER that day, and Duna suspected she knew why. From her vantage point in her study overlooking the bay, she could see the caskets spaced out perfectly, the result of a carefully orchestrated ceremony carried out by Cortus Venn himself. The Stoneborn was walking the length and breadth of the solemn formation, inspecting each casket as if he were a gardener tending crops.

In a way, Duna realized, he was.

"He's as good as they say he is." The voice from behind her almost sent her out of her seat. It was Aldis Tennech, and Duna had no idea that he was in the castle—let alone the room.

"Gods, General, you scared the life out of me! I thought you were supposed to be down on the shore with the Commander."

"I was." He gave a chuckle and absentmindedly traced the scar on his neck. "Until I realized that there was nothing I could do to add to the order and balance of the ceremony. Venn is a master, and I don't just mean in battle." He walked up alongside her to join her by the window.

"You mean with . . ." Duna said, nodding to indicate the ceremony that was taking place before them, no doubt for the first time outside of Lash'Kargá.

Tennech nodded. "I mean with all of it, really. The way he leads, the way he displays compassion for those beneath him. You couldn't ask for a better man to be doing what he's doing."

Duna was silent as Venn paced between the caskets, pausing at regular intervals like a soldier on patrol. His lips were moving, but thanks to the breeze from the bay, Venn's words didn't make it past the caskets they were no doubt meant for. He had been ritualistically pacing and chanting for almost six hours now. He had started at dawn, and it was just past midday.

"How much do you know about Stoneborn?" Duna asked, not

taking her eyes off the Commander.

"Only what I've heard in stories, and what I've seen with my own two eyes," Tennech replied. "And most of both is Venn." He chortled.

Duna felt the corner of her mouth curl into a half-smile. "Then I find myself in the strange position of being able to educate you," she answered. "They were just a word to me, these Stoneborn—a myth—until Venn showed up at my doorstep. He came to me in Khala Val'ur, volunteering his services as we marched against the chovathi." As she watched the careful and calculated movements of the man on the shore below, she found it hard to equate it to the daring and headstrong Stoneborn who had thrown himself from the back of an airborne beast into the midst of a chovathi horde. "The one thing I can say about myths now," she said as she glanced back to Tennech, "is this: his will carry on into eternity."

Tennech nodded. "He is quite the warrior," he said.

"That is an understatement, General. Before him, I had never witnessed anything like it in my life: his fearlessness in combat, his recklessness that was somehow so carefully controlled. He was a force with no regard for his own life. Everything he did elevated the lives of his men—our men."

"That is the very definition of a leader," Tennech said, placing his hand on Duna's shoulder. "It is good that you have figured that out early. As queen, that knowledge will serve you well—and as a general, it could mean the difference between victory and defeat."

Duna felt her smile slip away as the weight of responsibility crept in and took its place. She was grateful for the opportunity to lead, but she never thought that it would have come about this way—or this fast; there had never been a more meteoric rise to power as quick as hers: from second-in-command of an army to general to queen in less time than it took for the moon to change phase. As she looked over at the hand on her shoulder, though, she let herself feel relief. Tennech was a man who had dedicated his entire life to combat and leadership, and for him to be saying these things about her now made her sit up straighter and exhale the doubt.

"Thank you, General." She tore her attention away from Venn for the first time in a while. "The best lesson I ever learned was that if I am the most capable person in the room, I am in the wrong room."

Duna stood up to make her way to the far wall of her study. She approached a deeply stained mahogany desk that likely weighed more than some horses. A sleek brown with candleholders on both sides, it had a prominent carving of a bear in the center standing on its hind legs, paws up in the air and jaws wide, ready to strike.

"This desk was a favorite of my father's," she said, tracing the jaw of the bear with her fingers. The piece had been dutifully carved into the desk itself—made from a single, massive piece of lumber. "Even when I was young, I knew why." With a sly look back to Tennech, she pressed down on the jaw. There was a click, and the carving opened, revealing a spacious holding place with a glass decanter and two chalices. She reached in and picked up the decanter, placing the cups on the desk, and pouring a little bit into each.

"Say what you will about the raiders of Hjorl," she said, holding out a cup for Tennech, "but they make some damn fine mead."

"They fight like they brew: recklessly."

Duna grinned and held her cup high. "Then we should drink that way as well."

Tennech returned her grin and raised his cup to hers. The two of them clinked cups. Duna raised hers to her lips, letting the sweet heaviness of the mead splash onto her tongue and down her throat.

"Agreed," said Tennech as he tilted back his own. He held it out to look at the yellow-brown perfection in the art of distillation that rested in his cup. "When one approaches drinking the way one approaches fighting, the only disappointment comes in surviving."

Duna laughed and gave a nod of agreement. "Gods, General," she said. "No one told me you were funny."

The general paused and looked at her with a twinkle in his eye. "I'd die before I let that secret out."

Duna was so caught off guard by the joke that she nearly missed it as it flew over her head. "You'd—" she started to say—and that's when it hit her. She breathed in a lungful of air and sputtered it out with gusto. "You'd die!" she cried. "But you did!" she squealed, pointing at him with her cup of mead. She laughed so hard that found that she needed to steady herself on the desk.

After her laughter finally subsided, she caught her breath and her balance. She smiled. "Shaper forbid I be the one to spill it, then."

She raised her cup, and Tennech returned the gesture. Each of them took a long pull of mead.

How this man—feared warrior of legend and perhaps the brightest military mind alive—could be so calm against the specter of all that they faced was beyond her. Maybe it was *because* of the impending doom that Tennech focused on something else.

Either way, he was welcome company.

Walking back to her perch by the window, Duna sat down to keep watching Venn. There he was, meticulously going about his paces: stopping by a casket, raising his hands to the sky, taking out a blade and drawing it across his open palm. No blood came out of course—Stoneborn did not bleed the way mortal men did—but it was all a part of the ritual. Each time he drew the blade across his palm, he thrust it into the dried wood of the casket where it stood upright as he chanted. Once his chanting was complete, he dug the blade out of the wood and moved on to the next casket. He had repeated this, without deviation or rest, for the better part of a day. Duna wondered how much longer he would keep at it . . . and how much of the ritual was left.

"They're not all like him, you know," Tennech said.

"All soldiers?"

"All Stoneborn."

These words came as a surprise to Duna, who was under the impression that Venn was the first Stoneborn that the man had met. She turned back to look at Tennech. "I thought you said Venn was the only one you knew."

"I said he was the only one I've seen, but he was not the only one I knew. Those stories I told you about?" he said, leaning forward. "They started with a man I never met, but knew as well as a Khôl knows his horse."

At this, Duna took a deep drink from her chalice that left it empty. She placed it down on a small table by the window and crossed the room for the decanter, picking it up and bringing it back to have a seat again. Tilting the glass Vessel into her cup, she let the liquid flow until it nearly overflowed. "Then I would say that a man who intends to accompany me into battle should tell me of this Stoneborn who has influenced him so."

Tennech looked at her for a hard and silent moment. Without taking his eyes off of her, he raised his drink to his lips and upended his cup, placing the empty chalice with a thunk on the table beside the decanter. Tapping the table with a finger, he said, "That will cost you at least one more cup."

Duna smiled, and poured. "You know," she said, topping it off, "when you're queen, they just *give* you mead."

Tennech chuckled and sat down beside her. "Why do you think I came here first?" he asked with a sly grin. He swirled the mead around in his cup and brought it to his nose, breathing in deeply and closing his eyes. "Mmm. Lilac and . . . sandalwood. A hint of brown sugar."

Duna brought her own cup and did the same. Her olfactory pallet was not as robust as Tennech's clearly was. The man was painting with hues that she had never even heard of, and here she was stuck with black and white. When she opened her eyes again, Tennech was taking a drink.

He lowered the cup and looked at the ceiling.

"I never knew my father," he said. "I knew of him, but I never knew him. Never knew the sound of his voice or the color of his eyes. The only things I knew about him were the things my mother told me."

He produced a small dagger from a sheath on his thigh, raising it up to admire it. "They say," he continued, eyes on the blade, "that you can learn a lot about a person by the way that he fights." He flicked his eyes over to Duna. "Do you believe that?"

She thought for a moment, then nodded.

"For people like us," he said as he looked back at the dagger, "it rings truest of all. The way they carry themselves on the battlefield, the way they hold a sword, the way they strike. Are they cautious? Are they reckless? Do they focus on one enemy at a time, or do they see the whole army?"

He pressed the tip of his dagger in the heel of his palm, whitening the skin around it as it tensed. "My father saw the whole army," he said, and the dagger broke skin. "But he was also reckless."

He drew the dagger across his palm and Duna winced as he did. Then she looked closer, blinking to make sure she was not seeing things. There was no blood. Her eyes went wide.

"And he was reckless because he did not bleed. He fought his way through too many battles to count, and always emerged without a scratch." He held up the palm that he'd run his dagger across for Duna to inspect.

"He was Stoneborn," Duna said, to which Tennech nodded.

"Something that I never was in life," he replied.

"But . . ." Duna began, puzzled. She looked again at his bloodless palm, then stared up at him in confusion. He did not have the marble-hued skin of a Stoneborn, yet . . . "You don't bleed. You—"

"I made a bargain with the Holder," he interrupted. "Because I am like my father in another way as well: I, too, see the whole army. The whole field of battle. I know what must happen to overcome this foe, and I am prepared to give it."

"So the Holder agreed to bring you back as a Stoneborn?"

"As something better, among other things," he said, sheathing his dagger.

Duna narrowed her eyes. "What other things?"

"Nothing that concerns you," he said. The words were not harsh but soft, almost gentle. "But what does concern you is what waits for us in Kienar. It was the reason I was brought back, and why I made the deal that I did."

Duna chewed on the words. She didn't like the fact that Tennech had made a deal with the Holder, but there was nothing she could do about it now. She was not sure that, had she been in his shoes, she would have done the same. Then again, she had not seen what he had seen, did know what he knew—and he knew more than he was letting on.

"Very well. I—"

Before she could finish her sentence, the door to the study flew open. Eowen, her messenger, stumbled his way into the room and knelt.

"Majesty," he said between breaths. "My scouts . . . from the south . . . have returned."

"Relax, Eowen, breathe," Duna replied. "What news?"

The blond man breathed in deeply. The red on his cheeks told Duna that he had sprinted to her. Whatever it was that his scouts had discovered, it was urgent.

"Four riders travel north from Beyond the Wastes," he said. "And with them . . . are two gwarái."

Chapter 40

Khala Val'ur

Yetz

FEAR IS RARELY SO PALPABLE as in the hours before a battle. Yetz had been riding along the inner path that led through the mountains, and in doing so, he'd passed by postings of soldiers waiting to meet the enemy; each of them wore their fear like blankets. Most of them knew about chovathi and how to deal with them, but the vast majority were inexperienced, with their only real knowledge of the inhuman monsters coming from the reports of the battle for Ghal Thurái—knowledge that, Yetz reflected, was indistinguishable from fear.

He tried to look encouraging as he made his rounds, and had barely left the inner ring when he saw Commander Aurin LaVince coming toward him on horseback, waving and smiling.

"High Khyth Yetz," LaVince said as he brought his horse to a stop a few feet away. "The men are inspired by your presence."

After being hand-selected by Duna Cullain as her second in command, then-Captain LaVince had done well to fill the power void created when Duna left to assume her rightful post as Queen. Now, in her absence, he had been raised to the highest rank in the Valurian army. Yetz hoped he had even half the tactical prowess that Duna had shown herself to possess by surviving Ghal Thurái.

"That is the idea, Commander," he said, and gave him a thin smile. "We are going to need all the inspiration we can muster."

"Then come with me to the front lines," LaVince said, nodding to a group of horses and riders nearby. "My men and I were just about to head out that way."

"As was I," Yetz said.

"Excellent. I hope you don't mind company."

Yetz was not used to a human being not only unafraid of him, but downright friendly. He reflected on the fact and thought it bade well for how LaVince might be in battle: fearlessness was a valuable trait among warriors—doubly so in a commander.

"Not at all. I hope the men will be equally encouraged by your presence as much as mine," he said.

They pointed their mounts down the path that would take them further away from the mountain, and rode.

✦ ✦ ✦

The path leading out of Khala Val'ur was narrow—no more than five men could pass through, shoulder to shoulder. As they pressed on, Yetz looked up to see some of the Valurian elite manning the rocky walls, fidgeting nervously with their weapons and armor.

"Are they ready?" It was more of a rhetorical question than anything; Yetz already knew the answer.

"As ready as they can be, High Khyth." There was hope behind the words, but also uncertainty. "We have a few men among us who served under Aldis Tennech. They've been making sure his tactics have been passed down—as well as reminding them that only cutting off the head of the chovathi can stop them."

"Good. A reminder that they can be killed."

LaVince nodded. "It's the one thing keeping a lot of them here, I'm afraid," he said, shifting his gaze to the mountain ridges above. "Most of them are veterans of the Battle for the Tree, whose only experience is fighting Athrani. There's barely a handful of them who have ever patrolled with Tennech on chovathi raids." He made a face. "It was never the most desirable duty—and definitely more dangerous than sparring. I'm afraid that our inexperience is going to be our undoing."

Yetz looked on down the path, which disappeared around the mountain as it retreated to the northwest. He would continue that way to see the rest of the men and aid them in their preparations as best he could—among other things. "As long as they can hold their ground," he began, "we stand a chance."

"I hope you're right."

Yetz silently agreed.

+ + +

As the riders continued along the mountain path, they were greeted by group after group of soldiers lining the walls, dutifully manning posts which had been manned for generations. Occasionally, Commander LaVince would get off his horse to speak to their troop commanders: senior lieutenants or young captains who had proven themselves worthy of the promotions that came after combat. Every one of them had been tempered by the flames of battle—and also defeat. The fact that they were alive following any loss spoke of their survivability—a trait that would come in handy in the battle to come. No army had ever had the audacity to attack what was commonly known as the most defensible position in Gal'dorok, perhaps even the continent.

That notion would soon be put to the test.

+ + +

Finally, after hours of riding, Yetz, LaVince, and his men approached the southern end of the outer mountain ring. They had made it all the way out, beyond the protection of the great mountain walls. As the path opened up into the wilds of Gal'dorok, the ridges on both sides formed a natural gate about seventy feet high that rivaled any of the great cities—and at its top stood dozens of archers ready to rain down death on the coming invaders.

Out past the edge of the gates, the bulk of the Valurian forces waited. There were a few thousand men—all that remained of a once mighty army—and they would be the ones to engage the chovathi head on. About a quarter of the forces were cavalry, and Yetz was thankful now more than ever that he had listened to Aldis Tennech when the general had insisted on bulking up their numbers. They were the linchpin of the strategy that they would need to employ against the chovathi; this was no ordinary human army, and could not be treated as such. Mobility was not just key—it was essential.

From the edges of the front line came two men riding toward them in full battle regalia. As they got closer, Yetz recognized them: the first was Lieutenant Commander Thuremond, commander of the cavalry, and de facto leader of the first line of defense; the second, Lieutenant Commander Haldir, commanded the archers.

Coming to a stop, both men rendered crisp salutes.

"High Khyth Yetz," said Thuremond. "Commander."

Yetz nodded.

"Gentlemen," said the commander, returning the salutes. "How go the preparations?"

Haldir spoke first, taking off his horned helmet to reveal a long mane of blond hair. "We've done all we can, I think. We've lined the walls just as you asked, though I know that will only slow them down."

"That is the plan," LaVince replied. "Which is why the initial contact is so crucial. We have to do everything we can to bite into their numbers."

Thuremond flinched at the use of the word bite. "And once we do?"

"We hold out as long as able," LaVince said. Pointing at archers that lined the path from there to the mouth of the Sunken City, he said, "Then, we begin the strategic retreat into the mountain pass. The cavalry and artillery will have to work flawlessly together to maximize the effectiveness of the retreat, to ensure we hold out until reinforcements arrive."

"Against a human army, it would be more than enough," Haldir replied. "For these chovathi, I fear, it may be all we can do just to stay afloat."

"My cavalry will handle them," Thuremond said, with a barely detectable waver in his voice. "Though we'll be sure to leave some scraps for the archers."

Haldir snarled, "My men will be grateful for the target practice."

The other two laughed, and Thuremond made a remark that Yetz only half heard. His attention was focused further out on the preparations being done on the battlefield.

Mixed in with the cavalry and outnumbering them nearly three to one were the infantry: the backbone of every army and the greatest weapon against the chovathi. They wielded the swords that would cut off the heads of the creatures—the only way to truly stop them. While arrows from the archers were sure to do damage, they did not hold a candle to the flame of the infantry—and flames, Yetz knew, would be another thing that would be on their side. He did not know firsthand how the chovathi reacted to fire, but he knew what it did to everything else—and all of it ended in ashes.

The army as a whole seemed to exude an air of nervous excitement, and Yetz could tell that all of them were taking their role as defenders seriously. Turning his attention back to the commanders, he noticed that all three were now turned to the east, in the direction of Ghal Thurái. When he shifted his own gaze in that direction to see what might have grabbed their attention, the breath caught in his throat. Even this far away he knew what it was.

Rising above the world like a shadow was a great cloud of dust and dirt, coming toward them and threatening to block out the sun. Under any other circumstances Yetz would have doubted its existence at all—even the largest dust storms in Gal'dorok dissipated when they met the mountains of the Great Serpent—but this one was certainly real . . . and it was not just any dust storm.

"Commander LaVince," Yetz said, grabbing the attention of all three men. "The time for preparation is over—now it is time to act, and to pray to the Breaker that we have done enough."

The commander looked pale at the sight of the cloud, but shook it out as he looked back at Yetz. "Spoken like a man who knows what is coming."

The empty shell of a laugh escaped his lips. "Indeed," he said, fixing his gaze on the east. "And I hope your men know as well: the chovathi are upon us, gentlemen—and I do not think they have come to talk."

Chapter 41

Do'baradai

Asha

THE DREADFUL WALK UP THE stairs leading to the tower was beyond any level of discomfort that Asha had ever experienced. Lining either sides of the stairway were Priests of the Holder, their faces upon her in baneful stares. She could feel the eyes on her from the ones that she had passed, knowing full well their disdain for wolves; it was why she had stayed in this form. Her descendants—the Wolfwalkers—had always been a thorn in the Holder's side, and the thought gave her a glimmer of satisfaction.

The wind howled behind her as she neared the top, where she paused to take a look back.

It was . . . magnificent. She stood fast to take it in. From this high up, it was very easy to lose her sense of scale and place, and walking the stairs had put her in a kind of trance that made her very surprised to see just how high she was. Spread out below her were the endless reaches of the Wastes of Khulakorum, dead desert dunes stretching out to disappear beneath the horizon. It was like looking down at the world from the back of a bird. She felt so removed from the world, yet intrinsically part of it at the same time—a feeling that all Wolfwalkers knew too well.

Turning again to face the top, she looked upon the great twin iron doors that barred her way to the palace. They were old, yet not worn away with time. Gold filigree that looked like it had been placed there yesterday lined the borders, tracing its way up and down the massive doors that were perhaps thirty feet tall. They had seemed so small from her vantage point on the ground, but she knew now that it was just a matter of perspective. Below them, the two Priests manning the doors looked like children, even as they pushed them open.

The doors yawned wide to reveal an entryway of polished marble and quartz. A reverberating clang accompanied their fixation in place as a ton of wrought metal was set on immovable stone.

Asha took her first few steps into the entryway and watched her shadow stretch out to greet the darkness of the tower. A sense of dread came with it as she watched it disappear. Her padded feet made no sounds as they carried her across the marble, but she knew that silence was not her ally in here. She was expected.

As if on cue, the voice of the Holder rang out. "I would tell you that it was foolish of you to come here, but foolishness seems to be a common trait."

The words came from far away, but due to the vast emptiness of the tower, it was impossible to tell from just where. Further in, toward the center, was a spiraling staircase lining the great chasm around which the tower was built; it was the central staircase up—and down. Asha approached.

"The only foolish thing I did was fall for you, Ahmaan," she said into the darkness. Her words echoed off the walls and tumbled their way down into the deep. She listened as they fell, and tried to gauge how deep the cavern was, to no avail. She had never been in the far depths of the tower—the truly deep recesses where darkness and emptiness thrived—and had no desire to go. She craned her head upward, tracing the spiraling stairs up, up, up toward the top. That is where the Holder would most likely be.

"Yet you did bear me a son," came the hollow voice of the Lord of the Dead, "which may be the wisest thing you've ever done." The laughter that followed echoed through the dark, but Asha had no trouble discerning its origin. He was above.

+ + +

Asha ascended the spiraling staircase that was carefully carved into the wide, circular shaft that ran the length of the tower. The climb was unnerving as there was no handrail or safety measure to keep one from falling, but the steps were wide enough to not induce vertigo in Asha as she climbed. She did not know exactly where the Holder was, but if his grandiosity had remained unchanged since she last saw him, he would certainly be in one place: the very top.

The tower of Do'baradai was impossibly tall and straight but for the top, where two massive columns jutted out like antlers, supporting the two towers of its namesake; the whole structure vaguely resembled a man holding out two stone goblets above his head. The head, in this case, was most likely where the Holder would have been waiting for her—with his twin brother Lash'kun hopefully nearby.

She continued her ascent up the winding stone stairs, never looking down to see just how far she had climbed. She preferred not to think about it.

+ + +

After a while, when Asha was sure that the climbing would never stop, she looked up to see the stairs begin their final spiral to the top, like an upside down whirlpool above her head. The stairs, she knew, terminated at the Eye of the Two Brothers: a great circular turret with windows all around it, providing a complete view of the city from any angle. She had not been up there in quite some time and realized that focusing on the climb had alleviated the feeling of dread for what awaited her at the top. As she rounded the corner that brought her into the Eye, though, the dread came flooding back. There, seated on the far end of the room, was the Holder.

"I was wondering how long it would take you," he said.

The circular stone floor that formed the base of the Eye was about a hundred feet from edge to edge, and sparsely decorated. It had been a watch tower when it was first built, but as the urgency to watch for invaders had steadily decreased throughout the centuries, it had become little more than a stopping point for those passing through to one of the two towers branching off. To the left and right were entrances to each tower—a short ascent through the massive columns that supported their weight—and toward the back was a semicircle of thirteen wooden chairs. Seated in those chairs were Priests—and in the center was the Holder himself. Lash'kun, however, was notably absent.

"Couldn't make the trip without your pets, I see," she sneered. Still wearing her lupine form, swept her gaze over each of them.

The Holder laughed. "Says the wolf," he snarled.

She knew the words were supposed to be mocking, but they only reinforced her own sense of power. She felt strong—she *was* strong—in this body, and the form fit her perfectly.

The Holder leaned forward, eyeing her and the entryway behind her. "I'm surprised you came alone."

He doesn't know about Ulten, then. Good.

"I had no choice. I had to get out of Khadje Kholam quickly," she said, pausing. "Although, in the end, I suppose it didn't matter."

"You may be wiser than I give you credit for," said the Holder as he leaned back again. "Yet not so wise as to venture into my city unescorted. And my brother—the fool!—walking practically right up to me. Did you not think that I would find you? That I would not be able to follow you, to track you? Surely you must know that I can sense you, just as you can no doubt feel my presence even as we speak." The Lord of the Dead tilted his head and, for a moment, Asha thought he was smiling. "You feel it," he went on, "don't you?"

Asha had tried to push out the trepidation that had been clouding her mind, but now she recognized it for what it actually was: the presence of the Holder. She closed her eyes and tried to shake it off, knowing full well that it would not help, yet doing it anyway.

"It's no use here," he continued, "in the heart of Do'baradai. Even if this city didn't hold the ancient powers that give us strength, the Three are together again after more than a thousand years of waiting. You cannot shake it off any more than the night could shake off blackness. We are linked, you and I, and you know it."

"That doesn't mean I have to like it," she growled. The Holder was right, though: there was power in the resting place of the Three, and now that their spirits all inhabited the ancient city together again, that power was taking on a life of its own.

"Your opinions are of little concern to me," said the Holder as he stood up. "What matters is that you are here—*we* are here—and that we three are awakened."

"Where... is..." Asha began, realizing that she was struggling to even talk under the weight of the palpable power in the room, "Lash'kun?"

The Holder put his hands behind his back and turned to walk casually to one of the many windows throughout the Eye. The one he approached was toward the back, so he faced away from her as he talked. "One thing they never tell you about power," he said as he stared out the window, "is of the ebbs and the flows; it is never static. Even now, I am sure you can feel it surging, growing."

"Where..." she started again, but this time it was even more difficult.

"That surge is because you are here—you and my brother—inside the walls of this tower. Separate, we are each but a little flame," he said as he reached for a small, white candle that was mounted between the windows. He cupped the wick with his hand, and a tiny flame began to burn. "Harmless for the most part, but," he said as he placed his finger in the flame, "still able to do some damage."

He walked over to another candleholder on the wall and took the candle from it, doing the same with a second, and then walked back to the first candle.

"But," he said, lighting the wicks one by one with the first candle, "when you put them together," he said, and he brought the three flames together as one, "they become greater than any one flame could have been by itself."

As he said this, the flame from all three candles erupted, shooting improbably high—high enough to lick the ceiling of the Eye itself. Asha's eyes went wide, as she knew it should have been impossible; no candles, no matter how much wick or wax, could have produced a flame like that.

"How—" she began, but choked on her words.

"I already told you," the Holder replied, snuffing out the flames. "The power of the Three is great—but to gather it all in one place, here in this tower, well . . ." he said, splaying his fingers as he trailed off. By now, Asha was nearly nauseous. The Holder was right: there was power here—too much power. "But I haven't even told you the best part."

He began walking toward her. Every fiber of her being told her to turn away, but not a single muscle in her body would comply. What was he doing to her? How was he doing it?

"This city is more than just a fortress, Asha, and this tower is more than just stone and mortar. It is an amplifier, a focus." Suddenly she felt the tower tremble. She had felt earthquakes before, many years ago in the mountains of the Spears, but never this far west. "A Vessel."

At that word, Asha froze. She looked up at the Holder, whose eyes were burning with madness and power.

He couldn't possibly mean—

The thought was cut off by another tremor, this one more forceful, followed by a small yet consistent quaking that Asha knew was more than just the shifting of the earth. It almost felt like it was straining, a tree branch bending in the wind. As the thoughts were tumbling around in her head, there was a violent crack, and the tremors stopped—only to be replaced by . . . something else. Asha could not reconcile the strange sensation below her feet. She looked out a window at the world beneath her—and what she saw made her sick with dizziness and fear.

✦ ✦ ✦

Ulten

THERE WAS SIMPLY NO TWO ways about it: Ulten was not getting in. The tower of the Two Brothers was too well guarded by the Priests of the

Holder—he'd never seen so many in his life, or knew that many even existed—and it would be impossible to slip by without being noticed. Even though he knew that it would be fruitless, he made his way to the tower to look for any hidden entrances or back doors, or other things that only happened in stories.

The night made for good camouflage as he pulled his dark cloak tighter, doing his best to blend in with the blackness. Above him loomed the tower, mighty and tall, that seemed to reach forever into the sky. Looking up toward the top, he could barely make out the branching towers that were its namesake, climbing away in the pale moonlight.

If I'm going to get inside and get the blade, he thought to himself, *I need a plan.*

Just then, the world began to shake. A crack like a lightning storm made him cover his ears and he thought his other senses might be betraying him. Nothing that he had seen before prepared him for what he was seeing now: the tower of Do'baradai, longstanding beacon in the middle of an endless sea of sand, was flying.

Chapter 42

Haidan Shar

Cortus Venn

It had been too long since Venn had learned the ritual to make Stoneborn—the very same one that the gods had used to usher the first one into existence. He hoped he wasn't forgetting anything. So much was at stake. He watched the sun continue its descent below the horizon and knew that it was time.

He turned to face those gathered before him, whose faces were as varied as their age and skin. Most of them he had just met; others he had known since the battle of Ghal Thurái. It would not matter in the end: familiarity would not make them into Stoneborn—only one thing would.

"Just as the sun sets on this world," he began, "so do your lives fade into darkness." He drew out the last word, along with his dagger. "Yet each of you will rise again, as surely as the dawn, to fulfill your purpose on this earth." As he spoke the words aloud, he raised his hands up, dagger held across his palm. He looked out at the assembly of men and women and slid the blade down over his skin. Though there was no blood, it was a symbolic beginning—and symbols played just as much a role in the ritual as blood itself. He sheathed the dagger and began to walk.

"There are things in this world that the light cannot touch," he said as he made his way through the ranks. "Things that even the gods have turned their backs on. Things that should not be. Things that *must* not be. Things that only Stoneborn can hope to defeat."

As he walked, dusk continued to fall. The shadowed faces of the brave Sharians were unwavering in the face of the coming night. *They will have to be brave*, thought Venn. *And they will face much more than just the darkness.*

"You have heard," he continued, now walking horizontally through the ranks of men and women, "that the chovathi have begun to gather their forces." He stopped, dead center of the formation. "But what you may not have heard is that they threaten more than just us," he said, beginning to raise his voice. "They threaten all living things." His words carried as well as he had intended, and saw a few ripples of fear run across the face of the army of soon-to-be-Stoneborn. *Just as well,* he thought. *Better they come to grips with their fear now, than to have it sneak up on them in the midst of battle.*

"But I have some good news for you." His voice was softer now, quieter, yet still had an edge. "After tonight, you will no longer be amongst the living."

He turned on his heels and walked to the front of the formation, allowing the words, like the sun, to sink in. When the final rays had left, he knew it was time. He faced them again.

"Blood," he said, "and fire. Both life, both warmth. Both sacred." He took his place by a coffin that was offset from all the rest, the head of the formation. Upon it were placed two items: a sword, and a burning torch standing upright in a steel holder. He reached for the torch.

"This light represents hope," he said. He picked it up, holding it high above his head with his back to the east. "It burns brightest in the dark. This sword," he said, leaving the torch raised up and reaching for the blade, "represents willpower." He raised the steel weapon, its polished surface reflecting the light of the torch's liquid, dancing waves. "It cannot be bent or broken in the right hands.

"And this darkness," he continued, voice steady and calm, "represents everything that will fight to smother those first two." He spun around to face them, sword crossed over torch before him. "We will not let them."

He steadied himself, allowing no more than one breath of hesitation. There was no turning back, and if he so much as blinked, all would be lost. The time was now. There was no room for waiting.

In a graceful and seamless motion he threw the torch at the man closest to him.

"Stoneborn do not bleed," Venn said as the man caught the torch. With deadly precision, Venn thrust forward, catching him in the throat. The man's eyes went wide as his life and warmth spilled out, sending him to his knees in a ragged, sputtering gasp. Venn pulled the sword back and, with barely any effort, sliced through the neck of the second man standing before him. There was no time for thought—just steel. "Tonight, I will show you why."

Whirling forward, Venn swung his sword in perfect arcs as it slashed and bit at the soft, fleshy shells that these men and women had been born in. He was unstoppable, unwavering, cutting through muscle and bone like air. His strokes were flawless, his timing perfection—they had to be. Though these Sharians had prepared for this moment, visceral fear was much more powerful than any devotion to duty or pursuit of an ideal. Stoneborn were born in battle, yes, but even the bravest of warriors could balk when facing the edge of his own death. It didn't matter; Venn was relentless.

The darkness surrounding him gave him no pause as he stalked forward with care and precision, bringing his blade up in an arc, down in a counter slash, sideways in a vicious stab, forward in a thrust. It was a dance that Stoneborn had performed for generations. The steps may have changed, but the rhythm was the same. No movement was wasted. No life was spared.

Slashing. Turning. Driving. Twisting. The flash of steel was all that caught the light as the master maintained his advance. One by one they fell as culled chaff from wheat to be reaped.

Five. Ten. A dozen. A score. None were spared; none were meant to be. Every single one had to die in order for the ritual to be complete. Venn knew this—yet it did not make it any easier.

All around him were the sounds of death: sharp, choking gasps; ragged breaths. Victory always came at a price, and every man on these sands was paying it now, including himself.

Slash. Turn. Drive. Twist. The savage, bloody pattern repeats. Slicing. Stabbing. No force on earth could stop him.

Finally, after what seemed like ages but was no more than mere seconds, the last sword fall came with the same ruthless grace with which it had started. It was done. He could rest. They were felled.

Venn stood and was still.

There was nothing left but the sound of his breathing and the sea. His blade hung loosely in his grip, its polished steel edge dulled by blood and bone. He dared not wipe it clean. There was only one thing left to do: the slow and toilsome task of taking the bodies of each of the men and placing them in the coffin, letting their blood run dry, their bodies empty.

The final step in the rite.

+ + +

Hours passed; one does not rush such things as these. Venn took care to follow the ancient ways, taking painstaking measures to see everything through to perfection. It was his labor, his great purpose, and he did so gladly.

+ + +

The bodies were laid in their coffins to face the sky. The still-burning torch, once held by the first man who'd died, had been placed back in its holder at the foremost coffin. Its flames now made shadows of the still and lifeless.

Venn stood for a moment and watched. Listened. All before him was cold: the wood of the coffin, the bodies of the men. They were shells, now, of the things they once were—but soon, by the time the sun rose again, they would be so much more.

These bodies would be hope; these broken shells, life.

They would be fury, come again. They would be rage.

They would be light.

They would be fear.

They would be Stoneborn.

Chapter 43

G'hen

Elyasha

SHARING HEADSPACE WITH THE SHAPER of Ages was as uncomfortable as it was frustrating. Sometimes their thoughts would run together in a confusing cacophony of chaos, two waves crashing into each other. Other times it was deathly silent, and Yasha had to do her best to keep her private thoughts just that. Miera had told her that it took more effort for her to exist outside of Yasha's mind, but Yasha was constantly wishing for her to do so. It was better than the alternative, she reasoned: Miera could have taken her over completely like any other god would have done, turning her into a mindless Vessel for her to control. The Traveler had done it to their friend Rathma back in Théas, and it was . . . unsettling. Yasha didn't like to think about the fact that she was teetering on the edge of having her consciousness erased if not for Miera's willpower. It was like hanging by a worn, thin rope over a bottomless chasm: one false move and she would plummet to the depths below, never to return.

She hoped that the rope would hold.

+ + +

We need to find Kethras, Miera said.

Easier said than done, Yasha thought back. *He could be anywhere out there.*

They were looking, through Yasha's eyes, into the forest that surrounded G'hen. While not nearly as extensive as the Talvin Forest to the northwest where they had first met him, it was certainly large in its own right. Thick oaks on one side and sturdy maples on the other formed the outer layer of trees that line the road stretching from G'hen back toward Théas.

If I know Kethras, Miera began, *he will be by the oaks.*

Yasha, remembering that the tree of his home forest, Naknamu, was a massive oak itself, felt foolish for not realizing that immediately. The two of them, as one, set off in that direction.

✦ ✦ ✦

What's it like being the Shaper? Yasha asked. She couldn't help herself; she knew the question was going to come out sooner or later, and she preferred to ask it now on purpose instead of later on accident.

A blur of Miera's thoughts filled her own, images that Yasha could barely make out or comprehend, emotions and feelings that were as foreign to her as dying. It was at that moment that Yasha realized: Miera wasn't preparing to answer her question—she was answering it. Yasha tried to focus on the flurry of thoughts that flew around, a cloud of sound and fury.

It's . . . a bit like looking at the sun, Miera finally said. The chaotic display had gone on for—well, Yasha couldn't quite figure that out. *Yet also a bit like falling asleep. One day I just woke up and . . . remembered.*

Yasha had been with her when she had ascended to the godhood that had always waited for her inside the Otherworld, the realm of creation where she and the Breaker, and the Binder of Worlds once called home. It was so strange to watch the transformation happen, too: one moment she was Miera, and the next she was the ancient goddess who'd been responsible for bringing the world into being—yet they had always been one and the same. It was like watching the stars come out at night: they had always been there, but now they could be seen for what they were.

The inkling of power and memories that Yasha was feeling now were a strange sort of comfort: there was limitless knowledge contained in them, hidden in the spirit of the Shaper. Walking beneath the great canopy of trees, she felt doubly protected from the world, both by the branches above her and the goddess inside her. It was . . . nice.

There, Miera said.

Distant enough to blend into the shadows, but close enough for Yasha to be able to make out the faithful dagger by his side, Kethras

242

rested in the shade of an ancient-looking oak, seated on the ground in a meditative stance.

Should we . . . wake him up? Yasha asked with a hint of hesitation. Even though he was their friend—perhaps because he was—she was afraid of him. She was even more afraid of him when he was angry.

We have no choice, Miera replied, pushing away the fear that spread through Yasha's mind. *He will understand.*

Fortunately for both of them, they didn't need to. At that moment, Kethras opened his eyes as if he'd been summoned. "Yasha," he said. He sounded tired, like he had just got done walking a great distance. "And, I assume, Miera?"

Yasha nodded.

"Good," he said. "I need you with me in Kienar. I have spoken to Ynara, and I have seen it for myself. Thank you for delivering the message to me, Miera."

Yasha heard Miera's reply in her mind and suddenly found herself in the strange position of playing interpreter to two beings who spoke the same language. "She says you're welcome."

Kethras stood up, stretching out his long limbs and nearly touching the branches that hung above their heads. "We should retrieve Alysana and make our way to the forest."

Yasha opened her mouth to answer, but heard Miera speaking. She closed her mouth, and shook her head at Kethras.

"What?" he asked.

"She says we can't take her with us. Her place is here."

Kethras blinked. "Why?"

Miera's voice was silent in her head. "She, uh," Yasha stammered. "She isn't answering."

"Well," he said with a grunt, and began to walk away. "I disagree. We need her."

"Kethras."

The Son of the Forest stopped in his tracks. It had not been Yasha's voice—it was Miera's. "You know it must happen," she said. "And you know it must happen a certain way."

He stood there, unmoving, and Yasha heard him inhale sharply. "I do," he replied. "And I hate it with every fiber of my being."

"I know," Miera said. "I do, too. As does your sister."

Kethras snapped his head around. "Do not lecture me about my sister."

Yasha took a step back. She had seen him angry before, and it was always frightening. She could feel her heart racing as her body was telling her to flee. Even knowing that he would never hurt her, she was afraid. She could only imagine what his enemies must feel when they face him.

"I . . ." Kethras said, lowering his head. "I am sorry. I should not have snapped at you like that." He turned his back to them and looked to the trees.

"No apology necessary," Miera said. She had manifested herself beside Yasha, but was walking toward Kethras now. "We are all under a lot of stress, and your forest is in danger. You have every right to be upset."

She stood beside him now, gazing up at the towering black hunter with a look which Yasha knew was genuine compassion.

"It's just—" he started, and looked down at the ghostly form of the Shaper beside him. "You know. You've seen it."

"I have," Miera said as she broke eye contact with Kethras. She looked to the northwest, to Kienar. "Which is why you know we need to leave now. The puzzle pieces have started to fall into place; it's up to us to make sure they form the picture we want them to—and not one that some would form themselves."

"You are right," Kethras said, turning to face both of them. "I am sorry for delaying us even this much. We should be off."

"I'll secure a horse from in town, then," Yasha said.

"Very well," Kethras said. "Meet me to the north of G'hen. We will begin the journey back to the forest."

After he said those words, Miera disappeared again, but Yasha knew that she was only gone to the rest of the world. She was hiding out, waiting for the right time to emerge again.

Walking back to G'hen intent on getting a horse to ride to Kienar, Yasha knew without a doubt that Miera had buried herself inside her mind—as the vision of Kienar that came into her mind, unbidden, almost made her collapse.

Chapter 44

Kienar

D. C. Jennings

Ynara

IT WAS A STRANGE SENSATION, the feeling of knowing one's own fate, but one that Ynara was familiar with nonetheless. To her, the fate of the Binder of Worlds was as plain as the leaves beginning to blanket the forest floor, the first tidings of autumn. Yes, the weather had grown colder and the days had grown shorter, but those were just feelings that change was coming. Now that the oranges and reds had begun to creep into the leaves, there were finally signs that everything was about to change.

Everything.

+ + +

As she walked among the forest that she had always called home, Ynara let its sights and sounds comfort her. Although she knew them all by heart, they were different now through the lens of the Binder of Worlds, like looking at an old friend and seeing details that had never been obvious before. The bark of the ancient oak, Naknamu, had a quality to it that resonated strength and resolve—but through the sight of the Binder, Ynara could see all the way back to the tree's infancy, when it was still just a sapling. Her eyes showed her its future as well, mixing tangible with abstract in a path that was tangled, yet clear.

The vision of a god did not come without consequences, however. When her new and expansive consciousness was first birthed, Ynara could barely comprehend it. Even though she was not the true reincarnation of the Binder of Worlds—D'kane had seen to that by destroying her in the mortal realm—she now wielded the power and gifts which her mother had left her with her dying breath. Ynara, so used to seeing with her mortal eyes through a mortal mind, could barely reconcile the vast reaches of the cosmos—and even time itself—that stood suddenly unveiled before her; it was too much for her to bear all at once. She was still slowly learning to control it, like the pupil of an eye contracting to

229

control the flow of light. If she were to open her eye completely . . .

She shuddered at the thought: all that power, all that knowledge . . . terrifying—and it should have been, she knew. Knowledge like that was a flame: easily controlled on a small scale and useful while controlled in such a manner—but allow it to grow too large too fast and it could ravage the earth. She had seen exactly how it could destroy someone.

. . . Someone whose presence she felt growing ever closer.

+ + +

Ynara found herself standing at the outer bounds of the forest of Kienar, the entirety of its living, breathing, interconnectedness behind her. She felt it moving and pulsing together, a hundred thousand voices that sang as one. Looking out over the plains that lay between her and the great Talvin Forest, she found herself at peace with the events that were beginning to unfold. Even now, she felt the footsteps of the approaching army. She knew the scrambled, chaotic thirst that bubbled below their surface. She watched, and she waited.

The chovathi were not so different from her own forest, she mused: many creatures acting as one, a collective consciousness that grew out of the darkness, growing and changing. It was a dark reflection of how the Binder of Worlds had orchestrated the growth of her forest, but a reflection nonetheless.

They grew closer, and the presence in her mind grew stronger; it was one that she had not felt in . . . how long had it been?

Not long enough, she decided.

+ + +

Ynara felt the great wave of chovathi come to a stop, like water hitting a dam. She knew that they would not be able to pass through and into her forest so long as she was alive. She took a small comfort in that fact. The power that held the very threads of the universe together were present inside her, and inside her forest. So long as there was a Binder of Worlds, that power would hold.

"So," Ynara began, standing up from her meditative posture on the forest floor, "you have returned."

The chovathi army before her seemed to shudder in a strange and furious reply — and from that reply emerged the presence of Zhala, matriarch of all chovathi, the head of the terrible snake that had slithered and slid its way to the edge of her forest. Striding forward with terrible, twisted legs of rock and flesh, Zhala towered above Ynara in the same way that Naknamu towered above all other trees. She was fearsome, determined, and strong—and she reeked of hunger.

"I have indeed." Coming to a stop before her, Zhala's eyes did not meet Ynara's; they were on the Tree, Naknamu, the Old One, and they burned with a fiery rage that seemed to flare up at Ynara's words. "Returned to the forest from whence I was banished," she spat.

Ynara could feel the presence of a power-corrupted entity connected to Zhala. The presence had surely been human—once—but now it was something . . . different.

"You were banished by us for the same reason that the Khyth were disavowed by humanity: wanton disregard for the lives of others."

Zhala sneered at this and finally looked down, a looming monstrosity that Ynara hardly recognized anymore. "The time of the Kienari is coming to a close, dear sister, and the chovathi have come to claim that which is rightfully theirs."

Ynara locked eyes with the force of nature that once called this forest home. She knew that Zhala had marched all this way with a purpose, and she knew that she would not leave until that purpose was fulfilled—and, worst of all, she knew that the chovathi matriarch was right.

Chapter 45

The Otherworld

Thornton

It all felt like a dream. Thornton had come to accept the chilling fact that his body was no longer his own. When the Breaker had seized control, the feeling of powerlessness had enveloped him completely. He struggled and pushed against the influence of the ancient god, but it was like trying to move an oak tree by blowing on it. There was nothing to be done . . . yet Thornton was never one to quit so easily. He poked and prodded at his cage, probing for weaknesses, and searching—hoping—to find something, anything, that could mean his freedom. The first glimmer of hope came as a direct result of this searching, and it had almost cost him his sanity.

He found that, quite by accident, he could gather what he came to recognize as his own consciousness and move it around. He thought to himself that it felt a bit like catching smoke in a jar, and was mildly amused by this finding. Up until then, he'd had no real "form" in his mental prison—he was just a jumbled collection of thoughts floating around in a cage, unable to leave. Now, he could form his thoughts into a body—or at least what passed for one here. He looked down and saw what he had indeed expected to see: two hands.

It's progress, I guess, he thought.

He paused and looked around again.

The walls of his prison were solid, gray, and imposing, with not so much as a crack in their façade. They reminded him of the walls of the old Athrani prison where D'kane had held Miera before trying to siphon off her essence to wield the Hammer of the Worldforge. The only difference was that these walls had no ceiling—or at least not one that he could see. They just went up and up and up until they disappeared from sight. An infinite prison with infinitely high walls. The perfect place to keep someone whom you never wanted to get out.

The more he thought about it, though, the more certain he was that it *was* the Athrani prison—or at least a version of it that the Breaker had used when first subduing Thornton's consciousness. It was a curious thought that gave him an idea.

He walked over to the wall. Reaching out his hand, he touched it. It was smooth, cold. Just like he remembered the walls being in the real world. Looking up, he squinted to see if there actually was an end in sight to the walls. No such luck.

He closed his eyes, and reached out for the feeling again. His thoughts, flying around chaotically and with no pattern or reason, suddenly jolted as if grabbed by an unseen hand. He could feel them—and his makeshift body—begin to align. The frenzied swirling began to take shape. If this place was a prison in his own mind, that meant that somewhere deep down, he was its architect as well. He would use that.

The world around him began to tremble as Thornton reached out. He touched the wall again, but this time it felt different, like dipping his hand in a stream. The sensation was jarring, and almost made him lose his concentration. He felt his thoughts start to scatter. He reeled them in, though, locking down his focus and shifting it back to the wall of his prison. He pushed his hand further into the stream. Suddenly, the tip of his fingers felt cool. Curious, he inched his hand further, and it was like the sensation had stopped. *No . . . not stopped.* He was vaguely aware that something, in the distance, clicked into place.

He continued to reach, tilting his head as he tried to figure out what it was that he was feeling. The odd, rippling sensation was surrounding his whole arm except for . . .

He opened his eyes. He'd reached the other side.

Chapter 46

Derenar

Sera

THE JOURNEY FROM THE WASTES was tiresome, but the moment Sera's feet touched grass, she knew it was worth it. North of the Wastes, the land lay in stark contrast to the dead scenery of the south. It was like someone had drawn a line between Derenar and Khulakorum: on one side were hot, lifeless barrens; on the other was a lush, verdant green.

Sera, overcome with joy to see this much plant life again, paused to take it all in. "We should rest," she said. "We've come a long way."

"Aye," said Dhrostain. "And this seems like as good a place as any."

A small stream further in provided the perfect opportunity to let their mounts replenish themselves, along with allowing a bit of a rest for the weary travelers. Riding wasn't easy—Sera had never liked it—and riding in a desert was among the world's most difficult undertakings.

"I'd almost forgotten about the color green," said Dhrostain as he dismounted. "Much better than—" he waved his hands back in the direction of the Wastes "—whatever that was back there."

"Agreed," Sera said, and she took a deep breath in through her nose. It even *smelled* different here! It had only been a few short weeks since they'd arrived in Khulakorum, but somehow it had seemed much longer. Their entire existence, sunup to sundown, had been spent monochromatically, surrounded by nothing more than beige sand dunes and beige huts holding beige horses and colorless dreams. It was refreshing to see such a vibrant and varied color palette again. "Was Derenar always this . . . alive?"

"It was," said Hullis as he refilled his flask. "But it's like having water after going thirsty for days," he said, raising the flask to his lips and taking a deep drink. Wiping off his mouth, he added with a smile, "More satisfying when you're deprived of it entirely." He reattached the flask to its holder on his hip and patted it.

Sera smiled and let the serenity of it all comfort her—until it was broken by the grating voice of the Priest of the Holder.

"When you informed me that you needed to stop for a rest," he said from behind them, "I did not expect there to be such a…lack…of resting."

The blue-robed priest was staring at Sera with his cold, empty eyes. Even though she had been around his kind since her arrival in Khulakorum, she was still not used to how they made her feel. There was something beyond unholy about them, despite the fact that they were mere men. The power of the Holder coursed through them and sustained them, making their skeletal faces all the more terrifying because of what lurked behind them: darkness.

"Talking and resting are not mutually exclusive, priest," Sera said. She turned her back to him and walked along the stream to find a quiet place to sit. She had her eyes on her horse, who was still drinking, and found a spot in the shade to have a seat. She could feel the priest's eyes on her even as she shut her own. "See? I'm doing both right now." Any opportunity to forget about what lay ahead—and what was traveling with her—she took.

Clasping her hands behind her head, she laid down in the cool, green grass and listened to the brook babble by.

✦ ✦ ✦

"Sera, wake up."

The voice was Dhrostain's, and Sera had no doubt that the hand jostling her shoulder belonged to the bearded Thurian as well.

"I'm awake," she lied. She could have used more rest, and her body was definitely upset at being disturbed. "What is it?"

"The priest," Hullis said from down the road. "He left about an hour ago."

At this, Sera opened her eyes. Dhrostain was bent over her, but stood up when he saw that she was awake.

"Did he say where he was going?"

"He did. But he said we had a different destination—one where he could not follow."

Gathering herself, Sera stood up. She had really been enjoying the peace and quiet that a stream-side slumber had brought. *Of course it had to be cut short,* she thought bitterly.

"Very well," she said, dusting herself off. "Where are we headed?"

Dhrostain looked back at Hullis, who shrugged. He turned back to Sera. "Haidan Shar," he said with a grimace.

When the words finally sunk in, Sera was furious. To begin with, Haidan Shar was at least a three day ride, if not more. They had been riding almost due north of Khadje Kholam since they left, when they should have been traveling east, or at the very least northeast. Secondly, she had no idea how warmly they would be greeted at the gates of the Gem of the East—though she suspected the answer was "not well." Third, the priest had left no instructions on what to do when they got there; should they beg for help? Should they demand cooperation? They were children tossed to sea and told to swim; Sera hated swimming.

The journey would take them through the lands under the influence of the Khyth in Khala Val'ur—the last place that she wanted to be since she and Tennech had essentially fled in the midst of battle to escape to the Wastes.

+ + +

"How convenient for him to leave us now," Sera said to Dhrostain, who was loading up the last of their supplies on the back of the gwarái.

"Fine with me," he said. "Those priests are more unnerving than Khyth—and you know how I feel about Khyth." He shuddered, as if to prove his point.

Sera cracked a smile. "I do. And I assume captain Hullis feels the same?" She turned to look at the blond Thurian, who was already saddled atop the gwarái and ready to ride.

"Let's just say," he began, "that I would rather walk through the sands of the Wastes by myself for a week than have to ride another day with that—" he made a face like he was smelling sour milk—"thing."

"I'm glad to hear that we are in agreement," Sera said. She put her left foot into the stirrup of her horse's saddle and climbed up, pausing to take one more look around Derenar while she still could. Everything east of here—Gal'dorok as a whole, all the way to the Tashkar Sea—was rocky, jagged, and dull. Sure, the mountaintops were nice to look at from afar, but she had spent too many years beneath the surface of Khala Val'ur to ever feel at home in such terrain. She looked northwest, toward the land of her birth, Ellenos. It had been so long since she left its gates to venture forth with her mother that the memories seemed more like a dream than a life. "We might as well get started."

The two Thurians, atop their gwarái, nodded in agreement.

Sera clicked her tongue twice, spurring her mount ahead to the path toward the foothills of the Great Serpent, Gal'behem.

Chapter 47

Do'baradai

Ulten

ULTEN STOOD WITH HIS JAW slack as the tower of Do'baradai floated away, wondering if what he was seeing was the truth. He blinked a few times to make sure. He'd seen visions sometimes as his people wandered the desert in search of new places to settle—hidden lakes or patches of green, mostly—yet all those visions had been insubstantial, illusory. But this one? This one was solid and convincing. In short, it looked real—*very* real.

Tearing his eyes from the sky, he walked over to where the tower had split from the ground to see a very real-looking hole in the ground, too—a hole where the mighty structure had once stood, like mighty structures are supposed to do. Peering down, he saw nothing but black.

He searched around for a rock. Finding one close by, he picked it up and walked to the edge where he tossed it in, listening for it to hit. Nothing. He waited. Still nothing! Could the hole be that deep? His mind reeled at the magnitude—and at the idea that what had been so firmly rooted once could just break off and fly away. He had to steady himself to make sure, in his musings, that he didn't fall in. He knelt down and peered over the edge again, into the black and featureless void below.

The original architects of the tower had clearly understood things like counterweight and balance as they must have dug into the ground nearly as deeply as the tower was tall. Looking up, Ulten could see the tower still floating through the air in its agonizingly slow retreat—yet it was noticeably further than when he had looked before. Its sheer size, he knew, made it look like it was not even moving at all; Ulten thought that it felt like watching a mountain erode. He shook his head, still unable to make sense of what he was seeing.

"I can't believe my eyes," he said out loud to hole in the ground.

Much to his surprise, he got a response.

Believe them, said a voice in his head. If Ulten hadn't been so close to the ground, he may have tumbled off into the hole.

"Who said that?"

Who do you think?

Ulten tilted his head, replaying the voice in his head. It was one that he recognized, barely. Haltingly, he called out. "T-Traveler? Is . . . is that you?"

The disembodied voice gave an annoyed grunt of affirmation. *While I appreciate being recognized, I'd rather be found. Where are you?*

Ulten looked around. "Right where the tower used to be," he answered. "It just . . ." he began, swirling his hands about frantically, "up and left."

So I heard. Lucky for me that you weren't with it.

"Lucky?" he asked. "Lucky how?"

Well, my brother would prefer that I stay here, in the one place that I can truly be bound—and that might have been the case if you'd been in that tower when it left too.

"Bound?" Ulten asked. The word found the sides of the cavernous walls that plunged into the hidden depths, echoing as it fell. "Are you—" he gulped, "—somewhere down there?"

Ulten had the strange sensation that the god was smiling. *I am. And I would be grateful if you could help me fix that.*

He peered out into the darkness again and, just then, swore that he heard a faint *crack* that echoed upward and into his ears. He blanched. If that was the rock that he'd thrown, then . . . Oh . . . he felt dizzy at the thought. "How far down are you, exactly?"

Far, was the Traveler's response.

"Can't you, ah . . . poof yourself up here?"

There was the sensation of a smile again, with more than a hint of amusement. *Believe me, I would if I could. But my brother had me placed under iron the moment he captured me. No poofing for me, I'm afraid.*

"Well, I don't know how to say this, so I'll just say it: I'm not sure what to do," Ulten said, sitting down on the ground by the hole. "I can't see a way down; the walls are too steep," he said, peeking over the edge again. "And I doubt I'd survive the jump."

Ulten's mind was quiet for a moment, and he realized that the Traveler must have been thinking about what to say. Every time the god spoke to him, it was like listening to an echo in reverse—an odd sensation that Ulten didn't care for. He would be happier when they were standing face to face and could talk the way the gods intended: with voices.

There is a cave entrance, the Traveler said after a silence. *Well to the east of here. It looks out over the Tashkar Sea.*

"The Tashkar Sea!" Ulten shouted. "That has to be days from here!"

Two, if you don't stop. Three, if you do.

"Two days," Ulten repeated. He closed his eyes and rubbed them in frustration. "Let's say I get to the cave," he replied, "what then?"

Climb inside and walk back. The great river that once flowed through and emptied into the sea carved out a trail over the centuries. It will lead you back here.

Ulten surprised himself with the laugh that came forth; it was not one of glee, but of disbelief. "You want me to walk for two days, only to walk right back? You have to be out of your mind."

Technically I am, answered the Traveler. *I'm in yours.*

"And I have never regretted it more."

Just trying to lighten the mood.

Ulten waved it off. "Let's say I do make this journey," he said with resignation. "I walk the two—possibly three—days toward the sea, through the Wastes and past the Spears, and somehow manage to find this cave that you speak of. Then I just, what, walk in a straight line until I find you?"

I can guide you, was the Traveler's quick response. *All you need to do is tell me when you get to a crossroad or a branch in the path; I'll be able to focus on where you are and tell you the correct path to take.*

"Will I be able to hear you all the way out there?"

A fair question; the answer is, "Probably."

"Not very reassuring."

It's the best I've got, the Traveler replied. *Our mental connection is strong, but the further you get from me, the more tenuous the link will be.*

"I see," Ulten replied. He looked back up to the sky to see the tower of Do'baradai continuing to drift away as it slowly shrank from view. "And I suppose no amount of persuading could convince you that you like it down there?"

A sensation reverberated through Ulten's mind and he realized that the Traveler was laughing. At least he was a pleasant houseguest.

It wouldn't be so bad, the god began. *At least it's out of the heat. But I am afraid, were I to stay here, that my brother would accomplish just what he set out to do, and that would not be good for any of us—not you, not Asha . . . not even the other gods.*

The words hung in Ulten's mind as they seemed to have a weight attached to them that made them seem larger and somehow more dense. He did not want to ask the Traveler to elaborate for fear of what he might say if he did.

"Then I suppose I should get a move on," Ulten said. He stood up and looked back to the gates of the city. Through the dark, he could barely see the silhouette of his camel, still tied up outside. "Two days there and two days back is no easy task," he said.

Well, if you need some company along the way, you know where to find me.

"Indeed," he said as he began to walk back.

There was a pause. *Are you . . .* began the Traveler. *Are you saying everything out loud?*

Ulten wasn't sure what to make of the question. "What do you mean? Am I—" he stopped. Whirling around to the opening of the chasm, he shouted, "What do you mean?"

I mean . . . The sensation of laughter again. *I mean that I can hear you. You don't have to shout. In fact, you don't even have to speak.*

"Why didn't—" Ulten started to say, then stopped. *Why didn't you mention that earlier?*

You were doing so well, I didn't want to interrupt.

Ulten hoped that the Traveler could feel how hard his eyes were rolling at the moment. *I probably would have figured it out eventually, right around the time I reached the cave.*

Probably.

After he finished untying his camel, Ulten whispered some soft words of reassurance in the creature's ear. He had a thought and reached out to speak to the Traveler through their mental connection.

When I return, he asked the Traveler, *do you want a camel?*

Quite a kind offer, came the response. *But I won't need one where I'm going. I could, however, use a lock pick and a shemagh.*

Ulten paused and looked around. *I'll see what I can do.*

✦ ✦ ✦

Putting his foot in the stirrups of the polished leather saddle, Ulten climbed on top, taking the deep purple reins in his hand and urging the beast forward with two clicks of his tongue. *Two days east to the Tashkar Sea*, he thought to himself. *I must be mad.*

If you are, said the Traveler, *do try to keep it to yourself. It's terribly quiet down here, and I'm afraid you'd just take me with you.*

Ulten wasn't sure whether to laugh or cry, but he knew one thing for sure: it was going to be a long trip. If he wasn't mad now, he thought that he might be by the time the journey was through.

Chapter 48

G'hen

Alysana

THE BODY THAT LAY BEFORE her was one that Alysana knew. She had known him when he was alive: knew how he talked, how he fought . . . knew what sounds he made when he died. She knew these things, of course, because she had been the one to kill him.

Yuta? she thought in confusion. *Why would Mordha bring his body here? There is just no good . . .*

Before she could complete the thought, the door down the hall crashed open, and her uncle Ezna spilled out. "I demand an explanation," he said. "One does not simply defy Ghaja Rus without facing repercussions."

His footsteps grew louder as he drew near, leather sandals tapping on stone.

Hovering over the body with the monogrammed Théan dagger of Ghaja Rus beside it, Alysana realized that there was simply no talking her way out of this. She was trapped . . . and her sister had been the one to orchestrate it. Mordha, the one who had raised her and loved her and taught her to defend herself. Was everyone she loved simply out to betray her?

Ezna was practically on top of her now. "So there had better be a good . . ."

His words trailed off, and Alysana knew that she was going to have to face whatever consequences came with not only defying Ghaja Rus, but murdering one of his bodyguards—and then, apparently, bringing the corpse with her to G'hen.

Her uncle's next words were whispered. "What . . . have . . . you . . . done?"

She stood up. "It wasn't me, uncle, I swear it."

Ezna looked at her skeptically and laughed. "The word of the daughter of a liar and a thief is not one I trust. Besides," he said as he crossed his arms, "it's not me that you'll need to explain it to."

The cold silence that hung in the air left a void that only one name could fill— and that name now sat on the tip of her tongue like a prisoner about to break free. *Ghaja Rus.* She didn't give the name the satisfaction of being spoken out loud.

"I have nothing to say to him."

"He certainly has a lot to say to you," Ezna said, looking at the body. He gave a soft, low whistle. "Especially in light of . . . this." He tilted his head to the side, as if noticing something. Stooping down, he picked up the dagger by the tip and held it up as if he were showing off a fish. "And this."

Alysana could plainly see the haughtiness in her uncle's eyes. She knew that there was no way out. The trial would be quick—almost laughable—and Ghaja Rus would certainly be the one to pass the sentence. Not only that, but he might even want to carry it out with his own two hands. Her shoulders sagged in defeat. She looked around at the solid stone walls of the prison: impenetrable, inescapable. She was trapped. Why had Mordha done this?

Her uncle was standing now, dagger hanging loosely in his hand. "Don't you have anything to say for yourself?"

Alysana, mute with the shock of it all, simply shook her head. This was no time for bargaining, for begging.

"Well, you're going to have to think of something," he said scornfully. "Or don't, I suppose." He shrugged. "You'll go to the gallows all the same. Ghaja Rus will see to that, I'm sure."

Alysana could feel her cheeks burning. She ground her teeth together, clenching and unclenching her jaw. He was right, of course: Ghaja Rus would stop at nothing to see her family destroyed. First her father, now her. Even her uncle had been twisted to that abhorrent man's will. The only one left was Mordha—and, looking down again at the corpse before her, Alysana wasn't even sure about that much. "You're right, Uncle."

Ezna's smirk grew into a wide grin. He closed his eyes and cupped a hand to his ear. "Say that again."

Alysana laughed. "No. I'm sure you'll hear it before the day is through—just not from me."

Her uncle dropped his hand and opened his eyes again to look at her. "I'll ride out the satisfaction, don't you worry." He turned the monogrammed dagger over in his hand, casually inspecting it. "Which will only be compounded when Ghaja Rus finds out what has transpired."

A few thoughts raced through Alysana's mind as the branching paths of possibility unfolded before her. She watched each of them, tracing their lines as well as she could along their nebulous and uncertain pathways. The future was never certain, nor was it easy to discern. She would do her best now, though. She mentally recounted her options.

One: deny it all, and blame her sister. This was certainly the truth, and would probably be the easiest option—but on the other hand it would be difficult to prove and nearly impossible to defend in a courtroom led by Ghaja Rus.

Two: fight her way out. She liked this option, as it presented her with quick gratification in doing what she had to in order to neutralize her uncle. There was a very good chance that meant killing him. She could live with that—although not for long if she was caught on her way out.

Three: surrender. This, of course, was the hardest road, and the one that she liked the least. It took everything out of her hands and placed it into the hands of fate—hands she neither understood nor controlled. They were hands that had delivered her to cruelty after cruelty, coldly thrusting her from one hopeless endeavor to another. It sickened her to think of, and she resented whatever god or force or being was behind it. If fate had been the driving force behind her life, it certainly resented her.

. . . Or did it?

She paused for a moment, tilting her head in silent thought. All this time—all these years—she had been tossed into the fire again and again. Yet . . . here she was, not only living, but thriving. Growing. Changing. What was it that Thornton used to say? About tempering steel? As if on cue, the blade in Ezna's hand glimmered with a flash of light so brief that

Alysana wondered if it had even happened at all.

The best blades come from the hottest flame.

She looked down at her hands. They were calloused and strong, the end result of years of training with her sister and the Guard of Annoch. She balled her hands into fists, flexing her fingers and feeling her muscles and tendons ripple with raw strength. She thought about being sold as a slave, growing up in the shadow of war in the city of Annoch, fighting for her life against the giant half-eye, Thuma, surviving the encounter with Ghaja Rus again, even summoning the Traveler.

All these things had been the fire that was tempering her into the blade that she was becoming—*had* become. Perhaps now all she needed was one final thrust into the furnace.

"I killed him," she said flatly. "And I don't regret it."

Her uncle was silent for a time and seemed to be choking on any words that he might have been trying to conjure. That, it turned out, did not matter, as the next voice she heard was the last one that she wanted to.

"Thank you for saving us a lot of time." Shedding the shadows as he stepped into the room was a brooding and menacing Ghaja Rus. "It will make your trial and execution that much shorter and sweeter. Guards, place her in chains." With a grin, he added, "And kindly deprive her of her weapons."

Chapter 49

West of Haidan Shar

Sera

IT SEEMED LIKE AGES SINCE Sera had first traveled from Ghal Thurái with the captains in tow, leading them back to the gates of Khala Val'ur under Tennech's watchful eye. She had dragged them away from their commander, Caladan Durakas, before the man had surprised his army by showing them he did indeed have a brain, as evidenced by the fact that bits of it were now scattered over the forest floor of Kienar. Outside the walls of Khala Val'ur was also where Sera had met Durakas's feisty second in command. What was her name? Dina? Vana? Something like that.

Hullis, ahead on his gwarái, turned his head back to her. "How long do you want to ride before stopping for the night?"

Sera considered this before she answered. While she detested riding, she disliked tardiness even more. Now: the priest had not technically told them that they were in a hurry, nor did he leave them with instructions as to when to arrive at Haidan Shar. Better to play it safe, she reasoned.

"Let's ride on till dark. No sense in dragging our feet—even though everything in me wants to."

Hullis gave her a nod.

The sun in the sky told them that night was a few hours away, and they still had a long way to go – but at least she was traveling with two men that she had come to know well by now. In fact, she realized, there was only one man in the world that she knew better than these two: Aldis Tennech.

✦ ✦ ✦

Two sunsets had come and gone, with just as many sunrises following on their heels. The third day of their travel toward the Gem of the East was eerily uneventful. Sera didn't like it. The dull tingling at the base of Sera's spine was her body's way of telling her that something was off.

"Captains," she called out.

The two Thurians did their best to coax their gwarái to a halt—a difficult task for a creature larger than most trees.

"Aye?" Dhrostain replied from atop the black beast.

"How much further would you guess that Haidan Shar is?"

Dhrostain shielded his eyes with a hand and surveyed the rugged and uneven terrain. This far into the mountains of the Great Serpent, only those who spent time learning every crest and valley would have any hope of discerning their position. Lucky for them, Dhrostain was just such a man.

"I would wager that we could reach it before nightfall if we keep this pace, which I recommend we do," he said.

Sera furrowed her brows for a moment and began to ask him why, when she suddenly remembered what had befell them the last time they three rode through here.

Chovathi, she thought with a shudder. She had almost forgotten about the white-skinned horrors that roamed the night, waiting for wayward travelers to make an easy meal for their hungry jaws and empty stomachs. "Then let's press on," she said. "I'm not one to question a sensible recommendation like that."

Just as she was about to spur her mount forward, though, the hiss of something flying through the air made her draw her sword. Landing a few feet to her right and piercing the ground with a thud, a blue-and-white fletched arrow made its presence known—along with whatever silent archer had loosed it from his bow.

"Come no closer, strangers. I don't know where you got those gwarái from, but you have some explaining to do."

The voice was a man's, but Sera couldn't tell where it was coming from. Though it was daylight out, whoever was shooting at them had concealed himself well.

Sera, knowing that she could defend herself if she had to, sheathed her sword and put up her hands. "We mean you no harm. We're just on our way to Haidan Shar."

"What business do you have there?"

Sera opened her mouth but realized that she didn't have a good answer. *Saying that the Holder of the Dead commanded us to go would probably be a poor decision,* she thought. "Dhrostain," she whispered. "A little help?"

Clearing his throat, the Thurian projected his voice as well as any diplomat. "We've been sent to raise an army."

Sera shot him an angry look, expecting both of them to be shot full of arrows before they could say "Uprising" . . . but, surprisingly, arrows didn't come. Instead, a chainmail-wearing blond man stepped out from behind some cover and approached them, short bow strapped to his back.

"That's what the queen had thought," he said, stopping a few feet short of Sera's horse. "She sent me to make sure."

Hullis scowled. "So the insufferable Queen Lena still sits atop the throne in Haidan Shar, eh?"

The messenger looked up at him, puzzled. "Queen Lena . . ." he began, tilting his head. Then, realization seemed to dawn on him. "Queen Lena is dead."

Hullis and Dhrostain both looked shocked, but Sera couldn't have cared less. The words meant nothing to her.

"Then who," Hullis began, "is Queen in Haidan Shar?"

"Duna Cullain," came the reply.

Duna! Sera thought. *That's what it was! How funny that this new queen shares her name.*

"And," the messenger went on, "there is someone there she would like you to meet."

Chapter 50

Kienar

Ynara

THE CHOVATHI MATRIARCH, ZHALA, PACED back and forth like a tiger in a cage.

Ynara simply watched and waited on the forest floor, legs crossed, as the towering white terror before her lumbered her way back and forth across the invisible boundary of the forest. She stopped, mid-pace, and turned her back to Kienar. Ynara had seen her do this before several times, but this time something seemed different. She stood there, silently, as if in defiance of the forest itself.

In the quiet passing moments, Ynara began to wonder what she was doing—when a sudden, muted crack sounded from somewhere along the barrier to Ynara's right. She turned to see what had caused it. Lying on the ground was a chovathi drone—male, judging by its size—who looked to be in pain.

"You and I both know," Zhala said, still with her back to the forest, "that all things with a beginning must also have an end."

Ynara considered her words for a moment; mere metaphor? Was she speaking of . . .

The barrier.

Ynara swallowed hard when she realized that the chovathi matriarch was indeed speaking literally—and that she was right, too: the forces that kept those of Zhala's blood from setting foot into Kienar were ancient and powerful—but they were not without their limits. Ynara knew very little about them, including how long they would remain intact—hours, days, centuries—wishing with every ounce of her being that she would never have to find out. She watched another drone approach the barrier, stopping short as if he could sense the invisible wall. He skulked back and forth like a spectral wolf, crawling on all fours, sniffing at the ground and the air. He approached the area where Ynara was sitting—and suddenly reared up on his hind legs. As if sensing her presence, the drone craned his head right toward where she was sitting, and gave a low, guttural growl.

The action made Ynara shiver—not from the perceived threat, but because a creature who was essentially blind had been looking right at her. It made her wonder what else they were capable of.

"It is only a matter of time, sister," Zhala said from her place outside the boundary. "Either my brood will figure out a way through, or I will." Finally turning to face Ynara, the matriarch had a dark and sinister smile on her lips. "And I would wager that you do not want to be here when we do."

Ynara shut out the voice out of Zhala and instead embraced calm. She reached out to feel the forest, tapping into the power that her mother had left behind as her inheritance. She hoped that doing so might help ease her mind, or perhaps give her some insight into the strength of its defenses—but what she felt instead made her recoil in fright. When she reached out to touch the essence of the forest, her forest, she realized that it was shaking. It was not a physical shaking like when the earth would shift and grow—but the tremble of a child beneath her mother's comforting touch, fresh out and shivering from the cold. Her forest was . . . afraid.

"You can feel it, can't you?"

The words from Zhala forced Ynara's eyes back open—and she was horrified to see the grin of the chovathi matriarch mere inches away from her face. Zhala, all hundred feet of her, was hunched over like a lion waiting to pounce on a weakened gazelle.

"I can feel it," she went on, "and if I can feel it, I know that you can too. It is breaking. Weakening. Fading."—

Another drone threw himself at the barrier. Then another, and another. Each one was repulsed, yet Zhala's grin only widened.

From her vantage point inside the barrier, Ynara could see the shockwaves of pure light and energy that radiated outward from each collision—invisible, she knew, from the outside, but disconcerting nonetheless. It was like watching from beneath as rocks were dropped onto the surface of a frozen pond: each collision, while small, left behind a remnant in the form of tiny, light-streaked scars.

"The strength of your forest is waning, sister," Zhala hissed. "And my strength grows." As if to demonstrate her point, she reached out to one of the male drones posturing beside her. She laid her hand flat on the ground, palm toward the air, in a gesture of invitation. Ynara watched, curious, as the drone climbed calmly onto the outstretched hand, big enough for two full-grown male chovathi to lie on side by side. Zhala closed her hand around the male—gently, almost lovingly—and stood up.

It was a spectacle to watch: the giant mountain of white rising to her feet. She was a great pale conifer, standing head and shoulders above the canopy of Kienar, rivaling even the mighty Naknamu in height.

"We chovathi are creatures of brute force, and our strength lies in numbers—not strategy." Saying this, she brought up her other hand and gripped the upper torso of the chovathi while still clutching his lower body in her first hand. "And each of my brood is willing to die for the cause. *My* cause."

As fast as the blink of an eye, and with just as much effort, Zhala ripped the male in half, tossing the pieces of his body to the ground like a pair of twigs. The two halves of the body twitched and seized on the ground like a dying fish. The creature screeched, arms clawing wildly at the air.

Ynara looked up at Zhala, who showed no hint of remorse. "Our mother was right to banish you," she said, her voice soft and weak. She tried, but could not fully swallow her shock. "You care nothing for any life that is not your own."

Zhala knelt down, making eye contact with Ynara but still towering above her. On the ground below, the body of the male still twitched.

She glared. "That is where you are wrong," she said. "I am my brood, and my brood is me. You are blinded by your own false superiority if you think that the essence of this forest does not still fill us in some way."

Ynara, from the corner of her eye, saw the male moving again, and fought back waves of disgust, nausea, and rage. It was like looking at a struggling deer brought down by an errant hunter's arrow. The creature must be put out of its . . .

She stopped. Turning to look at the creature directly, Ynara's rage was replaced by fear. This creature wasn't in his death throes. In fact, he wasn't even dying at all—he was . . . growing.

"The longer we wait," Zhala said, "the greater our numbers become."

Both the upper and lower parts of the severed chovathi torso were beginning to form new flesh, right there on the forest floor. The depth of Ynara's horror now rivaled even the vastness of time and space as she saw the walls of her own fate beginning to close in.

"And here I can wait, even to the ends of the earth," Zhala added with gravitas.

Ynara swallowed. *The ends of the earth.*

The thought made her shiver. All this time Ynara had thought it was merely an expression, the hypothetical recognition of some point in the future, vague and undefined. Now, in the face of one she once called "sister," she realized that she was wrong: the ends of the earth was not a time at all—it was an event.

She looked up to Zhala and knew right away that the matriarch could sense the growing dread inside her. There was no use in denying it, and there would be no hope when the event was manifest. The chilling thought that followed was like the snuffing of a candle in a darkened room: the ends of the earth was here, alright—and Ynara was staring right into its eyes.

She reached out with her mind across the vastness of Derenar—a plea to anyone with the power to stand against the chovathi threat. She hoped it would be enough.

Whatever came with the dawn would determine the fate of the world—and the fate of the gods themselves.

Chapter 51

Khala Val'ur

Yetz

THE SHEER SIZE OF THE chovathi horde was the first thing that over-whelmed Yetz. It reminded him of the great blizzards of Hjorl: massive, churning tides of white, unrelenting and unopposed. The three commanders beside him were silent, no doubt trying themselves to reconcile this angry, swirling mass coming toward them.

Haldir, who had silently placed his horned helmet back on his head, was the first to speak. "I had no idea that the chovathi had such numbers," he said with a touch of awe in his voice.

"I don't think anyone did," Lieutenant Commander Thuremond said. "In all the stories I'd heard, there were never more than a hundred or so, scattered throughout lairs and caves of Gal'dorok."

Yetz looked over at LaVince, who had been so stoic and fearless when they had spoken, only to find a blank look on his face that complemented his empty stare. "Commander," Yetz began, seeming to snap the man out of whatever trance he was in. "You and your men have prepared for this. I suggest you do not let that preparation go to waste."

LaVince coughed and said, "Of course, High Khyth." Turning his horse around to face the southern pass, he looked back at Thuremond and Haldir. "You both know what to do," he said, and gave his mount two quick taps with his heels.

Yetz watched the commander ride through the pass and disappear through the curve that would lead him back to the mouth of the Sunken City. There he would pass along meticulously detailed orders to his men, making sure that no command was wasted, no solider ill-prepared. These men were, in the commander's own words, as ready as they could be. That was not any cause for celebration.

Yetz turned his eyes back to the approaching horde, and its advance almost caught him off guard. For something so large, it was moving at an alarming pace. It was like watching a thunderhead speed its way across the sky, a dreadful payload behind the menacing, tumultuous front.

"There must be three thousand," Haldir said in a near whisper. "Maybe more. How could this be?"

"Well," Thuremond began, still looking at the horde, "when Ghal Thurái fell, the chovathi did what they do best." He looked over at Haldir. "They multiplied. It's why Tennech took it upon himself to thin their numbers the entire time he drew breath: he knew what a threat they would be if they ever reached a critical mass."

Haldir scoffed. "Well, it looks like that mass has been reached—and surpassed." Into the distance, to no one in particular, he said, "And where the hell are you now, General?"

"In the grip of the Holder," Yetz said with no hint of emotion. "And of no use to us now. Come," he said, turning his own horse back to the chokepoint. "We have a battle to win."

✦ ✦ ✦

Thuremond and Haldir flanked Yetz as the three of them rode to the entrance, passing scores of infantrymen who all looked nervous but ready. Most of them acknowledged the commanders; only a few made eye contact with Yetz. He recognized their looks; it was one he knew quite well.

"They are afraid," Yetz said to the commanders. He thought he heard one of them laugh. Looking back, he read contempt on Thuremond's face.

"Of course they're afraid," he growled, trying to keep his voice down. "Look at what's coming for us. They've never seen anything like it—hell, *I've* never seen anything like it." He urged his mount forward so he was even with Yetz, and looked him in the eye. "Preparation and training can only take you so far, High Khyth, and experience is a bridge that few manage to get across. It's only when you've passed over it and are looking back from the other side that you can see how valuable it was. There's no telling when you're on it how useful it may be."

Yetz allowed a smile to cross his lips. "I can see why Commander LaVince chose you," he replied. "There is wisdom in your words. I hope it will serve us in the battle to come."

"As do I," Thuremond replied, now scanning his cavalry. They were formed up, like the rest of the army, but it was apparent that some of the riders were restless. Whether it was from excitement or fear—or both— Yetz could not tell. "We shall soon see. Excuse me, High Khyth," he said. Saluting, he rode off to the front of the cavalry.

Yetz returned the salute with a nod of his head. Without looking at the other man, he said, "What say you, Haldir? How do you think your men will fare?"

The commander of the archers was behind him—Yetz could hear his horse snorting nervously as the great white cloud approached—and had still not found his voice after having it softened by the sight of the chovathi horde.

"I'm afraid I don't know, High Khyth." He sounded like every human who had ever addressed Yetz: meek and uncertain.

"'Afraid' is certainly the word. There is a quality in your voice that all humans share when confronted with fear. It's like a dog that barks at the darkness." He turned in his saddle faced the commander. "It knows there is something out there—perhaps it can hear it, perhaps it can smell it—yet its only instinct is to cry out. To make noise. To make itself appear vicious and fearless."

"But I am not fearless. None of us are."

"And just what has fear ever availed you?"

Haldir sat there in his saddle, wavering a bit, as he seemed to ponder the question. "I'm afraid I—" he began, and then caught himself. "I don't know, High Khyth."

"I can tell you, Commander: nothing. Fear has no purpose save one: control. Look again at the enemy bearing down on us." Haldir shaded his eyes with his hand, looking out over the vastness of Gal'dorok, that fierce and inhospitable land from which the mountains of the Great Serpent had sprung. "Tell me what you see."

"A few thousand chovathi coming from the—"

"I don't want a scouting report, Commander. I asked what you *see*."

Haldir flinched, glancing quickly at Yetz, and looking again at the advancing army. He was silent for a good while as he scanned. Finally, he dropped his hand and looked at Yetz.

"Targets."

Yetz smiled. "Targets," he agreed. "Something your archers are good at shooting, I should hope." Haldir nodded. "Then remind them of that."

With a crisp salute and renewed energy, Haldir turned his horse around and pointed it toward the cliffs where his archers stood. Yetz watched him ride off and felt something tugging at his chest—a feeling that was so distant and foreign to him that he almost didn't recognize it. He turned his attention inward, focused, like a sailor searching for a lighthouse in a storm. He knew it was there; he could feel it.

Ah, there it was. Of course. He had hardly even recognized it when it came. It was the light above men's heads when darkness bore down, the sword to stave off defeat. The fire in winter, the tree in the desert, the promise of rest, of relief.

Yetz looked again at the approaching horde and, to his surprise, felt it once more. He felt the crackling of the Otherworld course through him as he touched his power—more practical than some long-forgotten sensation. Yet, as he began to call upon the earth in the face of the on-coming horde, he realized at last what it had been.

Hope. He smiled wryly to himself, and the light inside him pulsed strong. *May it be as useful to me as it is to them*, he thought as he raised his hands, *or we are all doomed.*

Pulling his hands apart, the earth cracked before him in response to his arcane call. Just like almost everything they would throw at the chovathi, it would not stop them—it would only slow them down.

Yet, as a rain of arrows flew over his head and toward the advance horde, he thought—perhaps even hoped—that it might be enough.

Chapter 52

The Otherworld

Thornton

THE FIRST TIME THAT THORNTON found himself outside his own body, it had almost unraveled his sanity. Floating outside himself, looking down at himself had been an experience that he never knew he didn't want. It was a strange sensation, watching someone else steering his body around, like a puppet master—only there were no strings on him . . . at least none that he could see.

He watched as this hollowed out version of himself traversed the Otherworld with purpose in his step. Wherever he was headed, the Breaker apparently knew. Thornton floated alongside him, watching with growing curiosity as he trudged on.

Even here, manifested outside his own body, he knew the will of the Breaker, heard his secret thoughts. He saw the destruction that the ancient god was capable of. He saw what he had done to Miera—to the Shaper—and saw flashes of what the god meant to do to her followers.

Thornton had a vague notion of where he was, despite the Breaker's attempts to conceal such information. The landscape around him, ethereal and haunting, was familiar. He'd been here before, a lifetime ago. How long had it been? He wasn't sure that he could begin to answer that question: a moment spent in the Otherworld seemed like a lifetime—and may very well have been. Memories blurred together; eternity stretched and shrunk. The single searing thought that radiated in his mind, though, was this: power. It wasn't his thought, he knew, but the Breaker's. The moment the god had entered his mind—after Thornton struck down D'kane in Khel-hârad—he had felt his attempt to snuff out Thornton's spirit and make him a hollow Vessel, the way that the Traveler had done to Rathma. Yet Thornton had resisted, pushed back. It had taken everything in him not to succumb to the overwhelming power of the ancient god of creation, but he had done it, somehow. And while he still existed, even if it was in this mind-prison, he thought that there was a chance—a chance of what, exactly, he wasn't sure. But it was a chance.

They walked on, toward the beckoning power.

+ + +

They had been walking up a steadily rising landscape, and Thornton had grown more and more aware of a presence that was gnawing at the back of his mind. It felt familiar somehow, but he couldn't quite say how. As they crested the top of a hill, however, Thornton immediately knew why.

Looking down at the bottom of a chasm, impossibly deep and wide, Thornton realized exactly where they were. He had been here before. For the first time since the god had taken over his body, the Breaker turned his head and acknowledged Thornton, a sneer on his face.

"The first rule of power is this: consolidation."

Below them, untouched since his battle with the Shaper, was the gargantuan body of the Breaker of the Dawn—and the massive, hulking chains that bound him.

The god reached back, to where the Hammer of the Worldforge was strapped, and wrapped his palms around its handle. The instant he did, Thornton felt power coursing through his body—power that had been present at the dawn of creation. The Hammer, he knew, was simply a conduit for the god's power. An amplifier. A focus. It was a tool, but even a tool was capable of incredible things in the hands of a master.

Thornton felt dizzy as he watched the Breaker, in Thornton's body, cover the distance between them and the great empty shell of a god that lay still on the surface of the Otherworld. With every step that the god took, a sense of dread washed over Thornton, pooling at his feet, and making his way up his body, threatening to drown him in it. He wanted to call out, to tell him to stop, to demand him to reconsider—but the knowledge of his own powerlessness kept him mute and still. The Breaker walked closer, and the sense of inevitability froze Thornton in place.

He could only watch as the Breaker approached the base of the massive chains which held the body of the ancient god. He lifted the Hammer of the Worldforge into the air, and Thornton saw that same familiar blue glow that had come when he brought it near the Anvil of the Worldforge in Annoch. The whole of the Otherworld trembled.

"At last, at long last, the chains that bind the Breaker will fall."

The words were the Breaker's, and they sprung from a well, deep and vast—older than time, beyond comprehension.

There was an ear-splitting *CRACK* as the first of the chains broke apart. The great metal shackles around the god's wrists and ankles fell to the ground. There was nothing restraining the ancient god any longer, and his hulking, empty form fell forward. When it hit the ground, the earth-rending boom made Thornton think that reality itself was about to come apart as rocks flew into the air, and a cloud of dust rose around them. A tiny voice in Thornton's head said that perhaps that was right.

The blazing blue Hammer of the Worldforge was still aloft, but its light was so much brighter, even through the haze. Thornton could do nothing but watch as the same blue light emanating from the chains seemed to seep out of them—and into the hammer. A great flash of light was accompanied by a chest-rattling blast . . . and the Otherworld was once again still.

"Thank you for everything, blood of the Shaper," said the ancient god. "You brought me the Hammer," he said, turning to the great black figure on the ground, "returned me to the Otherworld, and reunited me with my true Vessel." He turned his head back to where Thornton was watching and, smiling, said, "I no longer have need of this one." He dropped the hammer on the ground and, as he did, blue light began to stream from his eyes. Mixing with the light of the hammer, it swirled into the air. He was kneeling, hands raised, as the unbridled power of a god poured out. His skin began to blacken, char and split. A scream of pain pierced the air, and was suddenly cut off as his human body slumped to the ground.

The silence that followed was the worst thing that Thornton could ever recall feeling, and the sense of dread that had been building up finally covered him completely, twisting his stomach in knots. If he could have choked in the Otherworld, he would have.

The next thing to move was not Thornton's body—it was something much, much worse.

For the first time since the Shaper had given her gift to the world, the Breaker stood up, unbound by his chains. He rubbed at his wrists, free of their fetters, and gave a laugh that was deeper than the Tashkar Sea.

"You have served me well, blood of my blood. It was always your fate to set me free." He looked down at the Hammer of the Worldforge, still burning with blue fury . . . and it began to grow.

A twisted smile worked its way onto the ancient god's face as he reached down to pick up a hammer that was now perfectly suited for a gargantuan god to wield. "Your body was strong enough to contain me, so your Breaking is my parting gift to you." He looked at Thornton one more time, both his spirit and body, then turned to leave.

The Otherworld, as infinitely expansive as it was, still held many bridges to the world of mortals, and Thornton felt one of them now. In the distance a gate appeared, its opening draped in blazing light. On the other end of the gate was the outline of an anvil. The Breaker thundered toward it, and his footfalls echoed throughout the Otherworld.

Thornton looked back to his empty body, freshly scarred with the power of the Breaking. Before, he could at least hide his heritage, so long as no one looked him in the eye. Now, his body was covered from head to toe in the marks of Khyth power, skin charred black like a burnt-out log. He knew that there was no going back; his life was irrevocably changed.

He shifted his essence back into his body, once again reclaiming it as his own.

And, as he stood up and watched the form of the Breaker retreat, he also knew that he had no choice: he had to follow.

Chapter 53

Annoch

D. L. Jennings

Aldryd

ALDRYD, KEEPER OF THE FORGE of Annoch, woke from his sleep
with a start. His forehead was coated with sweat, and he dug his palms
into his temples. His head felt like it was being blasted with fire.

"Denna," he gasped, hoping the servant girl was within earshot. No
answer. "Denna!" he called again, louder. This time he heard something.

Footsteps, coming down the hall.

"Yes, Keeper?" Her voice sounded like it was coming from the direction of her quarters—and not from the chamber of the Anvil where she
should be. He would talk to her about that later; right now, there were
more important things to discuss.

As her footsteps finally made their way into his room, a bright-eyed
young Athrani poked her head in. "What is it, Keeper Aldryd?"

Still in his bedclothes, Aldryd ran his fingers through his white-gray
hair and looked at Denna. "Go and fetch Speaker Deyhan. I need to
speak with Sh'thanna."

Denna nodded and disappeared around the corner.

Standing up, Aldryd conjured a flame in his hand with Shaping and
used it to light a candle near his bedside. He picked up the candle and
crossed the room, shedding light onto the piles of books and scrolls that
cluttered his normally neat desk. He sighed and placed the candle in a
brass candlestick.

"No amount of study could have prepared me for this," he mumbled
aloud to no one in particular. He idly flipped some pages in a book enti-
tled *The Night Sky and its Names*. Next to it was a text on creation myths
of the world, and an aged tome that detailed all the prophecies, stories,
and ideations regarding the supposed end times. The words on the spine
read *Days of the Dark*.

Aldryd closed the *Night Sky* and picked up the candlestick.

✦ ✦ ✦

Having changed out of his bedclothes and into the traditional silver robes of the Keeper, Aldryd had tried to tame the wild hair that was a result of a fitful night's sleep, but he hadn't put much effort into it; Sh'thanna had been his friend for decades and would certainly understand if he looked a bit disheveled. If anything, it might add to the urgency. He reached up and tousled his hair a little more.

He was walking down the hall toward the chamber of the Anvil when the sense of dread—which had been nothing but a mosquito in his ear—suddenly changed into a roaring lion. He stopped and looked around, as if he expected to find someone there, perhaps the source of the dread. Seeing nothing, he pressed on.

The candle that he had been using had done a good job of lighting the dark hallways of the Temple of the Shaper, but as he approached the chamber of the Anvil, he quickly found that he did not need it. Even from this far out, he could see the bright blue light spilling out from the chamber. Stepping inside, he was reminded of the power of the Shaper all over again, as if She had never left.

The Anvil, larger by far than any of its mundane counterparts, was draped in luminescent blue. It was bright enough to fill the room, and to make Aldryd cover his eyes in order to see. He had never seen it so bright!

He blinked a few times and squinted to try and let his eyes adjust. After a few moments, it worked, and he was able to look around—but his eyes were drawn right back to the Anvil of the Worldforge, whose surface was covered in the ancient script of the Athrani people, thought to have been passed down from the Shaper of Ages Herself. He approached the Anvil, not quite sure what he was looking at. For thousands of years, the words on the anvil had read, *AS MY DAUGHTER, I LIVE.*

As he got closer, the writing came into focus—and his eyes shot wide open. Not all of the words were illuminated.

He rubbed his eyes to make sure it was not just sleep playing tricks on his eyes. When he opened them again, clear as day, were two words in the ancient Athrani script:

I LIVE.

The candle he'd been holding fell from his hand, and the metal clink resounded throughout the chamber.

"Oh, this can't be good," he said. "This can't be good at all."

Chapter 54

Haidan Shar

Sera

SERA HAD NEVER BEEN TO the so-called "Gem of the East," Haidan Shar—and, if she was being truthful with herself, she wasn't impressed. They were riding through the city and had just passed what was very clearly the center: a large fountain surrounded by merchant stands that served as a sort of gathering point. Ahead of them lay the castle, and to either side were roads that stretched out into two very different looking districts. Even from this distance, Sera could tell that the district to their left was run down and shoddy; the district to their right looked like it had been built the week before: clean, towering, and flawless.

While the castle was not the opulent, imposing building that Sera had envisioned, from this angle—rising above the fountain that was the centerpiece of the town—it at least looked regal.

"Honestly, I thought it would be bigger," she said. Behind her she heard Dhrostain snicker, followed by Hullis clearing his throat. She whipped her head around and gave them both a glance that could have melted the glaciers of Hjorl. "The castle," she said through her clenched teeth.

The blond messenger—Eowen, as he'd introduced himself to them earlier—seemed to take personal offense to her remark. "There is of course a reason for that," he began. "The castle—the city itself, even—is strategically placed, so there's no real need for some huge, gaudy wall," he said, nodding toward the castle's location overlooking the Tashkar Sea. "And Haidan Shar has always been historically neutral. Sharians pride themselves on being able to travel freely between all cities—whether they be Khyth, Athrani, or human. So could it be bigger? Perhaps," he said with a shrug of his shoulders. "But does it need to be? No."

Sera had to give that to him. It was sometimes better to simply be no one's enemy rather than everyone's friend.

+ + +

As they passed through the city, Sera felt a sense of calm. This city knew war . . . yet it did not bear the scars of it. There were children playing in the streets, merchants shouting about their wares, a general hustle and bustle that she had not seen in some time. It was like the people of Haidan Shar were oblivious to the state and events of the world around them. Did these people not know that their very existence was being threatened?

She opened her mouth to say something, then thought better of it. Just because she had known conflict her whole entire life was no reason to force it on other people. She looked around some more as they rode quietly through the road to the castle, watching the people go about their lives . . . and she smiled. This city was how the world should be. This city wasn't the exception—it should be the rule! She hoped that whatever army the Holder had waiting for her could change things for the better.

+ + +

Eowen quickened the pace on his mount as they made their way past the massive fountain, and on to the road leading up to the castle. It was a simply paved road of cobblestone, with carefully cultivated shrubs on both sides forming a natural green aisle that seemed to usher them right into the castle. It truly was a lovely sight, Sera had to admit. Looking past the castle and out to the sea, she couldn't even think of anywhere that may have rivaled a view like this. Soaring white stone that overlooked the sea, circling gulls diving for food, and freshly tended flowers lining the vast green gardens that were the jewel in the crown of this royal city. It was breathtaking! She was lost in it all, caught up in the seemingly unending beauty.

Dhrostain had said something, but Sera was too busy admiring the scenery. She was shaken out of her daydream when he called her name.

"What is—" she began to say, but the words caught in her throat. As she had turned her head to look at him, she saw something out of the corner of her eye that she knew to be impossible. Her mount, not knowing any better, had continued to walk toward the castle—but Sera's mind had already been left behind.

There were two figures standing by the open gate of the castle—both of them known to her. Her jaw fell open. The sound of the horses' hoofbeats on the cobblestone echoed through the air.

Eowen, who was closest to the castle, dismounted as he approached. With a deep bow, he said "Your Majesty."

Queen Duna barely acknowledged him, instead turning to the man beside her.

"I told you my spies were right, General," she said with a smile.

"You did indeed, Majesty."

The man standing beside the queen was nothing short of an impossibility. His voice rang in Sera's ears—the first time she'd heard it since . . . since . . .

Well, since . . . "You died." The words dropped from her mouth as easily as she dropped from her horse, eyes fixed on him.

"So I've been told," Tennech replied. "But when has that ever stopped me?"

Sera was seeing it, but she certainly didn't believe it. She approached the man who had practically raised her, sure that she might find some flaw that would expose him as a fraud—some errant scar, or eyes that were too dark. As she stood next to him, though, close enough to touch, she found no such thing—just the ghost of the last man to die in defense of Khadje Kholam. A ghost who was very much alive.

"You died. I watched you die." The emotions that coiled around her heart were numerous and confusing, and her words came out hoarse and broken. "I buried you." She put her face in her hands. "I buried you." She dropped to her knees, too weak to stand. Holding back no longer mattered; she let the tears come. Great sobbing gasps and painful exhales reminded her of how she felt when she saw his body up close, lying there on the sands of Khulakorum. The man who brought her up—who'd been with her almost as long as she could remember—had drawn his last breath. Yet here he was, standing before her again.

The tears were hot on her cheeks. She thought she had mourned him; the trembling breaths she took between sobs told her that, no, she had not. The pain was still as fresh as ever. Yet . . .

She felt a familiar hand on her shoulder.

"I'm sorry, Sera."

Tennech always knew what to say—and just how to say it. His voice was calm, barely above a whisper, but it still held the authority of a man who commanded legions. The words were meant to help, but they only made the tears flow more.

"You left me," she said, looking up at the closest thing she had to a father. "I thought I was ready, but I wasn't." Her breathing was mostly under control now. She struggled to keep her voice steady, though. "I wasn't ready."

She felt him squeeze her shoulder even tighter. "I didn't leave you, Sera. I could never leave you—not for good. Not even death could keep me from coming back to you."

Sera looked up at him, right into his eyes, and saw the faint tracings of a smile on his lips. She stood up and embraced him, putting her face in his shoulder.

Tennech held her tight. Just as he always knew what to say, he also knew when not to say anything. He let the silence speak for both of them. The sound of fast-moving footsteps was followed by an out-of-breath messenger.

"Your majesty," the messenger said, stopping and giving a quick but respectful bow. "Cortus Venn sends word . . . the Stoneborn are ready."

Sera's eyes shot open. This was . . . unexpected.

Chapter 55

Khala Val'ur

Yetz

YETZ COULDN'T EVEN REMEMBER THE last time he felt so alive. The power of Breaking flowed through him, coursing through his veins, empowering him, rejuvenating him. The Breaker's strength, after all, was not just in the destruction that it wrought, but also in the primordial power of creation itself: a power that was present at—and responsible for—the birth of the universe. It was a wildfire born of the very spark that set the stars in motion. To use it was to touch the gods.

Yetz breathed in the power, bending and breaking the earth to his will. It was almost enough to make him forget what the power of Shaping had felt like.

Almost.

"Archers! Blanket them with arrows!" Haldir shouted. Behind Yetz, the thundering footsteps of the approaching chovathi horde filled the air. "I don't want to see even a speck of white on those filthy hides."

In place of words, the archers responded with arrows loosed from countless bows that fell on nearly as many chovathi.

Yetz, between his strained efforts to splinter the world, caught glimpses of whispered death raining down from above. As skilled as the archers were, though, he knew the difficulty of trying to get an exact hit from the distance they were firing from; it was a lot like trying to push a thread through the eye of needle—only the needle was across the room, and the thread was frayed and split. That being said, there were apparently some seamsters among them, as more than a few arrows found their marks, lodging themselves in the skulls of the oncoming chovathi.

The encroaching storm of white, like the foam of a crashing wave, was peppered with arrow-strewn corpses that were swallowed up by the tide.

The dead were nothing to the chovathi—and Yetz knew it.

Yet what more could they give besides their all?

+ + +

"Pikemen!" Commander Thuremond shouted. "Prepare yourselves! May your blades and wits be sharp!" He was shouting at his men while his mount carried him, blazing, across the face of his waiting army. "Your time for glory draws near!" He waved his saber in the air like a man possessed.

The archers behind the pikemen were firing as fast as they could nock their arrows, and a few dozen fletchers worked tirelessly to together more for their older counterparts. Though young, the future of the Valurian army were an indispensable part of the defense, too: if any arrows broke or misfired, they were the ones who would rush to replace them, as well as refilling the quivers of any archer who ran out of ammunition. They were but one link—yet even a link that small could be enough to hold an entire chain together.

Yetz looked past the front lines at the chovathi creeping ever closer, only slightly slowed by the biting rain that fell from the sky.

He reached out with his power again and, with a mighty pull, split the earth in two, sending a few hundred chovathi plummeting down below. With a grunt he pulled his hands together, doing the same to the chasm he had just created and crushing the chovathi with several tons of rock. It took a lot out of him to expend such power—but with each heaving breath that followed came a sense of satisfaction: satisfaction in destroying his enemies, and in wielding the powers of his god. Or, at least, one of them.

"Spears!" Thuremond bellowed, "Now!" Following the words was a volley of deadly steel that vaulted overhead, landing in the skulls, shoulders, and guts of the bloodthirsty creatures. The chovathi who caught them in the skulls went down, never to rise again; the ones who caught them elsewhere, though, merely slowed. Yetz watched more than a few of them pull them out like so many splinters, seeming almost annoyed at a wound that might fell even the mightiest of men. "Throw like your lives depend on it—and know that they do!"

The commander rode back and forth, whipping his troops into a frenzy. The physically largest of the troops, the swordsmen, were practically frothing at the mouth to get at the chovathi—but that would not happen before the horde was softened as much as possible by the archers and spearmen behind them. The commander was utilizing his artillery to the fullest extent before loosing his valuable foot soldiers upon them— for as strong as his warriors were, they were almost hopelessly outnumbered . . . and in a battle such as this, numbers meant everything.

Almost everything, Yetz reminded himself with a smile, breaking off splinters of earth and forming them into makeshift spears to fire at the chovathi. He could almost feel them sink in as they hit their mark, and suddenly understood why men like Tennech craved battle. What a thrill it was to exercise this level of control over Breaking once again! Up until now, Yetz's use of the art had been boring and superficial, like a painter coating a canvas in nothing but black: simple, repetitive motions; mundane, boring, and bland; he was certain he could do it all in his sleep. Now, though—finally!—he was able to reach deep into his palette, vibrant and bold, casting reds and yellows with deadly precision, leaving his mark on the world like the true artist that he was.

It felt so freeing!

A flick of his fingers sent serrated stone slicing through skin, flaying flesh and felling foes. Almost effortlessly he broke and reformed rocks, using them as weapons more deadly than the arrows and spears which flew overhead. The earth was his paintbrush—the rocks, his paint. Even the Breaker Himself would have smiled at the bleeding death and chaos being sown by such a master. If there had been a dozen needles on the other end of the battlefield, Yetz would have threaded them all with a wave of his hands and a smile.

The thrill of it made his heart race. If it wasn't for the shouts of the men behind him, he might have forgotten that this was a battle that they were not expected to win—that fact, of course, was one that he had kept to himself, although he suspected that a good number of soldiers knew it too.

A glance back at Commander Thuremond, though, told him no such thing.

The commander, resplendent in his armor, was fury made flesh. He galloped back and forth across the formation of battle-crazed soldiers ready to fight and die for the fate of the human race. Yetz could not recall a time he had seen a more impressive display of battle-hardened rage since Tennech himself—and almost all of written history would agree that the venerated general was among the finest to ever live.

✦ ✦ ✦

Kunas

OF ALL THE POWERS IN all of creation, none is stronger than instinct— and, as Kunas's chovathi bore down on the outskirts of the Sunken City, theirs became a razor-sharp blade that was being dragged across the neck of humanity.

Show them no mercy! he commanded. His instinctual link with the horde, made possible by the grace of Zhala, made for lightning-quick execution of his will: commanding thousands became as easy as lifting an arm, or making a fist. *And leave not a trace.*

He could feel the bloodthirst of the horde—his horde—and it gave him strength. When the first of his foot soldiers met with the first of theirs, he could almost feel the world tremble. Chovathi dominion had begun with the reclamation of Ghal Thurái, and now it was continuing on to the bosom of Khyth culture. One by one, the cities of men would fall, and one by one the chovathi would be there to pick them back up.

Kunas could hear shouting over the melee as the two sides spilled first blood—"Archers! Loose!"—and he scanned the battlefield trying to pinpoint the source of the noise. He spied a horn-helmed man in plate mail barking orders to his men. No sooner did the words leave the man's mouth when hundreds of arrows filled the sky, biting their way into the tough white hides of Kunas's brood brothers. He could feel the pin pricks of searing pain that echoed across their collective consciousness, dulled by distance and scale, but very real nonetheless. The strength of the chovathi was also very much a liability when it came to pain and senses.

"Again!"

Before him, the battlefield was alive with the scents and sounds of combat, and Kunas was able to "see" it all at once through the minds of his foot soldiers: every individual's experience in the moment came flooding into his brain, pieces of an incomprehensibly large puzzle that assembled itself effortlessly. It almost felt like a new sense to Kunas—and in a way, it was: he did not have to command the puzzle pieces to assemble themselves into a picture, nor did he have to command the horde to react—it simply did. He could exercise as much or as little control over the brood as he wished.

Red hot pain shot through his mind again as a second volley of arrows found their marks. He felt the life slip away from a few of his broodlings, like so many grapes dying on a vine. Their consciousness was shut off to him, and the multi-colored picture of the battlefield dimmed slightly.

Do not give them the satisfaction of thinking they can hurt you, Kunas prodded. He felt the horde's anger in response, a vicious and aimless mass that he tried to keep focused. *Where one falls, two rise up. Do not forget what makes us strong.*

He felt the cold, hard metal of the human soldiers' plate mail as the claws of his brood brothers dug into them. They were a tough outer shell that housed a soft and vulnerable underbelly. As swords bit into his broodlings, so did his broodlings bite back. Many of them found flesh, drawing forth blood and screams from the Valurians; others had no such luck, and found their teeth and claws barely able to scratch the armor that protected the mortal Vessels inside.

Kunas narrowed his focus, honing in on the broodlings of the front line who were now clashing directly with the Valurian forces. He let his consciousness drift along the edge of the battle, commanding several chovathi at once and letting the others swarm as they will, drawn like sharks to blood. He heard a shout and felt more pin pricks of pain as yet another volley found flesh. The Valurians were targeting the forces further away from the front lines, not wanting to make casualties of their own men now clashing with the chovathi.

Kunas pulled his consciousness back and shifted his focus again. The sounds of battle were jarring, and he willed himself to block them out, opening his mind to the pinpoints of heat that every man emanated.

There are two—no, three—commanders, he thought. *Find them, bring them down, and the battle will be ours.*

He felt a ripple of understanding and acknowledgement in the aggregate mind, and felt the flow of battle shift ever so slightly. The horde was like a single, unified body, and Kunas was exercising flawless control over each of the limbs. One arm was being used to tear through Valurian swordsmen; the other arm now reached out to the earth that gave birth to the chovathi, moving and manipulating it like only they could.

"They're tunneling!" came a shout from further back. "Ready yourselves for when they emerge!"

Below the surface, the chovathi hunted by sound and smell, picking their way through the dirt and rocks as easily as a sailor follows the sun. While their brothers above took arrows and swords, the ones below sought the pinpricks of light that Kunas had identified among the palette as being commanders. There was something about the weight of the air around them, the way their voices carried, the way the Valurian men reacted to them; it was like watching the flow of a river redirect over a sunken stone: even if the stone was not visible, its presence certainly was.

Kunas put himself in the mind of one of the lead chovathi tunnelers, guiding his movements as he swam through the rock. No matter which way he turned his head, the three pinpoints of light were there like a beacon. He could not miss, and they could not escape.

There, he thought, as the first of his brood brothers came closer to the first commander. The chovathi warrior in the lead burst from the ground and was followed swiftly by a dozen others flooding from the freshly bored hole in the Valurian ground. *Spill his blood, and the blood of those around him.*

His horde obeyed. One chovathi warrior in the front—the largest of the ones who had just emerged from the ground—sped toward the commander looking like a mountain lion chasing down prey. Although he moved on all fours, his movement was fluid and lightning-quick, looking almost more natural than when he walked on two. Arrows riddled his tough hide, but Kunas felt his relentlessness. He was bearing down on the commander, and nothing short of death would stop him.

"Coming at me will be the last mistake you ever make, beast," the armored man growled.

Through the eyes of the foot soldier, Kunas could see he was poised and battle-ready, sword drawn and held in front of him, waiting to strike. He reached in and guided the movements of the chovathi, slowing him down and preventing him from leaping onto the man like he was preparing to do. Kunas felt the urge—the bloodlust—and fighting against it was like trying to swim upstream.

"What are you waiting for?" the man barked.

Kunas let back on his control and filled the minds of the other warriors surrounding him. Despite being pelted with arrows, they stood their ground. They had formed a semicircle around the commander, and were closing in. All fire had been momentarily concentrated on them. Kunas smiled. *Advance*, he commanded.

At his word, he felt his horde push forth, tearing through the ranks of men who, until just now, had been protected by the cover fire of the archers now guarding the commander. They stood no chance against the bigger and more numerous chovathi, who had no concept of either lenience or mercy.

Dimly, on the edge of his consciousness, Kunas felt a few of his brothers fall to the blade of the man in the plate mail, but he knew it was a worthy sacrifice. There would be more chovathi to rise up and take his place. And, as he felt the tide of his warriors push forth towards the shore of humanity, he smiled.

The time of the chovathi was nigh.

✦ ✦ ✦

Yetz

TURNING AGAIN TO HURL ANOTHER dozen shards of sharpened rock at the skulls of the oncoming horde, Yetz nearly lost his concentration as he felt a hand grab him by the shoulder. Surprised and infuriated, he whirled around to find out whom he was about to plunge into the earth—only to find himself staring into the wild and swirling eyes of a Khyth. Not just any Khyth, either—this was one he knew well.

"One second more, Kostas," Yetz began with a growl, "and you would have found yourself buried deeper underground than the river K'Hel."

The Master Khyth blanched, but only for a moment. "My apologies, High Khyth, but it is time."

The feeling came like a smack in the face. Hearing the words was, to Yetz, like realizing he had fallen from a great height, and he was only now opening his eyes to see the ground rushing up to meet him. Bitterness spread on his tongue as he looked around, knowing what came after the fall, but not wanting to embrace it or accept it. "No," he whispered, tongue suddenly dry. He licked his lips, but it did him no good. "No, not yet. I need more time."

To anyone listening, the words could have easily been mistaken as ones meant for Kostas—but anyone that heard them would know that they were meant for fate, and the gods. Yetz's stomach twisted into knots. *Was this how it felt? The moment before hitting the ground? This was no way to die. Not at all.*

"We don't have more time," Kostas replied, and his grip on Yetz's shoulder tightened.

Yetz resisted with every fiber of his being. He gritted his teeth and narrowed his eyes. Looking around at the fallen Valurian warriors and the strengthening chovathi horde, though, he realized that Kostas was right.

"Fine," he said, and felt the Master Khyth's hand slip away. The knot in his stomach, though, persisted.

His waiting steed seemed eager to retreat from the fray, bowing his head as Yetz approached and letting him mount with ease. Tugging at the reins, Yetz turned away from the front lines to join his subordinate who was already riding back to the mouth of the Sunken City, to the last bastion of Khyth and men.

Looking over his shoulder one more time, Yetz watched the white wave of chovathi crash against the rocks of men, a tide that would continue to pound and break until the ends of the earth—a time, he realized with a chill, that was bound to come sooner rather than later.

Just as he was about to turn toward the Sunken City, though, something caught his eye. It stood out because, whatever the figure was, it was not clad in the colors of Khala Val'ur, or even any colors of their closest allies.

There, perched atop one of the many peaks of the mountains surrounding Khala Val'ur, was a single, solitary figure dressed in a dark blue robe with a white border.

Chapter 56

Wastes of Khulakorum

Ulten

R'HAQANS WERE MASTERS OF THE desert, and the well-traveled Ulten was no exception. As he crossed the desert on his camel, he wiped the sweat from his forehead and took another drink from his water skin.

Be glad you can't feel this heat, he said mentally to the Traveler. His thoughts, through some incomprehensible means, raced across the desert as effortlessly as raindrops falling to the ground. At first it had been an odd sensation, directing his inner monologue toward the god inside his head, but after about an hour or so of travel over the barren sands, he found that he not only had gotten used to it, but was even starting to enjoy it. His inner monologue had suddenly become a dialogue.

I would prefer the heat to being trapped in here, the Traveler replied. *They don't call me the "Stays-in-one-placer," after all. I'm the Traveler—it's my whole identity to move around! It would be like me taking your goats and camels from you. Where would you be then?*

Ulten chuckled to himself. *Fair point,* he conceded. *I suppose your brother burying you down there was more than just a way for him to accomplish his goals . . . it was also a way to punish you while doing so.*

Exactly. Which is why I am grateful to have your assistance. Your being here was more than just fortunate: I believe it was fate.

The idea rattled him, and Ulten was quiet for a long time after hearing that. He had never thought of himself as a man whom fate would favor, let alone use as its agent. He glanced up at the clear sky and wondered how much of a hand the gods had in moving the sun across it—and if they did the same with human beings: moving them across the open sky of time, putting them in place to be where they needed to be, and when. Thinking of himself as just another piece to be moved was almost comforting, like it was meant to be, and he could not fail in his task. He rather liked that concept.

He knew by now that the Traveler would not have heard these

deeper thoughts—he had already learned that he had to direct his surface thoughts in order for the god to hear him—and briefly considered asking him about them. He stopped, though, when he realized that hearing the opposite—that he was in charge of his destiny, and it was up to him to change the fate of the world—would only make him more nervous. What chance did a simple goatherd stand against the powers that shaped the world?

Not much, came the answer from his inner monologue—and with that, he suddenly realized why he preferred the Traveler to talk to.

He wiped off his forehead again, and continued riding in silence.

✦ ✦ ✦

After a few more hours of travel, the sun had finally reached the horizon, and the blue desert sky had begun slipping into the purples and oranges of twilight. It was already making a difference in the temperature, and for that Ulten was truly grateful. He would not normally have journeyed across the desert during the day, but the tone in the Traveler's voice had been one of urgency when he'd suggested he make the journey. Ulten was not one for shirking responsibilities—after all, when it came to things like tending to his flock, procrastination could mean losing his livelihood. That was why he had chosen haste over comfort—and it had meant drinking more of his supply of water than he would have liked.

The camel would have no problem at all going without water. Ulten had seen some of them go as long as two weeks without water, and right now he was starting to envy that ability. Taking his water flask in hand and weighing it, he estimated that he would have enough to last him one more day—which meant he could make it as far as the Spears. He did not know the area well—only what he'd seen in maps—but he had heard that there were mountain streams among the low-lying peaks that he could use to refill his flask.

He hoped that what he'd heard about the streams was true.

✦ ✦ ✦

Riding at night was one of the few pleasures that Ulten knew in the desert, and this night was a pleasure indeed. The clear night sky meant that each and every star had come out to greet him. Great clusters of purplish-blue interspersed with sharply defined points of white made up one of the most beautiful nighttime sights that he'd seen in recent memory. Each celestial brushstroke that made up the heavens was now visible to him—perhaps the only living soul looking up at it in this particular part of the desert. A quick glance down at his mount confirmed that camels still cared nothing for stars, as the two of them steadfastly made their way across the desert. Ulten readjusted in his saddle and looked back up at the sky. *He doesn't know what he's missing,* he thought to himself. *The Traveler too,* he added. Realizing that they had been largely silent these past few hours, he opened their mental link again.

You really should see these stars, he said quietly.

There was a moment of silence followed by a sort of stirring that Ulten quickly recognized as the feeling one gets when one wakes from slumber. The Traveler had been asleep!

I didn't know gods slept, Ulten said.

Oh, all the time, replied the Traveler, and the thoughts seemed sluggish but somehow still very sharp. It felt like picking up a red-hot coal with gloved hands: the heat was still there, but mercifully kept at bay. *It's one of the benefits of these mortal Vessels.*

Benefits? Ulten shot back. *You mean to tell me that you enjoy being asleep?*

Immensely, said the Traveler. *Because with sleep comes dreams, and even dreams are something we gods do not possess.*

Ulten raised his eyebrows in surprise. *But what do dreams offer one with your power?*

Many things, the Traveler replied, and Ulten could feel the slight ripple of laughter coming over their shared mental link. *Tell me: how does it feel to you right now, borne on the back of your camel below the night sky?*

Ulten looked up again at the heavens and a smile crossed his lips. *I quite like it,* he admitted.

That is how it is with us and dreams: like sailing on a Vessel across an open desert, looking up at the sky as it passes above you. It is the feeling of letting go, of being carried when all you are used to is bearing a burden instead.

Ulten glanced back down at his camel and suddenly completely understood what the god was trying to tell him. For most of the Traveler's existence, he was just like the camel: pointedly wandering toward a destination with no care to stop and glance at the marvels of creation above. But, in dreams, he could be like Ulten: gazing up at a celestial canvas that was there seemingly for just his enjoyment. The two viewpoints, he realized, were very different in feel and in weight. He sat up straighter in his saddle, a new appreciation dawning on him.

That makes sense, he admitted. *Although I feel like I could get a lot more done if I never had to sleep.*

Inside his mind he felt the Traveler chuckle again. *Are you really that concerned with accomplishments that you would give up dreaming to do so?*

Ulten gave a long, hard blink. *I . . . I never thought about it like that. Is that why you gods seem so keen on taking Vessels?*

That is not the primary reason, though it is a most welcome side effect.

Well, I am sure that when you dream, it is of the day that you get your hands on the godkiller, Ulten said with a bit of a sneer. *It must be down there with you somewhere, buried under Do'baradai, like the stories say.*

The Traveler was markedly silent. To Ulten it was like feeling the warmth of the sun only to have it abruptly cut off by the cold night of the desert.

What . . . what is it? Ulten asked, breaking the mental silence.

How do you know about the godkiller? The Traveler asked. His tone was solemn, and in Ulten's mind it felt like a sword being dragged over gravel.

Growing up in the shadow of Do'baradai, you hear stories, Ulten began.

Stories about gods and those who serve them. Some of these stories are just that: stories. But others seem to have some grain of truth to them—and one such grain is the story of the godkiller: a weapon—maybe a sword, or a dagger, or something else—that exists for one purpose, and one purpose alone.

Ulten felt the Traveler shift uncomfortably. *It is a weapon,* he began. *Your stories are right in that sense. But there's more to it than that.*

Like what?

It is . . . complicated. Like most prophecy, the meaning is shrouded in ambiguity and half-truths. This, of course, is done on purpose—after all, prophecy is just we gods telling you mortals the way that things end up. We like to drop hints. After all, half the fun of telling a story is watching it play out, he said with a mental smile. *But I digress. This was always one prophecy that my brother tried to stifle for many reasons . . . but in the end, it always came out. Tell me, R'haqan: what do you know about the godkiller?*

Ulten shifted in his saddle. He was growing uncomfortable, in more ways than one.

I have only heard stories, like I said, but they all speak of a weapon buried in the depths of Do'baradai, forged by the gods themselves, powerful enough to make mortals into gods—or make gods into mortals and snuff out their fire forever; deadly and secret, with the power to bring even the Holder of the Dead to his knees.

The Traveler was silent again, as if he was waiting for something. After a punctuated silence, his voice once again sounded in Ulten's mind. *All that you have said is correct.*

And I believe you. . . Yet I feel you are holding something back. What are you not telling me?

Nothing that you won't eventually figure out for yourself, the Traveler answered, words as restrained as the god himself.

The words were like the slowly rising sun, illuminating the pre-dawn sky of Ulten's mind. *The godkiller is not a "what," is it?* Ulten asked. His only answer was the warmth of a smile that Ulten had become familiar with. *The godkiller is a 'who.'*

Chapter 57

Haidan Shar

Sera

WISPY SHARIAN CLOUDS CLASHED WITH the purple-orange of the darkening ocean sky. As she emerged from the castle, Sera knew right away why the first Sharians had chosen this place to build their city. She was barely two steps out of the castle when she'd been stopped in her tracks by the scene above.

"We don't have sunsets like these in Khala Val'ur," she said breathlessly to Duna. The queen was a half-step behind her, eyes on the sky as well. Turning, she chuckled. "In fact, we don't have sunsets at all. If you're lucky, you can leave the city for half a day to catch one from the Spine."

Duna came to a stop beside her. Clasping her shoulder, the queen said, "Then I'm glad you get to see one. I think you'll find there's a lot more to Haidan Shar than what you've heard in stories."

The two of them heard a quick cough from behind them.

"Ah, if I may, Your Majesty." Sera and Duna both turned to see the messenger standing there, a look of worry on his face. "The commander seemed rather urgent when he told me to go find you," he said. "I would respectfully convey that same urgency to you now." With this, he added a hesitant bow, as if to punctuate his point.

"I swear, Edris," Duna said as she waved it off. "What did I tell you about bowing?" Without waiting for an answer, she turned to the rest of them and said, "Follow me, everyone. Apparently the great Cortus Venn waits for no man."

There was more than a hint of sarcasm in the word "great."

✦ ✦ ✦

Sera rarely got excited about much these days, but the prospect of meeting Cortus Venn—*the* Cortus Venn—was enough to make her match pace with the queen. Dhrostain had talked about the man enough for her to feel like she knew him already.

She was walking briskly beside Tennech and Duna, with Hullis and Dhrostain following close behind. "I've heard a lot about him," Sera proclaimed, hoping she had concealed her excitement as well as she thought she had. "I look forward to finally meeting him in person."

Duna didn't much care for royal pageantry—something that Sera appreciated her for— and had insisted that they walk together, as equals. The two of them had only met once before, and Duna had been but a lowly second-in-command to Caladan Durakas, but Sera could tell that this woman was somehow different than the one she'd exchanged heated words with outside the walls of Khala Val'ur back then. The fact that she had risen to such a high position in such a short amount of time meant that she had surely done some growing up. Sera knew all about that.

"I am eager for you to meet him as well," Duna said. There was a noticeable amount of pride in her voice. "I've been nothing but impressed with him in the time that I've known him. You should have seen him in the battle of Ghal Thurái. He was like a force of nature."

Tennech chuckled. "Before I met him, I'd heard nothing but good things. He was commander of the Lonely Guard when I was just a young captain, and anyone who can stay in command that long—let alone in a place like Lash'Kargá—has got to be damned good."

"You know very well he's not just good, General," Duna said. "He's better."

Now *this* Sera had to see.

✦ ✦ ✦

They made their way out the rear of the castle and down a path paved in white, leading toward the shore. Sera could see two figures—a man and a boy—standing front and center of two dozen wooden boxes. She was fairly certain she knew what they were, but her curiosity got the better of her.

"Are those . . . caskets?" She asked.

297

Duna nodded. "It's part of the ritual, and I only know that because Venn himself had to explain it to me. Stoneborn can only be born—made, really—after they've died."

"Died?" Sera echoed. "But . . ." she began, but her thoughts never found words.

"I know," Duna replied gravely. "Each of the men and women in those coffins was prepared to give their life. Venn told them the risks. Every single one of them agreed."

The words tumbled over and over in Sera's mind. As she looked out at the sea of caskets, the weight of it all began to sink in. It was one thing to be marched into battle under a banner, with your brothers and sisters beside you—but it was another thing entirely to die alone in a casket for a cause that could very well be hopeless.

Hullis broke the silence, pointing at one of the standing figures. "Is that him? Is that Venn?"

"In the flesh," Duna said, "in a manner of speaking."

"And who's that beside him?"

Squinting, Duna replied, "That's his armiger, Benj—although I don't think the term 'armiger' really applies anymore." Turning to Tennech, she explained, "Benj is Stoneborn, so I think Venn looks at him more like a son than just someone to carry his sword."

Tennech glanced at Sera. With a smile, he said, "I certainly understand that sentiment."

Sera felt her face flush.

"Commander!" Duna shouted as they drew nearer to the shore. "Did everything go as planned?"

Venn motioned to Benj to stay put as he approached the party. He cut through the line of caskets to come out the middle, meeting them a few dozen feet from the arrangement. "Your Majesty," he said, giving a nod so slight that Sera barely noticed it. "General," he said, with a proper salute to Tennech. "We will soon find out. You've arrived just in time, right before the sun sets."

Venn's eyes wandered over the others—and suddenly came to a stop. Recognition washed over his face as his eyes went wide. With a shout of joy, he threw his arms out. "Well, look what the gwarai shat out!"

"You're the one who looks like bird shit, old man," Dhrostain said as he moved forward to greet his former commander. The two of them embraced in a hug hard enough to dent Dhrostain's armor. "I heard you had a little chovathi trouble near Ghal Thurái," he added with a grin.

"Trouble! Ha!" Venn shouted, throwing his head back in laughter. "Not as much trouble as you gave me, Lieutenant. How many wenches did I catch you trying to sneak on post that night?"

"First of all, it's Captain now," Dhrostain grinned, pointing to the three scars on his left forearm, marks of rank in the Valurian army. "And second of all, if you hadn't personally inspected those barrels of Hjorlian ale we were using to smuggle them in, you'd never have known!"

The two of them howled with laughter, and Venn clapped Dhrostain on the shoulder. "It's good to see you again, old friend." His smile faded as quickly as it had come, though, and he turned to the others. "Though I wish the circumstances were different," he said with a glance at the sunset. "I'm afraid we haven't much time. Has the queen brought you up to speed?"

"She's told us about the chovathi threat, as has General Tennech," Sera said, stepping forward. "Is there anything else we need to know?"

Venn turned to look at her and seemed to linger on her face for longer than normal. Then, much to her surprise, he gave a gracious bow and extended his hand for hers. "Cortus Venn, my lady, at your service."

Sera saw Duna and Tennech exchange surprised glances, but gave them no mind. She placed her hand in his. "S-Seralith Edos," she said. She tried to sound confident.

Venn raised his eyes to hers and gave the back of her hand a kiss, letting it go and standing upright. "A pleasure to make your acquaintance, Lady Edos. It's been some time since I've seen one of your kind outside of the First City," he said, eyes still locked with hers.

"Sera is . . ." Tennech began, then stopped. "Well I believe you will find her to be quite exceptional, Commander."

"Is that so?" Venn replied with a grin. "Well if her swordplay is as lovely as she is, I'd say we stand half a chance against these chovathi."

Sera took her hand back and turned away, crossing her arms. She looked at him from the corner of her eye and said, "I was trained by the best, Commander."

Venn stood up straight. "That's impossible. I don't remember training you."

Sera rolled her eyes so hard that for a moment she thought she might never see normally again.

"Commander," Duna said, rolling her eyes just as hard. "Care to share how the ritual went?"

With another glance at the sinking sun, Venn said, "Ah, of course. Right this way. I was just having Benj ready final preparations." He turned back to the arrangement of caskets, where Benj waited. Now that Sera saw him up close, she realized that the boy could not have been more than thirteen—and that his skin was the same marble sheen as Venn's. "Benj, have you laid out all the scabbards?"

The boy nodded and approached the group. "I have, Commander Venn, just like you asked."

"Good lad." Over his shoulder, to the queen, he said, "Now it's time to pray to whatever god might listen." He spun on his heels and was off toward the first row of caskets with the rigidity and poise of a soldier.

Standing in the middle of the first row, arms held by his side in the position of attention, Venn barked an order to Benj, who dutifully attended, marching in the same fashion to join the commander. Below the spot where each of them stood was a black scabbard with a sword in it, and Sera could see, lengthwise facing the shore, swords and scabbards were set to the right, laid against the dark, solid wood of the caskets.

"May the fallen now rise," Venn said, "stronger than before."

Benj reached down to take the scabbard before him in both hands, then stood back up, holding it out in front of him like he was presenting it. Venn knelt down and did the same. He stood back up, resuming the position of attention. Neither he nor Benj moved, nor spoke.

The sun sunk lower behind the mountains to the west, and the purple of the sky began to fade into black. Silence hung in the air long enough for Sera to get uncomfortable. She looked at the faces of the others with her and saw the same concern reflected in their own eyes.

Duna turned to Tennech and whispered, "What's happening?"

"I'm not sure," he whispered back, "but they're waiting for something."

"For what, exactly?"

Tennech didn't need to reply, because just then, one of the casket lids began to move.

Sera though that she saw a flash of relief on Venn's face, but it was too dark to be certain. He showed no sign of movement as the casket lid was pushed off.

The man inside it stood up. "What . . . what happened?" he asked. He was a sturdy looking man with jet-black hair and raggedy-looking clothes. Sera could tell that he had grown up poor. "Is this Khel-hârad?"

Venn said something to Benj that Sera couldn't make out, and Benj double-timed it to the casket of the man who had just stood up. The boy held the scabbard out with both hands. Confused, the man took it in one hand and clasped it over his waist. After he did so, Benj did an about-face and marched back to his place next to Venn.

Sera had to admire the boy's military bearing. He was so young, but still managed to carry himself like a seasoned soldier. She started to wonder if he'd ever been to war, then remembered what Venn had said about Stoneborn. Not only had this boy—*boy!*—been to war . . . he had died.

Still at the front, Venn was motionless. He barely even looked like he was breathing.

The sound of wood against wood pierced the air again, and a disoriented woman stood up from her coffin. Benj repeated his actions from before, then swiftly took his place beside Venn once again. This happened two more times, with every occurrence being accompanied by a look of relief from Cortus Venn.

After the fourth one clasped the scabbard around his waist, Venn and Benj once again waited.

And waited. And waited.

And waited.

As the sun dipped down below the mountains of Gal'behem, Venn seemed to finally exhale. It was not an exhalation of relief, Sera noted; the man's sagging shoulders showed defeat.

"All of you," he said in a voice loud enough for all to hear, "were found worthy, by me, to be Stoneborn." He paused, and swept his gaze over the remaining coffins, each of them undisturbed. "But only you four were chosen by the gods."

Sera, from the corner of her eye, saw Duna mouth the word "four" questioningly to Tennech, but the general put a finger to his lips and re-directed her attention to Cortus Venn.

"I urge each of you to let these words ring in your ears," Venn said, pausing for effect. "You were chosen . . . By. The. Gods." Each word was spoken precisely and with great weight. He then made his way, slow-ly, to the center of the arrangement of coffins. "Though we mourn the passing of our brothers and sisters, there is still a reason to celebrate—for each of you has entered into the ranks of a fighting force so few, so rare, that each of your names will be etched into history by virtue of just having survived."

He reached for his scabbard and pulled out his sword, thrusting it into the air.

"Join me in this, the final step in the ritual, and your first act as Stoneborn," he said, sword aloft. The others, including Benj, did the same. "A hope for the future; a lament for the past."

As they held their swords aloft, Sera caught a fleeting glimpse of movement beside her.

"You represent the good in humanity," Venn said, and a silhouette walked toward him with purpose. "The best in this world; you epitomize life, embody light, and objectify hope.

"You are Stoneborn," he said—and as he did, Tennech pushed past him.

"This sword," Tennech said, grabbing Benj by the wrist and turning it toward him. "Where did you get this sword?"

The boy looked confused, looking from Tennech to Venn and back. "II—" he stammered.

"Where did you get it?" Tennech repeated, louder. Turning to Venn, he nearly shouted, "Where did he get this?"

Sera couldn't remember the last time she had seen him so frantic.

"It belongs to the boy, by way of his mother," Venn said, sheathing his sword and walking toward the general. "He had it in his possession when I found him, crushed beneath the rubble of Ghal Thurái." Stopping beside Tennech, he crossed his arms and said, "He fought bravely, I'm told."

Tennech gathered himself for a second, like he was thinking about something. He looked back at Benj . . . and a look of slow realization washed over him. His features softened, and he let go of Benj's arm. Looking more carefully now, Sera recognized the look on Tennech's face: it was one of calculation, contemplation. He was putting together puzzle pieces, she knew, like he did on the eve of a great battle—but what these particular pieces showed now was a mystery to her.

To Tennech, though, the picture was always as clear as day. "Of course he fought bravely," he said. His tone was hushed, and the corners of his mouth were raised into a smile. "Not only does he have the sword of a Stoneborn . . ." he began. Dropping to one knee, he looked Benj right in the eyes. "But he's the son of two Valurian warriors." Looking back up at Cortus Venn, Tennech added, "One of whom just happens to have been a general."

Sera saw the same realization sweep over Venn as he took in the scene before him. He raised his fist to his shoulder in a salute. "General Tennech," he said, "I will take my leave and prepare the Stoneborn for battle, along with whatever other soldiers we can muster in defense of Khala Val'ur."

Tennech stood up and returned the salute.

Venn turned on his heels and headed toward the rest of the group. Sera was the first to approach him.

"I'm sorry," Sera said, putting out a hand to stop him. "Are you going to tell us what just happened?"

"I will, I promise," Venn said, continuing on toward the castle. "But for now, all I can say is that General Tennech needs to spend some time with his son."

If Sera's jaw hadn't been attached to her skull, it would have fallen clean off, then and there.

Chapter 58

Khala Val'ur

Yetz

YETZ CLIMBED DOWN FROM HIS mount at the mouth of Khala Val'ur, where he was greeted by the stoic faces of the Master Khyth before him, assembled at his command. Kostas, who'd been riding behind him, trotted over and dismounted by the group of five other Master Khyth: Yuras, Caledeus, Enero, Mentaphet, and Hruz.

"Thank you for coming, Master Khyth," Yetz said from a few paces away. He knew full well that a summons from the High Khyth himself was not a request, but in times like these, nothing was certain. "Your presence here means a great deal to the city, and to me."

"When the City calls, we answer," Master Hruz replied. The eldest of the Master Khyth gathered, Hruz had trained as an apprentice under Yetz before being sent across the Tashkar Sea to become Master Khyth of Ylia'sa-Bor. "No matter whose voice is behind the words," he said solemnly.

Yetz gave a mirthless smile. Each of these men—Master Khyth of the Breaking, to the last—had spent most of their lives in service to the Breaker as Master Khyth in cities of their own. Yet each of them had returned to the city of their birth, beckoned by the one Khyth to whom each were beholden, to the city they'd now defend with their lives.

It was the first time that so many Master Khyth had been gathered in one spot since . . .

"High Khyth!"

Yetz whirled around as a shrill cry pierced the air behind them, accompanied by frantic hoofbeats. A young rider, no more than a boy, was making his way toward them. "The chovathi," the boy said breathlessly, "have breached the outer gate."

Yetz breathed in and let out a sigh. He'd expected the news, but hearing it was still unwelcome. He put on a smile for the messenger. "Thank you, boy. Who sent you?"

"Commander Haldir," the boy replied as he commanded his horse to a halt. "I'm his messenger, Alyn." He gave a halting and awkward bow.

"Then you may pass along my thanks to Commander Haldir for the message, Alyn. Your message has been received."

The messenger boy did not break eye contact, though. "There . . . ah . . ." he began. "There is more," he said, looking to Yetz for permission to continue.

"Go on."

"Commander Haldir said he recognized the one leading them. He is—was—a Master Khyth. Kunas, they called him."

Yetz felt the color disappear from his face as his smile did the same. He turned to look at these men of the Breaking, and saw the determination in their eyes. Each of them had survived pain beyond imagining when their powers first manifested; they had looked death in the eye and had survived. They would do it once more by the time the sun rose again.

"This does not change our plan," Yetz said. "But it does makes it more urgent."

+ + +

Kunas

LIKE THE OUTER SHELL OF an egg, the gates of Khala Val'ur had cracked open, revealing the treasure inside. Kunas—and his chovathi—could taste it.

Forward, he commanded, licking his lips in anticipation. *Give them no time to regroup. Their destruction must be swift and complete.*

There was a sensation, quiet and dull, in the back of his mind that seemed to say how odd it was to be back in this place that he once called home. Khala Val'ur, the Sunken City, home to Khyth and human alike, was now being broken by the very creatures they once sought to destroy—sought out by none other than the so-called Dagger of Derenar,

Aldis Tennech.

Tennech.

A deeper, more primal part of Kunas snarled at the thought, shifting in revulsion. The memory of his people flowed through his blood, and that memory ran deep. It fueled the hatred that Kunas now felt—that all of his horde felt—and it hastened their advance. Pressing forward through the biting of steel and the stinging of iron, the chovathi moved forth toward the burning center of Khala Val'ur.

✦ ✦ ✦

Yetz

YETZ COULD HEAR THE SOUNDS of battle off in the distance: the sinking of metal into armored chovathi skin and the sounds of claws and teeth piercing manmade shells; shouts of pain, cries of war. It was a losing battle, despite his best efforts, and he knew that it would not be long until the armored horde spilled into the inner ring of the mountains of Gal'behem.

This was what they had prepared for, though. This final contingency in a long list of final contingencies. The work that Tennech had begun long ago with the culling of the chovathi numbers was now coming to a head—and it was no blemish on the legacy of the general that they were here now. Tennech had seen them as a threat long ago and had done what he could do cut down their numbers—but the strength of the chovathi was in their chilling ability to reproduce. Cutting off their head was the only way to kill them. Kill them, not stop them; no one living had found a way to stop them. Today, however, Yetz and his Khyth hoped to do just that.

"How much time do we have?" Yetz was looking at the retreating sun as it dipped below the peaks of Gal'behem to the west.

"It's impossible to say for certain," Kostas said, nervously clasping his hands together. "Thuremond and Haldir—"

"Thuremond and Haldir have never faced a chovathi horde commanded by a Master Khyth," Yetz interrupted, glancing sidelong at the Master Khyth. "How long?"

"Hours, High Khyth. Our warriors are strong, but the chovathi outnumber them two to one . . . and they only grow stronger with each errant cut of the sword."

Yetz closed his eyes and rubbed his temples, attempting to soothe the headache that had begun to set in. Gathering power was one thing; focusing and redirecting that power was another thing entirely. "Then we have put this off as long as we possibly can." He opened his eyes and blinked away the blurriness, looking again to his second in command.

Kostas, who seemed to know what was weighing on his mind, said, "We are ready, High Khyth. Our ancestors laid the blueprint long ago for the legacy of the Khyth. Today we shall honor that legacy."

A twinge of sympathy pierced Yetz's heart as he looked again at the men before him.

Men.

Khyth.

Were they really so different from the people that they had diverged from? From the Athrani they had once called brothers? It had never been Yetz's place to question the will of the Shaper when he was first ordered to Khala Val'ur, but it was certainly his right to do so now, in the face of certain death.

Yetz's faith in the Shaper was once strong enough to move mountains—today, with the help of the Master Khyth surrounding him, he would be doing just that, with the full might of the Breaking behind them.

Chapter 59

Wastes of Khulakorum

Ulten

THE DAY DRAGGED ON SLOWLY, yet still Ulten pressed ahead, making his way across the eastern part of the Wastes—to a cave he'd never seen in a mountain range he'd only heard of. He shook his head at his own foolishness at such an undertaking; gods must be more persuasive than he realized. He took a look backward at all the ground he'd covered, marveling at how far he'd come. He swiveled his head back around, forward to his destination. Squinting, Ulten's heart skipped a beat when he realized he could make out the gray outline of a broken and craggy horizon. The Spears! They were in sight! Though only barely distinguishable in the distance, he knew from here that he had just about a day's ride to go until he reached them.

He reached out and tugged at the mental link with the Traveler.

I think I see them! he thought.

You do? You see the Spears? The Traveler's reply was laced with a bit of something Ulten recognized as hope.

I believe so, Ulten said after a pause. *It's hard to tell. I've never seen them before.*

The Traveler chuckled. *Fair point. But you're close then?*

Closer than when I started.

Well, I suppose that's something, said the god.

Ulten tapped his heels, and his camel's gait quickened ever so slightly. They could very well reach them by nightfall if he kept this pace.

+ + +

During the journey, Ulten and the Traveler had been trading tales to pass the time—for Ulten it was to keep his mind off the heat, and for the god it was to keep from going mad. It had gone better than Ulten had expected, and he'd learned a few things about gods that he never knew: their nature, what drove them, and—in some instances—what could be

311

their undoing. The Traveler had been surprisingly forthcoming about his own nature . . . yet still Ulten's curiosity pervaded.

There is something I've been meaning to ask you, Traveler, if you'll indulge me.

Ask away, the god replied.

Why didn't you destroy the Holder when you had the chance?

There was a silence, like a great thunderstorm suddenly dissipating. *There are many layers to that answer,* the Traveler began.

Glancing up at the sky and looking back at the sinking sun, Ulten gave a mental shrug. *It seems I have time for such an answer,* he said.

The next thoughts that came into Ulten's mind were not so much thoughts, but images—images of the Otherworld and of Khel-hârad, Land of the Dead. He saw the gods of creation—the Shaper of Ages, Breaker of the Dawn, and the Binder of Worlds—in their ancient and shapeless forms. They were not just gods; they were the essence of everything they would go on to create. Then, more images fluttered into his mind—too many to count—like flashes of light in the night sky. He didn't know how he knew, but something told Ulten that they were lesser gods—but still gods nonetheless—and among them were the Traveler, the Ghost, and the Holder of the Dead.

Our nature, began the Traveler, *is a complicated thing. We are not mortal, but we share many qualities that you mortals do: we live, we love, and we seek out meaning. That search for meaning can consume us—both god and mortal. Some of us can go our entire existence without finding it, where others find it the moment they are formed. My brother and I were long into our own existence when we were burdened with our purpose, and that, we thought, was to be the end of it.*

But purpose, the Traveler went on, *is not so easily discerned. It turns out that there was another purpose for me, lying dormant, waiting for the right time to manifest.*

Ulten cocked his head. *But how did you know?*

That is a questions I cannot fully answer, for I do not understand it myself, the Traveler answered plainly. *I don't know what caused the change either, but I felt it immediately. Something in the universe moved . . . and I was born a second time. Up until then, I hadn't even known what I was; I thought I was nothing but a ferryman, taking the souls of the dead to their final resting place in Khel-hârad. After that, though, I felt something growing inside me that told me I was part of a much larger plan—something that perhaps not even the gods of creation themselves knew about.*

There was silence as the two minds were left to their private thoughts, which both seemed to intermingle on the surface, like streams of air colliding. Ulten's head spun at the idea. If there was something else acting in the shadows behind the gods . . .

He rubbed his eyes; it hurt to think about.

When he opened them again, he saw something move, just out of the corner of his eye. It was a ways away in the distance, but something was definitely there. Ulten wondered if the Holder of the Dead had left him some parting gift—perhaps a priest or two who'd been ordered to keep tabs on him. The Lord of the Dead was certainly devious enough to have planned for such a contingency. Or perhaps it was just some desert animal making its way toward the Spears in search of water—a desert fox at best, or a wolf at worst.

Either way, the pace that Ulten was traveling suddenly felt sluggish. He tapped on the reins once more and his mount once again sped up.

"Don't worry boy," he muttered as the beast's exertion at the quickened pace became evident. "There will be some fresh mountain springs to drink from when we get there, and all this effort will pay off."

With another glance behind him, he hoped that he was right.

More importantly, however, he hoped that he was safe.

Chapter 60

Annoch

D. L. Jennings

Aldryd

ALDRYD'S HAND TREMBLED AS HE reached for the Anvil. Before he could touch it, he heard a familiar voice coming from behind him.

"I understand you wish to speak to the High Keeper."

It was Deyhan, son of Yaden. Aldryd turned to greet him. "I do, Speaker. Thank you for coming."

Deyhan bowed gracefully. "When the Keeper calls, the Fires of Ellenos answer," said the younger man. He was dressed in the orange and red robes of his order—an order whose members once numbered in the hundreds but had dwindled to less than a dozen just in Aldryd's lifetime. His dark hair was tied back neatly in a knot.

"Thank you all the same," Aldryd replied. "I am ready whenever you are."

With a nod, Deyhan went about the ritual of opening the fabric of reality in order to link two places in space: in this case, Annoch and Ellenos.

Aldryd watched as the young man wove his Shaping in a way that was as mysterious to him as Breaking was to a human. Despite tapping the same energy source which was the gift of the Shaper, Deyhan's application of it was different than how Aldryd used Shaping. It was a manipulation of energy on a much grander scale, and one that Aldryd sometimes had trouble comprehending. The ease with which Deyhan altered reality was truly a thing to behold.

A dull boom filled the room as a tear in reality formed—with its twin also having manifested in Ellenos, the First City, inside their own Temple of the Shaper. The portal shimmered as it grew, and Aldryd watched with admiration as Deyhan finished his elegant dance.

"It is done," Deyhan said, bowing and stepping back. "I will leave you to speak with her."

"Thank you once again, son of Yaden. Your father taught you well."

The words of the order brought a smile to Deyhan's face. He bowed again and exited the room, leaving Aldryd alone with the translucent portal into Ellenos. Before he could even turn back to the portal, though, the voice of an old friend greeted him from the other side.

"I've been waiting since I felt it, Aldryd. I knew you would reach out."

Turning, Aldryd saw the face of his old friend, Sh'thanna, High Keeper of Ellenos, leader of the Athrani people. Her blue on blue eyes were as lovely as he remembered them . . . yet today they did not exude beauty—only fear.

"I suspected that I was not alone in feeling her plea," Aldryd began, stepping closer to the portal to get a better look at her. It was like gazing into a pool of gently rippling water. "But I am afraid that she waited too long."

Sh'thanna grimaced from the other side. "While I share your fear, I am confident that the power of the Binder of Worlds holds strong in her daughter, Ynara—and within her beats the heart of the Kienari."

"Will that be enough to face what is coming?"

Aldryd suspected that he knew the answer, but he wanted to hear Sh'thanna say it anyway. Her voice comforted him, and today was no exception. He just wished that he didn't have to always hear it under such dire circumstances.

"I do not have that answer, old friend," Sh'thanna replied after a silence. "But my faith in the Shaper is strong, and I believe that She has seen the end of all things. Only She truly knows how this all plays out."

Aldryd's hand trembled again, and he glanced back at the glowing words on the anvil. Looking back through the portal, he gazed upon the soft features of Sh'thanna who, despite her long rule, still maintained the beauty of her youth. "Everything that has happened lately," he began. "The awakening of the Three, the battle of the Tree, the fall of Ghal Thurái . . ." His words trailed off.

Sh'thanna must have somehow read his thoughts because she spoke them aloud. "These are the days that we all feared would come, Aldryd, with the Holder's grip tightening, and the chovathi descending upon Kienar. We knew they would arrive, and we have done our best, truly, to prepare for them. I have already sent word to my generals that they will be needed at the Tree."

"But we both know that will not be enough," he said curtly.

Sh'thanna cleared her throat and sat up straight, and Aldryd immediately regretted voicing the words. He had no way of knowing who might have been listening behind the portal in Ellenos.

"The coming battles are what the Athrani were made for," Sh'thanna said. Her dignity and grace shone through as once again Aldryd was reminded why she had been chosen above all others to become High Keeper so long ago.

"Then why can I not overcome this feeling of dread?"

The High Keeper shifted in her throne. "I feel it too," she said. "I haven't felt it since . . . since . . ." Her words trailed off, and a distant look filled her eyes. "It is some ancestral fear, I think, something in the back of my mind. I don't know it, but my blood does—and right now it runs cold."

Aldryd turned his attention inward; his blood, too, ran cold. He hadn't been able to shake the overwhelming sensation that something was wrong. It had come just before the Binder had reached out to him—and to countless others, no doubt—but something inside him told him that it wasn't her. The sensation he was feeling was coming from some other source, some other—

A muted boom like a clap of thunder resonated through his chest, and the very Temple around him began to shake.

"Aldryd, what—" Sh'thanna began. Her mouth hung open.

The feeling of dread that Aldryd had felt before now enveloped him like a shadow. From the corner of his eyes he could see the flickering blue words on the anvil turn a sickening, hellacious red.

I LIVE.

Aldryd turned, hoping not to see what he feared he would—but hope, he knew, was merely the other side of the coin of fear, and only one of them could come out on top.

From the middle of the Anvil of the Worldforge, a hand came forth. Then a second. The two of them gripped the sides like they were bracing for something . . . and then Aldryd saw it.

In all his years spent in service to the Shaper of Ages, Aldryd had seen many horrors and atrocities—some committed in her name, others in the name of peace or war, or any multitude of reasons to impose the will of One upon the will of Many. But what he saw now, emerging from one of the artifacts of creation, was something so profane and unholy that Aldryd could not find the words for it. His skin crawled in revulsion. His heart pounded in fear.

Sh'thanna called to him through the portal. "Aldryd," she said. The word was calm despite the horror that was emerging on the other side. "Run."

The command registered in Aldryd's mind, but he was frozen in fear. He never thought that he would be here, in the temple of his goddess, staring face to face with the one thing that should not—that could not—be allowed in this hallowed place.

Now fully emerged from the portal in the Anvil, one thundering footfall preceded a second as the Breaker stood. Rising up to his full, terrible height, the ancient god spread his arms and, with hardly even a show of effort, burst through the brick of the temple that was as old as the city of Annoch. Daylight cascaded down along with the falling debris as the Breaker of the Dawn made his presence known.

"Hear me and dismay, O mortals!" His voice was a volcano, and the world around him trembled like leaves in a storm. "Your god, the Breaker of the Dawn, has come for his claim!"

He was a black mountain, blocking out the sun. And in his hand was . . .

Was . . .

Could it be?

Aldryd's knees were weak, and he felt them collapse beneath him. He looked around at the wreckage. His beloved temple, which had been his responsibility since birth, was in ruins—desecrated by the very god who was its antithesis.

"And my claim ... begins ... *here!*"

The Breaker raised a massive hand to the sky.

Aldryd could do nothing but watch as the Hammer of the Worldforge—once used in the very creation of this world, and all that it contained—came crashing down in a terrible arc toward the anvil. He closed his eyes. He couldn't watch.

He braced himself.

... And waited ...

... And waited.

There was no grand crash, no cacophonous roar like Aldryd expected. Instead, there was merely a small sound, hollow, like a body surrendering. An exhale, a sigh. A relief. He opened his eyes, rubbing them to see through the haze. He blinked a few times to confirm what he was seeing, but he knew deep down that he didn't need to.

When the dust had cleared and the trembling had stopped, two things were immediately apparent to Aldryd: one, standing in the ruined Temple of the Shaper was none other than the Breaker of the Dawn ... and, two, the Anvil of the Worldforge was no more.

Chapter 61

Haidan Shar

D. L. Jennings

Tennech

As Aldis Tennech looked down at Benj, a million thoughts ran though his mind—but only one of them mattered: *I have a son.*

The words carried with them the weight of his absence. He'd lived his entire life without knowing this fact—his final thoughts before he died, he recalled, were of how alone he was—but now, all of that had changed, and the change stood before him in the form of a thirteen-year-old Stoneborn child.

He found himself staring at the boy: his porcelain skin that no blade could ever pierce; his eyes that looked so much like Nessa's, a woman he knew an entire lifetime ago; his hands, covered in the callouses of someone who knew not just how to wield a sword, but how to use it.

This boy . . . this boy was so much more than he could have ever hoped or expected. He realized he was staring and tore his gaze away. Tennech, a man who never found himself lacking the right words to say, was suddenly struck mute.

Lucky for him, Benj was there to exceed his expectations yet again and say the first words to break the silence. "She talked about you all the time." His voice was soft, and Tennech almost missed the words. "It was her favorite story to tell, the story of the day you saved her."

Tennech had the words to a response in his head, but somewhere between his lungs and his mouth they got stuck. He cleared his throat, hoping to coax them out.

It worked.

"Did she now?" he asked. It was more than he thought he could manage at a time like this. He sat down, close enough to the water to hear the light lapping of the waves.

Benj nodded. "She said it was the most beautiful thing she'd ever seen—and this sword," he said as he held up Glamrhys like a mother cat showing off her newborn kitten, "was what did it."

Tennech looked over at the blade with a fond admiration. "That sword belonged to my father." And, as the realization struck him, he looked at Benj. "Your grandfather."

Benj's eyes went wide as saucers and he hurried over to sit beside Tennech. "My grandfather! Was he a Stoneborn too?"

"Yes, he was. Just like you. I suppose that's where you get it from," Tennech said as he looked out from the shore. The light of dusk had since faded, leaving just the glow of the moon rippling across the waves of the Tashkar Sea. "And much like you, I never knew my father either. That sword," he said with a nod to Glamrhys, "and its sheath was all that he left me with."

Benj sat down beside him to look out at the sea.

It was not lost on Tennech that both of them had lived and died without having known their fathers. Both of them had found themselves in the profession of arms, and both of them—Benj more so than even he—had been forced to do a lot of growing up.

He looked again at the boy—at his *son*, he had to correct himself—and wondered where to even start. How does one make up for a life of lost time? He found himself staring again, but this time he didn't look away. It was with a mixture of admiration and wonder that he now saw him. Benj was his son. Though his age might mark him a boy, he had seen and done things that some men might go their whole lives without. He had trained in the art of war, gone into battle against the chovathi—*like father, like son,* Tennech thought—and had doubtlessly taken lives before his own was cut short. This was no boy, Tennech finally concluded. Benj was a man in everything but name.

Benj must have felt his stare. He looked up at Tennech. "Do you . . . want to see her?"

The words smacked Tennech right in the face, and he almost recoiled at how much they stung. His mouth hung open. "She's . . . she's alive? Nessa's . . . alive?"

Benj gave him a look like he'd just asked if it snows in Hjorl. "She was this morning when I left the stables." He stood up suddenly and tugged at Tennech's arm. "Come on! I don't know how long Commander Venn will let us stay here before we march for Khala Val'ur."

Tennech, for at least the third time since he started keeping track, was stunned. Nessa was here! In this very city! He stood up slowly as the thoughts rattled around in his head.

"I . . . I don't know," he stammered. "I'm not sure that's a good idea." His heart was racing. Of course it was a good idea. Why would he say that? Was he nervous? He'd commanded armies—*armies!* One lone woman shouldn't be a . . . He stopped himself. *Oh, gods. What if she hates me? Is she angry at me? Does she resent me for having to raise Benj by herself?*

He felt another tugging at his arm and realized Benj was a lot stronger than he looked. "Come on!" he said again, dragging Tennech toward the castle and forcing his feet to catch him to keep himself from falling. He couldn't remember the last time that he'd been taken anywhere against his will, but he was sure that the circumstances were just as frightening.

✦ ✦ ✦

The two of them had left the paved road of the castle and were now traveling on a road caked with dry mud and dust. Looking around, Tennech could scarcely believe the poor quality of some of the houses when hardly a quarter mile away was some of the greatest wealth in all of Gal'dorok.

"This is where you live?" he asked, and could hardly believe he'd just said it out loud.

"Uh-huh!" Benj answered excitedly. He'd been talking his ear off for the whole walk from the castle, spent in a sort of half-jog, half-walk, bouncing around Tennech as he brought him up to speed on absolutely everything. By the time they had rounded the corner onto Benj's street, Tennech even knew what size saddle Benj's horse wore. "Isn't it great?" Pointing, he said, "There's our stable."

Tennech felt himself being pulled by Benj once again as they got closer—and with every step, his own heartbeat grew louder in his ears.

"Wait here," he said as they approached a modest looking, single-story house with shutters of copper and white.

The colors of Ghal Thurái, Tennech noted with a smirk. *Once a warrior, always a warrior.*

He stood in the street right where Benj had told him to, admiring the night sky and wondering just how much longer he would be able to enjoy it before . . . before . . .

He closed the door on the thoughts, allowing his mind to drift to simpler things. Before he died, he recalled that his final thoughts had been one of loneliness—but the ones right before that had been of her.

Moments later, Benj burst through the door, dragging a figure behind him by the arms.

"I don't see why you can't just tell me what you're—"

Tennech turned and looked to see where the words were coming from, and he froze. There she was, looking just like the day he'd last seen her: beautiful, tall, and strong.

"Nessa," he said, and the word itself was like a breath of fresh air. "They told me I'd find you here."

"They said—" Nessa began, barely able to get the words out. She pulled her hands up to her face and covered her mouth for a moment. Moving them away again, she started again, this time more softly. "They said that you died. Beyond the Wastes. There were messengers . . ." Her words trailed off.

There, by the light of the moon above, Tennech saw the same woman that he had loved all those years ago. "Rumors," he said with a wave, finally able to find his feet again. He took a step toward her, haltingly, as he felt the weight of uncertainty pushing back against him. "Nothing but rumors."

Without looking at her son, Nessa said, "Benj, go feed the horses."

Benj started to protest but was immediately waved off. Reluctantly he made his way to the stables.

Still standing where she had emerged from the house, Nessa was like a statue to Thurian greatness: silent, unmoving, strong. She stood there so long without saying a word, that Tennech nearly jumped when she finally spoke, in a voice barely above a whisper.

"I didn't think you'd even know who I am, let alone remember me."

The words were a dagger to his heart. Here he was, face to face with the one woman he had ever found the courage to love—the woman whose name had been on his tongue when he died, the woman who had borne him a son—and she tells him she thought she was an afterthought. Nothing could have been further from the truth. If Nessa couldn't move, he resolved, it was up to him to banish the distance between them.

"Those words are viler to me than the ones that proclaimed my own death," he said as his feet carried him to her. "I never stopped thinking about you. Do you know how many times I sent runners to Ghal Thurái looking for a woman matching your description? How many excuses I made to visit that place in the hopes of running into you?" Nessa covered her mouth with her hands again and shook her head. "Too many to count, Nessa." He loved saying her name, he realized. It felt so warm and wonderful, like sliding his hand into a woolen glove in winter. "Too many to count. I spent my whole life waiting for you." He was mere feet from her now, and he could see that she was trembling. "I wasn't about to lose you again."

He was close enough to her now that he could hear her heavy breathing through her hands, feel the weight of her longing. It was like a rope, pulled taut and about to break.

She closed her eyes, reached out, and put her arms around him. Tennech leaned in.

When his lips met hers, it was like feeling the sun again. He kissed her deeply and long, the kiss of a man who had been given a second chance at love—and life. When he finally pulled back, he saw that her hazel eyes were wet with tears.

"What is it?" he asked softly.

"I didn't know," she said. "How could I have known? When I came back as the sole survivor of my regiment, I was labeled as a coward and a deserter. So I fled. It was the only way. I had to leave everything and cut ties with my old life."

Tennech held her tighter. "Oh, Nessa. My Nessa. I'm so sorry. If only I'd known . . . if only I'd . . ." He searched for words. "I've lost so much in my life, but my greatest loss was something I never even knew I had." He let her go and took a step back, still holding onto her arms with his hands. "If I lived a thousand lifetimes, I could never make up for the pain I must have caused you, and for that I am sorry."

Nessa wiped away the tears from her eyes.

Just then, Benj emerged from the stables and triumphantly announced that the horses had been fed.

"Thank you, my love," Nessa replied, still staring deep into Tennech's eyes. She let her gaze linger, then turned to her son. "Will you put on the kettle?" Turning back, she furrowed her brows and asked, "You do like tea, don't you?"

As a smile began to form on his face, Tennech felt uneasiness rise in his stomach. "I can't stay," he said, and the words nearly broke him. "If I'd known . . ." he started to say, then caught himself. "Nessa, you changed my life . . . but I owe a debt to a much higher power, and that debt will soon be called in. I'm sorry, but I cannot stay."

The look on her face as he said those words made him feel like he had lost her all over again.

"But you've only just got here," she protested.

"I will come back for you," Tennech said, and he knew in the very depths of his soul that he meant it. "No matter what it takes, Nessa, I will come back."

She looked at him for a long moment, and in her eyes raged anger, fear, love, and regret. Love, though, found its way to the surface, and she reached out for him. "I used to lie awake at night and wonder what it would be like to hold you again," she said as she pressed her cheek into his shoulder. "Please don't make me lie awake and wonder that anymore."

Tennech squeezed her tight. He tilted his head down and kissed her on the forehead. He wasn't sure just how long he stood there holding her, but he was vaguely aware of the sound of hoofbeats approaching from behind, followed by the distant words of a breathless messenger.

"General Tennech! General Tennech!" the man shouted as he pulled his horse to a stop. "They've been looking all over for you. Commander Venn is ready. You are to leave at once."

Tennech looked from the messenger and back to Nessa, who still had her head pressed against his body. "I will come back for you," he repeated. "And as for you," he said, pointing to Benj, "take care of your mother while I'm gone."

Benj nodded exuberantly, rendering a salute so crisp that it even surprised Tennech. He returned it and spun on his heels toward the messenger, who had a second horse waiting nearby.

"I-I'm sorry, General," said the messenger as Tennech approached. "But Commander Venn explicitly said that Benj was to come too. All Stoneborn are—" he began, but Tennech waved him off.

"Very well," he said as he climbed into the saddle of his mount. "But you're going to be the one to break his mother's heart and take him from her," he said, and he dug his heels into the ribs of his mount. "Good luck!" he called over his shoulder as he sped off toward the castle.

The messenger, holding the reins to his own horse, could only stare as he rode away.

✦ ✦ ✦

As Tennech neared the castle, he could see that there was already a small force gathered outside, no more than a dozen. Drawing closer, he saw faces he recognized—Duna, Venn, and the four new Stoneborn—but noticed that a few were conspicuously missing.

"Where are Sera and the captains?" he asked, coming to a halt just beyond the collection of soldiers.

"Thank you for coming so quickly, General," Duna said. She was garbed in light chain mail but carried no weapons. "She is with the rest of the conventional forces. They'll be the bulk of the charge. But," she said, nodding to the Stoneborn, "our first attackers are here."

Tennech eyed them skeptically, letting his eyes drift over to Venn, who was beaming with pride. With a skillful dismount, he walked over to the commander and took him by the elbow, away from the group and prying ears. When he felt that he was sufficiently far enough away, he looked Venn in the eyes.

"While I am overjoyed at the idea of using Stoneborn to stave off the chovathi," he said quietly, "they are by no means battle tested." He peeked discreetly over his shoulder to steal another glance at the four new fighters, still mere volunteers in his eyes. They wore little more than rags—any armor would have been strictly for show—and nervousness bled through their assumed exterior of fearlessness and strength. "I know they're impervious to harm, but what good will it do us if they can't even wield a blade?"

Venn, in a voice equally low, replied. "Yes, they are new, General, and, yes, they have never faced chovathi, but you forget one thing." He paused, crossing his arms over his chest, and gave Tennech a look smugger than a Kienari in a tree-climbing contest. "They have me."

Tennech held Venn's stare for a long, silent moment. Then, he let the edges of his mouth curl ever so slightly into a smile. Turning back to the queen, he said in a voice loud enough for all of them to hear, "Who is ready to make some chovathi heads roll?"

A resounding shout came from the crowd, small but mighty.

Tennech surveyed those gathered before him. He had worked with fewer, and he'd worked with less. This would be a challenge. He loved a challenge.

"Then, Majesty, I have two questions," he said as he turned to Duna.

"When do we leave, and will you be joining us?"

Duna smiled. "I think you know the answer to both, General," she said as she turned to her messenger, Eowen. "Bring them," she said, and he disappeared inside the castle. "After my sister perished in the battle of Ghal Thurái," she went on as she approached Tennech, "crushed beneath the rocks with most of her army, we thought her body—along with her greatsword—was surely lost. But thanks to the tireless effort of men like Cortus Venn, we were able to recover both."

Venn nodded. "Never leave a man behind," he said, "or a woman."

Just then, Eowen reappeared, carrying two sheaths in his arms.

"Now," the queen continued, "Lena was a lot stronger than I am, and I had no hope of wielding the sword which she used so effortlessly, but it seemed like a waste of perfectly good steel to simply put it on display over some mantle. So do you know what we did?" she asked with a grin.

"I think I know, but I've a feeling you're going to tell me anyway."

Duna's grin held as Eowen approached, kneeling formally and presenting her with the twin sheaths: blue, with a thick white line down the center of each—the colors of Haidan Shar.

She reached for the first one and held it in one hand.

"You're right, General, I am going to tell you—but not so I can bore you with details of how we melted down the steel of my sister's single sword and poured it into twin molds, which my best blacksmith worked furiously to complete." She smiled. "No: I'm going to tell you because I need your help. You see," she said, holding the sheath out in front of her, grabbing the hilt of the sword that it held, and pulling it out to reveal the blade, "I was classically trained in the art of fencing." She eyed the flawlessly sharpened edge as it caught the moonlight. She let her eyes snap to his. "Which, as you know, only uses a single sword." She snapped the sword back into its sheathe and strapped it around her waist.

Tennech caught her gaze but furrowed his eyebrows. "Majesty, we don't have time for me to train you in the art of two-sword combat," he said. "We're on the eve of—"

Duna held up a hand, shaking her head at him. "That's not what I mean, General," she said, and nodded to the other sword, still in the outstretched hands of Eowen. "I mean that the second sword belongs to you."

Tennech felt his jaw go slack. "M-majesty," he stammered, "I can't, can't possibly—"

"You can and you will. And would you take the sword already? Eowen's kneeling is driving me crazy."

Tennech hurriedly took the sword from the blond messenger, who made it a point to find his feet as fast as humanly possible.

"Thank you," Duna said. "You honor me by sharing steel with me."

"The honor is mine, Queen Duna," Tennech said, making sure to emphasize her title as he did.

"Now . . ." Duna began, "there is the issue of naming them. A sword given by royal decree must have a name."

Tennech nodded and strapped the sheath around his waist. "I have a few ideas."

"Good. Then find me and tell me after you land."

"Land?" Tennech asked. He couldn't begin to comprehend what she meant. Khala Val'ur was to the west of them, not over the sea to the east. There's no reason to . . . His thoughts were cut off as a great, loud whistle came from the mouth of Cortus Venn.

"Aye," the Stoneborn said with a wild grin on his face. "Land."

Tennech gazed in confusion at the former commander of the Lonely Guard, who had a grin plastered on his face like he was about to reveal a plot for treason.

"I still—" Tennech started to say, but found that his words were cut off by the mighty beating of wings. "Don't . . ." he said, looking for the source of the sound. When he found it, he simply uttered, "Ah."

Coming toward them like falling stars were two pale yellow eyes, affixed to the body of the largest gwarái that he'd ever laid eyes on. The courtyard they were all standing in was large enough to hold a warship, but Tennech wasn't sure if that would be enough.

The great creature circled above them, wings beating slowly and strong as it began its initial descent. Gliding through the air like an eel through water, the gwarái worked its way closer until it was directly overhead. Then, suddenly, it reared itself up with a great flap of its wings, ceasing its forward movement and bringing it nearly perpendicular to the ground, limbs hanging beneath it like a striking hawk. Its fall from the sky was both controlled and smooth for a creature its size, with every wingbeat blasting the ground with gale force winds. Tennech found himself blinking and shielding his eyes from the dust being kicked up.

"Where in the Holder's hells did you find one of these?" Tennech shouted to Venn. His words were barely audible over the maelstrom.

"Lash'Kargá holds many secrets, General!" Venn shouted back. "Perhaps one day you'll see them for yourself."

Tennech let his eyes drift back to the great beast, which had nearly reached the ground. Its hind legs made contact first, and the wingbeats were smaller and more controlled as its forelimbs came down soon after. Even with a soft landing, the ground shook.

Tennech stood and stared. The creature before him was familiar, yet also unlike anything else in this world. "Absolutely marvelous," he said. "And you're telling me this creature lets you ride?"

Venn walked toward the gwarái, which was slowly swiveling its head—on an impossibly long neck—around the courtyard, as if determining its next meal. When the gwarái spotted Venn, it closed its eyes and, in what Tennech could only guess was a display of affection, raised its head over the commander, exposing its chin along with the inky black scales beneath it.

"Me, and anyone else we can fit," he said as he reached up with both hands—the creature's chin was still a good seven feet from the ground—and began scratching. A low rumble came from the gwarái as Tennech realized what was happening.

"Is it . . . purring?"

"She," Venn corrected, "is doing nothing of the sort! She's simply . . . expressing her gratitude to me in a . . . purely . . . audible fashion."

"Right," Tennech said. He watched Venn continue to scratch the creature below the chin. "Not purring." He felt a hand on his shoulder and turned to see Duna standing beside him. "I believe we have everything we need to depart."

"This is where we say farewell," she said, and extended her hand.

Tennech clasped it in his own and struggled yet again to understand her meaning. "You're not coming along?"

"Not on that thing," she said, nodding at the gwarái and ignoring the protests of *she can hear you!* from Venn. "I am not a frontline fighter like my sister was. My place is in command." Patting her sheath, she added, "This is more for show than anything. If I have to use it, something has gone terribly wrong."

Tennech joined her in a well-deserved chuckle. "But you did say you'd be joining us."

"And I will be—but my presence is not needed as imminently as yours. You," she said, gesturing to indicate the Stoneborn before her, "will be the key to victory. You are sorely needed, and I have every faith that Tennech and Venn will be the ones to guide you there." As she spoke those words, something seemed to catch her eye. She leaned slightly over to look past Tennech. "Ah, the final member of your war band has arrived."

Tennech turned to see, dressed in a smaller version of full battle regalia, his son, Benj, riding on horseback on his way to the castle. He rode the horse as far as it would go—not far, given the great winged gwarái in the courtyard—and ran the rest of the way, holding his chain mail coif to his head as did so.

"Sorry I'm late, Your Majesty," Benj panted. "My mum insisted on a proper goodbye."

Tennech shook his head and laughed—not at the comedy, but at the absurdity: that a thirteen-year-old boy, the last piece of this great, bloody puzzle, was nearly late to war because he was saying goodbye to his mother. Were it not for the winged gwarái before him, it would have been the most incredible thing he'd seen that day.

"You're not late, Benj," the queen said with a smile. "They wouldn't have left without you." The boy gave her a gleeful salute, which she returned. "Go on then," she said, nodding to the gwarái. "Get on."

Benj's eyes lit up. "You mean it?" he asked.

"Well, I certainly say it's alright, but you'd better ask Venn," she said, nodding to the commander who was apparently whispering words of encouragement to the great winged beast.

"Commander Venn!" Benj shouted. "Can I ride with you?"

Venn stopped what he was doing and looked over at the boy. "Of course you can," he shouted back. "Come over here and introduce yourself. It makes for an easier ride."

If Benj's eyes had opened any wider, Tennech was sure they would have fallen straight out of his head. He walked over, cautiously, to where Venn was standing.

"Put out your hand," Venn said as the boy approached. "She has a great sense of smell, and she uses it to identify you."

Benj complied, stretching his arm out with his palm toward the sky, like he was looking to feed a carrot to the world's largest horse. As he got closer, Venn began scratching her below the chin, which seemed to relax her.

"Atta boy," Venn said, his voice quieter. "Don't be shy." The gwarái opened her eyes in between scratches but regarded Benj indifferently. He looked to Venn for reassurance. "You're doing fine," said the commander.

Benj was only a few feet from where Venn was standing when the gwarái moved her head toward him. Venn's hands were now free from her completely. The head of the gwarái dwarfed Benj as she positioned her nostrils—two great slits on the front of her snout—right by him. She took in a quick breath that even Tennech felt, as far away as he was. Seemingly satisfied, she puffed the air back out and swiveled her head right back to Venn, who resumed his scratching.

"I think she likes you," Venn said in a conspiratorial whisper. "Now get on. We've got to make it to Khala Val'ur while the Khyth are still able to fight."

Benj happily obeyed, practically sprinting to a large rope ladder that was hanging down from the back of the gwarái. Secured to the creature's back, like saddlebags on a horse, were leather pouches large enough to hold a man—and it was clear to Tennech that these pouches were meant to hold them as they flew. They were arranged in two rows of four, facing forward, so that each person would lay down and slide in, feet first.

"Interesting design," Tennech said as he looked at what he could only think to describe as a people carrier. "Who thought of it?"

"That would be me," Duna said. "Venn had offered me a chance to ride with him on the way to Ghal Thurái, but what he was using then was barely more than some leather straps tied together. There was absolutely no way I was going to bet my life on the grip of Cortus Venn to keep me from falling off."

"She's a clever one, that Duna," Venn said. "All brains, with a little bit of brawn thrown in for good measure."

"Well, let's hope it holds," Tennech said. He started making his way to the gwarái, then stopped. "I don't suppose you'd allow me one last goodbye," Tennech said over his shoulder to Duna.

The Queen didn't have to answer as, instead, a strong Athrani voice came from the path leading away from the castle. "And just who would that be for?"

Tennech turned and was more than pleased to see Sera riding toward him. From head to toe, she wore the silver and black plate mail of Khala Val'ur, battle-tested and timeworn. She'd been gifted the armor nearly a decade ago; it fit her as perfectly then as it did now.

"I haven't seen you wear that since the Battle for the Tree," Tennech said as she approached. Sera pulled off her helmet and shook out her long, brown hair.

"I haven't had a need to," she said. "But if you think I was going to let you leave without saying goodbye, you're duller than this armor is." Grinning, she added, "General."

She got down from the horse and walked over to him. The smile faded slowly from her face.

"I never got to say it to you last time," she said in a quiet voice. "The regret nearly tore me apart."

"Well, you can say it to me now."

She looked at him, as if gathering her words. She took a breath, started to say something, and then stopped. Looking away, she began again. "If I could go back to that day, the day when the Tribes invaded. The day that you—" she said, choking on her words, "—the day that you died . . ." She turned to face him again, and looked him in the eyes. "I would have told you that I love you.

"I would thank you for everything you did for me—everything I didn't understand . . . that was your way of making me stronger. Every late night and early morning you spent with me, trying to make me the best version of myself; every laugh, every tear, every patched up scraped knee, every bruise, and every scar. It was all for me—all of it. And even though you wouldn't say it out loud when it was happening, you were saying it in another way: you loved me. Because even though it isn't by blood, I am your daughter. Nothing in this life or the next will ever change that." She had tears in her eyes as she spoke, and Tennech found himself having to blink away his own.

He reached out and placed his hand against her left cheek, covering part of the scar that ran the length of her face. "You are my daughter," he reaffirmed. "I can't imagine why the gods saw fit to give me such a blessing, but they did." He smiled and continued, "And here I was, foolish enough to think that I was the one who was good with words."

Sera laughed through her tears. "You still are," she said. "I've just been bottling mine up for too long; it's time I let them out."

Tennech sighed. "I should probably do the same—though you are right about one thing," he answered. "I didn't say it out loud; I always let my actions do the talking for me. But sometimes, actions alone aren't enough, especially in matters such as these." He reached up with his other hand, gently holding her face as he looked at her and smiled. "I love you, my daughter."

The words hung in the air. He couldn't remember the last time he said them—and for that reason, they carried weight.

Sera collapsed into him, embracing him like the father he was, and Tennech held her right back, making sure that this time they had a proper goodbye. He had seen the toll it could take when such words were left unspoken.

He wanted to savor the moment, but he knew there were greater things at stake. There would be time for saying these things again later; he would make sure of it.

"Now," Tennech said, letting her go and taking a step back. "You have your orders, and I have mine," he said, lowering his voice to a near-whisper for the next words, "as well as a tailored purpose as to why we both are here."

Sera nodded knowingly. "Understood," she said. "I will see you again on the battlefield."

"That you will," Tennech said with a smile. Turning to the gwarái, he said, "Now let's finish what I started."

There was a smattering of applause from all those gathered, including a small crowd of curious passersby who had stopped and stared at the spectacle that had made its way into their normally quiet city. And, as he climbed up the rope and slid into one of the pouches on the back of the gwarái, he could clearly hear the words of Duna as she turned to Sera, despite the distance between them.

"He's better at leading armies than he is at giving speeches." She elbowed Sera gently in the ribs. "And, by the gods, can he give speeches."

Tennech smiled as he fastened himself in.

This was going to be one hell of a ride.

Chapter 62

Kienar

Kethras

IT HAD BEEN A LONG and grueling road from G'hen to Kienar, but the two of them had managed to do it at a respectable pace. Kethras was constantly glancing back at Elyasha to make sure she was keeping up, and it was absolutely to her credit that she surprised him every time.

Even though she was on horseback and he on foot—the Kienari were as fast as any creature on four legs, and faster by far than any on two—riding a horse this far and for this long was no small feat. That fact became evident by how often she asked for the two of them to take a break. Kethras had felt sympathy for her horse and, at least the first few times, had immediately relented. The further along they got, however, the more reticent he became—and it was more than just a love for the land of his birth that compelled him. It was something much, much greater.

"I'm not sure how much further my horse can make it," Yasha called from behind. She'd been pleading her case for a few miles now, and her voice was becoming more urgent. "He's starting to breathe a little funny."

Kethras was more than a dozen paces ahead of her and feeling fine. He was constantly having to remind himself that not every creature under the sky was built for speed like the Kienari were. He stopped in his tracks and looked back.

Squinting, Yasha and her mount came into focus, and Kethras saw that, sure enough, her mount was fatigued. Turning back to the north, though, he could see the faint outline of Naknamu as it towered above the earth. They were close enough to his ancestral home that they might even be able to walk the rest of the way . . . depending on how urgent his sister's situation was. If it was as bad as the hairs on the back of his neck seemed to indicate, a horse dropping dead from exhaustion would be a small price to pay to get them there on time.

Just as the thought to press on was taking root in his mind, something darker and much more powerful took its place.

Whatever it was, Yasha felt it too. She looked up at him with eyes of chaotic and cacophonous green that were wider than the gap between Athrani and Khyth. "What . . . what was that?" she breathed.

Kethras had an idea, but he hoped with all his might that he was wrong. The rational part of his mind, however, reminded him that he was right. "It's the barrier," he replied, his eyes still on Naknamu. "It's beginning to fade."

From behind him, he heard the slow but sturdy hoofbeats of Yasha's horse as it approached. "What barrier?" she asked, voice heavy with anticipation and dread.

Without looking back at her, he began to recall the painful and terrible memory of the last time he had seen his younger sister, Zhala, before her lust for power had driven her mad—and out of the forest of Kienar forever. "Have you ever wondered where the chovathi came from?"

The grass bent softly underfoot as Yasha slid from her horse. She walked up beside Kethras and shared his gaze toward Naknamu. "The elder Khyth always used to say that they were formed from the blood of the earth when they upended the mountains to make Khala Val'ur. It's why they hated us so much, they said: hatred was in their veins."

"That last part is certainly true," he said, and walked over to Yasha's horse. He unhooked the saddle and tossed it to the ground. Raising a hand to the horse's face, he caressed it, raising the creature's forehead to his own. After a silent moment he stepped back. The animal, clearly exhausted from the ride, gave a whinny of relief as it folded its legs beneath it and laid down on the ground.

Yasha looked at him in amazement.

"What did you do?"

Kethras smiled. "Come," he said. "I will tell you, but it must be on foot."

✦ ✦ ✦

The two of them hurried toward Naknamu, close enough to see yet far enough away that Kethras was yet to feel the power that emanated from the ancient forest he called home.

"When we were young," he began, "before the rift between the Shaper and Breaker, my mother stood as the gatekeeper between worlds—between gods and men, and between the living and the dead. It was a different world back then, and—sad to say—it was a better one, too. We Kienari lived among the humans in peace, and the selfishness of mankind had yet to mar the land. My brothers and sisters were many, and we walked among you." He looked over to Yasha and was quickly reminded of how different she was than the humans he talked about when he said 'you': her power-cracked skin was gray with streaks of black and orange running through it like a burning log. As a Khyth of the Breaking, Yasha was part of an elite subset of an already scarce population; she had touched the power of the Breaker and survived.

"I heard stories of the Kienari living outside of their forest," Yasha said as she walked beside him. Her smaller legs, relative to his own, were pumping hard against the ground to keep up with him. Kethras did his best not to smile at the sight. "But I thought they were just stories meant to keep children in line."

"Sadly, they were not," Kethras said, adjusting his pace by a tiny fraction to allow Yasha to keep up without passing out. "They were tales of how the world once was, before the corruption of the Breaker spread through every crack and crevice to turn brother against brother in the bloodiest war this world would ever see."

"Then what happened? What changed?"

The memory was a bitter recollection: more than the split between humans, Khyth, and Athrani; the split between Kienari and chovathi was closest to his heart. It was a tale that few knew because the shame of its truth was greater than the pain of its existence.

"Pride happened," he said, and he felt his lips curl down in a frown. "And my sister, Zhala, happened. She saw how quickly the power of the Breaker had spread. She thought that the power of our mother, the Binder of Worlds, could elevate us, the Kienari, above the humans that we were created to live amongst. She longed for it, for a separation, for something to set us apart. She sought it out . . . and she found it.

"The very power that pulses in the heart of Kienar is present in Zhala to this day: the interconnectedness of the forest; its existence as a single, living entity—it remains in her, unchanged . . . yet twisted into a state almost unrecognizable from what it once was."

Kethras heard Yasha's footsteps come to a sudden stop.

"Wait. Zhala? The chovathi matriarch . . . is your . . . sister?"

Kethras sighed and nodded.

Yasha cocked her head, like she was listening to something far away. "I'm not going to ask him that," she said in response to an invisible Miera, whose spirit was coexisting, inexplicably, inside her. "But I will ask him who put the barrier in place." She straightened her head, flicking her eyes back to Kethras like she expected an answer.

"My mother. The Binder. When she learned of Zhala's desire to separate the Kienari from humans, she knew that she no longer belonged in our forest. And, since she could not bring herself to imprison her daughter like she did the Breaker—in eternal captivity—she did the next best thing that she could."

Their footsteps through the grass were quick and firm. Yasha was doing a good job, short though her legs were, of keeping up with Kethras, who was nearly twice her height. He looked down at her and marveled for a moment at the fact that the spirit of the Shaper inhabited her body as well, knowing full well how impossible that fact was. In every other case that he knew of where a god chose a Vessel, he or she had burned away their host's essence completely, like a flame turning tinder to ash . . . but in Yasha's case, the tinder had just kept burning, almost like the flame wasn't even there. She existed—tinder and flame—in a balanced and perfect equilibrium. She was special, this one. Special—and powerful.

"The barrier," Yasha said hesitantly, "was never meant to be eternal?"

Kethras winced. "No. It was shortsighted and foolish, but merciful." The very words hurt him. "Sometimes mercy can punish the judge as much as the sentenced."

"Then what you're feeling now . . ." Yasha began.

"Is the barrier coming to an end," Kethras finished. "It has held all these years, across countless generations and for longer than most humans can measure time. But all things that are not eternal must one day cease—and I am afraid that time is now."

Chapter 63

Gal'dorok

Tennech

ON THE BACK OF THE winged gwarái, wind rushed past like a river. For a creature of her size, she was surprisingly aerodynamic. There were long stretches of time where her wings would not beat at all; she would just glide along, wings outstretched, like a sail atop the sea. Other times, though, it was like she had to fight to stay aloft—especially over mountains, it seemed. Tennech suspected that it had something to do with the weight and consistency of the air, but he knew next to nothing about flight. Besides watching the rock sparrows that lived in the craggy peaks of Gal'behem, he had no exposure at all to creatures of wing.

Riding, however, was something he was intimately familiar with, and this gwarái, huge though she was, was nothing more than a mount—a mount that, somehow, Venn exuded command over. Tennech looked up to see the Stoneborn fully out of his holder, saddled at the base of the creature's neck. The man certainly trusted the creature not to let him fall. Or, more likely, he didn't care if he did; Tennech had heard about his daring dive-bomb at the battle of Ghal Thurái. When death—true death—was no longer an imminent possibility, one tended to act with reckless abandon.

They'd been flying through the night, and Tennech found it incredibly difficult to get any bearing on where they were, or where they were headed. He knew that they were needed in Khala Val'ur, but something inside him told him that is not where they were bound . . . and that "something" was the voice of the Holder—the one to whom Tennech still owed a debt. The voice spoke in visions, and this latest one had been a series of the same images over and over: leaves—thousands of them, rippling in a breeze; a horde of hungry chovathi; soil; blood; steel. No matter how many times he shut his eyes and tried to fill his mind with some other image, the will of the Holder pushed itself right back in. It had been like that ever since the Holder had brought him back when their bargain was first struck. Tennech was now nothing more than a puppet, and the Lord of the Dead was pulling the strings.

Unstrapping himself and pulling free of the leather holster that held him down, Tennech reached out for handholds, finding them in the massive scales of the gwarái. Each teardrop-shaped scale was roughly the size of a human hand, and Tennech found that they were strong enough to hold onto. Looking forward, he realized that's how Venn had secured himself to the creature's neck: by slipping his hands between the large, sturdy scales, and hanging on. Tennech did the same, "climbing" his way forward, closer to Venn.

When he reached him, the Stoneborn looked back and smiled. "There's no better way to ride a gwarái," he began, "than the way the gods intended: with your bare hands!"

Up here, outside the comfort and safety of the holster that had secured him to the side of the creature, Tennech felt the dizzying realization that there was nothing more between him and a plummet to earth than a loose scale or two. His heart beat a little faster, a remnant of his former mortality. Even though he knew that a bodily death would not mean the end of Aldis Tennech, it was still a lot to contend with. He tightened his grip on the creature's scales.

"Does she have a name?" he called out. The air was still rushing by, but he found that if he pressed himself against her, it would flow over him instead of crashing into him like it had been—like water over a flattened stone.

Venn gave a quick laugh from up ahead, then craned his neck to look at Tennech. "Aye, she does—two, in fact. She's got the one that my men gave to her, and she's got the one that she was born with." He paused. "The one she was born with is the reason that she answers to me, so if you'll forgive me," he grinned, "I'll tell you the one that you can call her."

"That's reasonable."

"The first time the men saw her fly, they said she looked like a dagger flying through the air: sleek, deadly, and quick." He reached up and patted the creature gently on the neck, and she gave another "not purring sound" in response. "All they could do was point, and say, 'Udadi-hai, rata khajara.'" He glanced back at Tennech. "In Khôl it sounds a little rough, but it basically translates to, 'There flies the dagger of night.'"

Tennech gave an impressed nod. "Dagger of Night," he said, looking down at the creature of pure black. "It certainly fits."

"Aye, it does. Isn't that right, Khajara?"

At the sound of her own name, the winged gwarái gave a great, rumbling cry that shook Tennech to his core. Even from up here, thousands of feet off the ground, he swore that he could see the earth tremble.

Just then, the images from the Holder flashed in his mind again, more sharply than they ever had before. He knew what it meant.

He frowned and looked back up at the Stoneborn. "We need to change course, Venn."

The Stoneborn commander of the Lonely Guard gave him a quizzical look. "What? Why? We're headed right for Khala Val'ur."

"I know, and that's the problem. We need to alter our course to the northwest."

"Northwest?" His eyes narrowed. "Are you sure?"

Tennech nodded. "I am."

"What reason could we possibly . . ." Venn began, but his words trailed off as the realization struck him.

Tennech, knowing the commander would only be satisfied with the truth, spoke it aloud. "The forest of Kienar. The Binder of Worlds. The chovathi matriarch," he said. "And something else—something big that I can't quite discern. It's out there, among the trees. And it's hungry."

Venn was silent.

After some hesitation, he reached his hand forward, giving a slow series of taps on Khajara's scales. The creature responded with a shrill cry of acknowledgment, and Tennech felt the great beast shift slightly, dipping her body to the right and turning toward what he assumed was a northwesterly heading.

"It's done," Venn said. "Kienar is a little further than Khala Val'ur, so we will have to stop to rest along the way for Khajara to gather her strength, but it won't be long."

"Can we reach it by dawn?"

Venn furrowed his eyebrows and looked up in mental calculation. After some thought, he nodded. "Aye. By dawn."

"Good," Tennech replied. "We are sorely needed, and every moment we spend not moving toward Kienar is a moment wasted."

"She'll get us there," Venn said, turning to pat Khajara on the neck. "Won't you, girl?" The gwarái gave a short, rumbling growl. Venn flashed a smile back at Tennech. "Lucky for you, she listens to me."

"Lucky indeed."

Venn faced forward again and continued to watch the ground as it sailed beneath them, a blur of jagged lines and twisted shapes.

Heading back to the security of his makeshift saddle, Tennech paused for a moment, and turned. "Venn," he called, and the commander looked back one more time. "Thank you."

A smile came over the bearded warrior from Lash'Kargá. "Anything for the Dagger of Derenar."

Tennech gave a wry laugh. Two daggers, soaring through the air, on a collision course with Kienar. He only hoped that, when they landed, each of them would find their marks.

Chapter 64

Kienar

D. C. Jennings

Ynara

YNARA HAD SPENT THE LAST few hours between waking and dream; nothing was real anymore. Reality seemed to shift and break, crumbling to pieces before her, only to reassemble again before her eyes.

Her exiled "sister," Zhala, had returned with blood on her breath and conquest in her heart, stalking through the woods like a tiger. At times, Ynara could have sworn that she saw chovathi breaking through the barrier. More than once she had seen herself—felt herself—being swarmed by the pale-skinned creatures. She could feel their teeth on her flesh as they sunk in, meeting no resistance, like stakes pushed into softened earth. She screamed . . . and the next moment they were gone.

She felt her arms in a panic. No blood. No teeth marks.

. . . And then suddenly teeth marks would appear—only to fade again like they were never there. The whole thing was like a fever dream that came and went.

Maintaining the integrity of the barrier was taking a toll on her, and she wasn't sure how much longer she could maintain it. It was already taking all her strength—and the forest's strength—to keep it in place. The power that was present at the beginning of time, the beginning of creation, had found its way into the body of Ynara, passed down by her mother. But all power has a limit—even that which shaped the worlds.

"I can feel your life force waning," Zhala shouted from the dark. "How much longer do you think it will hold? How much longer will you hold?"

Ynara knew the answer. Both of them did: not long.

✦ ✦ ✦

In order to keep her focus, Ynara had to block out all distractions from the outside world. She shut her eyes tightly and blocked out all sound—but doing so took as much a strain on her body as it did on her mind. It was like trying to hold a fist for hours at a time. She could feel the fatigue setting in and had to take breaks in order to replenish her already diminishing strength—and each time she would gather her strength, the chovathi would gather theirs. It felt like, for every one step she took forward, she was being pushed back by another two.

She was resting now and could feel the barrier weakening with every breath that she took. She almost wondered if it was worth it, this break for her body. It meant that she could hold out for longer, but to what end? She sent her mind out to the edges of her forest, probing, seeking. Was anyone out there? Did anyone hear her plea?

Was it the Binder's fate to die alone? The very thought made her flinch.

No, she thought, steeling herself. *While I still hold breath, I will not surrender.*

She closed her eyes again, gathering her will, summoning her strength, pushing it out into the forest, to the invisible barrier that the Binder had erected after Zhala's expulsion.

There, Ynara said, finding again the familiar feel. With invisible fingers she combed over it, soothing it like a frightened child. It was beaten, broken—like she was—but it was still there, and holding firm. No chovathi had breeched its protection. Not yet, anyway.

✦ ✦ ✦

The pushing became greater. With every violent thrust of the chovathi against the barrier, Ynara felt her body reeling back in anguish. It was like she had exhausted all her strength on trying to push a boulder uphill, only to have it roll right back on top of her. She felt the crushing weight, the violence of inevitability—yet she stood firm.

I... will not... surrender.

She repeated the mantra in her mind, forcing her focus to the edge of the forest. It felt like a thousand burning raindrops colliding with her skin.

"Not much longer now, sister," Zhala taunted. "You and I both know it. Soon your barrier will fall, and the passage to the Otherworld will be mine."

A chill ran down Ynara's spine. Here she had thought Zhala's sole aim had been to reclaim the forest that she once called home; this new revelation was much, much worse.

"You . . . can't," she gasped, struggling to even get the words out.

"I can, and I will. And with the power of the Otherworld at my disposal, creation itself will tremble at my strength."

Unbidden in Ynara's mind came images of which Zhala spoke: images of death; of endless, countless dead throughout the world. In every city in every land, chovathi burst forth from the ground, covering the earth like a plague. The skies darkened as the teeming white masses grew and grew.

The ends of the earth. Now Ynara had seen it herself.

She swallowed hard. With every moment that passed, Zhala's power grew—and Ynara's was a candle that had burned down to the wick; nothing remained but the leftover wax and a bit of string. Her strength was fading. Her light was dimming.

All around her, she felt the barrier weakening, groaning. Straining. Dying.

She felt it falter.

She felt . . .

Thwip!

It was a tearing sensation. She looked up with bleary eyes, unfocused.

Thwip-thwip!

Twice more the feeling of tearing, and the pressure on the barrier almost seemed to lessen for a moment.

Suddenly, a voice came from somewhere in the dark. "There's too many of them! I've never seen this many before."

Ynara was doing her best to focus her eyesight through the

pain-wracked effort of maintaining the barrier, but she didn't need her eyes to tell her what she already knew. Hope was out there, and its name was . . .

"Kethras!" she cried. She heard the sound leave her mouth, but she didn't even recognize her own voice. It was weak, desperate. Broken.

"I'm here," he called back. His voice, on the other hand, was strong and foreboding, rumbling like a landslide—everything that she needed him to be right now.

Ynara was about to call out again but stopped; the warm sensation that she felt spreading through her mind and her body was unmistakeable. Here, on the outskirts of her forest, was the fragmented, missing piece of power that the Binder of Worlds wielded. Once, she knew, it had been whole . . . but the Breaker of the Dawn, in his careless audacity, had splintered it apart and cast it out, like three pieces of a sword—hilt, crossguard, and blade—spread to the corners of the world.

But here, now, the blade had found the hilt.

"Ynara, can you hear me?" Strange. It was the Shaper's power she felt—there was no question about that—but it was not her voice. It was . . . someone else's. It was a voice she knew, though not well. It belonged . . . to the young Khyth girl! "Ynara!" Yasha called again.

This time, she answered. "I hear you," she said weakly. "I'm here."

Ynara felt a surge of strength course through her as the power of the Shaper of Ages flooded in; it was like opening the doors of a raging furnace. The power that shaped the world was once again finding its footing.

"We're going to try to work our way to you. Can you hold the barrier?"

Ynara was, at this point, fighting just to remain conscious. "I—I can try."

"That is all I ask."

With great mental effort, Ynara exerted her will over the barrier once again, gritting her teeth and heaving. Her color vision began to dim as the world around her faded, sapping her strength—but empowering the barrier.

"Hang on," Ynara muttered to herself. "Hang on."

Her power was a tightly woven rope, stretched to its limits. One by one, strands of it had been frayed and broken by the strain, leaving precious few remaining. Now, those few strands were being tested to their absolute limit.

She felt a trickle of blood from her nose but ignored it. The barrier was all that mattered. The Shaper was close. Kethras was close.

"Hang on."

Snap. Another strand was tested and broken.

Snap. Another. Another.

"Hang..." *Snap.* "On."

Dimly, Ynara was aware of the struggle going on before her. She saw the form of the young Khyth girl, steeped in the power of the Shaper, felling chovathi like gnats as she waded through to the forest.

Snap.

The white forms of countless chovathi swarmed over the Shaper, the beacon of eternal power who formed the very stars they stood beneath. Wave after wave of creatures tossed themselves at her, hoping to overwhelm her with numbers and brute force.

Snap.

Ynara felt herself being pushed to the brink of spiritual and physical exhaustion.

"Shaper," she cried weakly. The word came out as no more than a whimper. "Guide me."

Snap.

Ynara felt her consciousness give way. Her rope had broken; the barrier, breached. Strangely, though, she did not feel fear. What she felt was more like . . . relief.

Relief to be finally able to rest—or, oh, she was so tired. To sleep. To dream.

To die.

Ynara slumped to the ground. Strength flowed forth from the body of Ynara Once-Binder, abandoning breath and life as the whole of Kienar surged with fading might. In anger and sadness, it trembled. Lost, broken. Afraid. Its protector lay still, its barrier shattered.

The mantle of Binder—the power of the gods of creation—was forfeit.

. . . And that power, rising again, made its way to the Vessel that it had always been destined for.

The Binder of Worlds—the Last Kienari—Kethras. Now—under the watchful eye of the Shaper of Ages, in the forest of Kienar—they were one and the same.

The earth trembled . . . and so did the chovathi.

Chapter 65

Khala Val'ur

Yetz

"THEY'VE BREACHED THE WALLS!"

The shout came from an approaching runner, voice lined with panic. It was not the voice of a battle-seasoned warrior; it was the voice of a man who had been thrust into a conflict with no discernible way out—none, save desperation. Yetz turned to his assembly of Master Khyth.

"Kostas, Caledeus, we can wait no longer. I am counting on you two to keep them at bay as long as possible. I know that you know your roles. I will delegate nothing further."

The two Master Khyth nodded and immediately began preparations for battle.

Kostas pushed back the sleeves of his robe, and Caledeus closed his eyes in a meditative stance. Every Khyth draws upon his power in different ways, and the contrast in the two styles made Yetz pause in appreciation. When the time came that the first of the pale-skinned terrors lumbered into the open valley where they now stood, they would be met with the full fury of two Master Khyth.

"The four of you," Yetz said to the others, "come with me," and he began his walk toward the mouth of the Sunken City.

+ + +

The five Khyth were gathered at the cavernous entrance to the depths of Khala Val'ur, spread out like points on a star. Yetz was the furthest point in, facing out.

"Each of you," he said to his men, "have distinguished yourself in service to the Breaker, not only by surviving the ritual of your own Breaking, but by training young apprentices in their service to Him as well. For that, I have no doubt that you will be rewarded in the next life—and after today, I have little doubt that we will see those rewards sooner rather than later." He paused and looked at each of them individually before speaking again. "It is all we can do to forestall the inevitable—but in doing so, we will secure victory."

Victory for whom, exactly, was purposefully omitted.

The sounds of combat continued to grow ever closer. At this range, however, the clear difference could be heard between shouts of intimidation and screams of terror—and there were increasingly fewer of the former than there were of the latter. The chovathi were bred for destruction, and they were sowing it freely upon the warriors of Khala Val'ur. Freely, that is, until they came face to face with Master Khyth. Yetz looked on in admiration of their handiwork as the two of them met the horde head-on.

Caledeus, eyes blazing with furious might, had lifted a boulder off the ground with his Breaking and ripped it apart into hundreds of jagged projectiles. He stalked toward the chovathi, encircled by his spinning dome of death, and one by one commanded the spears of rock through the necks of the encroaching creatures.

Behind him, Kostas had reached back into the brazier for a weapon of his own, gathering the flames like a coat of orange that swirled menacingly around him. He moved his hands in a practiced flourish that sent the flame rising to the heavens, growing and twisting as it did, going from a flame of dull cherry red to a column of blazing hot white. The Master Khyth surged forward, surrounded by the hellish tornado, and the errant chovathi that were not taken down by Caledeus's spears were incinerated, one by one, by the flames of Kostas.

The two of them would stem the tide—but would not stop it completely. That was *his* job. Yetz turned his attention back to the Master Khyth gathered before him. "Our time is now," he said, as he felt the weight of responsibility settle onto his shoulders. "Our predecessors left us with a monument to their greatness in the Sunken City itself—and now it is our turn to leave our mark on the world as well."

With that, he raised his hands in the air and the others followed suit. Each Master Khyth was to be a conduit for the power of the Breaker, and each point on the star was a focus. As the power ran through one, it would be redirected back toward the others, fourfold, in a feedback loop that would see the power build, and build, and build. Yetz quieted his mind—and as he did so, he felt the first sparks of power as they winked into existence.

So it began.

Touching power had always been easy for Yetz. In most men, there was always an initial resistance to it where one's body tends to fight back, like touching a hot stove; Yetz was not born with that reflex, though, which is why, to him, it was so easy to embrace the power of Breaking. His own Breaking ritual had been less of a test of endurance and more of a test of will. Could he hold his hand to the flame long enough? Could he do what it would take to feel the full power of the Breaker? He had little doubt that his body would survive . . . but would his mind? Most found themselves either dead or mad from the sudden and violent influx of the full power of the Otherworld, consumed, like parchment over a flame.

But then again, he was not like most—in more ways than one.

"More yet come!" shouted Caledeus from outside. Before them, scores of chovathi poured in from the gap, with Caledeus and Kostas there to greet them. Piles of pale, headless bodies laid on a ground covered in ash—a testament to the skill of these two Masters.

"Then let's give them a warm welcome," Kostas shouted in return.

The retort gave Yetz a fleeting grin, yet he knew that the chovathi's power lay in numbers. These foot soldiers were just the tip of a frightfully sharpened spear, set to strike at the very heart of Khala Val'ur. And they would never stop coming—ever.

No two Master Khyth could ever stop an army of chovathi. Perhaps five could, though.

"Focus, Masters," Yetz said, turning his attention back inside. He could feel beads of sweat starting to appear on his forehead. "It will only grow more difficult from here."

The power of Breaking swelled among them, magnified by each Master and fed back into the others in a dizzying orchestration. The chovathi were clawing their way in, the outer wall of men having been completely overrun. Only Kostas and Caledeus stood in their way now. Yetz knew he was watching the last stand of Khala Val'ur.

"Focus, and hold," he reiterated. The beads of sweat on his forehead multiplied as his blood ran hot, filled with fire. The trickle of power that had started between them had now turned into a stream. Before long it would be a torrent.

Yetz intended to use that torrent to break the world.

Chapter 66

Kienar

Kethras

THE STRENGTH OF THE BINDER of Worlds burned as it enveloped Kethras, and he dropped to his knees at the weight of unbearable power. Eternity permeated his mind, and the cosmos unfolded before him. He saw his sister and his mother—both of whom once held the mantle of Binder—as the lifelines of their existence raced backward, to the beginning of time. Stars collapsed in on themselves; the universe shrunk; life, in its entirety, was reduced to the single thought of three deities.

Kethras retched and vomited. He felt the hand of Elyasha rub him gently on the back.

"I know," she said softly. "It's a lot to take in. You did better than most Vessels, if I'm being honest. This one got sick four times before she finally got her head right."

Kethras wiped his mouth and looked up at Yasha—and nearly fell over again at what he saw. It was the body of the Khyth girl—but enveloping her like a cloak was the ghostly form of the Shaper of Ages.

Suddenly, a rumbling came from the distance. "Zhala," Kethras growled.

From the corner of his eye he saw Yasha's hand, outstretched and waiting for him. "The barrier?" she asked as she helped him up.

"Gone."

"Then we don't have any time to waste."

Yasha's body was draped in an otherworldly glow. Kethras had to shield his eyes; it was like looking at an eclipse. He turned to Naknamu, where he knew that Zhala and her brood would be headed.

"We have to get to the Tree," he said. "We can't let her set foot inside that gate. I've seen what will happen if she harnesses the power of the Otherworld."

"I have, as well," said the Shaper. Her voice, to Kethras's mind, was the perfect fusion of Yasha and Miera's, with a ghostly echo that trailed behind. "Let's make sure that doesn't happen."

Kethras nodded and unstrapped his bow. Beside him, the form of Elyasha was blazing with an effulgent glow that grew brighter and stronger with each step she took. Kethras had to shield his eyes once again as her feet left the ground.

Rising into the sky like the sun, the voice of the Shaper of Ages was thunder. "Zhala, daughter of light, bringer of dark, heed my words: today you will fail, and the chovathi line will end."

By now, she had risen higher up than all the other trees in the forest, but Kethras still had to protect his eyes when he looked at her. Her blazing light had turned the dark night of the forest into broad daylight.

The next sound that he heard, though, made him swirl his head back around toward the heart of the forest. Zhala's voice, stronger than he had ever heard it before, pierced the air.

"Come and try." The rumbling of the matriarch's words was followed by a similar quaking, the source of which Kethras immediately knew.

Chovathi.

They burst forth from the ground on all sides, surrounding him. There were dozens—maybe hundreds—and they were hungry. They closed in.

Instinctively Kethras reached for his bow, but something in the back of his mind made him stop. Dropping it to the ground, he said a silent thank you to his mother and his sister, both of whom had sacrificed their lives and their power for this moment in time: for him to lay claim to the power of the Binder of Worlds—and, in doing so, securing the future of the very world they swore to protect. Somewhere, in that vast and overwhelming influx of understanding that had come with inheriting the mantle of Binder, was the very knowledge he sought. The darkened corners of his mind lit up, infused with new strength as he searched. His mind was a forest, and somewhere in the middle of it was one tree that held the answer. Before he found it, though, the first of the chovathi were upon him. He felt claws dig into him.

Faster than he could think, Kethras had drawn his twin daggers and brought up one to the throat of the creature. His newfound strength surprised even him as his blade burst out the back of the chovathi's neck to take the head clean off. The white, headless body crumpled to the ground in a heap. He knew one thing about fighting chovathi: land a killing blow, or don't land one at all. He had to be lethal to a fault.

Come on. Where are you? Kethras thought in frustration as he whirled around, daggers gleaming in the moonlight. It was like being handed a treasure map with no compass, orientation, or scale. He knew that the prize was there; he just had to find it.

He kept digging as another chovathi slashed at him; he felt the blood rush to the surface where the creature's claws dug in. A second set of claws from another chovathi came in. He dodged and slashed, but pulled back at the last second, seeing the blade almost land errantly. It would have meant spawning another chovathi and, even if it would have been a minute or two later, he could not afford to make the enemy stronger. There were already too many of them, and too few of him.

He tried to focus inward, to grasp the power of the Binder. He let his body take over. Instinct drove him. He focused on his senses—smell, touch, hearing — to "feel" where the chovathi were. His hands flew on their own, landing right where they needed to, slashing, biting, cutting. His body, after centuries of training, knew just what to do. On his own he was a lethal killing machine; with the power of the Binder he had the potential to be much, much more. But there was still the problem of fully accessing the power of the Binder.

He danced and swayed, dodged and thrust, feinted and parried.

I know you are in there. Reveal yourself!

His anger turned to pain as chovathi claws raked down his back. Along with it, Kethras felt something that he had not felt in a long time—fear—as clawed hands grabbed him from behind and pulled him down. He tried to twist out of the way, but was immediately met by more, pulling him to the ground.

Jagged teeth bit at his flesh, and razor-sharp claws tore at him down to the bone. Sharp pain shot through him as his vision began to go dark. They were on him like jackals on a carcass.

His mind went to the pain. He was losing blood—a lot of it. He coughed, choking. The agony was almost too much to bear. He was being ripped apart.

Blackness seeped in. The world around him began to go silent, cold. He never screamed though—not once. Not a single time. He simply stilled his thoughts, and . . .

✦ ✦ ✦

Miera

THIS CLOSE TO THE OTHERWORLD, Miera felt her full power returning.

Just beyond her lay the path to the realm of the gods, carved beneath the surface of Naknamu, throne room of the Binder of Worlds. Miera's host body was overflowing with strength. Yasha had already been a powerful Khyth of the Breaking before Miera had chosen her as her Vessel—and now, with the spirit of a goddess inside her, that power was pushed to near-cosmic capacity. She scanned the surface of the forest below her. All around, dotting the landscape like a million grains of rice, were the chovathi.

Miera, however, was only looking for one of them.

There.

Lumbering toward Naknamu at a thundering pace was the great behemoth Zhala. While Miera knew that chovathi walked upright but ran on all fours, it was still incredible to watch a creature of her size move so swiftly, like a wolf chasing prey.

A mere thought sent Miera hurtling toward her, with the power of the Shaper now seeping through every pore of the Khyth who acted as her Vessel. She felt it as it awakened, like blood returning to a limb numb from disuse.

Miera slammed into the ground about a hundred feet in front of Zhala, who skidded to a halt mid-stride. The matriarch gave a grunt of annoyance, and gathered herself up to her full height, brushing away branches and breaking off tree limbs in the process. She stopped and glanced down, her broad shoulders towering above the treetops.

"So, Shaper." Her words came out in a menacing growl. "You think you will succeed where my sister failed? Even the Binder of Worlds, in the heart of her forest, was not enough to stop the might of the chovathi."

The words stirred up a sharpness inside Miera, which she had not previously known was there. She floated up into the air until she was even with Zhala's sight line. Barely the size of one of the chovathi's eyes, Miera certainly felt small—but the power that welled up inside her urged her onward.

"I don't have to stop you," she said. "I just have to slow you down."

"Slow me down?" Zhala laughed; the forest shook. "You? You're a gnat! An insignificant speck. I could crush you right now and not even give it a second thought. What could even stand in my way between me and your precious tree?"

"Kethras," Miera said as she crossed her arms. "The Binder of Worlds."

Zhala's eyes narrowed . . . and she threw her head back in laughter again. "You don't know, do you?" she said, when her laughing had finally ceased. "Even as we speak, my broodlings are feasting on his flesh. I can taste his blood in their mouths." She cocked her head in thought. "It is . . . almost sweet. Aged, like a fine wine. Fitting, given that he was the oldest of us."

The blood drained from Miera's face as she reached out to grasp at the twin of her own power. It was like groping around in the dark. She brought her hands up to cover her mouth as she suddenly felt heavy. *Very* heavy.

"You can feel it, can't you?" Zhala began. "The power slipping away. Soon, nothing will be left of the first son of Kienar, and all that will stand between me and the Otherworld is a broken shell of a tiny god."

Miera trembled as she hung in the air. Stand and fight or leave and save her friend: these were Miera's only options.

"If you're thinking of going to him, I would hurry," Zhala said through her teeth, "before there is nothing left."

Miera could only watch in frozen horror as Zhala lumbered past, her great white form drawing closer and closer to Naknamu—closer to the entrance to the Otherworld.

As the first light of dawn illuminated the sky overhead, though, a shadow stretched across the world. The first of the Athrani arrows began to fall.

Chapter 67

Khala Val'ur

Kunas

THE SMELL OF BLOOD HUNG in the air over the battlefields of Khala
Val'ur as Kunas's chovathi horde continued their slaughter of men. The
goal of annihilation grew ever closer—the first step in reclaiming the old
world in favor of the new. Now, all that was left was the handful of Khyth
who defended the heart, and Kunas was determined to throw everything
he had at them in pursuit of this goal—down to the last chovathi, should
it come to it. He focused his thoughts inward, and pushed them out to
the horde, making his will theirs.

*The human soldiers are of no concern to us now. All that matters is
defeating the Khyth.*

He felt a shift in the awareness of his chovathi, who turned their attention to the seven figures standing between them and the entrance to
the city. Two of those figures had been masterfully and mercilessly defending the other five, who seemed to be doing little more than standing there. A feeling in the back of Kunas's mind—no more than a tingle
of instinct—told him that they were doing more than that, but it was
impossible to say just what. He did, however, feel a great deal of power
among them. If they were waiting for something, Kunas could not see
them waiting much longer. He pushed out a signal of urgency to the in-
terconnected minds of his brethren.

The chovathi descended, snarling and bloodthirsty.

+ + +

Yetz

THE POWER OF BREAKING BURNED like the sun; it's heat and intensity were nearly too much to contain. No mortal should have been able
to wield such power; it was only the combined might of the five Masters
that kept it in check. Even Yetz, as powerful as he was, struggled with

the task.

There was no going back now. The power that they had gathered had to be released or redirected—anything else would be cataclysmic.

They were nearly there.

There was just one problem.

✦ ✦ ✦

Kunas

OVERWHELM THEM! KUNAS COMMANDED TO his troops. *Hold nothing back!*

In response, every living chovathi warrior descended on the mouth of Khala Val'ur like a swarm. Victory was now so close that he could taste it. It tasted of blood.

As he traversed the mountain path that led to the city, Kunas smiled at the carnage that his warriors had strewn: bodies in armor—from chain mail to full plate—lined the path. The defenders of the city had been slain where they stood, some still even clutching their weapons. No mercy was given, and no survivors were left.

You have done well, my warriors, he began. *Zhala will reward you, so long as you carry out her will, down to the last man.*

The last man, he mused, smiling to himself. It turns out that the so-called last man was, in fact, a Khyth.

✦ ✦ ✦

He rounded a bend in the path and suddenly knew that he was close: a part of his consciousness recognized it. He had trodden the path before, in fact—but that was in a former life: before he had become . . . what he became. Before Zhala; before real, true power.

A noise to the left of him caught his attention, and he stopped.

It was a voice, almost too weak to make out, and he wondered for a

369

moment if he had even heard it at all. He looked around, trying to discover its source.

That was when he saw it, lying on the ground in a pool of blood: a man in full plate looking back at him, sword in hand. Kunas recognized him. *LaVince,* said a voice in the back of his mind.

He approached, kneeling in order to look the man in the face—and as he did, he saw movement out of the corner of his eye. It was the man, attempting to raise his sword. In his weakened state, however, LaVince wasn't nearly quick enough to catch him off guard, and Kunas swatted the weapon away like a fly. The blade clanged as it hit the ground.

"A fighter to the end," Kunas mocked. "What a shame that your effort is wasted."

He was breathing on the man's face, who winced as it hit him.

"You'll ... never ... succeed," LaVince choked. His voice was strained and broken, a near whisper.

In contrast, Kunas's words rumbled out like a landslide. "And just what makes you say that?" he asked with a toothy grin.

"Yetz ... will never ... allow it," LaVince said between breaths. "He'll fight ... to the end ... or bring ... this whole place ... down."

Kunas gave a guttural chuckle, and stuck out a long, bony finger. His razor-sharp fingernail grazed LaVine's cheek. "Yetz could stop me no more than you could stop Yetz, you insignificant speck," he began, and ran his fingernail down LaVince's cheek, leaving a trail of crimson behind. The soldier winced but said nothing. "Even as we speak, my chovathi are bearing down on him and his men, the last bastion of hope for your people."

He pulled the finger back and brought it to his own mouth, placing it on his tongue to get a taste of the man's blood. It was sweet. He smiled in satisfaction.

LaVince said nothing, turning his head to spit on the ground. "Damn you ... and ... your horde," he wheezed. "Holder ... take ... you all."

Kunas laughed again, moving his face even close to LaVince. The man's pupils dilated in fear. "The Holder?" he scoffed. "When we're done, even he will answer to us."

LaVince looked like he was about to speak when a coughing fit took him, staining his armor with flecks of blood and spittle.

Kunas stood up and looked at the sword that he'd swatted away. He considered its edge and looked back to LaVince. "Speaking of whom," he said, reaching down to pick it up, "send him my regards."

LaVince's eyes went wide as Kunas lunged, driving the blade into his stomach all the way down to the hilt. The stench of death mingled with blood, piss, and fear. LaVince's jaw went slack. He looked out, eyes glazed, unmoving. They closed.

His breathing ceased.

Kunas pulled the sword back out, its blade streaked deep red. Up ahead, his warriors were closing in on the seven figures who stood in defiance of Zhala's will; beneath him, a death rattle sounded in LaVince's throat.

Kunas would see to it personally that these Khyth met their end, and his matriarch would be well and truly pleased.

He smiled in anticipation and walked on.

Chapter 68

Kienar

Tennech

DAWN WAS APPROACHING, AND THE wings of the gwarái beat as steadily as the sun rose.

As they drew closer and closer, Tennech saw flashes of light coming from the ancient forest of Kienar. He was on the back of Khajara, and he shouted for Cortus Venn, who was in his usual place on the gwarái's neck.

"Did you see that?" he asked.

"Aye."

"What do you think it is?"

"I was hoping you might know."

Tennech frowned. It was a clear morning with no thunderclouds in sight, so he knew it wasn't lightning. Whatever it was, it was powerful— and most likely not of this world. "We should approach with caution," he warned.

Venn turned, a look of recklessness in his eyes and his grin. "What, and spoil the fun?"

Tennech gave his best attempt at stern disapproval—the kind he used to give Sera when she skipped out on her riding lessons. It did not seem to have the same effect on Venn. He held it nonetheless.

"Bah, fine," Venn relented. "Have it your way." He moved his left hand under the neck of Khajara and gave a few quick pats followed by a pattern of motion with his palm. The nonverbal communication clearly meant something to the gwarái, who began to fly noticeably slower— and quieter. She was gliding now, flapping her wings only once or twice a minute as they descended.

"There," Tennech said, and pointed to a clearing on the edge of the forest. "Take us down there."

Venn looked where Tennech was pointing and nodded, giving Khajara another series of nonverbal gestures. The great gwarái responded by giving a low, rumbling assent.

✦ ✦ ✦

Stepping down from Khajara, Tennech had an uneasy feeling as he set foot in the forest of Kienar for the first time since Sera was nearly killed. He'd been in almost this same spot back then, showing around a hapless Caladan Durakas—who met an unfortunate and arrow-filled end on the forest floor. *Well . . . unfortunate for him,* Tennech mused—it had certainly been a stroke of good luck for Duna, who shortly thereafter found herself Queen regnant of Haidan Shar.

"So? What do you think?"

Tennech was surprised by the words from Venn, who had snuck up soundlessly behind him.

"About?"

"Our ingress," Venn replied. "You have more experience in these woods than I do."

Tennech scanned the tree line. It was unlikely that any waiting Kienari would attack them on sight, as they most likely had bigger problems to worry about—namely, the chovathi. Turning to Venn, he said, "I think our best bet is the direct route: we make our way as best we can toward Naknamu as a single file. The enemy should be preoccupied and therefore will not be expecting us." Looking back at the tree line, he added, "I hope."

Venn smashed a fist into his palm. "I'm ready for whatever they'll throw at me."

Tennech didn't have to see the look on his face to know that the Stoneborn meant it. "Gather the others, then. I have a few things I'd like to say."

Venn gave a silent nod of agreement and walked off toward the rest of the contingent. After a few moments, they were all gathered before him.

Tennech was trying his best to give them a reassuring look, but he wasn't sure how well he was doing. He wasn't used to commanded novice troops: all his soldiers—man and woman alike—had always been hand picked because they were the best. It had been a long, long time since he'd had to lead amateurs. In fact, the last amateur he had to train was . . . Sera? He smiled to himself—and again at the next thought: the person among them with the most combat experience?

Benj.

His son. The thought brought true warmth to the smile on his face.

"So the rumors are true," Venn said, shaking him out of his daydream. "Combat does strange things to the Dagger of Derenar."

Tennech shot him a look, turning back to address his troops. "I want to start by stating the obvious," he began. "You were not forced to be here. You did not have a knife held at your throat to become Stoneborn. You didn't climb aboard the gwarái under duress. Are these things all true?" He had been looking at the new Stoneborn, who all nodded in unison, but saw that Benj was nodding as well. This was not just their fight, Tennech had to remind himself—it was his, as well. "Then on that we agree," Tennech went on. "And those facts are important because we are not fighting for just ourselves. Remember this as you charge into battle: this fight is not for us, but for every man and woman who lives, breathes, and bleeds." Looking back at Venn, he added, "And even some who do not."

The commander flashed a toothy grin.

"This was never about individuals," Tennech went on, holding up a finger to emphasize his point. "Not about Haidan Shar, Ghal Thurái, not even Gal'dorok. This is about a menace that threatens us all, and everything we hold dear." He clasped his hands behind his back and looked at the four Stoneborn, locking eyes with the one on the left. "Are you prepared to fight to defend us all?"

The man nodded.

Tennech moved his eyes to the second one, a woman. "And you?"

She gave a nod as well.

The third, another woman. "And you?"

Another nod.

The fourth, a man. "And you," he said, more statement than question. A nod, slow and deliberate.

Finally, he looked at Benj. He didn't even get a chance to ask the question.

"I'm ready," he affirmed.

Tennech put a hand on his shoulder and gave him a smile. "Then we are all in agreement," he said. Looking back at the rest of them, he said, "I, too, am prepared to fight and die—once again, if need be—for the protection of everyone who draws breath . . . and all those who ever will after us, long after we have become dust."

"Then what are we waiting for?" Venn asked, stepping forward. "I can almost feel myself turning into dust already."

Benj snickered.

"You know," Tennech said as he looked at Venn, "I hear Gal'dorok is looking for a general. I can pull some strings for you after this is all over."

Venn pulled out his sword. "Do I get to kill chovathi?"

"If there are any left."

Venn grinned. "Then let's get started on these."

✦ ✦ ✦

Tennech led the way through the forest, with Venn following close behind. The four Stoneborn followed him, and Benj brought up the rear.

They moved silently, using hand signals to communicate, in the hopes that it would allow them to get as close as possible to the chovathi before being detected. Stoneborn, as Tennech understood it, had no detectable scent to the creatures, which is part of what made them so deadly. Stealth was their strongest ally; surprise, their greatest weapon.

What they did with that weapon when faced with chovathi, however, remained to be seen.

They had been making their way toward the heart of the forest for nearly an hour, by Tennech's reckoning, and there were still no signs of the invaders. He wondered if they were too early—or, worse, too late. Just as he was beginning to question whether they should turn back, another flash of light came from up ahead—the same flash that he had seen before from the air.

He tapped Venn on the shoulder and signed to him: two fingers pointing at his own eyes, one finger pointing in the direction of the light.

Look. There.

Venn signed back: tapping his ear, moving his hand back and forth. Tapping his eye, moving his hand back and forth.

Hear. Nothing. See. Nothing.

Tennech spread out his fingers and pushed them down in a sign that meant "wait here" and made his way through the tall grass toward the source of the light.

After nearly a minute of crouched walking, and covering a good distance, he came to a clearing—and nearly fell over at what he saw.

There, in the middle of the forest of Kienar, were nearly two dozen chovathi. Their numbers weren't what alarmed him, though—it was what they were doing: they looked to be mobbing a single, dark figure.

Tennech's eyes widened as soon as he realized what the figure was: a Kienari.

He whirled around toward the others. With one finger in he air, he made a circle and emphatically pointed to himself, repeating the action over and over again to both signify urgency and to make sure they understood: *Rally on me. Now.*

As soon as he saw movement from them it was good enough to let him know that they'd seen his signal. He put his hand on the hilt of his sword and drew it. Standing up, he dashed from the tree line toward the mob of chovathi. His lips curled into a smile as a single thought entered his mind: *Just like old times.*

And, just like that, the Dagger of Derenar had been unsheathed.

✦ ✦ ✦

Kethras

. . . REACHED INSIDE FOR A LAST, desperate grasp. The burning throughout his body told him that he'd found it. The power of the Binder of Worlds, finally, was his to command. For how long, though, was Kethras's prime worry. His body—that frail outer shell—was being ravaged by the fangs and claws of chovathi. His spirit was still intact, but he knew that one could not exist without the other. His sister and his mother had both proven that. He needed to hang on—for them, and for Kienar.

He opened his eyes again to see the face of a chovathi staring him down, mouth open, exposing the razor-sharp fangs that had shredded his flesh to ribbons. As the creature looked at him hungrily, it suddenly seemed to stop, eyes glazing over. An ear-piercing shriek stopped as soon as it had started as the chovathi's head separated from its body. Suddenly the feeling of claws and fangs on Kethras ceased, and the creatures surrounding them turned their attention to something he couldn't see. Whatever it was, its presence was sending the creatures into a frenzy.

The taste of blood filled Kethras's throat and he still had trouble breathing . . . and an odd, tingling sensation began to fill him. It started with his back and worked its way up to his chest, which was facing the sky. It felt like bleeding, but . . . in reverse. He couldn't make any sense of it until he looked down at his ribs, where his wounds felt the worst, and saw nothing but green around him. He blinked a few times to clear his vision, and that was when he realized: the forest itself was tending to his wounds. It was healing him!

His eyes drooped closed again. His loss of blood was severe—he was surprised that he wasn't dead, in fact—and hanging on to consciousness took a greater toll on him than he was comfortable with. With the healing sensation of the forest spreading throughout him, he let his eyes close completely, allowing himself to be swallowed by the darkness. It felt like being lowered into a warm bath. It was good. It was right.

This, he thought as his mind went dark, *is the power of the Binder of Worlds.*

✦ ✦ ✦

Tennech

IT WAS JUST LIKE RIDING a horse. Killing chovathi was the one thing that Tennech excelled at and would be his legacy on the world—and for good reason: no living being had a greater chovathi head count than the Dagger of Derenar.

His sword sprung to life in his hand, stinging, slicing, cutting. He was grossly outnumbered, but it didn't matter; he was doing what he was born to do—and he knew that help was on the way.

"Leave some for me, you selfish prick!" It was Venn, leading the charge of Stoneborn into the clearing toward the chovathi. He dove into the fray, war hammer in one hand and gleaming sword in the other. "Nice trick back there, trying to get a head start. It almost worked!"

Tennech smacked away an encroaching chovathi with the flat of his blade, taking a step back before surging forward at the creature's throat. Even out of practice, he was still the best at what he did. "You sure did take your sweet time getting here," he said with a grin.

Venn returned it, swinging his hammer at the head of a nearby chovathi, knocking it to the ground and stunning it. He walked over and, near effortlessly, took the creature's head clean off.

Tennech tipped his sword in admiration. "Interesting technique, Venn. But perhaps a little slow." In a breath, he spun around and decapitated two more who had managed to stalk their way behind him. "If you had a sword in that other hand instead of a hammer, with enough practice, you might someday get close to felling as many as I have."

Out of the corner of his eye, Tennech saw the straggling Stoneborn joining the fray—and, to his pride and delight, Benj had unsheathed Glamrhys and was brandishing it like the Stoneborn he was.

A few errant strikes from the newer Stoneborn had opened the door for more chovathi to spawn from the forest floor, but Venn was on them in the blink of an eye. *He may have a mouth on him,* Tennech thought, *but his actions do more than enough talking.*

It felt good to be back on the front lines, Tennech realized. It almost made him feel young again, despite his labored breathing. He had previously been unsure about whether Stoneborn could sweat, but now he was certain: if he wasn't sweating now, he was entirely incapable of it.

Planting his sword in the exposed throat of a chovathi on the ground, Tennech stood up and took in the battlefield. He and his Stoneborn had made quick work of the chovathi mob that had attacked the—

He froze. Where was the Kienari?

He looked back over to where he had first seen him, surrounded like a fresh kill among wolves, but saw no evidence of his presence. He walked over, moving aside a few bodies of fallen chovathi to clear a path.

There was absolutely no question about it: the Kienari was gone.

Chapter 69

Khala Val'ur

Yetz

THE BURNING! IT WAS ALMOST too much. Yetz could feel his own body failing at the power of Breaking that coursed through him—and the other Master Khyth who helped keep it in check. They pushed themselves closer and closer to the precipice of power: the threshold of energy they would need to accomplish their goal—their last, desperate heave against the chovathi horde. The energy pulsed and roared, burning like wildfire, heating him up from the inside. They were nearly there.

Nearly . . .

He felt a shift inside him, like a key clicking in a lock—and for a moment, eternity stood still.

✦ ✦ ✦

Kunas

THERE WAS AN EERIE STILLNESS about the battlefield as Kunas walked. Death and power filled the air. Up ahead was the mouth of the Sunken City, and guarding it were seven points of blazing light, crackling with strength. *The Masters*, he thought. All that stood in his way of conquest. He tightened his grip around the hilt of the sword that he had taken from LaVince, looking more like a dagger in his massive hands.

The normally cacophonous thoughts of his brothers were muted in his mind, no more than a dull gray drone that scratched at his consciousness. His focus, now, must be on these Khyth that lay ahead of him. Nothing else mattered.

He stepped to the edge of the battlefield, and everything around him seemed to stop. It was the eye of a hurricane, and Kunas was witnessing its wake. He let his focus drift onto the five figures that guarded the mouth—and the one wielding the bulk of the power was one whom he knew very well.

"Yetz," he bellowed, and his voice shook the earth. His old master—and the reason for his exile to Khala Val'ur. "I've come to end your line."

A voice from the mouth shot back. "Then come!"

Kunas felt his lips curl back in a snarl. He did enjoy a challenge.

✦ ✦ ✦

Yetz

HE HARDLY EVEN RECOGNIZED THE abomination before him as his former pupil, Kunas, Master Khyth of Ghal Thurái. What he saw before him now was a giant, hulking mass of muscle and bone, bleached white and covered in rough, spiky armor. He looked like a chovathi, but he was also something more—much more. This creature—this *thing*—was something new entirely.

"What have you become?" Yetz called out as the creature, Kunas, slowly advanced. Out of the corner of his eye he could see Caledeus and Kostas eyeing the creature uncertainly as they dealt with his ilk. Chovathi continued to pour from the earth—from the rocks themselves it seemed at times—and it was all they could do to keep them at bay.

"Something you could never dream of, old fool. Something beyond your comprehension: a joining of Khyth ferocity and chovathi resilience; expansion, improvement . . . perfection."

As he walked, the very ground seemed to give way. There was a swaggering certitude to his step: a haughtiness that said that he couldn't be stopped.

The sword at his side was a jarring contrast to the rest of him: it was sleek, sharp, and uniform; Kunas, on the other hand, was huge, bulky, and rough. A creature with his makeup had no business wielding such an instrument of grace and precision—yet here he was, striding toward the opening of the Sunken City doing just that. There was a certain majesty to it, a disturbing and beautiful blending of the simple and complex.

All around him, chaos reigned. The two Master Khyth wove their Breaking through the air, cutting down score after score of chovathi—yet they kept coming. And Kunas walked calmly through them without a care in the world.

Yetz knew that their time grew short. He felt the power stirring within him and knew that it would be enough—it had to be. He looked to the Khyth beside him, forming the five-sided star which focused their Breaking, and saw the effect it was having on them. Being this close to such raw power—drinking from the very source of creation—was doing so much more than the ritual of the Breaking ever did: it was consuming them. A hand can only be warmed by a flame for so long before it gets burned.

"And now comes the end," he said in a voice barely above a whisper. It was time to plunge it into the fire.

As Kunas drew ever closer, Yetz threw open the floodgates which had been nothing more than a crack before. The Master Khyth furthest away from him, Enero and Hruz, cried out in pain—and were swiftly silenced as their life essence burned away, severing the ring that had been used to concentrate their power and funneling it in towards Yetz.

It was like nothing he had ever experienced before, this influx of power. His senses sharpened, and his body surged with power. Breaking of this magnitude was only ever reserved for the gods—and right now, Yetz certainly felt like one.

Something stirred. Yetz wasn't sure what it was, but it almost felt like . . . recognition. Like a hand reaching out that had suddenly found him. He drew upon the power again, like drinking deep from a burning stream. Yuras and Mentaphet cried out as they collapsed, suddenly stripped of the power they had helped cultivate—and along with that power came the forfeiture of their lives, as the emptiness left a void too great for mortal man to ever fill.

Yetz felt dizzy, almost sick. The power roiling within him had been gathered for a singular purpose, and it was about to be unleashed. All he had to do now was focus, and it would be done. Breaking would do the rest; he was simply a cog in a wheel.

On the edge of his distorted vision was Kunas, the white blur, who had been stalking his way toward the other two Masters, Caledeus and Kostas, sword in hand. Yetz could barely keep focused as he wielded the power, like trying to dam a great river with nothing more than a handful of sticks; it was far too great for him to do anything of consequence. He simply had to hope, and aim.

A muffled scream told him that one of the Masters had been overtaken by Kunas. No matter, he told himself. It was all building toward this moment, this release. He was hammering a nail; it didn't matter to him how many boards were splintered in the process.

The power swelled and tossed within him, a vast, churning ocean.

He turned to the mountains that surrounded Khala Val'ur, monuments to the greatness of the Khyth, and spread his arms. In his mind he saw it clearly: using the power of Breaking to lift each and every peak around them for miles, and dropping them down again, driving every living creature within a sparrow's breath of Khala Val'ur into the ground for all eternity. Wave after wave of energy slamming into mountains, trees—a cataclysmic release, its rival never known. The depth of its violence unending; its savagery, unparalleled. Mountains upended, streams diverted, boulders split.

The world, remade. Nothing would survive. Nothing would be the same.

... unless ...

He opened his eyes to the razor-sharp teeth of Kunas. It was both the last thing he expected, and the last thing he ever hoped to see. There could be no more hesitation, no more waiting. The time was now.

Yetz let go of his grip on the otherworldly power that clawed at him, relieved to finally be free of the terrible and tremendous burden. The power pulsed from him in waves. As he did so, though, something felt ... off.

He looked at Kunas—and realized too late what was happening. All this time, Yetz had looked at him and seen a chovathi, when the truth was much more complicated. Kunas had even said so himself: this was not just a chovathi—this was a Master Khyth with the body of one.

"In the depths of Ghal Thurái, I was born anew," Kunas said. He was standing mere feet from Yetz, towering over him. "I touched the source, and the source filled me. I became one with my Lady, Zhala, and she opened my mind and my spirit to the possibilities of the world. At first, I could not even begin to comprehend what was happening, as my body fought against the change—but when I finally let go, the secrets of existence made themselves known to me."

Right as Yetz let go of the power he realized that the recognition he felt was Kunas's own control over Breaking—and he was redirecting the power into himself.

"This new body was a gift," Kunas went on. "I shed my old shell, a weak and fragile thing, and transcended. The power of Breaking is but a candle to the true potential that the chovathi have inside them. Their bodies do not break like human bodies; they either die or grow stronger. There is no regression." Kunas flashed his teeth in a twisted grin, and Yetz felt the sudden and terrifying sensation of being drained. He was a sieve, and Kunas was catching everything that came through.

"You . . . can't . . ." Yetz croaked. The words were all he could muster as his very strength was being pulled from him. He tried to redirect the power, but Kunas was too strong, too focused. He felt like a tree being stripped of its bark, knowing that he would soon be felled and hollowed out.

"I can feel you struggling, my old master," Kunas growled as he lowered himself to look Yetz in the eye. "But it's too late. The path is set, and the power has been set free. You can no more stop it than clouds can stop falling rain. You are a Vessel," he said with a grin. "And I am the end."

Kunas stood before him, arms outstretched, basking in the power of the Breaker. Yetz felt a tremor surge through his body, and dropped to his knees. Blackness began to creep in, spreading through his vision like ink in water. Yet, in the blackness was something familiar, right on the edge of his mind. Something near. Something . . .

Sera!

The thought filled him with hope—and fear. He knew that her destiny was drawing near, but if she were to arrive too soon, it could all fall apart in an instant. She alone could face what was coming—but not as she was right now. He knew that she wasn't ready. He had to give in. The sooner that Kunas contained the power, the sooner he would set off for his mistress in the forest of Kienar.

This was it. This was his time.

Yetz took a breath. He summoned the last bit of strength he had in order to look around, to feel his final moments before they slipped through his fingers.

The images came, filling his vision.

Ellenos. Playing on the streets with his younger brother, Aldryd. Blossoming in the ways of Shaping; learning; listening; growing. Becoming Tallister to the High Keeper. Meeting Coraline. Fathering a child that he knew he could never keep. Seeing her raised under the watchful eye of another man—a man whom he both respected and resented for his relationship with his Lilyana. Leaving the city he loved for a chance at peace, to one day see a plan come to fruition whose seed was planted long, long ago. All hopes lay on her now—not just the hopes of Yetz, or the Athrani, but all those who lived and died under the stars.

He looked up at Kunas, still siphoning off the unbearable power of the Otherworld. It was filling him, changing him. He was already more monster than man; what would this new power do to him?

As the last bit of energy left him, Yetz felt a great burden fall from his shoulders. It had all come down to this moment—and, even though it seemed hopeless as Kunas surged with new power, something inside him told him that his faith in Sera was well placed. Above all else, though, he had to make sure that Kunas left for Kienar before Sera crossed his path.

He looked up at the hulking monstrosity, rife with power, and spoke. "You may have defeated me," he said with the remainder of his strength, "but there exists one greater than you—you, or any of the gods. She is the judge and the executioner. It is She alone you must fear."

The words gave Kunas pause. Absorbing all of that power had left his body swollen and twisted, like a python's belly after a meal. Yet even snakes fear something. Yetz could see it in his eyes—but only for a moment. In an instant, the fear was gone . . . and replaced with something far more sinister.

"When my work is complete, even the gods will not be able to stop me, nor comprehend what I have become."

He turned his head very slightly, almost imperceptibly, and Yetz felt a rumbling all around. A shadow stretched over both of them as Yetz realized what was happening: Kunas had broken off a piece of the mountain and was raising it above their heads.

"Impossible," Yetz said as his eyes went wide. "That kind of power—"

"Is only reserved for the gods," Kunas said, cutting him off. "Witness the birth of a new one."

The last thing Yetz felt before ten thousand tons of earth came crashing down on him was the unbridled fear that the High Keeper could be wrong.

✦ ✦ ✦

Kunas

THE MAELSTROM OF THOUGHTS AND sensations inside Kunas was far beyond driving him mad—it had pushed him past it, submerged him in it, and absorbed it; another piece of clay in a twisted, writhing sculpture. Now, the consciousness that called itself "Kunas" was as distant from the man as the stars were from the earth. It was a force, an entity, an abomination; one voice among thousands, shouting for control from a prison of anguish.

He felt himself pulled—called—and he answered.

He moved toward Kienar.

Chapter 70

Khala Val'ur

D. L. Jennings

Sera

THEY HAD BEEN MARCHING FOR the better part of a day, and Sera was impressed with not only the endurance of the Sharian army, but with its leader, Duna. The queen had kept pace with them this whole time, despite not needing to; Sera knew full well that if she so desired, Duna could have made the entire army wait for her—or go ahead without her. This was a woman who led by example, though, Sera realized. She respected that.

It reminded her of *him*.

"We're nearly there," Duna said over her shoulder, leaning slightly backward in her saddle to look at Sera.

Sera stifled a grin. She had ridden the Khala-Shar pass more times than she could count. She knew its ins and outs, its twists and turns—and she certainly knew how far they were from the city in which she grew up. But she didn't speak any of those words aloud to Duna. Despite their heated first encounter outside of the Sunken City, Sera's opinion of the queen had shifted almost as radically as Duna's status. After all, she had the ear of the man Sera admired most—Aldis Tennech—and for that, she would give her the respect that she deserved. She simply nodded and said, "Thank you."

"Of course. I just thought you'd like to know. You were looking a little . . . preoccupied."

"Me?" Sera asked, now fully turning in her saddle to face the queen. "Preoccupied?"

"Yes, you," Duna affirmed. "It's none of my business so I won't ask, but I'm willing to listen if you think it will help."

Sera's opinion of Duna took another great leap forward. Here was the Queen regnant of Haidan Shar offering Sera—nothing more than an appointed soldier being asked to help lead her army—an ear. It was beyond respectable. It was downright . . . human.

"Thank you," Sera said. Her mind went back to the thoughts of everything she had been through recently. Her service to the Holder, the death and rebirth of Tennech, her exile from Khala Val'ur in everything but name. "Perhaps recent events have taken more of a toll on me than I realized."

Duna looked at her expectantly, waiting for her to continue.

"It's just something the Holder said that I can't get out of my head," she went on.

"I'm afraid I have little experience in dealing with gods," Duna began. "But I have known a few men in my time who thought they were one. Maybe I can offer some insight. What did he say?"

Sera wasn't sure where to start. Everything the god said was enigmatic. "He called me 'Seed,'" she said, making eye contact with Duna. "He called me that, as did the Ghost of the Morning . . . and, though she was the first one to speak the words, he somehow knew me by that name when we met."

Duna furrowed her brow. "Seed?" she considered. "I guess that would imply that you're supposed to grow into something—or that something is growing in you."

Sera had near-endlessly entertained the possibility of the first thing—but had never even stopped to consider the implications of the second. She blanched. *Oh, gods. What has he done to me?* She found herself unconsciously moving her hand to her stomach when suddenly there came shouts of confusion and surprise from the men behind her.

Her eyes went immediately to the horizon, westward, where the Khala-Shar pass emptied into the foothills of Gal'behem, and the entrance to Khala Val'ur. Instead of the usual company of guards standing watch outside the gates, she saw nothing but . . .

"What in the Holder's hells happened?" Duna asked in a whisper filled with fear and trepidation.

This was not at all what Sera had expected. She dug her heels into the ribcage of her mount, spurring it onward toward Khala Val'ur in the fractionally small chance that they were not too late. She knew deep down that they were, but that didn't stop her from getting there as quickly as she could. If nothing else, they would be able to get a jump on whatever it was that did this.

Only, she knew exactly what did this.

Behind her, twin hoofbeats matched her own as she looked back to see Duna on horseback, thundering to keep up with her. "Just because you're better with a sword than I am doesn't mean you get to go storming off on your own!" the queen shouted over the hoofbeats.

Sera smiled to herself and pulled back ever so slightly on the reins, allowing Duna to catch up. "Old habit," she said.

The two of them raced down the road toward the entrance to the Sunken City and, as they drew closer, Sera's fears grew slowly into focus. Every hoofbeat drew them closer to the meaning of true horror.

+ + +

Pulling back on the reins, Sera slowed her mount to a walk. "Breaker above," she swore under her breath. "There's nothing left."

Duna came up beside her and silently shared in her despondency. The look on her face told Sera that she was thinking the same thing: they would not find any survivors.

Before them lay the corpses of the freshly dead, thousands and thousands of defenders of Khala Val'ur, beneath the mountains that they had given their lives to protect. It was a grisly scene: men torn in half, missing limbs, or drowned in blood and guts. Some of them were clutching weapons, looking like they had fought to their last dying breath; others did not seem so brave, but were lifeless all the same. The bodies knew no formation or semblance of direction—it was chaos, through and through.

Perhaps most chillingly of all, though: there was not a chovathi corpse to be seen. Sera didn't have time to think of the implications— nor, did it seem, did Duna.

"I . . . I didn't know that the chovathi were capable of this," the queen breathed.

"Neither did I," Sera admitted. She had seen smaller bands of them attack outlying towns and hamlets for food, but it had always been out of necessity, and never as savage as this. "This was not just an attack—this was a slaughter."

Duna got down from her horse. Walking over to inspect one of the bodies, a young soldier who couldn't have been much more than twenty. She knelt and placed a hand on his face. She looked back up at Sera. "This was a *message*."

Sera took a breath and looked deeper in toward the city. Something caught her eye. She squinted, trying to make it out. A lone figure, it seemed to be . . . moving toward them! She drew her sword. "Arm yourself," she said to Duna, who looked up at her in confusion. Seeing where she was looking, Duna stood up and turned her head to do the same.

"What is it?" she asked. "Do you think it's . . . do you think it's what did this?"

"I'm not sure, but I'm not taking any chances." She turned toward the rest of her waiting army and waved them off, making sure they knew damn well to stay where they were. If this creature was responsible for such a level of carnage against the entire standing army of Khala Val'ur, she reasoned, the fledgling army of Haidan Shar stood about as much chance as a fish in the desert.

When she turned back to get a better look at it, she almost dropped her sword.

"Son of . . ." she began.

"What?" Duna asked. "What is it?"

Sera sheathed her sword. While she was not alarmed to find that she recognized the figure as it drew closer, she was uncertain whether she should be relieved. "It's the Priest," she answered bitterly.

She would not, she decided, be relieved.

Chapter 71

Kienar

Miera

THE ATHRANI LEGION COULD NOT have picked a better time to arrive. As Miera sped off to meet them, a torrent of arrows streaked overhead to the front lines, followed shortly thereafter by the thick thumps of success as they buried themselves into their targets.

Zhala.

They were going to need help. She soared over the underbrush, dodging trees as she went, finally catching a glimpse of the Legion. When she did, she heard Yasha's voice in her head, rife with excitement.

It's Endar! I know him!

Who? she asked, but the question went unanswered. As she flew toward the front lines of the army, she felt Yasha take over. The sensation of not being in control of her body was both frustrating and strange, but Miera tried not to be upset—after all, she was technically a guest of Yasha's.

"Endar! Hi!" she shouted, waving as she came. "It's me, Yasha!"

This was a man whom Miera had never seen before, but clearly meant something to Elyasha. The great warrior, clad in plate mail and wearing a purple cloak, was busy hacking apart a few chovathi when he looked in her direction, confused.

"Yasha? The Khyth girl?" he asked, lowering his sword, and idly shoving a lunging chovathi out of the way. "Is that really you?"

"It is."

"But you look so . . . different."

"Oh, this?" she answered sheepishly, spreading her arms out and dimming the light that was shining from her. "I'm sort of . . . the Shaper? It's weird."

Endar nodded absently. "Ah," he conceded. Hacking at the neck of a nearby chovathi without even looking, he said, "Well, you look great."

Miera felt herself blush, and immediately heard Yasha's voice in her head say, *Don't you dare say anything.*

"Anyway," Endar went on, putting his boot to the chest of another chovathi and sending it flying backward, "Sh'thanna said you might need some help."

"Oh, definitely. Yes. Yeah. Is that why you're here?"

Miera felt her cheeks flush again, and Yasha's presence retreat. *Can you steer?* she asked sheepishly.

I've got this, Miera said, doing her best to suppress the grin that was forming in her mind.

"Don't answer that," Miera cut in. "We've been doing our best to hold off the chovathi, but they've been overwhelming us with sheer numbers. And Zhala, their leader," she said, pointing to the great matriarch, "is drawing strength from the forest. I know she means to cross into the Otherworld—and it will spell doom for us all if she succeeds."

Endar flashed a grin that rivaled the great Naknamu in size. "I can definitely help with that," he said. Turning his head, he shouted over his shoulder, "Legion! Focus your fire on the big one!" Looking back at Miera, he said, "That should help."

In response, a hail of arrows soared through the air, piercing the skin of the mammoth white chovathi. Zhala thrashed about, then let out a roar that almost seemed to dim the sun.

"It will at least slow her down," Miera said. "But the goal is to stop her. And I'm worried that the one being who can just disappeared on us."

Endar gave her a quizzical look. "But you're the Shaper. Surely you of all people could stop her."

Miera felt her light dim. "She is strong, and her power rivals my own—especially here in this forest, where she was made. I would have a better chance in the Otherworld, where my own power is strongest . . . but that is a risk I am not willing to take."

"Then we stop her here, together."

Her light returned. "Together," she affirmed.

"Then," came a voice from behind her, "may we offer some assistance?"

Miera turned around to see standing before her one of the very last men that she had ever thought she would see again.

"Tennech," she breathed. Thoughts surfaced of the last time that she'd seen him—being dragged against her will into the depths of Khala Val'ur—and she reflexively took a step back.

"Indeed," he answered, and gave her a nod that bordered on a bow. When he looked up at her again, he cocked his head as if trying to figure out the answer to a riddle. The answer apparently dawned on him, and a smile began to form on his lips.

"So it is true. The spirit of the Shaper has found a home in the body of a Khyth." Grabbing a part of the black cloak that hung from his shoulders, he flung it out as he took a knee before her.

"What . . ." she stammered. "What is this?"

"Just a few stones to add to the dam, my lady. I commanded armies before, in a past life," Tennech said. "I hope you will allow me to offer mine to you now."

Miera watched a half dozen, gray-hued humans emerge from the trees and take a knee behind him. She looked over at Endar, who seemed just as caught off guard as she felt. Turning her attention back to the general, she blinked a few times to try and clear her head.

"We will take all the help we can get," she said, continuing to herself, *even if it comes from the most unlikely of places.*

Chapter 72

Khala Val'ur

Sera

THE SKINLESS, SKELETAL FACES OF the Priests of the Holder never failed to make Sera uneasy. The one walking toward her now, eyes caught in a lidless stare, was looking right through her, and it took everything in her to not turn away. She held his gaze, though. She'd learned long ago that facing down her fears was the only way to overcome them—and this was one fear that she fully intended to overcome.

"So you decided to join us after all," she said through gritted teeth.

The priest, as always, showed no hint of emotion. "I told you that beyond the dunes of Khulakorum waits the greatest army ever assembled, did I not?"

"You did. And?"

"And the time draws nigh for its assembly."

Sera looked around them at the endless sea of bodies and pursed her lips. "Looks like we got here a little late for that."

"No," the priest rasped, "we did not. Look." After he spoke the words, he pointed a finger behind her toward the sky.

Sera turned around to see what he was pointing at, and her heart nearly stopped. Moving toward them, eerily silent, was a massive column of stone and sand hundreds of feet high, with two great towers at its head. As it approached, it blotted out the sun.

She had seen its like in terms of size, but had never seen any of those towers do, well—*this*. She fumbled with her words. "Is that . . . is that tower . . . flying?"

Duna was equally stunned. "How . . . how is that even possible?" she asked, gawking at the colossal floating structure.

"The power of the Three is beyond your comprehension," the priest replied. "And what you see before you is but a trifle to the Holder of the Dead."

If that was a trifle, Sera thought, *I would hate to see a show of effort.*

She was caught in rapt attention at the tower, held up by an invisible force that she could neither see nor understand. The tower itself looked as if it had been torn from the ground—and, when Sera looked closer, she realized that it probably had: the base, which would normally have been solidly connected to the ground, was jagged rock and crumbling stone, like a marble column that had been cracked in half and uprooted. Stairs, which now led nowhere, jutted out the front like penitent hands.

The entire thing moved at a glacial pace. Watching it gave Sera an odd feeling, like she was floating down a river toward a great mountain—only in this case, the mountain was the one moving, and she was standing still. The scale of it all hurt her head. She rubbed her eyes—and when she opened them again, she found that it had finally come to a stop above the mountains of Gal'behem. She watched expectantly, glancing over at Duna, who was similarly enrapt.

"What . . . what do you think it wants?" The queen asked.

"Silence," said the priest. "He comes."

Sera looked back at the tower and squinted, sure that she was missing something—when suddenly, fleeting movement near the base of the tower caught her eye. Two iron doors, impossibly tall, began to creak open . . . and when they came to a stop, she saw him walk out—the Holder of the Dead—looking every last bit of the god that he was.

The Lord of the Dead had always struck Sera as peculiar, though, affecting a regal air with his flowing robes and extravagant white staff. Today, however, he seemed to hold himself differently than he did in the throne room of Khadje Kholam—almost as if being there, in the tower, was giving him strength. He stepped forward, descending the stairs that led to a precipitous drop—and as he did so, the tower moved toward the ground in kind. As his foot reached the last step, the tower, too, met the ground, and a muted tremor shook the earth. He took another step forward, into the soft grass of the Dorokian landscape.

He took a minute to look around, a king surveying his kingdom. "Ah, the rugged and discordant land of Gal'dorok," the Holder said. His multi-colored left eye, which betrayed the half-eyed Athrani nature of his host body, gleamed with a terrifying confidence. "How anyone managed to settle here is beyond me." He looked over at Sera, then past her to the mountains of bodies of the defenders of Khala Val'ur. "It seems that violence and death have spilled over into the land of the Khyth. How . . . *unfortunate*."

The deep, rumbling laugh that came forth from the skeletal figure was at once both terrifying and unwelcome, and filled Sera with exactly the kind of dread that she expected from the Holder. She hated it—she hated every moment she was around him—and wanted nothing more than to put and end to that horrific laughter.

. . . Only she had no idea how she would even do that in the first place. How does one kill a god? Could it even be done? Would his spirit simply inhabit another body? The Priest's body? Or worse . . . hers? She shuddered as she dropped the thought and noticed the Holder's attention shift past her to Queen Duna.

Duna, who had been silent the whole time, had a look of mild curiosity on her face. "You know, you're the first god I've ever met in person," she said, looking the Holder up and down. "I thought you'd be taller." The Holder held his lidless stare as Duna placed her hands on her hips, as if waiting for him to say something. Sera was positive that he had never been spoken to like that before. *Damn, that woman has balls*, she thought as she bit her lip to stifle a laugh. "Oh well," Duna went on. "What's all this about an army?"

The Holder looked like he was about to boil over. From behind them, the Priest spoke. "You would do well to give the proper respect to the Lord of the Dead, Queen Duna." His tone, as did the Holder's eyes, trembled with rage. "This is not one of your peers or subjects to be spoken down to and disrespected."

"Respect," Duna snapped, turning around to address the blue-robed figure, "is earned, Priest, not taken, and so far, the only thing I've seen him do is land a flying rock near some other rocks." Turning back to the

Holder, she looked him in the eye, as if daring him to speak. "When he does something that earns my respect, he shall have it."

The laughter that erupted from the throat of the Holder of the Dead told Sera that he planned to do much more than that—and the shifting of the earth under Sera's feet told her exactly what that plan was meant to be.

Chapter 73

G'hen

Alysana

THE WIND HOWLED. A SOLIDER shoved her from behind. "Keep moving," he grunted. Alysana had no intention of doing otherwise. She looked up at the sky that was darkening with the evening, and frowned.

If Mordha is planning something, I hope she comes through soon.

She was being led by a chain connected to manacles around her wrists; from there, another chain was connected to a shackle around her neck. The soldier in back of her, who had given her the point of his sword a few times already, made Alysana feel like the most closely guarded person in all of G'hen. Looking up the hill to the gallows, she suddenly knew why.

"How are those restraints?"

Putrid words from a putrid man, Ghaja Rus's voice made Alysana cringe more than his pleased and arrogant demeanor.

The guard in front of her stopped, turning around to inspect the manacles that bound her wrists. As he did so, he looked at her with a hatred reserved for kinslayers. He gave her restraints a solid yank that nearly sent her tumbling forward.

"They are as tight as they get, Magistrate."

"Good. Bring her." The words dripped like sap from a tree.

Alysana felt the point of a sword in her back once again and knew that was her cue to move. She did as requested without so much as a word in return.

+ + +

Standing beneath the tree where all executions in G'hen were carried out, Alysana couldn't help but think of the path that had gotten her here. The dirt trail that led out from the city was so much like her own journey all those years ago: rough, unpredictable, and long. It had been difficult, yes, but it had also been rewarding. In what other life would she have accomplished all that she had, and met all the souls that she did? She allowed herself a weak smile at the thought of the first time she met Thornton, hunched over his bowl of stew, mouth burnt from impatience.

Thornton. The memory seemed as distant as he did.

"Only a fool smiles in the face of certain death," Rus scoffed, breaking her out of the reverie.

"Then I suppose a fool is what I am," Alysana shot back. "After all, there was a point in my life when I didn't think you were a *lying coward*."

Ghaja Rus backhanded her, hard, across the face.

Alysana reeled but did not lose her footing. She stumbled a bit, catching herself before her knees buckled. The ear that took the blow was ringing, and she tasted copper. She spat on the ground and saw more blood than spittle. With a side-eye at Rus, she craned her head toward him . . . and smiled again.

The fat G'henni took a step back as his eyes opened wide—but the look faded as quickly as it had come. He stepped forward and grabbed the chains around her wrists, violently pulling her towards him. In the span of a breath his face was against hers, and Alysana could feel the heat as he whispered through his teeth, "Once again, somehow, you find your life in my hands; I would not be so quick to mock the one who holds the chains." He looked at the guard who was escorting her. "Unshackle her."

"But—"

"I said do it! I want to enjoy this."

The guard fumbled with some keys on his belt, holding one after another up to the light to inspect. After five of them, he looked nervously at Rus, who gave a nod. The guard inserted it into the lock around her neck, turning it with a *click* and repeating the same with her wrists.

The shackles dropped to the ground, and the guard jumped back, shakily pointing his sword at her. Alysana stood there in silent defiance, her face a mask of granite. Not once in her entire life did she give Rus the pleasure of showing him fear. Before, it had been an act—now, it was real.

"I'm not afraid of you, Rus," she replied, her voice calm and low. "I'm not afraid of what you can do to me—or even what you think you're capable of doing." She turned her eyes briefly to the forest. "And do you really think that killing me will be the end?"

Rus's pupils widened for a split second, and Alysana recognized his fear. Whatever happened here, now, she knew that a singular seed of doubt had been planted in Rus's brain. He turned to the guard and snatched the rope from him. Looking Alysana in the eyes, he said, "I intend to find out." He slipped the noose over her head and brought the knot nearly to the back of her head, stopping just short of tightening it completely. Grabbing the rope with both hands, he pulled her closer to his grin, then spun her around and pushed her. "Forward," he said.

She walked to the wooden steps of the gallows, placing a foot on the first step and stopping. Turning her head slightly, she looked at Rus. "Don't I get any last words?"

Rus swiped the sword from the guard and pointed it at her. "You will," he said with a sneer. "Whatever I want them to be. Now go."

Alysana laughed and tugged at her noose. "You threaten me with a sword with this around my neck? How many weapons must you have on me before you feel safe, Rus?"

The fire in Rus's eyes was almost hot enough to melt the sword he held. He stormed over to her, faced her toward the stairs, and pushed. Alysana fell forward, bringing her hands up to brace herself—but just as she did, she felt the violent pull of the rope on her throat. She gagged audibly as Rus yanked her backward to him, catching her with his body. He pulled her against himself, and Alysana felt his breath on her face. She retched and choked as he whispered in her ear.

"How you haven't learned to keep your mouth shut after all these years is beyond me," he sputtered, "but I am not about to teach you manners before I kill you."

He let go of her and shoved her again—only this time, he didn't catch her. Alysana crashed into the wooden stairs with a thud, clawing at the noose to breathe. A long, gasping breath filled her lungs with air and her body with relief. She heaved and spat on the ground. One of her eyes was starting to swell. Inhaling sharply, she rubbed at her throat where the noose had been. Rolling onto her back, she saw Rus standing over her with a grin.

"Now how about you listen to me, hmm?" She wiped some blood and spit from her mouth but did not reply. "Now stand up and get moving before I pull you by that rope again."

Alysana did as she was told, turning around and resuming her slow march up the gallows. As she walked up, each creaking step seemed to mock her. How could she be so stupid? How could she leave her fate in the hands of Ghaja Rus? She should have killed him in Théas. The noose on her neck seemed to tighten with the thought. She looked again to the forest, hoping that, like last time, a Kienari might come to her rescue—yet deep down, she knew that none would be coming.

Her time was running out.

When she felt the sword point in her back again, she knew it would be her only chance.

She took it.

Whirling around, she caught the dangling rope, wrapping it quickly around the sword that was now pointed at her chest. In one fluid motion, Alysana brought up her free hand to smash it into Rus's, flicking the wrist of the hand on the rope to rip the sword away and flip it toward her. She caught it with all the grace of a Kienari and leveled it at Rus.

His eyes went wider than the Mouth of the Deep. "Guards!" he shouted hoarsely.

"Don't," Alysana countered, turning her head to the guards but keeping her eyes on Rus. "Come any closer and his blood is on your hands. From this range," she said, slowly moving the blade closer to Rus's throat, "even *he* couldn't miss." She shot them a look. "Swords. Ground. Now."

The guards exchanged nervous glances, then did as they were told.

"Good choice," she said. "Now go. Tell my uncle Ezna that he's needed here."

The guards stood for a moment looking confused. When Alysana punctuated her request with a "Now!" they nearly tripped over themselves on their way back into town.

She looked back at Rus, whose stoic face told of a man who had been hardened by greed and transgression. This was a man who had built an empire on the blood of slaves and had not even batted an eye at separating children from their parents to further his own ambition.

All of that was about to change. "Kneel," Alysana said, still pointing the sword at his throat.

Rus got on his knees slowly, keeping his hands in the air as he did. "Those guards are going to bring the full force of G'hen with them when they return," he said. "What do you hope to accomplish in these few short moments?"

"Only what I've waited an entire lifetime to do," she replied. She cocked her head as her eyes were drawn to something hanging around his belt. "Unstrap that," she said, pointing with her sword, "and place it on the ground."

Rus reached for his belt, unhooking the leather holster that was connected to it. He laid it at her feet. Alysana bent down to pick it up, never moving the sword from its lethal position at Ghaja Rus's throat. When she stood, a wry smile spread across her face. It was her dagger—the one they had taken from her before placing her in chains . . . the dagger that she had kept her entire life as a reminder.

She threw the sword aside, drawing the blade from its sheath. It gleamed in the sunlight. Even after all these years, it still had an edge.

"Do you know what this is?" she asked, still admiring the craftsmanship.

"It's the dagger my men took off of you," Rus replied.

"Yes, but do you know how it was passed to me?"

"How would I know such a thing?"

She glanced down at him, and old emotions came bubbling back to the surface. Something in the pit of her stomach stirred. "It's a story

I don't often repeat, because it brought with it a lifetime of trauma—a trauma that, even seeing your face nearly two decades later, I realize I still feel." She locked eyes with Rus. "Your men—men that my father paid to keep me safe—tried to sell me as a slave when I was just a girl. But do you know who came to save me? Who answered the panicked cries of my sister and me? It wasn't the Athrani Legion, or the Guardians of Lusk, or even the Guard of Annoch. No—it was a Kienari, a daughter of the forest." Her voice trembled at the retelling. "Ynara is her name, and she is the reason I am alive today."

Rus was stone-faced, saying nothing.

"When I saw you again in Théas," she went on, "I thought for sure my time had come. Finally," she said, throwing her arms up in mock triumph, "I thought I was being gifted a chance for revenge!" She lowered her arms again and pointed the dagger back at him. "But then I never would have seen the man you truly are; the man who the rest of the world knew as 'Magistrate Rus.' All I had was my own experience, and my own reason for wanting you dead, but this—*this*—was so much more."

"Justify it however you like, girl. It's not so easy to take a life—and if you choose to take mine, I have no doubt that your conscience will keep you awake."

Alysana knelt down, getting at eye level with Rus. She wrapped her hand around the back of his neck, and pulled him close, pressing her forehead into his.

"On the contrary, Rus: I think I'm going to get the best sleep of my life." The dagger slid into his throat like fingers dipping into the surface of a lake: gentle, easy, without a single thought for the disturbance it would make. Rus choked and tried to look away, but Alysana held her grip. "I want my eyes to be the last thing you see," she said coldly. She held his gaze with the same mercy that his men had shown her when she was a little girl: none.

Rus opened his mouth to speak, but nothing more than a gurgle came out. His eyes, wide as moons, were fixed straight ahead in a lost and vacant stare. Then, something rattled in his throat, and Alysana knew that he had just taken his last breath. She stood up and backed away, letting the fat G'henni slump over, into the dirt of the land of his birth.

Looking down at the knife, now streaked with the same blood that was pooling in the soil below, Alysana had a half a mind to leave it as a reminder, but she knew that it would be better served as a weapon than as a trophy. She pulled out a cloth and began to wipe it clean.

"You must surely know that half the world will celebrate when they learn of his death." The words took her by surprise, but not the voice. She whirled around to see Jinda, Captain of the Guard of Annoch, standing beside her. "I certainly know it will be a better place with him gone."

"How long have you been standing there?" she asked, trying to contain her shock.

"I never stopped watching; your sister insisted on it. I almost stepped in before you got to the tree. I was pleased to see that you have not lost your fighter's instincts."

"You know," Alysana began, wiping the last of the blood from her dagger and putting it back in its sheath, "I told myself a long time ago to stop being surprised when a Farstepper shows up unexpectedly," she said with a grin, "but I still haven't gotten over it." She looked around. "Where is Mordha?" she asked as she scanned the trees.

"In Kienar," he replied. "I will take you. You are both needed."

The sounds of footsteps and shouting made them both look down the path that led to the city. Sure enough, just as Rus had said, the entirety of G'hen's soldiers were making their way to them in a hurry.

Alysana looked down once more at the body of Ghaja Rus and felt an odd sense of loss—not for him, but for a part of her. The revenge that she had sought for most of her life was now complete, like climbing up a mountain and reaching the summit: she had made the journey, yes. . . . *But what now?*

She glanced at the tree from which Rus sought to hang her, and then to the dagger in its sheath. Patting it, she offered her hand to Jinda. "Then let's take this blade home. I have a feeling it has not outlived its usefulness."

Jinda took her hand and smiled—and the two of them vanished like Rus's breath.

Chapter 74

Kienar

Miera

MIERA WATCHED AS TENNECH DIRECTED his troops with surgical precision: though few, they were mighty. He barked out orders like the general that he was, almost seeming to thrive in the thrill of combat. Looking back at Endar, he said, "We could use some cover fire if we're to advance."

"Then you shall have it," answered the big half-eye. "Archers! Redirect. Cover the ingress of the Stoneborn."

His archers' answer came in the form of the twanging of bowstrings and the slinging of arrows, followed by the abrupt yet orderly departure of Tennech's troops toward Zhala.

All around them, the battle raged. The chovathi had not stop coming since their incursion into the forest, and Miera was beginning to think that their supply was endless. How many of them were there? Soldiers from the Athrani Legion cut down score after score of them—but just as she they thought they were making headway, a new batch of them seemed to appear from the earth itself.

Almost as if . . .

"It's the forest!" she suddenly exclaimed, whirling around to Endar. "I don't know how, but it . . . feeds them somehow."

"I don't understand," said the commander of the Legion.

"Kethras told me that Zhala—the chovathi matriarch—was a Kienari once. I think being this close to the forest again is giving her some kind of strength."

"What can we do to stop that?"

Miera's face contorted. She hadn't gotten that far yet. Before she could open her mouth and admit as much, though, she heard a rumbling—almost like a low growl—and felt the earth shudder. She looked around to see where it might be coming from, and nearly jumped from her own body with what she saw: rising from the ground was a . . . mountain?

The earth trembled as it rose, a great peak that extended toward the sky, shedding boulders and dirt as it grew. But then, like no mountain Miera had ever seen, this one did something most unexpected: it stretched out its arms and stood up. The mammoth black figure rivaled Zhala in size. It was draped in green—vines running up and down like veins—and stood tall, like the mighty Naknamu. Looking closer, Miera realized it looked like a giant version of . . .

"Kethras!" The word leapt from her mouth in a mixture of awe and confusion.

The great Kienari turned, but there was no look of recognition in his eyes—only rage. He turned back to Zhala and took a thundering step forward, brushing aside trees and chovathi alike.

Miera looked at Endar, who was similarly awe-stricken. "It looks like your archers have help," she said.

"Welcome, indeed," the half-eye said with a nod. "Press the advantage!" he shouted, pointing his sword in the direction of Zhala, and the impossibly tall figure of Kethras, Binder of Worlds, who was lumbering toward the heart of the forest . . . marching right toward the entrance to the Otherworld.

Miera had a sinking feeling in the pit of her stomach. She knew what Zhala was after, and it terrified her that she was this close. She hoped Kethras would make it in time.

+ + +

Kethras

KETHRAS FELT THE VERY WEIGHT of eternity coursing through him, driving him forward, ever forward, to the depths of the forest whence he came. The entrance to the Otherworld lay ahead of him, and everything inside him told him that was where Zhala was headed.

His body no longer felt like his anymore. The forest had done something to him—changed him—and his mind was foggy. Instinct alone drove him—instinct . . . and rage. With each booming footstep he drew closer.

Up ahead he saw Zhala, desperately clawing her way toward the entrance of the tree, swatting away defenders like flies. Her army of chovathi had done most of the heavy lifting in clearing the path for her; the defenders of the forest hardly stood a chance. It was almost too much to ask of mortals, defending against the unstoppable. After all, Kethras knew, no matter how many they cut down, there would always be more. Here in the heart of the forest, where Zhala's own bloodline began, she had everything she needed to spawn new chovathi with a mere thought. He could feel it every time she plucked a tree from its roots to form a new one. She was killing the forest to give herself power, but it didn't matter. If she wasn't stopped, none of it would matter.

He surged forward, feeling the urgency spread through him as the chovathi continued to spawn. He was nearly upon her. He could feel her footsteps, hear her breathing, and—

He stopped.

We meet again, brother.

The words echoed in Kethras's mind, clawing at him from the inside. It was a connection he had not felt in an eternity, and it was jarring to feel it now, like a cold knife in the back.

He steadied himself and reached back. *Leave this forest, Zhala. It's not too late. You and I both know that your presence here brings nothing but destruction.*

Yes, Brother. That is the point.

Up ahead, Kethras saw her turn to him, a wicked and twisted grin scrawled across her face. He recoiled at the sight; it was not just physically disturbing, but mentally as well. It had been countlessly long since he had seen her last—before she had become this unholy thing—and to see her now in this state was nothing short of revolting.

You have fallen so far, he said, sending his thoughts to the creature that he once called Sister. *I cannot stand to see you this way.*

You care nothing for me! Zhala screamed in his head, and the words sent him staggering backward. *You only care for this forest. You never cared for me at all.*

Along with the words, Kethras could feel the venom that Zhala sent with them. She truly believed these things that she said. Her emotions were bleeding into his mind, a consequence of the mental link that they shared. He began to move toward her again.

That is not true, and deep down you know it. You must remember how I could not stand to see you leave—it was the only way! After what you did, you and I both know that you had no place in our Mother's forest.

Kethras was nearly upon her now, and their mental link was so much stronger than he ever remembered it being, a bridge for the emotion behind the words—and it was something that they had shared since birth. When Zhala was exiled, her voice silenced, it had been like losing a limb; now that limb had grown back, twisted and strong.

She was facing him, breathing heavily. Looking closer, Kethras could see that it was not from physical exertion; instead, it was the anger that he felt welling up inside her, manifesting itself physically—along with something else. Her closeness to Naknamu made her elation palpable.

What she did next, though, was jarring to Kethras's core—only because of how unexpected it was.

She looked him dead in the eyes . . . and held out a hand.

Join me! she said, making Kethras step back. *You need not forfeit your life as our sister and mother did. We can rule, together, as deities of a new world. A world where Kienari and chovathi are one.*

Kethras paused and narrowed his eyes. *Look around you, Zhala,* he replied. *You know just as well as I do that we could never coexist. Your very presence feeds on life, and your children bring death. This forest is at odds with you and your existence. Surely you feel it fighting you, even now.*

He took a step closer, close enough to reach out and touch her.

But what if I told you, Zhala said as she held up a second hand in warning, *that there was a way?*

He stopped again.

A way for what?

In a burst of speed, Zhala grabbed onto Kethras's wrist—and a flood of images came with it. He saw the chovathi, saw their beginnings as the first children of Zhala; he saw them spread, and multiply, and grow; he saw them sinking into the rocks and the earth, becoming one with them; he saw visions of Ghal Thurái, of the blood of humans seeping into the rocks, and forming something new; he saw the chovathi seed spreading all over the world, washing it away and chasing away shadow. Every living thing—even the world itself—was being absorbed.

Everything. All of existence.

The images were so close, so vivid. It could only mean one thing: it was happening—right now.

He broke free of her grasp, horrified. *Zhala, no! This cannot be. This was not the way our mother intended!*

She glowered at him again, hunched over, and put all of her strength into a shove that sent Kethras tumbling backward. She turned away, facing the tree.

Then she should have never let it happen.

Kethras hit the ground hard enough to take away his breath, but all he could think about was the vision—and it mixed with a deeper sight that Kethras could not explain, only feel: Zhala's body was scarred and mangled, pocked with arrows of humans and athrani alike. He saw the mighty creature that she had become—but he also saw what she once was: a broken and scared Kienari, like she had been when their mother had first forced her out of their forest.

That creature now stood before him, in the heart of the Kienari forest, arms raised to the great tree in some twisted form of thanks.

The tide of arrows kept coming, burying themselves in her skin. It had seemed to slow her down at first, but as she stood before Naknamu, she looked like she was being held up, rather than compelling herself; she was a hollow shell, propped up by the strings of destiny.

Deep down, Kethras had hoped that he would have been able to stop her, either by physical means or by sheer force of will. He had not counted on her simply ignoring those two options completely. Yet, she was so close to the entrance to the Otherworld. Why was she not crossing over?

A panic began to rise inside him as realization set in: she had no intention of crossing over!

He turned his head and shouted. "It's the tree, Miera! She's after the tree!"

Zhala turned to him again, glancing at him sidelong—only this time, her eyes were full of pain, and sadness. She was the scared Kienari again. His sister, his blood. His regret.

She reached out for the tree.

It was never supposed to be this way.

Zhala, daughter of the Binder, howled in pain . . . and the whole world, as it would never be again, howled with her.

Chapter 75

Wastes of Khulakorum

D. L. Jennings

Ulten

I THINK I'M GETTING CLOSE, ULTEN told the Traveler through their mental link. *The air feels lighter here, like I'm coming to an opening.*

Well, I certainly hope you are, the Traveler replied. *I'm in terrible need of a stretch.*

Ulten laughed to himself and tried to see further ahead. This deep underground, no light reached; but the torches he'd brought along had come in handy for just such an occasion.

He had been passing through an underground tunnel that led westward from the Spears, back toward Do'baradai. It was large enough for him to ride comfortably on his camel, and that fact made him think that it had been carved by human hands rather than some ancient river, like the Traveler had suggested. It had taken him roughly the same amount of time to make the journey back this way, although it had been easier since there was a small stream to drink from whenever he needed.

It certainly made the journey less treacherous—and Ulten liked that just fine.

+ + +

With every step, the air became lighter and lighter. He knew he was nearly there. Dousing his torch, he let his eyes adjust to the darkness.

There, he thought with excitement. A speck of light up ahead—and an end to the tunnel! He had lost all sense of time after being in the darkness for this part of the journey; there were no stars above, no sun to guide him. For all he knew, it could have been weeks, but the growling in his stomach told him that it had been just about a day. It was probably early morning, by his best guess.

The nearer he drew, the brighter the light became. As he got closer, he could tell that it was coming from some sort of chamber. It was dim, but it was still light, and that suited him very well.

✦ ✦ ✦

Walking toward the mouth of the tunnel, Ulten was completely un-prepared for what he was seeing: a burial chamber, with columns and statues carved from stone, that looked to be centuries old. He looked up, to where the light was coming in, and realized just how far deep under-ground he truly was — the light at the top, where he had first looked in a few days ago, was nothing more than a pinprick above him. It gave him just enough of a reference to examine the chamber, though, which was massive, buried perfectly beneath the tower all those centuries ago. If the Holder of the Dead had overseen its construction, he had no doubt done it on purpose to hide . . . whatever it was that was down here.

"I realize that it is indeed impressive," came a stifled voice from the darkness, "but there will be plenty of time for gawking after you set me free." It was the Traveler, and Ulten realized that this was the first time he was hearing his voice out loud instead of just in his head. The voice was coming from deeper in the burial chamber, and his words were damp-ened—no doubt a result of the iron he was bound by.

"My apologies, Traveler," he called out. "I've just never seen anything like this."

"Well, get me out and maybe I'll give you a guided tour."

Ulten pulled out his last torch and lit it. Holding up, he saw for the first time the true scale of the place and felt smaller than he ever had before. The walls of the underground chamber went up higher than he could see, and the only way he knew that they ended at all was the sin-gular point of white far above, spilling down the sides like melted wax. Directly in front of him, a few hundred feet away, was a gargantuan stone figure poised over three slabs of granite.

As he got closer, he could make out enough detail on the face of the figure to realize who it was supposed to be: the Holder of the Dead—and the three slabs of granite below him were sarcophagi.

"I . . . I think I found you," Ulten said. His mouth felt drier than the desert he'd just walked through.

"I'd put my money on it," said the Traveler. His voice was certainly closer and seemed to be coming from the sarcophagus on the left.

As Ulten approached, he saw that it was different from the other two. While both sarcophagi to the right were made of solid gray stone with lids to match, the one on the left had a lid of metal. Iron, by the look of it.

"Well," Ulten began, "I made it. Now to get you out." He set the torch down on the ground, resting it against the sarcophagus, and rolled up his sleeves. Placing his hands on the iron lid, cold to the touch, he pushed.

It moved—barely.

"Oh, that is heavy indeed," he lamented. He took a deep breath and pushed again, straining with all his might. It groaned as it moved, sliding across the stone on which it sat; it moved a little further this time— enough that he could see inside. Picking up the torch and peering in, he was pleasantly surprised to see the familiar, red-eyed face, squinting at the sudden influx of torchlight.

"My thanks for blinding me," said the Traveler. "However, if you can manage to push the lid off the rest of the way, I could probably find it in my heart to forgive you."

Ulten grinned. "Of course."

He set the torch back down and resumed his labor.

A great deal of huffing and pushing later, the metal lid fell to the ground with a crash that resonated through the burial chamber.

The Traveler, now free to do so, sat up. "I can't even begin to tell you how good it feels to do this," he said with relief in his voice. Holding up his wrists, which were bound together in irons, he asked, "Did you remember to bring the lock pick?"

Ulten reached into his breast pocked and produced a thin piece of metal. "This was the best I could come up with."

"It will have to do. Here," the Traveler said, offering his hands, "give it to me."

Ulten did as he was told, and watched the Traveler go to work, sliding the flat piece of metal into the locking mechanism. Concentration showed on the god's face as he moved it back and forth with care and precision.

After a few tense moments, there came a click, followed by metal chains hitting stone. The Traveler stood up and rubbed his wrists. "It feels good to be whole again," he said. "Thank you, Ulten."

Ulten gave a deep and reverent bow. "It has been my honor, Traveler."

"It's just good to see your face and hear your voice," the god said. Turning his attention to the central sarcophagus, he said, "Help me with this one. My brother's Vessel is inside."

Ulten's eyes went wide. He looked at the sarcophagus that clearly contained the original Vessel of the Holder of the Dead. "And you seek to destroy it?"

"I do," the Traveler said, "but I need the Wolfblade to do so."

"The Wolfblade . . ." Ulten began, "is in the hands of the Holder."

"It is," said the Traveler with a wicked grin. "Which is why I am going to bring the Vessel to him."

Chapter 76

Derenar

Sera

STANDING INSIDE THE FLOATING TOWER while it moved was incredibly disorienting, and Sera had to look out one of the windows just to keep from getting sick. Her entire body was telling her that they were moving—the tower rocked gently up and down as it glided through the air—but her eyes were telling her that they were standing still. She had been on a boat once when she was growing up, and this reminded her of that. She tried to forget it, though—along with all the vomiting she'd done that day. "The sooner we get out of here, the better," she said to Duna.

The queen was standing across from her, looking out another window that faced behind them. "I don't know," Duna said wistfully. "It's not so bad up here. I've never seen Derenar from this high before." She looked over at Sera. "I don't think anyone has."

"No one was meant to be this high up," Sera said, making sure not to take her eyes off the passing scenery outside. "I hate it."

Duna looked over at her and walked across the room to sit down. The two of them were in a lower floor of the tower that had apparently been some sort of dining hall, long since emptied out. Most of the tower, in fact, was bare, and Duna had pointed out that it felt like a crypt. Sera was forced to agree—especially after . . . recent events.

"I think you'd hate it a lot less if we didn't have to share it with another army," she said, turning her eyes upward, to where the horde of the Holder was being kept.

Sera grunted. "They're too quiet," she said, matching Duna's gaze. "It makes my skin crawl."

"How do you think I feel?" Duna asked with her eyebrows raised. "The way he just called those bodies back into service like they were trained animals?" She shuddered. "I don't like any of this, especially not—," she brought her voice down to a whisper,—"him."

Sera looked toward the middle of the tower where the Holder was seated—he had made sure that his seat was the center of both the tower and attention.

"I don't like it either," Sera said, "but Tennech wouldn't have agreed to a deal with him if there were any other way; I know that in my heart. He always has a plan, no matter how insane it might sound at the time." She gave Duna a reassuring look. "Trust me."

Duna sighed. "I trust Tennech," she replied. "And I guess that means I trust you by proxy," she said with a smile. Suddenly, however, her eyebrows came together in confusion. She tilted her head slightly to look past Sera. "Oh! Hello," she said. "I didn't hear you come in."

"My apologies. I didn't mean to intrude."

Turning around, Sera looked to where the voice came from—and her heart nearly stopped. She was looking at the man who had killed Tennech.

. . . Only that was impossible, she reminded herself. That man was dead. She had killed him herself.

Sivulu Imha-khet.

The name rang in her ears as the man himself stood before her. She heard Duna clear her throat beside her when she realized she'd been staring. "I'm . . . I'm sorry," she said. "I thought I'd seen a ghost."

The pupils in the emerald eyes of the man before her went wide. "Ghost?" he asked.

"It's nothing," Sera said, waving it off. "I'm Sera. This is Duna."

"Ah, pleasure to meet you both. I'm . . . ah . . ."

After a silence, Duna snarked, "Forget your name?"

"It's not that," he replied. "I just sometimes . . . hmm. It's a bit . . . complicated."

"My lifelong mentor had his throat torn out and was brought back to life by the god of the dead," Sera said. "Try me."

The man put his hand against his mouth in a look of shock. "I'm . . . so sorry to hear about your friend. And even more sorry that you have to deal with—" he looked past them both—"*him.*"

Sera looked over her shoulder toward the throne of the Holder, the ersatz representation of the god himself. Looking back at the emerald-eyed stranger, she asked, "So you don't care for him either?"

"That, too, is complicated."

Sera crossed her arms.

"I'm sorry," the stranger said. "It's been a long . . . existence. Can we sit down?"

Sera looked around the mostly empty room and noticed a distinct lack of chairs. "Where do you suggest?"

"I know a place," he said with a smile. "And please . . . call me Asha."

✦ ✦ ✦

The three of them had been climbing the spiral staircase for far too long for Sera's liking. She and Duna had been exchanging eye rolls every time they came to a new floor but didn't exit. Sera determined that she was going to get off at the next one no matter what.

"Ah, here we are," Asha said, to Sera's eternal relief. "In here," he said, and stepped out of the stairwell and into a massive and well-decorated room.

Sera hadn't seen anything like it since Djozen Yelto's opulent chambers in Khadje Kholam, and she certainly hadn't expected to find something like it here, in this giant floating tower. Although, she had to remind herself, nothing should surprise her anymore after what she had been through.

The room felt surprisingly comfortable when she stepped in. It was drafty—to be expected inside a flying brick—but not terribly so. It was well-lit, with candelabra spread throughout. It even had a large area rug just past the entryway that almost made it feel welcoming.

"Did you really have to bring us all this way just to tell us what to call you?" Duna asked. She was already making herself comfortable in one of the large plush chairs near the far wall.

"Of course not," said Asha, taking a seat near Duna. There were three chairs by the wall, laid out around a small wooden table, that looked to be perfect for such an occasion. "But I wanted to get away from Ahmaan Ka."

Sera and Duna exchanged intrigued glances.

"Why not call him the Holder?" Sera asked.

Asha, still waiting by the door, gave them both a long, contemplative look. "That is part of why I struggled to tell you what name I am known by." He crossed the room in his flowing, silk garments and sat down in the middle chair, between Duna and Sera, who were now also seated. "The name I told you—the one I was given when I was born—is Asha Imha-khet." Asha studied the faces of Sera and Duna, apparently looking for some hint of recognition at the name. Sera gave none, but only because she already knew the name "Imha-khet" because of the Wolfwalker that had killed Tennech. Sera just sat there, waiting, and looking Asha in the eyes. "But the body that I now inhabit belongs to someone else."

Sera furrowed her brow at this. "I've seen what happens to those who are raised by the Holder," she said as she leaned forward. "They are lifeless corpses. I have never seen them talk."

Asha shook her head. "You misunderstand me. I have not been . . . brought back to life. This body is not dead. It belongs to one of my descendants—a brave young man named Kuu."

Sera studied the man once again and only now, upon hearing the name, realized that it was not, in fact, the man who had slain Tennech—but it resembled him to a T. If this Kuu was one of Asha's descendants, maybe Sivulu had been his brother; the resemblance was certainly there.

"Then if your body isn't dead," Duna said, leaning forward, "what is it?"

Asha stood up and spread out her arms. "A Vessel."

Sera turned to Duna. "A Vess—" she started to say, but something just beyond the queen caught her eye.

She looked back at Asha, stood up, and walked over to the wall where a large oil painting had been hung in a gold-laced wooden frame: a dark background over a light desert scene. But the thing that caught Sera's eye was the subject—or rather, the three subjects. Standing in the middle, between two male figures, was a thin, silver-haired woman. The way she was painted, almost translucent, made her look like a . . .

Ghost!

Sera snapped her head back to Asha, letting her jaw hang open. She looked at the painting again. "This . . . this is you," she said, whirling around to Asha. "I met you in Khadje Kholam! You're the Ghost of the Morning!"

Asha nodded. "Indeed," she said. "It is good to see you again, O Godseed."

The words hit Sera like a kick to the chest, and she thought she forgot how to breathe for a moment. She blinked a few times before she remembered how again. "What . . . what did you say?"

"You are the Seed," Asha said, sounding puzzled. "You know this name. Surely this is not a new name to you."

"No," Sera said, shaking her head to work out the shock. "The Holder had called me the Seed before, but . . . Godseed? He never said that part before. What does that mean?"

Asha scrunched her face up. "It . . . hmm. Well, you know seeds . . ."

Sera looked at Duna, who shrugged. "I am familiar with seeds," Sera said.

"Then you are familiar with their purpose?"

"They grow into plants," Duna offered helpfully.

Asha nodded and spread out her hands like it explained everything. "But 'Godseed'?" Sera asked.

Asha glanced sidelong at Duna, then back to Sera. "Because that is what you are to become, when the time is right."

"What does that even mean?" Sera asked with frustration, "And how will I know when the time is right?"

Before Asha could answer, though, Sera felt the floor shift beneath her. She felt weightless for a moment, and then incredibly heavy. Then, all was still.

"What was that?" she asked.

Duna was already out of her seat, looking out the window. "If I had to guess," she said, pulling her head back in and facing the two of them, "I would say that it was the tower we're standing in, landing just outside the forest of Kienar."

Sera took a breath and let it out slowly. She and this forest did not mix well.

Chapter 77

Kienar

Miera

SICKENING WHITE SPREAD FORTH FROM Naknamu like tendrils, creeping over the forest floor. Miera watched it with a horrified curiosity. The creep was slow but steady—and as it reached the first of the smaller trees by the great oak, they, too, began to turn white. Her eyes went wide as she followed the color change, seeping through the inner architecture of the tree and spreading out to the branches, ending with each and every last leaf turning the same shade of white as the chovathi.

"What's happening?" Miera shouted. She flew over to Kethras and put herself even with his eyeline.

"Zhala has merged her essence with the forest. She's one with Naknamu now . . . and I have a feeling that she's not done."

"Is there anything we can do to stop her?"

Kethras looked at her with fear and gravity. "Not without destroying the heart of the forest itself."

Miera looked back to Endar and the Athrani Legion, dutifully chopping down chovathi all around them—when a new horror made itself known. Inside the ring of corruption that was spreading out from Naknamu, Miera witnessed the earth itself breaking apart . . . and from those cracks in the world came even more chovathi.

"We have to do something," she said, calling upon her power of Shaping to form barriers over the cracks to slow down the onslaught—but it was only a temporary fix.

"Agreed, but what?"

Before Miera could answer, she heard several cries from the front line of the Legion. Focusing her attention, she had to rub her eyes to make sure she was seeing what she thought she was seeing. As the wave of white crept forth, it began to make contact with a number of soldiers, and the earth itself seemed to reach up to engulf their lower limbs, latching onto them like jaws. Screams of desperation came out of each of the men who were caught as they tried frantically to release themselves, to no avail.

Then, it happened. The white from the earth began to seep into their veins, ascending the same way that it had done in the trees: slowly, and purposefully.

"Kethras!" Miera said urgently, trying to grab the attention of the lone Kienari. Both of them had already come in contact with it, but were apparently unaffected, to Miera's relief.

"I see it," he replied, turning to face Naknamu. "You stop it out there. I'll try to cut it off from the source. It might be the only way to save the forest."

If it's not already too late, Miera thought to herself. She turned to see the spreading white plague devour fresh victims. Even in the short span of time that she had looked away, the first men of the Legion who'd come in contact with it had already been consumed. Now, where they once stood, were nothing more than statues posed in grotesque death throes, shells of the men they once were.

"Get back! All of you!" Miera shouted, and Endar echoed the command. Having seen what it did to the other men on the front lines, those of the Athrani Legion who were further back were quick to obey. She turned her head to see a small number of them advancing, though, clearly disregarding her warning. She took a deep breath to shout at them—when she realized it was not men of the Legion who were moving forward.

"You were born for this!" came the shout. "This is why you were made!"

It was Tennech, leading his Stoneborn in the charge against this new and uncertain enemy. They stepped forward, meeting the encroaching edge of the spreading white plague. Miera held her breath as they made contact, sure that they would suffer the same fate as the men who had gone before. She watched as they advanced, heedless of the danger that awaited them.

... And they walked on, completely unaffected by the corruption.

Miera looked back. The Legion was being pushed out, forced to retreat, as Zhala's corruption continued to spread. Trees were being turned pale white, their leaves falling dead to the forest floor as they were consumed by the plague. If left unchecked, Kienar would be consumed in a matter of hours. She shuddered as she considered the possibility—and hoped that Kethras would succeed at whatever it was that he was trying.

+ + +

Tennech

TENNECH EYED THE GROUND WITH contempt. He turned around to watch the whiteness push out, eyeing the horrific man-statues that dotted the outer edge. He spat. Tightening his grip on his sword, he walked further in, lunging at a newly emerged chovathi and sending its head rolling on the ground.

Seven, he thought. *Seven of us against an endless army*. He took a swing at another chovathi, felling it where the creature stood. *I've faced worse*.

He looked around for Benj, hoping his son was faring better than he. Finding the young armiger, he was pleased to see that being raised a warrior had seemingly paid off. Benj parried and thrust, using his small, round shield to fend off the claws of the pale creatures surrounding them.

Tennech's eyes went to the sword in Benj's hand—and a wave of memory swept over him. He was back on the outskirts of Ghal Thurái, with his sword, Glamrhys, fending off the chovathi horde that had surrounded Nessa, Benj's mother. The image was striking, and the more Tennech watched his son moving and slicing and feinting, the more he was sure he was watching the memory of himself come to life. He felt his jaw go slack in the rapturous remembrance. A sense of pride like he had never known before swelled in his chest.

It was a moment in time that he was more than happy to lose himself in. Feeling the rake of chovathi claws across his chest, though, snapped him quickly back to reality.

"I was having a moment," he growled, shoving the creature back and advancing. He swung at its neck, and the chovathi made a raspy gargling sound as it fell. Making sure to finish the job, Tennech sent the steel of his sword through the creature's throat. Standing up, he wiped both sides of the blade on his forearm, and said, "Don't interrupt me again."

He fixed his eyes on the enemies ahead and gripped his sword with two hands. He continued forward, making his way toward the other members of his small, yet fearsome squad.

Chapter 78

Kienar

Sera

THE LAST TIME SHE CAME here, she died. *Let's not make that a habit,* Sera thought as she took a step out of the tower to look around at the forest of Kienar.

Duna, behind her, spoke up. "You and I were both here. Remember?"

Sera turned to her and nodded. They had been on the same side, but under much different circumstances. "Oh, I remember. I also remember that I didn't like you," she snickered.

"Nobody's perfect," Duna parried, stepping down to be level with Sera.

The stairs leading down from the tower numbered somewhere in the dozens, and from where they stood, they had a fine vantage point from which to drink in the sights of the forest.

Duna took a breath and looked around. "You know, I never got to appreciate this view when we came here before. Durakas never took the time for things like that; he was all about marching and discipline and strength." She crossed her arms and looked back at Sera. "He was so focused on the destination that he never took the time to look around and appreciate the journey."

"Maybe if he had looked around, he would have seen that arrow coming."

Both of them laughed.

"Well, if he did, then I wouldn't be where I am today. So maybe I'll thank him for always rushing around when I eventually make it to Khel-hârad."

The scraping of iron over stone made both of them turn around to see the great iron doors of the tower opening up.

"Speaking of the dead . . ." Sera began and felt her skin crawl. Out of the doors came the soldiers of the Holder—"her army," the Priest kept saying—freshly risen and ambling forth.

The defenders of Khala Val'ur had been great in number and resolve, but neither of those things had mattered in the end when they met the teeth of the chovathi horde. Now they had been given new life—if one could call it that—and new purpose under the watchful eye of the Holder of the Dead. His command over the souls of Khel-hârad, and the bodies they inhabited, was both frightening and perverse. Sera shivered at the thought of being used against one's will for a cause that only the mad and power-hungry would support. But if Tennech had seen what he claimed to see—and Sera had no reason to think otherwise—it was the only way to overcome the threat which the chovathi presented.

"Let's get out of their way," Duna said. Taking Sera by the arm, she pulled her off to the side so the army could walk through. They emerged from the tower: shambling, horrific corpses brought back to life by the wretched power of the Holder—still wearing the weapons and armor that they had died with in life. Most of them Sera had known. She recognized their faces, even with their dull, lifeless eyes. Watching the casualties of her city stagger by twisted her stomach in knots.

"I hate that it had to be my city," she said to Duna as the soldiers continued to come out. "My men. My friends."

Duna put her hand on Sera's shoulder. "I can only imagine what you must be feeling. I'm sorry. I know if I had to watch my soldiers who died at Ghal Thurái come back to life and march under a different banner, I wouldn't be able to handle it." She took her hand away, saying, "You're faring a lot better than I would."

Sera offered a thin smile in return and looked back toward the forest. She paused and squinted, not sure of what she was seeing. "Look," she said, getting Duna's attention. "What is that?"

Duna peered off in the direction Sera was facing and shielded her eyes from the sun. "It looks like . . . is that snow?" she said, looking up at the clear sky.

"No."

The voice sent a shiver down Sera's spine. The two of them turned around to see the Holder of the Dead standing at the entrance to the tower, wearing long black robes with a cowl pulled up over his skeletal head.

"It is not snow. It is the influence of the chovathi, and it has already begun."

Sera turned back to watch the army of the dead marching into the forest, where a blanket of white was laid over everything in its path—and creeping ever closer. "Should we be worried?" she asked.

The Holder scoffed. "You two have nothing to fear; you are under the protection of a god. I cannot say the same for other the mortals with you, however." Sera and Duna exchanged nervous glances. "But now we must away. The transformation has already begun, and we do not have long." He stepped down from the apex, descending the stairs in a smooth gait that made Sera wonder if he was floating. "Come, Seed," he said, not bothering to look back. "You are needed."

Duna and Sera both shared a frown, then started down the stairs to follow the Holder of the Dead into the depths of the Kienari forest.

+ + +

As they walked deeper in, everything around them was silent—eerily silent. The crunching of twigs underfoot provided the sole sounds of what Sera remembered to be a normally lively forest. She leaned over and whispered to Duna, "Is it just me or is something . . . off?"

"You mean besides the walking undead army? Or the god with a skull for a face?"

Sera flashed her a look. "You know what I mean." Their hushed whispers penetrated the air all too easily. "There's something about this place, the weight . . . it's . . . different."

Just then, from off to their left, they heard a low growl followed by a crunching sound.

"Chovathi," Duna said, drawing her sword.

Sera did the same. "Let's hope these corpses remember how to fight."

She heard them come in from all sides as the silence that had pervaded the woods was suddenly shattered, falling to pieces on the forest floor.

Sera watched in horror as the chovathi seemingly came to finish what they had started in Khala Val'ur, ripping the bodies of the men to shreds—but that horror was quickly turned on its head as the men stood back up, reanimated by the strength of the Holder, to continue to fight. They fought with an unholy quickness that was nothing like their slow, ambling walk: their blades, carried by instinct alone, whirled and stung at the pale white creatures surrounding them. She'd seen nothing like it before, and said a silent prayer to the Shaper that she never would again.

"Do not slow down," came the voice of the Holder from behind. "This is their purpose; it is not a battle you were meant to fight."

Sera turned and looked at him quizzically. "But I thought that's why you brought us here: to fight the chovathi."

The Holder drew closer, though Sera realized it was not to speak to her—he was simply moving through the forest in a specific direction. "In a way that is correct, but you were meant for something greater." He passed her by, the black of his robes flowing around him like solid smoke.

Duna sheathed her sword and shrugged. "You heard the man."

+ + +

Deeper they walked through the forest, the distant sounds of savage combat punctuating the silence. All around them was the spreading white pestilence of the chovathi, devouring trees and life alike. Sera had reached out to put her hand on one of the trees and pulled back immediately; it was rough and cold, like the belly of a snake. It was alive, yes . . . but whatever it was, it was not a tree anymore.

"What happened here?" she asked, looking up at the forest canopy with renewed, morbid curiosity.

"Zhala has spread her corruption throughout this forest," answered the Holder, "by making herself one with it. If she is not stopped," he said, motioning around them, "this will blanket the earth."

Duna frowned. "So how do we stop her?"

"She is far too powerful now for any one god to stop her."

Sera furrowed her brow. "Then what do we do?"

The Holder of the Dead did not respond. Sera turned her head where he was looking, though, and saw something that surprised her enough to make her jaw go slack: the former Khyth apprentice, Elyasha, was bathed in light, and hovering about ten feet off the ground. She drew near, a blazing radiance in human form, stopping just before the Holder of the Dead.

She lowered herself slowly to the ground, letting her feet come in contact with the bleach-white landscape of Kienar. The two stood in silence, as if waiting for the other one to speak.

Now that Elyasha was closer, Sera realized that she looked different from the apprentice that she had known in Khala Val'ur: Her skin was cracked and burnt now, with fire running through her veins. It could only mean one thing: she had gone through the Breaking—and survived.

... Yet no Khyth of the Breaking had ever looked like this, draped in power and light. Something else was at play here.

Before Sera could figure out just what, though, the Holder spoke, his skeletal rasp crawling out of his mouth like spiders. "Zhala has sunk her claws deep in the roots of this forest, Shaper. Surely you must know that."

Shaper? What was he ... Sera's eyes went wide. *Was Yasha the Shaper of Ages?!*

"I do, O Holder," the Shaper replied. "It seems that even the Lord of the Dead cannot resist witnessing the corruption for himself."

The Holder scoffed. "Look around you. My army is clashing with hers. It should be clear to you that I want to stop this just as much as you do."

The Shaper narrowed her swirling green eyes at the Holder, neither moving nor blinking for what seemed like an eternity. "And it is just a coincidence that stopping her would mean approaching the entrance to the Otherworld—the very realm from which I banished you? Or did you think I'd forgotten after all these centuries?"

The Holder of the Dead was silent for a moment. "Nothing lasts forever," he began, and the eyes in his skeletal face seemed to glow with fury. "Not even the will of the gods."

The Shaper crackled with energy, the green of her eyes swirling madly. "Is that a challenge, Ahmaan Ka?" She lifted off the ground, and the air suddenly seemed hotter and heavier.

The god of the dead didn't flinch. "Perhaps it is, Shaper—but it is not just I who challenges you. Your reign has long passed. It is time for a new god to take your place at the head of the pantheon."

Sera watched as he pulled out a dagger from his cloak, eyeing it casually. She recognized it—how could she not: it was the blade that the Holder had used to brand her back in Khadje Kholam. She touched the scar on her chest, tracing the outline of the wolf.

"Do you know what this is?" the Holder asked.

The goddess didn't answer.

"No, of course you don't. You wouldn't know the first thing about the Wolfblade. It was forged in secret, after all." He looked back at the dagger, holding it up and inspecting its edge. The golden handle was carved into the likeness of a wolf, and all along the blade was a black and gold filigree that seemed to writhe and claw at the point of the dagger as if it were alive. Almost the instant that he held up the dagger, Sera felt a tremor, small enough to nearly miss but powerful enough to be concerning.

"And it was made," the Holder went on, "with the blood of not just one god—but three." Another tremor. She looked at Duna, who gave her a worried look. So it hadn't just been her who felt it. "And, while your Hammer of the Worldforge was impressive," he continued, "it was nothing more than a crude tool. This," he said, holding up the blade, "is so much more."

The tremors were growing stronger, and closer.

The Holder snapped his fingers. Sera turned to see the Ghost of the

Morning being led out of the forest by the Priest of the Holder, peace and tranquility on her face. She was dressed in the same white robes that she had been in the tower. "You see," he went on as the Ghost was brought to stand next to him, "not only is it a tool of destruction, but it is also a tool of creation." He walked over to the Ghost, and slowly ran his hand down her cheek. The Ghost pulled away, but that did not seem to bother the Holder. "And, most importantly, it is capable of doing something that you never could, Shaper of Ages."

He raised up his hand and brought it swiftly down as he plunged the dagger right into the heart of the Ghost.

"What are you doing?" screamed Sera, but it was too late. The Ghost cried out, falling to her knees as red began to spread from the point of the dagger.

Sera ran over to the Ghost and held her up from behind. The goddess's breath was labored, and she was shaking. "It's okay," Sera whispered into Asha's ear. "I've got you."

"Seed," Asha said, looking up at Sera. "This must be."

Sera blinked a few times, sure that she had heard the words wrong. "This . . . what?"

"It is the only w—" Asha said, before a blood-filled cough cut her off.

Sera's wolf scar began to glow, red-hot, like an iron in the depths of a forge. She jumped up, backing away from the Ghost. Looking straight over to the Holder, she pointed, and said, "You. What are you doing?"

"I told you: I need you. You are the Seed, and for a seed to grow, it must have sustenance."

Her scar began to pulse in time with her heartbeat. On the ground beneath her, the Ghost was bleeding out—yet, for some reason, she still had a look of serenity on her face. What could she have meant when she said that this was the only way? What good will dying do?

As if reading her thoughts, Asha locked eyes with Sera and smiled— then, suddenly, her eyes rolled back in her head, and she seized violently like her chest was being pulled to the heavens by some invisible string.

The blood around her wound began to rise into the air as well—and as it did, a blast of golden light shot out, bright enough to make Sera cover her eyes. When she opened them again, she jumped back—for, floating toward her like liquid smoke was a trail of red and golden light, streaming out from the Ghost herself.

"What are you doing to her?" Sera screamed. "What's happening?"

"You are taking the first step in your journey to become who you were always meant to be—who you were born to be."

"I—I don't understand."

The swirling light came closer as it poured out of the Ghost, reaching out for Sera with its glowing, wispy tendrils. She backed up, but the light persisted—and something caught beneath her feet. She tumbled backward to the ground, barely managing to catch herself. She looked up at the light that was streaming from the Ghost as it continued toward her, undaunted. The hairs on her body stood up, and she could almost *feel* the light. Her chest heaved as her breathing increased, along with her nerves. She winced as the light came closer, and she braced herself.

When it embraced her, nothing she could have done would have prepared her.

The wolf scar on her chest caught fire, a searing white hot, and she screamed from the pain as the light from the Ghost flooded into her. Flashes of eternity appeared behind her eyes as she felt her consciousness being lifted—elevated—as it filled her. She could barely form a coherent thought, let alone words, as the breath was pushed from her lungs.

"Holder!" the Shaper shouted from behind her. "Release her!"

"It is already done," the Lord of the Dead replied. "Neither you nor I can undo what is happening—what *has* happened."

Sera felt her body flooded with strength as the light from the Ghost continued to stream in. Every passing moment meant a new level of strength that she never thought possible before; every single moment that the power of Asha Imha-khet left the body of the Vessel crumpled on the forest floor, was a moment that saw Seralith Edos grow stronger.

The seed was beginning to blossom.

"What have you done?" the Shaper demanded.

Finally, the light from Asha faded, and the last of her power was siphoned into Sera. Sera could hardly move; she lay motionless on the forest floor, overwhelmed with shock and confusion. It was then, after the chaos brought about by the Wolfblade had finally subsided, that Sera felt the tremors again.

"I have filled an empty Vessel with power that was her birthright," the Holder replied, turning to look at the Shaper. As he did, his gaze moved up toward the trees. "But that was merely an appetizer. I fully intend for her to feast on the main course."

It was now abundantly clear to Sera what had been causing the tremors. Coming into view with legs like giant black sequoias was a being that Sera had never seen but recognized immediately. There was, after all, no mistaking the awful dread and earthshaking power that was wielded by one of the very gods of creation himself.

The Shaper turned toward the lumbering behemoth and was gone, taking to the air with a streak of light—right toward the Breaker of the Dawn.

Chapter 79

Kienar

Kethras

KETHRAS PLACED HIS HAND UPON Naknamu and reeled from the sensations. His forest was hurting.

The first thing he felt was the pain, then sadness—though he couldn't be sure if it was his or Zhala's. Emotion and reason were an indecipherable maelstrom that pulsed and expanded in the space of a thought. He felt the creeping white, Zhala's corruption, spreading out from the center of the forest like blood from a vein: flowing, diffusing, unending.

It would fall to him, as Binder of Worlds, to see that it was stopped. If only he knew how . . .

✦ ✦ ✦

For far too long, while the songs of war sounded around him, he stood with his hand on Naknamu's bark. He was searching—not just for Zhala, but for answers as well. He knew, deep down, that he must follow her inside; he also knew that it was a journey from which he would not return. He took his hand away and looked back at his forest with sadness, barely recognizing the corpse that it had become: white, skeletal, dead. Should he fail, he thought that it might be better that he never return at all if it meant that all of creation would soon look like this. He took a breath and gathered his strength and willpower.

He touched the tree.

The pain came fresh all over again; he fell to his knees as it coursed through his body. He forced himself back up, redirecting the sensation back into the tree. Zhala had managed to merge her essence with Naknamu somehow; Kethras intended to do the same. He reached out with his mind, looking for something—anything—that could give him some hint of where to go or how to get there. He was not having any—

There!

A small drop of light, like sunlight through closed eyelids, winked in and out in an instant. He focused, trying to force his thoughts to move toward it. It felt like trying to push through a thin layer of film: his body was resisting, as was Naknamu. He strained with the mental effort, so much so that his vision started to blur.

He was trying too hard. It had been so effortless for Zhala!

Perhaps that was the key . . .

He relaxed, letting the sensations from the forest come and go freely through the barrier of his mind. And, as if in exchange, he suddenly felt that the path before him was equally open. He began to move, and suddenly experienced the strangest sensation, like millions of tiny, delicate cords connected to his body were softly and gently plucked away. It felt . . . warm, not at all uncomfortable, like an eternal summer or a loving embrace. More and more cords broke off as he kept moving, separating from his body with little to no resistance.

Finally, he felt the last one fall away. It was an odd feeling, but something in the back of his mind told him that it was a *good* feeling. He was floating in a void now, having passed through some unknown and invisible barrier, when something deep inside of him—curiosity or instinct, he wasn't sure—urged him to look back.

He turned.

Looking at the barrier he had just come through was like staring up from the bottom of a lake—but there was no mistaking what he saw. There, slumped over at the base of Naknamu's trunk, was Kethras's lifeless body. There was no going back now, and he knew it—yet the prospect did not fill him with dread like he was expecting. Instead, it filled him with hope, courage, and determination. He knew what he was fighting for now, and he knew the stakes. He had no choice but to succeed.

Turning around toward the heart of Naknamu once again, Kethras felt himself being gently pulled in one certain direction. He let himself be pulled, and hoped with every fiber of his being that he would find what he was looking for.

He would retrieve his sister—no matter what it took.

Chapter 80

Kienar

Sera

SERA'S BODY PULSED WITH THE power of the Ghost. Every heartbeat sent new and terrifying strength surging through her veins. It was dizzying, disorienting—and, worst of all, addicting. It was like drinking from a mountain spring after dying of thirst. She must have more.

. . . And before her was a god who could make that happen.

"I see that look in your eyes," said the Holder. "It is the look of one who has had a taste of godhood—a look that all Vessels share." He walked over and held out the Wolfblade, hilt first. "I can offer you more, and the blade can help."

She took it and rose to her feet. The Holder was close enough to her now that she could have easily driven the dagger into his heart and claimed his power for her own.

He seemed to sense that and looked her in the eye. "That dagger was made with my blood," he said calmly. "Through it, I can feel your thoughts, your desires. I know you want to drive it into my heart and do to me what you have done to the Ghost." He stroked her cheek with the back of his fingers. "But the dagger will not let any harm come to me if I do not will it.

"There, on the other hand," he said, pointing to the streak of light left behind by the Shaper as she sped toward the Breaker, "is power that is ripe for the taking."

Sera felt her mouth water with the mention of fresh power. She looked off toward the streaking Shaper, somehow embodied in the former apprentice Elyasha, and the hunger inside her rose. Something else inside her, small though it was, fought against it.

"I have no love for the Breaker of the Dawn," Sera said.

The Holder looked at her, and Sera could see the anger behind his eyes. "Good," he said, and turned toward the heart of the forest. "The Otherworld cannot be breached without the power a god of creation."

After he started to walk away, he paused and turned back, speaking again. "And if you do not open the way for me, I will happily rescind my deal with you—and Aldis Tennech. Now, I shall clear the path . . . you will follow me if you know what is good for you."

He resumed his walk toward Naknamu.

Sera looked down at the Wolfblade, only to find the hand that held it shook with rage. A hand on her shoulder surprised her, followed by Duna's voice from behind.

"Look," the queen said, pointing to the body of the Ghost—said body was sitting up, looking around with a confused expression.

"What . . . happened? Where am I?"

Sera and Duna both exchanged glances.

"Well," Duna said, "'we watched you die,' and 'Kienar,' to answer your questions."

"Kienar?" He held up his arms, still draped in the ceremonial white—stained freshly red with blood. "What's with these robes?"

Duna smirked. "I didn't know the Ghost of the Morning had a sense of humor."

The emerald-eyed man looked up at her and his confounded expression only worsened. He hopped to his feet in a surprisingly acrobatic display. "The Ghost of the Morning," he said, as if recalling a distant memory. "That's . . . the last thing I remember. She . . . she said something about the Wolfblade, and then the next thing I remember . . . is nothing."

Duna looked back at Sera. "She did say that her body was a Vessel."

The man whirled around and looked at Duna. "No. That's impossible. Sivulu always told me that anyone who becomes a Vessel does so permanently. There's no going back."

"Sivulu?" Sera said, and felt the color drain from her face. "You knew Sivulu?"

"He's my brother," he answered. "Kuu Imha-khet, at your service," he said with a surprisingly graceful bow. "If you've got something that needs stealing, I'm your man. I've got this neat trick where I can turn into a fox—"

Sera cut him off. "You mentioned the Wolfblade. What do you know about it?"

Kuu's eyes went wide, and snapped to the dagger in her hand, which he was clearly noticing for the first time. "How did you get that?"

"The Holder of the Dead."

Kuu marched over and went to snatch the dagger from her hand—but, right as he was about to touch it, his hand snapped back, as if repelled by some invisible force. "Ow! What was that for?"

"I—I didn't do anything," Sera said. "It's the dagger. It . . . I think it's bonded to me somehow."

Kuu shook out his injured hand, flexing his fingers and inspecting them to make sure they still worked. "Well, I don't know much about it, but I do know that Djozen Yelto came back with it from Do'baradai about ten years ago." He looked around conspiratorially, leaning in to whisper, "They say that it can claim the power of the gods."

Duna, from further back, spoke up. "You're a little late on that part."

Kuu shrugged. "Just telling you what I know." He looked around the forest and scratched his head. "What is this place?"

Sera joined him in looking up at the forest, wholly unrecognizable from what it had been before. "It used to be the forest of Kienar."

Kuu looked at her skeptically. "Forest?" He gestured around. "Doesn't there have to be trees for it to be a forest?"

"These are trees," Sera said. "Or at least they were, until the chovathi got to them."

Kuu exhaled and puffed out his cheeks. "I have to sit down. Did you say 'chovathi'?" he said, taking a seat on a small boulder nearby. "What is a chovathi?"

"Look," Duna cut in, "we don't have time to catch you up on all this. The Holder of the Dead is already waiting on us to get him through to the Otherworld, and two gods of creation are about to come to blows, so if you don't mind, we have some work to do."

Kuu crossed his arms and turned his head. "Fine. I'll just wait here, on this rock."

Duna rolled her eyes and looked at Sera. "Thank you."

Kuu shrugged silently.

"Now," Duna went on, "I'm not sure how that is going to turn out," she pointed at the floating point of light in the sky that was the Shaper, "but I think our best chance is to follow the Holder to the tree."

The Wolfblade gave off a soothing warmth. "I agree, and so does the dagger, apparently."

"Then let's go." Duna said, grinning. "There's no telling what sorts of trouble we'll miss if we don't hurry."

Sera tucked the blade into her waistband, took a breath, and headed off to see just how much damage a war of gods could cause.

Chapter 81

Kienar

Miera

ARE YOU SURE THIS IS a good idea? Elyasha asked.

Do you have a better one?

Miera took the silence for a "no," and continued to move toward the Breaker. She didn't have to think hard about the last time they were on the same plane of existence together; it was just unusual for it to be this one, and not the Otherworld, where she'd had him imprisoned. The truly odd part, though, was that she had never come face to face with this incarnation of the Breaker—and he had never known this manifestation of her, either. Yet they both knew each other. Their relationship spanned the length and breadth of eternity, and even though they wore different bodies, their spirits were unchanged.

Have you thought about what you'll say? Yasha asked.

Not at all. He won't be happy to see me, so I might not even get a word in edgewise.

If you're unsure, you can always ask what he's doing here. Maybe he'll tell you.

Miera considered it. *If nothing comes to me by the time we get there, that will be my backup plan.*

She could feel Yasha's smile in the back of her mind, and she gave one of her own to match.

+ + +

The Breaker of the Dawn was the largest thing by far, even dwarfing the mighty Naknamu. As Miera came closer, she realized just how massive he was. She had already felt tiny in the presence of Zhala, who had towered above most of the trees in the forest; for something to tower above *all* the trees of the forest was something different altogether. He was a walking mountain, shaking the very earth with his footsteps.

As she got closer, she could see the ground quaking beneath him. She rose up, above his line of sight, and came between him and the sun. She hung there in the air looking straight at him. Before he looked up at her, she *felt* him do so; it made the hairs on her neck stand straight up. He craned his head and smiled.

"I know you," he said. The power behind his voice was the same power behind his steps, and behind his eyes. "Even though it has been millennia since I have laid eyes on you, Shaper of Ages."

Miera felt primordial emotions surging through her at the sight of the Breaker of the Dawn—her oldest enemy, and once, her closest friend. "And I, you, Breaker," she replied. "Tell me: how did you get free from your chains?"

A smoldering fire behind the Breaker's eyes erupted at the mention of the chains. It was gone in an instant—replaced with a sinister smile. "With this," he said, and he raised his hand high enough for Miera to clearly see that, caught in his grip, was the Hammer of the Worldforge.

Miera's mind raced. *If he has the Hammer . . .*

Thornton! Yasha said before Miera could finish her thought.

"What have you done with Thornton?" Miera asked.

A slow, rumbling laughter rolled from the Breaker as he inspected the Hammer. "I know you share blood with him, Vessel," he said, his eyes suddenly darting back to Miera. He was looking *through* her, though, and Miera knew that he could see Yasha as well. "He was useful to me, and held within him the power to set me free—power that comes from my blood, and yours, too, Shaper. He was nearly the perfect Vessel . . . almost as perfect as the one you were supposed to have been born into."

Miera felt a shudder pass through her that stole the breath from her lungs.

What does he mean? Yasha asked.

Miera had no response. She couldn't move her lips to form words.

"You thought," the Breaker went on, "that even from the depths of the Otherworld, I had no influence? My Khyth are loyal to a fault because of the power I gave them—even loyal enough to raise one of their own to the ranks of Revered Mother of the Athrani—and, when the time came for the Shaper of Ages to be reborn into the body of the Great Uniter, I made sure that she was present for the birth." He laughed and said, "Her loyalty was so great that she gouged out her own eyes so her Khyth blood would not be revealed."

What is he saying? Yasha asked. *Revered Mother? Who is that?*

Her inquiry was met with silence as Miera's mind still reeled from the Breaker's words.

"A Vessel like the Seed only comes around once every thousand years," he went on. "Maybe less. I could not let you have her. She was meant for greater things. Now," he said, turning his body slightly away from the Shaper, "I have a Vessel to claim." The Breaker twisted his gargantuan body as he brought the back of his hand screaming toward Miera. Miera barely had any time to think before she manifested a field of energy around herself, stopping the mammoth fist from doing any damage.

"Hnnh," the Breaker grunted, and brought up the hand that held the Hammer. He swung it down in a vicious arc, right at Miera. Compared to her, the Breaker was like a towering volcano—and he may as well have been, with how hard the Hammer struck her: the unstoppable strength of one of the very tools of creation combined the might of a god who had spent a thousand years gathering his power. Even if she had seen the blow coming, she could have done little to prevent it.

As she hurtled toward the ground, every fiber of her being crying out in pain, she only had one thought:

I hope the Seed knows what she is doing.

Chapter 82

Kienar

Sera

THEY WERE SURROUNDED BY THE clashing of armies, all three of them seemingly inexhaustible: the army of the dead controlled by the Holder, the rapidly spawning army of chovathi, and the small, yet unstoppable Stoneborn of Aldis Tennech. It was impossible to tell if one side was winning or losing, and Sera thought that they could all fight on until the end of eternity if left to their own devices. She also decided that she'd rather not stick around to find that out.

As she and Duna cut their way to the tree through the swaths of chovathi, aided by reanimated defenders of Khala Val'ur, Sera felt the Wolfblade grow increasingly warm in her hand—yet it was not uncomfortable; it felt more like power than heat. No matter how hot it became, it inflicted neither burn marks nor pain.

Suddenly, Sera sensed something behind her. She whirled around to see a chovathi closing in—one who had managed to break through the lines of the Holder's army. It lunged at her throat—but the creature never made it. Sheathing his sword a few feet away was Aldis Tennech, the Dagger of Derenar, standing before her in his full battle regalia.

"I thought I raised you to be more careful than that, Sera," he said with a grin that turned the edges up his mustache upward.

Sera returned the smile. "You did." She kicked the head of the creature away. "I had him right where I wanted."

"Of course you did." Turning to Duna, he said, "Do you believe her?"

"She is rather convincing sometimes," the queen said.

Tennech chuckled. As he did, his eyes went to the blade in Sera's hand. He looked back up at her. "You wield the Wolfblade," he said. "How? Only those with the power of a god can do that."

Sera's smile melted away. "The Ghost of the Morning, she . . . she gave up her power to me."

Tennech drew closer and put a hand on her shoulder. "This is a good thing. Her power will aid you on this day—and it is certainly better in your hands than in his," he said as he narrowed his eyes, looking in the direction of the Holder.

"Are you sure?" Sera asked as she matched his gaze.

Tennech looked back at her and gave her shoulder a squeeze. "I am. It may not seem like it now, but this is the way things must be." He took his hand away, and his expression hardened. "That is not to say that this will be without pain and sacrifice—because there is still much to come—but I assure you: I knew what I was doing when I struck that bargain with the Holder," saying with a wink, "despite what he may think." Sera gave him a weak smile. "Now go," he said. "There is still fighting to be done, and not all of it with steel and strength." With those words, Tennech turned around and drew his sword. Over his shoulder he added, "Make me proud," as he surged forward, wading into the chovathi fray, and disappearing in a sea of white.

"Well," Duna said from behind, "he always did have a way with words."

Sera kept her eyes where she'd last seen him, but she knew that a master was at work. If Tennech didn't want to be seen, he wouldn't be. "And with a blade," she said. "They don't call him 'the Dagger' for nothing."

"I can see that," Duna said, stepping over the body of the recently felled chovathi.

The blade pulsed in Sera's hand. She looked down, as if just now remembering that it was there. "Come on," she said, trudging forward, "we're nearly there."

✦ ✦ ✦

Up ahead, at the base of the tree from where Zhala's corruption was spreading, stood the Holder. As Duna and Sera approached, he turned to face them. There was a frightening light behind his eyes when he spoke.

"The Binder of Worlds has surrendered his Vessel. His spirit is now inside, along with Zhala's."

Sera walked closer but stopped far enough away to leave a good bit of space between them. Inside her, the power of the Ghost of the Morning seemed to recoil, like a hand too close to a flame. Even her spirit was repulsed by the Holder of the Dead.

"What does that mean for us?"

Before she was even able to finish getting the words out, the earth trembled again. Sera didn't have to look to see what it meant. The Breaker was close.

The Holder looked off to where the tremor had occurred. "It means the Breaker will have sensed the vulnerability of the Otherworld, and—even though he has no love for the Shaper of Ages any longer—it is his realm to lose."

Duna glanced at Sera. "That doesn't sound good."

Sera raised her eyebrows and shook her head.

"You have inside you the power of a god," the Holder said, "and before you stands another. You are no longer a mere mortal to be crushed beneath his heel—you are the Godseed, and now you must prove that you are worthy to wield the power that you have been gifted."

Sera looked at him for a long moment and had many, many visions involving the Holder and her dagger. She tightened her grip around it . . . and relaxed. She knew that it was useless to resist him here, now. She turned around to see the hulking form of the Breaker of the Dawn crest the skeletal trees as he drew near.

She looked over to Duna. "How do you feel about taking on a god?"

Drawing her sword, the queen said, "I'm not sure how much damage I'll be able to do with this," she said, holding it up in front of her and comparing it to the oncoming Breaker. "But I do want to see if he bleeds."

The Wolfblade now pulsed more strongly than it ever had before, seeming to increase with every step the Breaker took toward them. It was like holding the sun in her hands.

The Breaker was coming . . . and Sera was ready.

Chapter 83

Kienar

Sera

SERA STOOD, WOLFBLADE IN HAND, waiting for the Breaker to come. Across from her was Duna, who looked up at the ancient god.

"He's big," the queen said, "but we can equalize with numbers."

Sera turned around to see the army of the dead still battling with the chovathi. Both sides were still at an apparent standstill—when one of them fell, another would rise back up.

"We've got numbers," Sera replied, "but not for long. If we divert too many of them away from the chovathi, we risk being overwhelmed."

"We can deal with the chovathi after we deal with him," Duna said. "One threat at a time—and this one," she said, pointing her sword at the Breaker, "is the bigger threat."

Sera nodded.

"I'll try to get in a good position," Duna said, and headed for the Breaker, disappearing from sight.

Sera was mindful of the Holder of the Dead behind her, whose eyes seemed to bore through her back when she spoke. She knew she was linked to him now through the blade, and it made her skin crawl. Inside her, though, the power of the Ghost of the Morning gave her strength. Looking up, she watched the Breaker come fully into view.

"Godseed," the Breaker boomed. His massive body was slightly concealed by the skeleton-white trees now ripe with Zhala's corruption—but that hardly mattered for a being of his size. It was like looking at a mountain up close. "I have scoured eternity for you, for the one who will be my Vessel." He tilted his head, as if noticing the Holder of the Dead for the first time. "And it appears that I am not the first god to try to do so."

The Holder stared, unflinching.

Sera had to crane her neck to look up at the titanic god. She had never felt so small and insignificant before. "What makes you think I would be your Vessel?"

The Breaker gave a deep, menacing chuckle. "You mean you do not yearn for power? The power to unite Breaking and Shaping—the power of creation and destruction itself? You would turn your back on this?"

Sera felt the Wolfblade pulsing in her hand. "I would. I have no need for such power."

"Need? Perhaps not. But desire?" He leaned slightly toward her. "You desire such power. I see it in you already, thrumming and pulsing, calling out. You hunger for it; it drives you." He straightened up again. "Give yourself up to me, and it will be yours."

Sera shifted uncomfortably. She felt the gnawing in her stomach and the throbbing in her veins. The Breaker was right: she did want it. It was an urge, a compulsion, and it threatened to consume her . . . unless she consumed it first. She looked up.

"Why give myself up as a Vessel," she sneered, "when I could just take from you what I want?"

The fire behind the eyes of the Breaker of the Dawn became, for a moment, a blazing hellfire. "You speak to a god, *human!*" The forest shook with the power of his voice. "Your body does not need to be living for me to occupy it"—and he brought down his massive hand straight for Sera.

It was all she could do to dive out of the way, rolling to safety just outside of the impact area. When the Breaker's hand struck the ground, the world shook, and it nearly knocked out Sera's breath. She stood up, dusted herself off, and held the Wolfblade up high, her brown-on-blue Athrani eyes gleaming with defiance. "Who says I'm human?" She turned her gaze slightly past the Breaker. "Now!" she shouted.

One heartbeat later, the form of Duna came flashing into view as she leapt from the trees nearby, sword in hand, bearing down on the vulnerable back of the Breaker. She landed, driving in her sword, with a dagger in her other hand to do the same. The Breaker howled in pain as Duna began to ascend, using her blades like ice anchors.

That should keep him . . . she began, but her thoughts were interrupted by a strange sensation inside her, like a whisper begging to be spoken aloud. Turning her attention inward, she recognized it as the power of the Ghost of the Morning, yet she had no concept of what it could do. She felt it tugging at her, though, pleading to be let out. Sera felt no compulsion to resist. So, like setting a feather loose in the breeze, she let go . . . and felt the power of the Ghost wash over her.

The first thing that she felt change was her eyes: her vision shifted, colors became less saturated. Everything was somehow sharper, more focused. The scene in front of her warped as her narrow field of view expanded into a wide panorama that took in everything in front of her as well as to her sides. Her nostrils were flooded with a cavalcade of smells, some foreign to her and some known—but all of them telling her exactly where each object was as it meshed with her other senses. She felt her bones shifting and cracking. She tried to cry out—but her voice instead came out as a twisted howl that pierced the air.

She looked down, expecting to find her hands similarly gnarled in pain, but instead found a pair of massive lupine paws that were larger than her own hands had been. She was less concerned with their transformation than she was with what they had been holding.

The Wolfblade! she thought. *Where is it?*

She scoured the ground, using her newfound sharpened senses to aid in her search—yet, in her panic, she almost missed the familiar glow of the god-borne blade. It was like moonlight in the daytime—nearly washed out by the light of the sun—but it was there. She focused on it. It was . . . inside her! Merged with her essence. She was the Wolfblade, and the Wolfblade was her.

So this is the power of the Ghost, she thought, as she ran her tongue over her mass of fangs. *Let's see how it holds up.*

Springing forth, she sprinted toward the Breaker on swift legs that carried her quickly to the god. With a glance upward, she could still see Duna, ascending the Breaker like a mountain, going hand over hand with her blades in his back. Sera smiled to herself as she neared. Leaping into the air, she was grace, she was precision—she was death. She sunk her teeth into the Breaker's tough skin. Pulling back, she tore away a chunk of his flesh as she ripped it out. She leaped off, looking for the next target of opportunity . . . when, suddenly, the wind shifted. It was slight at first, nothing more than a breeze running over her coat, but it rapidly began to increase in strength and intensity.

It's him, she realized. Of course he wasn't going to go without a fight—and for the god of Breaking and Khyth, conflict was merely one of his attributes.

"I applaud your fighting spirit," the Breaker said as he stood up to his full height, "but it will only serve to prolong your suffering, as well as the inevitable."

The wind was picking up, swirling around the form of the Breaker like an invisible barrier that moved with him as he lumbered forth. Duna was whipping like a flag, desperately grasping at the blades that were lodged in the Breaker's back when, suddenly, she was ripped away and tossed into the forest, gone from sight in the blink of an eye.

"I think you underestimate my ability to deal with suffering," Sera growled, baring her teeth. She dug her claws into the earth, held in place by the familiar yet strange power of the Wolfblade.

"Then we shall test your limits."

The earth shifted beneath her feet, followed by a loud crack. Looking down, Sera realized that the ground she had been standing on was floating in the air—and rising quickly. She leapt from the rocks before they got too high, spotting a place in the undergrowth that was suitable for landing. As soon as her feet touched ground, though, a shadow washed over her, growing larger and darker. Without taking time to think, she leapt forward—and the deafening crash of rocks behind her told her that she had missed being crushed by mere seconds.

She looked up at the Breaker. She couldn't get to him without being tossed by the windstorm that raged around him. She needed to find some way to break through, either through . . . or over. She dashed into the forest to find cover.

Behind her, he bellowed, "Come out, little Vessel! You need not fight me in this."

She skulked in the underbrush, trying to find some way around when, suddenly, her senses were overrun. The sharp smell of blood clawed at her nostrils. She lifted her head up.

Duna!

She turned, taking off after the trail.

It wasn't long before Sera found her—still alive, much to her relief. The queen's armor seemed to have taken much of the punishment, but her body had still suffered a great deal of trauma. The sharp scent of almonds from her right arm told Sera that it was broken.

"Duna, your arm," she said, hoping that the words would scare her less than the lupine form she wore. She tried but couldn't grasp how she might revert to her human form in order to help.

"Landed funny on the way down," the queen said, wincing from the pain. She coughed, and a spattering of blood misted her armor. Her voice was calm despite the trauma. "It feels almost as bad as you look. More fur than last time."

"We need to get you some help. Endar and—"

Duna cut her off. "I'll be fine. I trained under Durakas, remember? He gave me worse wounds than this."

Sera crinkled her nose at the thought of the Thurian commander, probably rotting nearby. "Fine. But stay here. You did your part: you caught him off guard and drew first blood." A sound from the Breaker's direction made her turn to the clearing. With a quick glance back to Duna she said, "If you find the Shaper, tell her we need help." She took off in a sprint, looking to see exactly how fast these new legs could carry her.

✦ ✦ ✦

Duna

SERA—AT LEAST IT SOUNDED LIKE Sera—bounded off into the forest toward the sounds of the Breaker. Duna sat up and winced, drawing in breath through her teeth as the pain shot through her. She probably had a few broken ribs, and her sword arm was in awful shape, but she had been through worse. She would manage. She would deal.

She stood up—or tried to. Her legs refused to work at first, and she collapsed again under the weight of the pain. Frustrated but not beaten, she rolled over onto her stomach, pushing herself off the ground with her one good arm, and came to her knees.

Looking around, she tried to orient herself in the forest. It was daylight, but the heart of Kienar wasn't exactly navigable land. If there was one thing she was certain of, though, it was that Sera was right: they needed the Shaper's help. She wasn't sure how strong the Holder of the Dead was—or even the Ghost of the Morning—but she was willing to bet that a god of creation ranked higher on the power scale than a ferryman of the dead.

Duna saw her sword a few feet from her and determined that this time she would make it to her feet. She gritted her teeth and stood up, realizing that the new pain in her left leg meant that she'd probably broken or torn something there as well—possibly both. Limping over to her sword, she picked it up with her off-hand and put it back in its sheath around her waist.

"Now to find another god of creation," she said out loud to no one in particular.

She stuck her pointer finger in her mouth to wet it, pulled it out, and stuck it up in the air. Judging the way the wind was blowing, she said, "That looks like as good a direction as any," and shuffled off.

✦ ✦ ✦

Sera

SERA APPROACHED THE CLEARING CAUTIOUSLY. The chaos from the Breaker had apparently stopped, and there was a haunting silence throughout the woods.

As soon as she stepped into view, she found out why: the Holder of the Dead was standing in defiance of the old god, with his twisted, undead army filling out the ranks behind him.

The bellowing of the Breaker cut the silence. "So, Ahmaan Ka, you would take that which is mine? You seek to control the Vessel of the Godseed?"

The Holder stood defiant, a staff in his right hand. "What I seek is of no concern to you, Breaker." Just then, a breeze from the west caught his robes, adding credence to his words. "Unless you stand in my way."

The air in the forest felt heavier, humming with power. A rumbling preceded a sudden crack in the earth, separating the Breaker from the Holder.

"Stand in your way?" the Breaker shouted. The rage in his eyes could have melted steel. "Inside me lies the power which gave you existence, Holder. Even the blood in your Vessel's veins is kin to my own. Everything you are, you owe to me!"

The earth continued to tremble, but the Holder was not swayed. "Yet you and I both know that gods can be usurped. The power of the Otherworld has been dormant, and the realms of the living and the dead have remained separate for far too long." Defiance gleamed in the half-eye host of the Holder. "You did not have the power—or perhaps lacked the vision—to see to that in your lifetime. I intend to do it for you." With that, he raised his staff, and a tiny ball of fire winked into existence just beyond his reach. "It does not surprise me," the Holder of the Dead went on, idly admiring the fire, "that the Shaper of Ages was able to contain you in the Otherworld; her power feels so much more . . . robust . . . compared to yours. The power of creation; the power to make something from nothing." In an almost casual motion, the Holder thrust his staff forward, commanding the fireball toward the Breaker. As he did so, the horde of reanimated soldiers behind him suddenly sprang into motion, swords drawn and running for the god of Breaking. "You have squandered yours, Lord of Khyth! Give it to someone who will make use of it."

The fireball from the Holder splashed into the body of the Breaker, and the ancient god reeled from the impact. When the flames cleared, though, he was still standing.

"It will take a lot more than the light of a candle to stop me, Ahmaan Ka."

The earth shift again beneath Sera's feet. At first she thought it was due to the sheer numbers of the soldiers from Khala Val'ur, but looking up at the Breaker, she realized that it was *him*. He didn't have the Shaper's powers of creation, true, but he had something just as powerful: destruction. She could barely keep her feet as the forest floor seemed to come to life, thrashing and cracking, splitting and shaking. She looked up at the Breaker and then back into the forest toward where Duna had been.

Hurry up, Duna, she thought. *And you'd better not be alone.*

† † †

Duna

AS SHE LIMPED THROUGH THE forest, every breath was labored, and came with fresh pain. She knew by now, after several unsuccessful attempts at standing on it, that her right leg was broken. It hadn't pierced the skin, though, so at least she had that going for her. It was just going to be, well, a pain in the meantime.

She had been walking for a few minutes, not really knowing where she was going, but only knowing that the Shaper was out there, somewhere. She looked up, trying to get some idea of where she was; it was nearly useless this far into the forest. Even if it hadn't been tainted by Zhala's corruption, Kienar was a thick and mysterious forest, practically unseen by outsiders since sometime before the Shaping War. There were no maps of the area; there were no experts, save the Kienari who lived in its branches. It was just her, and the leaves, dead though they were.

"Why couldn't you have been lost somewhere with fewer trees?" she said aloud in frustration.

"Nnnnhh," came a faint response, echoing from somewhere off in the distance to her left.

Her ears perked up immediately. "Hello?" she called. "Shaper?"

The groan came again, but this time Duna was ready. She already had her head turned in the direction it had come from and was almost certain she could place its location. "I'm coming!" she said as she hobbled toward the sound. "Just don't hold your breath waiting."

✦ ✦ ✦

After an excruciating trek through the underbrush, Duna was finally closing in on where the noise had come from. The call and response had been working well thus far, and she was certain that she Shaper was close.

Finally, as she climbed over a fallen tree that led to a clearing, she saw her—or, rather, she saw the impact crater she had made.

"Is that you down there?" she called.

"Unfortunately," the Shaper called back.

Duna dragged herself to the edge of the crater, nearly two hundred feet across. She peered in, and, sure enough, saw the outstretched form of the Shaper at the middle of the point of impact. "Can you get out?"

The Shaper looked at the crater around her. "I can try."

Duna looked down at her broken sword arm. "Well, I'm only half as effective as I'd normally be," she said, "or I'd offer to help you out."

"It's fine," the Shaper replied. "I can get myself out. It's just . . . going to take some effort."

Duna watched as the goddess struggled to her feet. With a look to the edge of the crater, the Khyth woman was suddenly draped in a silvery glow that started at her eyes and ran the length of her body. Slowly, she lifted herself into the air. It was like watching a huge fish being reeled in: steady, but exhausting.

As the Shaper cleared the edge of the crater, she let her feet touch the ground, just beside where Duna was standing. She took to a knee to catch her breath. Looking up at Duna, she said, "I can walk the rest of the way . . . but I feel my strength in flux. I don't know what's happening, though I think it has something to do with what's going on up there," she said with a nod, indicating the furor near Naknamu.

Duna offered a hand. "Then I hope whatever strength you need is recovered by the time we get there. I don't know how well Sera is going to fare against the Breaker."

The Shaper clasped her hand and stood up. "She won't last long unless she has help."

Duna patted the sword in her hilt. "Then let's give her what she needs."

The two of them walked off, leaving the crater behind. With a glance back at the massive hole in the earth, Duna wondered to herself just how she had managed to get herself in this position—and what she would have to do to dig herself out.

Chapter 84

Kienar

Sera

THE HUM OF EARTH AND the crackling of air was all that Sera could hear as she sprinted toward the Breaker. The dead were all around her, and she could feel their compulsion from the Holder. They had but one thought: *swarm*—and they were doing a damn fine job, she thought; the Breaker was like a rotting body being overrun by ants.

Still wearing the form of the wolf that the Ghost granted her, Sera was able to cover the distance much quicker than she would have on two legs. Careening through corpses, she wove her way to the god of the Otherworld, who was thrashing about, trying to rid himself of the Holder's soldiers. Sera didn't know exactly how to bring him down, but she knew that she had to try. If he was weakened by the efforts of the Holder and his army, perhaps the opportunity would present itself. When it did, she would be ready.

The Breaker had just brushed off a half dozen soldiers who had been clinging to his leg. Sera heard the humming of the air drop an entire octave as the sky began to darken.

"Your hubris is great, Ahmaan Ka," the ancient god thundered, "but arrogance alone will not see you hoist the crown of the Otherworld."

Peals of thunder split the sky as the Breaker rose up, thrusting his hands to the heavens. What had been clear skies only moments ago had now darkened into a menacing, swirling storm that seemed to surround the god of creation. Blinding flashes of burning light came down one by one and struck the ground; some of them landed squarely on the soldiers of Khala Val'ur, leaving them hollowed out husks of smoking, charred flesh; others hit nearby, still doing damage, but not enough to stop their advance. Sera was nearly struck, as the singed fur and ringing in her ears told her. She continued on, though, legs pounding, as she hastened toward the Breaker.

"I bring more than arrogance," the Holder replied. "The Shaper's blood courses through this body! Even you must know that is a threat to your reign."

The windblown robes of the Holder accentuated his hand movements as he harnessed the power of Shaping, manifesting countless daggers of stone and iron which rained down on the Breaker of the Dawn. They struck several of the undead soldiers as well, but the Holder either did not notice or did not care. The rain of blades continued.

The Breaker raised his forearm to shield himself from the onslaught, catching some of the daggers, but most of them found their marks, burying themselves solidly in his tough hide.

"The Shaper's power is kin to my own, godling. Surely you must know this."

Ear-splitting thunderclaps rocked the forest as the Breaker brought down more lightning strikes, with one even hitting himself. *His concentration must be waning if he's grown that careless,* Sera thought—then she realized that the god had done more damage to the swarming soldiers that had been plaguing him than he had done to himself. Still, if it wasn't reckless, it was surely desperate. Sera thought that both possibilities boded well.

Corpses littered the forest floor, some of them still smoking from the lightning strikes, unmoving. Others had gotten back up and resumed their attack, heedless of the physical damage that had been done to them. These men had already given their lives in defense of their city once; it was only fitting that they give whatever was left in defense of humanity.

Humanity, Sera added darkly. *If that is what we are defending.*

She had found herself near the Breaker several times, looking for an opening for the right time to strike. Up until now, she had found none—but that was when she saw it. The Breaker had diverted nearly all his attention toward ridding himself of the swarming dead. In doing so, he had left himself exposed.

Sera sprang into the air, flying right toward one of his legs. Making contact, she dug her claws into him and sunk her teeth into the familiar-tasting flesh. Power spilled out of him like blood, fueling her hunger. She could feel the very source of Breaking inside of him, and the Wolfblade that was now a part of her called out for it.

She would make his power her own.

"You forget yourself, *dog*," the Breaker growled. He swatted at her but missed, with Sera barely managing to twist out of the way as she let go and fell to the ground. A flick of the Breaker's wrist sent a chunk of earth hurtling toward her—only this time, she was not quick enough to dive to safety. "You do not deserve a seat at the table."

"Perhaps she does not," came another voice, drowning out the tempest that was tearing through the forest. "But any table of yours would only be lonely and forgotten—just like you."

Sera looked up to see the shining form of the Shaper come screaming into view, soaring over the trees, well above the grasp of the Breaker. The glow surrounding her was brilliant, building into an orb of almost solid light. She hovered for a moment, then the light from her hands shot out in two directions, meeting the ends of the Breaker's arms.

The Breaker cried out in deep and sudden anguish as the light on his wrists glowed white hot. Then, just as suddenly as it appeared, the light was gone . . . leaving behind the outline of two great chains, which now hung heavily from the Breaker's wrists.

"And that," the Shaper said, pointing to the Hammer of the Worldforge, "is mine." She held out her hand, and the hammer glowed blue in response.

"No!" The Breaker shouted. He looked vengefully at the Shaper as he struggled against his bonds, desperately clutching the hammer. "The Otherworld is just as much mine as it is yours!"

"But you proved long ago that you have no place in it," the Shaper said, and she clenched her fist.

The Hammer of the Worldforge broke free of the Breaker's hold, flying toward the Shaper with precision and grace. She reached out her hand and caught it; it fit perfectly in her grasp.

"We were once one," the Shaper said as she descended. "Breaker, Shaper, Binder. Do you not remember?" Her eyes were glowing with the same bright blue that was coming from the Hammer. "One accord, one spirit. One mind." She stopped, floating in the air, her eyes smoldering. "But you chose to break that bond. You chose to betray us and everything that we had created together." She moved her hand downward, and the Breaker was forced to his knees by the chains. "All for what? A chance at power?" she said, a mix of anger and sadness in her voice. "We had made such beauty—such enduring beauty. And you chose to simply cast it aside."

Sera felt her lupine form receding as it gave way to her human flesh once again. It was a dull burn, but one that she bore with clenched teeth and a hardened mind. When it was over, she found herself holding the Wolfblade again.

"It was stagnant," the Breaker said. The fire in his eyes had died down into embers. "What you called beauty, I called weakness. There was no chance for improvement." He spat on the ground. "It was dull."

The Shaper drifted lazily down, finally making contact with the earth. She was dwarfed by the massive frame of the Breaker, prostrated before her by his otherworldly chains.

Sera walked closer, studying the face of the Shaper. To her surprise, the goddess's eyes were awash with tears.

"You would give up what we had for that?" The Shaper demanded. "For excitement? To watch our creation fight and die? All for your entertainment?"

The Breaker gave a weak chuckle. "But look at what that conflict has brought them: invention, ingenuity, innovation; the building blocks of the sprawling civilizations we see before us that now blanket the world—a world that we created . . . but never improved. Do you think such feats would have been possible if not for the push I gave them?"

Sera felt herself being drawn closer, and the blade in her hand gave off its familiar warm glow.

The Shaper shook her head. A single tear ran down her cheek. "Then you really have learned nothing from all your years of solitude." She sighed. "All you ever saw was hardened clay to be molded into a vase . . . So what did you do? You broke the clay—shattered it into a thousand pieces—and from those pieces you sought to rebuild your own." Crossing her arms, she turned slightly away. "The thing you never saw, though—the one thing that I was hoping you would see after all these millennia of reflection—was that the vase had been in front of you the whole time. You just chose not to see it."

Sera walked closer, Wolfblade in hand. She could feel the power pulsing from the god in front of her. It was nearly blinding. Her other senses seemed dull except for one: hunger.

"I regret nothing I did," said the Breaker. The embers in his eyes had nearly faded, a whisper of the maelstrom they had been. "And I would do it again given the chance."

"Then you are truly lost," the Shaper said, "and the Binder was wrong to spare you." She turned her back fully to the massive god. A gesture forced him even lower to the ground.

Sera's hunger rose, along with her dagger. She could almost taste the power before her, feel it pulsing in the veins of the god before her. The hunger was so great that it washed out her vision, but she didn't need sight to know what she was doing. She was driven by something else now: impulse. She knew that the power could be hers—*would* be hers. It was dizzying! All she had to do was take it—and take it, she would.

She reached out, Wolfblade gleaming in the sunlight, and brought the dagger down.

. . . Right into the back of the Shaper.

Chapter 85

Kienar

Sera

No! SERA SCREAMED, BUT THE words merely echoed in her mind. Her mouth wouldn't listen. *Why is this happening?*

The Shaper of Ages dropped to the ground, along with the Hammer of the Worldforge.

Sera felt the hunger of the Wolfblade drinking in the goddess's power as it bled into her own, out from the body of the Khyth before her.

It coursed inside her like a river.

A fleeting thought told her that she should stop it, but every fiber of her being shouted at her to let go. Accept it. Embrace it. It was hers: the power of creation. Breaking and Shaping, united. It filled her like a feast.

. . . Yet, in the chaos, that fleeting thought resurfaced. *Try to fight it, try to pull back!*—but it was like shouting into the wind. The urge to keep going was too strong, the thirst too great. Sera had opened the flood gates; it was infinitely more difficult to close them now that the waters had been loosed.

The Breaker, still in his chains, roared, "What have you done?" His words shook the earth. "Her power was not yours to take!"

Lightning split the sky—but this time, it was not from the Breaker.

"Perhaps not, but it is mine now." The Holder of the Dead was walking toward Sera, staff raised, with an eerie glow about him.

"You," the Breaker said accusingly. "You did this? How?"

The Lord of the Dead gave no answer. He simply stared as he moved closer, lidless eyes piercing the darkness.

Feeling the Holder's intent, Sera steeled herself against him. "No," she said. "I won't let you." Yet even as she spoke the words, she felt their futility. Her body would not respond, as if it were no longer her own, a puppet held up with strings.

The Holder laughed and planted the end of his staff on the ground. "Your will was mine the instant your corpse hit the forest floor. I never needed your cooperation—I had it the moment you died. Now," he said, and Sera felt her body turn toward the Breaker. "The final piece of the puzzle."

Sera's body shuddered, sending spasms of power throughout. Insider her she felt the soul of the Shaper, the goddess's power now fully hers. If the power of the Ghost of the Morning had been a single drop of water, then the power of the Shaper was an ocean.

She looked up. Before her knelt the Breaker, still confined to the forest floor in the chains that she controlled—and she, in turn, was controlled by the Holder. She could no more let the Breaker go than defy the Holder's commands, and right now she felt herself commanded forward.

"You foolish, trifling mortal," spat the Breaker of the Dawn. "You were meant to be my Vessel! Now one of the gods of creation lies dead at your hands. Stop this at once! Surrender to me before you endanger us all with your reckless arrogance."

The skeletal face of the Holder of the Dead was a good distance away from Sera, but his laughter was loud enough to make it seem like he was standing right beside her. "Bargaining is fruitless endeavor, Breaker, as is begging and pleading," he said. "But, by all means, continue. Your weakness is . . . delicious."

The Breaker pulled at his chains in anger, but they held fast. Sera could feel her strength keeping them in place—and the cold hand of the Holder driving hers.

"You style yourself a god, Ahmaan Ka, but you are still just another creation. You will never have what it takes to rule the Otherworld."

A low, throaty chuckle worked its way up from the chest of the Holder as he approached. "I was right about you, Breaker: you lack vision. I have no intention to rule the Otherworld. It was never mine to begin with."

Sera raised her hands above her head, clutching the Wolfblade tighter than a mother would a falling child. Compulsion drove her closer to the kneeling god, and the power of the Shaper lifted her up into the air, surrounded by light.

She held the dagger inches away from the chest of the Breaker of the Dawn.

"But the realm that is mine, and has always *been* mine," the Holder went on, "is the realm of the dead. Together, with the power of the Breaker and the Shaper at my disposal, I will join it with this one.

"The three shall become one, once again."

Sera drove the dagger into the body of the Breaker, and a bleeding surge of power began anew. The light that filled her vision was brighter than the sun. She clenched her teeth for the onslaught.

The Breaker thrashed violently, but the chains held him in place. Spreading outward from where the Wolfblade had been plunged in, waves of liquid fire washed over him as it looked like his very body was being ripped apart, draining into the dagger along with his power.

It was nothing like when the Shaper's power had entered her. To Sera, it was more like regaining the use of a sleep-drained limb—a sense of completion, a feeling of wholeness. It was awful and violent, yet calming, all at the same time; a whirling, frenzied wake. It was a boulder dropped onto the surface of a tranquil pond, and Sera felt each and every wave.

After wave.

After wave.

Then, just as suddenly as the rippling of power had begun, it ended. The pond was calm. Sera opened her eyes.

Before her was a pile of ash—all that was left of the body of the Breaker of the Dawn.

That which had been broken has been remade whole.

Breaking, Shaping—both of them, now one—were contained inside the Vessel of the Godseed.

Her body lurched forward.

"Now then, Seed," said the Holder, turning to Naknamu. "You have one more door to open for me, and then I will put the entirety of your powers to use."

Sera lifted her arms skyward—and her eyes went wide as power leapt forth, forcing her to her knees. Light poured out from her eyes, fingertips, and mouth. It felt like all the air was being squeezed from her lungs.

A sphere blinked into existence, liquid and clear. In it, Sera saw the whole of reality: a point with a single surface, yet simultaneously containing the vastness of creation; a nexus of power, flooding from inside her, drawing on both Breaking and Shaping alike.

The sphere grew before them in violent, pulsing surges; it was like staring into an orbicular pond—yet Sera knew that beyond it lay the Otherworld and Khel-hârad. The barrier between the two realms had already been fractured, and now the Holder intended to link them together, extending that link to this one—the realm of the living.

"And from this seed, a new creation shall rise," said the Holder, and he stepped toward the luminescent sphere, which continued to grow.

It grew, and it grew, and it grew . . . and then, when Sera felt that she had no more power left to give, it swallowed them both whole.

Chapter 86

Kienar

Duna

THE FAMILIAR SOUND OF STEEL meeting flesh filled the air as Duna drew ever closer to Naknamu. The Holder's army and Zhala's forces were continuing their endless dance. Somewhere out there, Tennech and his Stoneborn were making trophies of the chovathi as well, and Duna hoped that they would be enough to turn the tide. Only time would tell.

Duna approached the edge of a clearing when a sudden, loud crackling noise blended with an electric hum. Then a *whoosh*, a bright flash of light, and silence.

Duna frowned. Silence is rarely good.

Drawing her sword with her offhand, she approached the glade.

Nothing, she thought. *That explains the silence.*

As she scanned around, though, the nothing was quickly replaced with something that caught her eye: partially obscured by underbrush was what looked to be the outline of a body. She sheathed her sword and walked over to investigate.

The first thing she noticed as she came around the brush was the shock of red hair. That, coupled with signs of a body that had been through the Breaking, told her that it was the Khyth girl from earlier—the one that the Holder of the Dead had called the Shaper. Beside her was what looked to be a blacksmith's hammer, intricately carved figures dancing up and down the length of the handle.

Panic bubbled up when Duna got closer and saw blood. She hobbled over, kneeling to feel for a pulse—and as she did, a voice rang out behind her.

"She's fine. I checked on her earlier."

Duna whirled around to see where the voice had come from. "Who said that?"

"Kuu."

"Kuu?"

"Over here."

Duna looked in the direction of the voice, but all she saw was a little gray fox seated on a tree stump. Confused, she kept looking for the emerald-eyed man that she had met earlier.

"Seriously?" Kuu said—and this time Duna saw exactly where the voice had come from.

"Wh—" She started to say, then stopped. She rubbed her eyes. Opening them back up, she saw that nothing had changed. "You're a fox," she observed.

His ears drooped a little. "I'm meant to be a wolf," Kuu said, leaping down from the stump. He trotted over to Duna and sat down on his hind legs.

"A wolf, eh? You're kind of cute," Duna said, and Kuu's ears perked back up. "How long ago did you check on her?"

"Not long. But you missed a lot."

"Can you catch me up? I've got to clean this wound."

Kuu took a breath.

✦ ✦ ✦

After bandaging the wound several times and rolling her eyes at Kuu's story several more, Duna was satisfied. "There," she said, "She's still in bad shape, but she's better than she was. The good news is that it was a clean cut. Whatever did this was sharp."

Kuu's ears drooped again. "I know what made it," he said.

"What was it?"

"The Wolfblade."

"The W—" Duna began, then froze. Her eyes went immediately to the girl on the ground. She was silent for a long, long moment. "If she was the Shaper before," she said in a low whisper, "then she's not any longer."

Right at that moment, as if in response, the girl's eyes fluttered open. "Nnnh," she said. "My mouth. So . . . thirsty."

Duna lunged for her water flask. "You're awake!" She held the skin to the girl's lips. "Here, drink," she said. "You lost a lot of fluids." The red-haired Khyth drank in deep, greedy gulps. "Easy, easy," Duna said, supporting her head. "You'll choke. And we just got you back to health, so none of us want that." Putting away the flask, she said, "What's your name?"

"Yasha," she replied, "and this is . . " She froze as her words trailed off. She tilted her head slightly. "Miera?" Seemingly waiting for an answer but hearing none, she said again in a panicked tone, "Miera?"

"Who's . . . Miera?" Duna said, looking at Kuu.

"Miera!" Yasha repeated. "Where is Miera?"

"I . . . I'm not sure what you mean," Duna said, "There's no one else here but us."

"No," Yasha said, and she started to get up. "No, that can't be."

Duna and Kuu exchanged a worried glance. "I don't know how to tell you this," Duna started.

"Tell me what?" Yasha asked, her voice trembling.

"Miera's gone," came a voice from behind. Duna turned to see a well-muscled Khyth of the Breaking emerge from the forest, with swirling brown eyes and the beginnings of a beard to match. "I felt her go. And something tells me, deep down, you feel it too."

"Thornton!" Yasha cried and looked at him with trembling eyes. "Don't. Please don't talk like that. I don't want to believe it."

Thornton walked over and put a hand on her shoulder. His frown was as deep as a Thurian mine. "I'm sorry, Yasha. I don't either, but she's gone," he said with a quiver in his voice. "I loved her since we were kids."

Tears welled up in Yasha's eyes as she looked at Thornton. "She loved you too. She loved you very, very much." A choking whimper leapt from her throat, and she buried her face into Thornton's shoulder as a long, mournful cry broke the stillness in the forest of Kienar.

For the next few moments, grief was the only sound.

+ + +

Duna looked down at Kuu, whose ears had drooped further than she even thought possible. Looking up at the two Khyth, she cleared her throat.

"I'm . . . I'm sorry about your friend," she began, waiting for the words to hang in the air. It was in that moment that Duna realized a truth about herself: even though she had lost family, it had never been anyone she cared for. It struck her as even sadder that she had no idea what to say to comfort these two. She decided on the approach that she'd used for most of her adult life. "But the time for grieving is past. The Holder of the Dead plans to use the Godseed to unite the three realms: this one, the Otherworld, and Khel-hârad."

Thornton frowned, wiping tears from his sorrow-reddened eyes. "Tell me what you need, and I will do my best to give it."

Yasha, who quaked with a sadness cloaked in rage, added, "As will I."

"I don't know what we can do—if anything," Duna admitted. "The Holder has the Wolfblade and the Seed, and he's made it to the Otherworld. If there were any gods left, maybe we'd have a chance—maybe."

"You don't need just any god." The voice was a new one, one that Duna didn't recognize—but apparently Thornton and Kuu both did. "You need one god in particular: one who knows him and knows his weakness." Stepping into the clearing was a red-haired man with eyes and a beard to match, and a tan and black shemagh low across his face. "And who better than his own twin brother?"

Duna had met more gods on this day than she even knew existed—so, then, what was one more to add to the pile?

Chapter 87

Kienar

Thornton

THE TRAVELER HAD THEM ALL gathered in a semicircle.

"My brother, Ahmaan Ka, is a complicated being, yes," the god began, "but what drives him is simple: ambition. At the very heart of that lies his weakness, and I intend to exploit it. He seeks to unite the three realms and has the means to do it—but we can stop him. There is a way."

"Alright," Duna said as she crossed her arms. "Tell us how."

The red-haired god looked around at everyone gathered before him and took a breath. "Killing his physical form—the one that is in the Otherworld right now—is not enough to destroy him. As some of you may know," he said, looking at Thornton and Yasha, "killing a god—even their original Vessel—does not necessarily destroy the god." He paused and looked around conspiratorially. "To destroy a god, you need to destroy their spirit, along with their anchor."

"Anchor?" Thornton echoed. "This is the first I'm hearing of any anchor—and the Breaker even used me as his Vessel."

The Traveler gave him a patronizing grin. "It's the most well-kept secret of the gods," he said. "Do you really think we would just give away the key to destroying us?"

Thornton nodded his assent.

Kuu shuffled nervously. "Even so, it all sounds like a lot."

"It is and it isn't," the Traveler replied, "if you know where to look."

"Then let's start with the anchor," Duna said. "What exactly is it?"

"An anchor," the Traveler began, "is a god-touched relic of power that binds them to another plane of existence. For the Shaper of Ages, it is the Hammer of the Worldforge; for the Breaker, his chains."

"And the Holder's?" Thornton asked.

The Traveler smiled. "Fortunately for us, that will be the least amount of trouble to find." He turned his head, looking to the massive tower that lay just beyond the forest. "*Jurok'do'baradai*," he said, "the Heart of the

Two Brothers. It is the one thing that keeps his spirit anchored to his Vessel and his power. Destroy the anchor, and we have a real chance at beating him."

All of them looked up at the looming structure that was so out of place among the trees. The sand-worn brick from beyond the Wastes was hundreds—if not thousands—of years old. For it to find itself transported here, to the ancient forest of Kienar, was almost too much for Thornton to comprehend. He looked from the tower to Naknamu, which seemed to stand in opposition to the Holder's anchor, and back . . . Two giant reminders that gods walked the earth.

After today, only one of them would remain.

"You mentioned the 'original Vessel,'" Duna began. "You're not talking about the body he's currently inhabiting?"

"Unfortunately not," the Traveler said with a shake of his head, "because that would make our job much easier. The good news is that we know that the Wolfblade has the power to destroy it; the bad news is that it will only work if it is used on the original Vessel of Ahmaan Ka."

And just like that, the air went out of Kienar.

"The original?" Kuu echoed.

"The one in Do'baradai?" said Duna.

"You have to be joking," injected Thornton.

The Traveler put up his hands in a placating motion. "Please, everyone, stay calm."

"Calm?" Yasha said, nearly shouting. "How do you expect us to be calm when we're staring down the end of the world, and you just told us that our only hope of stopping the Holder is half a world away!"

Thornton could hear the desperation in her voice. She was trembling, and he wasn't sure if it was from anger or fear. Perhaps both.

The Traveler took an exasperated breath. "It's like you don't even know who you're talking to. Jinda?" he said, peering around the semicircle and into the forest. "Would you care to fill them in?"

Everyone turned around to see, stepping from the forest, the very red-haired, red-eyed man that Thornton had once found himself face to face with when he first entered Annoch.

"Captain Yhun," he shouted, shocked. "What are you doing here?"

Jinda smiled. "My duty," he said, walking toward the Traveler. "I ran from it once when I abandoned the Tribes, and now that my younger brother has taken up the mantle of Traveler in my place," he said, clasping the god's outstretched hand with his own, "it is only right that I do everything I can to help him."

The Traveler embraced him. "You should be proud of your brother. He had no fear, and did not hesitate."

"That sounds like Rathma."

"Indeed. He is a warrior, Jinda. And so are you, by the looks of it."

The captain of the Guard of Annoch chuckled. "It is in our blood, you could say." Looking past the Traveler to Thornton again, he continued, "Speaking of warriors, there's someone here who has been asking about you."

Thornton's eyes grew wide. "You don't mean—"

But before he could even finish his sentence, Alysana was bearing down on him. "Thornton!" she cried, barreling toward him and throwing her arms around him. "I didn't think I was ever going to see you again." She fell into him with a deep embrace, kissing him softly.

Thornton simply let it happen, kissing her back when he recovered from the shock. "I—I . . . " he stammered. "It's good to see you too," he said. He heard snickering from all around as he felt his cheeks burn with embarrassment.

As he held her, he realized that his mind had completely emptied itself of all words. He looked into her olive eyes and saw the same raven-haired girl that he'd met when he first came to Annoch—the one who he'd seen do everything from defeat an Athrani captain in single combat to breaking her father out of a Théan prison. He had realized some time ago that she was more than just an extraordinary woman, but now he knew the truth: she was extraordinary by *any* standard. Yet here she was, excited to see *him.*

The thought would have knocked him flat on his back if he wasn't being held up by her strong G'henni arms. He tried to wipe the stupid grin off his face, but his self-sabotaging brain wouldn't let him. Another peck on the cheek from Alysana preceded further blushing—and she must have known it, too, because she finally let go and acknowledged everyone else.

Thornton's heart was beating in his ears as he used the much-needed distraction to catch his breath. He watched her walking around saying her hellos, smiling, and giving the occasional hug . . . but none of them had been as impassioned as her greeting to him. His legs weakened again when he shook himself free. He could think about all of that later.

He had to focus. "Traveler," he said, turning to the red-haired god. "You told us about the anchor and the Vessel, but that still leaves—"

"His spirit," he said, finishing Thornton's thought. "Yes." With a grin and a pat on Thornton's shoulder, he said, "Leave that to me. When the time comes, the godkiller will do what must be done."

Thornton blinked a few times at the words. He looked around to see if anyone else had heard it, but it seemed like the god had been speaking to him, and only him.

+ + +

The Traveler had divided them up into three groups according to need and capability, and the planning had gone well, despite the overwhelming sense of dread and finality that pervaded the air around them. Each of them knew the risks they were taking on—there was nothing commonplace about going toe to toe with a god—and each had a sense of the danger that awaited . . . yet they also knew that there was little choice. Their hands were being forced; they just hoped to be on the right end of fate when the executioner's blade dropped.

Looking around at the familiar faces around him, Thornton felt a sense of warmth well up inside him—a feeling he recognized and had not felt in quite some time: hope. He embraced it. Savored it.

A dull chatter blanketed them as the sound of several soft conversations at once began to occur. The words and smiles were filled with optimism. Most of them, anyway. Thornton scanned the faces of the group. When he came to his sister, who was wringing her hands nervously, she immediately looked away. He got up and walked over. When he reached her, she was staring at the ground.

"What's wrong?" he asked and stooped down to catch her gaze again.

After a moment, she finally looked back at him. "Miera never prepared me for this," she said in a near-whisper. "She didn't tell me any of this. She didn't tell me I would lose her . . . and that I would have to just . . . pick back up where she left off." Her voice trembled, and she barely got the last words out.

"That's the kind of person she is," Thornton said. Catching himself, he winced. "Was. The person she was," he said, and the words were a dagger through his heart. "Come here," he said, and leaned in to embrace Yasha. The hug was just as much for him as it was for her. "I've been meaning to tell you for a while, but I just never got the chance . . ." he began, feeling his sister fight to hold back her sobs as he held her. "I'm really proud of you. And I'm proud to be your brother."

Yasha leaned in and began to cry on Thornton's shoulder. She didn't say a word, and Thornton didn't press her to; he just let her cry. If the two of them were going to be instrumental in trying to save all of creation, he reasoned, the least he could do for his sister was let her mourn the loss of a friend.

The time that went by after that was a blur, and Thornton barely remembered any of it, save that.

+ + +

"So," the Traveler said, scanning the faces of those gathered around him, "now that everyone knows their parts, I'm afraid the time has come."

The forest was silent, as was everyone else. Every one of them knew that they couldn't put it off forever, yet that was exactly what each one of them hoped to do.

Thornton knew that he was in good company—each of them a skilled and capable warrior—and they did have a god on their side . . . but he just couldn't help thinking of all the things that could go wrong. What if they did things in the wrong order? What if one of them couldn't finish their task? What if the Holder was too strong? What if? What . . . if . . .?

He closed his eyes and forced the thoughts from his mind.

When he opened them again, Alysana was standing beside him, looking at him expectantly.

He looked around nervously. "Did . . . did you say something?"

"I asked if you're ready," she said, placing the palm of her hand on his heart. "Are you?"

Warmth spread through his chest, and right away he knew the answer. "I am."

"I'm glad to hear that," she said with a smile. After a pause, she added, "I don't like seeing you leave after I just got you back, but I know it must happen."

Thornton felt his face flush. He scratched his beard in hopes of disguising it. "I feel the same way," he admitted.

"Well, then," Alysana said, drawing closer. She leaned in and kissed him. "For luck," she said, "and more when you return."

Thornton's heartbeat felt like a team of horses was parading in his chest. He put his hand to her cheek and kissed her back, deeply. "Then I'll see you back here to collect," he said with a smile.

"You'd better. I've managed to amass quite a debt somehow."

+ + +

The groups were set, and each of them appeared ready to go. Back beside the Traveler, Thornton looked around at them—Duna and Alysana and Jinda and Kuu—and gave them a nod. "Don't forget whey we're here," he said, "and how far we've come. This isn't about just us any-more—it's about everyone, everywhere."

Jinda gave him a solemn nod in return, and Duna raised her fist to her shoulder in a salute. Yasha looked—for the first time in a long time—like the confident Khyth of the Breaking that she was.

Thornton gave her a warm smile, and she returned it.

He clasped one of the outstretched hands of the Traveler, and Yasha grabbed the other. Turning to face the others, he said, "It's time to play the parts we were all born to play—in this world, or the next."

He nodded to the Traveler and gave Alysana one last look, then held his breath for the Otherworld as the three of them were transported through the newly formed rift between the worlds.

Chapter 88

Kienar

Duna

BONES MEND, DUNA HAD TO tell herself, wincing with the pain of every step. *Bones mend.*

While she appreciated the faith that the Traveler had in her to let her go with Alysana to find the anchor, she wished that he'd let her have more time to recover. "Awfully rude of the Holder to start the end of the world so soon," she said through clenched teeth. "Barely had time to catch my breath."

Alysana looked back at her. "Do you need help?"

Duna, holding her broken arm at the shoulder, tilted her head. "I'll live," she said with a placating smile.

"Are you sure?"

Duna didn't even answer; she just kept walking painfully toward the tower.

✦ ✦ ✦

As the two of them approached the colossal structure, Duna took another opportunity to marvel at what it must have taken to move something so massive all the way across Derenar. It was taller than anything they had in Haidan Shar, and just as sturdy as even the finest of Thurian craftsmanship. While she was gazing up, she heard Alysana engaging in her own appreciation.

"The sheer size of this thing!" The G'henni girl said—and Duna had to admit that she was right. "I don't know how he even lifted it. I wouldn't know where to start."

"Probably the bottom," Duna remarked.

Alysana said nothing as Duna limped past her, and up the stairs to the tower.

✦ ✦ ✦

Opening the doors to the tower was like unearthing a coffin. The stench of death hung in the air, and Duna was reminded of the time that she had spent inside it, a "guest" of the Holder.

Alysana, behind her, voiced her displeasure. "Ugh," she said, fanning her hand in front of her nose. "You rode in this thing?"

"Wasn't my first choice," Duna replied. "Now come on. We have to look for . . . what did the Traveler call it?"

"'The Heart of the Two Brothers,'" Alysana answered.

"Right. Now where do you think . . ." her voice trailed off as she looked up. Her eyes moved to the twin spiral staircases that climbed the length of the tower, remembering how long it had taken her to walk up them—and that was with two good legs.

"Where do I think what?" Alysana asked.

Duna took a breath and let it out slowly. "Where do you think the Holder of the Dead would place the most important thing in this whole tower?"

Alysana put a hand to her chin. "Well, if I were smart, I would keep it locked away somewhere—somewhere that no one could ever see it."

"And let's pretend for a moment that you weren't smart," Duna said. "Only for a moment," she added quickly when Alysana looked at her with suspicion. "Let's say that you were arrogant—more arrogant than intelligent. Where would you keep it then?"

Alysana shrugged. "I suppose . . . the throne room."

Duna nodded. "That was my thought, too," she said, looking again at the stairs. Her shoulders slumped. "I'm sorry," she began, "I'm afraid I won't be much use to you in my ... condition," she said, touching her broken leg. "Are you alright to go this alone?"

"I will manage—though I'm not sure what to looking for."

"The Traveler said we would know it when we saw it, whatever that means."

Alysana took a breath and let it out slowly. "Then wish me luck," she said, and headed for the stairs.

"Luck," Duna replied.

+ + +

Hobbling back down the entrance of the tower, Duna cursed at how little weight she could put on her leg. She felt so useless out here, a human among such powerful beings. Even Yasha, young as she was, could lift a mountain if she wanted to; Duna could barely lift her sword arm.

She sat down on the last step, figuring it to be as good a place as any to wait for Alysana to retrieve the Heart. Looking to the west, she could see the sun beginning its descent below the trees; it would be dark soon. She looked back east, toward her city of Haidan Shar—and, for once, found herself wishing she was back in that cold, accursed throne room. She would have to do something to make it more comfortable when she got back.

Glancing at the horizon, she thought she saw something move. *That's odd,* she thought. Was something there? She squinted.

Something was definitely there. Something big. She stood back up.

"You see it too, my queen?"

Duna spun around to see the Dagger of Derenar standing a few feet away. "Tennech," she gasped. "Don't sneak up on me like that!"

"My apologies," he said with a slight bow. "I came this way when I felt an energy that I recognized coming toward Kienar."

"What is it?" Duna said, looking back out to where she'd first seen the movement.

"Whatever it is, it emerged from the rubble of Ghal Thurái."

Ghal Thurái. Duna went pale. "Another chovathi matriarch?"

"No," Tennech replied. "I'm afraid it's worse."

Duna tried to swallow but found that her throat had suddenly dried up. "What could be worse than a matriarch?"

As soon as the words left her mouth, she regretted saying them.

"It appears we will soon find out."

+ + +

Alysana

SHE DIDN'T KNOW HOW MUCH time she had exactly, but something inside Alysana told her that she needed to hurry. As she made her way up the twisting, winding stairs of the Tower of the Two Brothers, she did her very best to ignore the burning in her legs and lungs.

Just reach the top, she told herself. *You can rest there. Then it's easy on the way back down.*

She kept telling herself that with every new turn.

At one point she tried her best to gauge how far she had until she reached the top, but it was nearly impossible. She also then made the mistake of looking down, and the near-vertigo she experienced almost made her fall. At least she knew that she was making progress.

+ + +

By now, her legs were burning. She had to take a rest before she collapsed. She dragged herself to a nearby window so she could at least get a view of the forest while she caught her breath.

She breathed in deep, relishing the fresh air, and looked out over the gently rolling hills of the neighboring Talvin Forest. She frowned, though, when she looked back toward Kienar, covered in Zhala's corruption, and wondered what it would take to fight it off. She thought of Kethras, telling herself that, if there was a way to stop it, he would find it.

As she looked back out toward the horizon, something caught her eye: white dots in a sea of green. She looked closer, letting her eyes adjust—and nearly fell backwards when she realized what it was.

No more time to rest, she thought in a panic. She redoubled her efforts to reach the top, knowing that she would have to find the Heart in time to stop the Holder—because judging by what she saw, the entire forest of Kienar was about to be overrun by a bloodthirsty chovathi horde.

Chapter 89

The Otherworld

Sera

THE FIRST THING THAT SERA noticed was just how incorporeal she felt—disembodied, detached—like she was watching her own body move, from within her own body. It was beyond strange. The sensation had not happened when they were in Kienar; it had come on the very moment they arrived in the Otherworld. It was a singularly unpleasant experience, like her skin itching from the inside.

The Holder of the Dead, behind her, was taking in the look and the feel of the Otherworld—a conquering king come to roost.

She felt the powers inside her roiling about in a potent and volatile dance, like a reckoning between two long-lost lovers. Powers separated for centuries, now violently reacquainted, torn from their host bodies and replanted in a new one.

Yet, still she thirsted for more.

Beyond them, in the distant horizon, was the fracture between the realms, put there by the previous Breaker of the Dawn, D'kane. Sera knew without asking that this was where they would be headed.

When the Holder of the Dead turned his skeletal face to hers, imposing his will on her to move, her suspicions were confirmed.

Onward they walked toward the rift.

+ + +

The place where the two realms met was a confluence of chaos: the energy from both sides came together, crashing into each other, but never mixing. They were as separate as two human bodies. Behind them, the passage that she had opened, was a similar rift to the mortal realm with the same chaotic quality. The Holder, she knew, sought to destroy the barriers that kept them separate, uniting all three under his command.

"This is where we shall begin," he said to her, pointing to the rift ahead. She felt his influence over her wane, like a tight grip on her shoulder suddenly relaxed—but not released. She knew it was still there, and she knew he intended that. "Where we join the first two realms into a new one." He turned his head slightly toward her. "You should feel honored to even be a part of this, the moment that will overshadow creation itself with its greatness."

The words felt hollow to Sera, and the clashing powers inside her seemed to agree. "You're upsetting a balance," she said, giving words to the feelings inside. "The realms are separate for a reason."

"That is how the old gods see it, perhaps," the Holder sneered, "but the lowly caterpillar cannot conceive of the butterfly. When the realms are joined as one, they will see that they were wrong . . . if I allow them to." He raised up his staff, and thrust it violently into the ground beneath them, sending out a shockwave that rocked the Otherworld. Looking over at Sera, he raised his hand—and suddenly clenched it into a fist. "As the living embodiment of the Otherworld," the Holder went on, "you are crucial to this joining—a seed from which a new world shall arise."

Her body spasmed as he touched the power inside her. As it released, unbidden, she felt the power of the Ghost of the Morning, forcing her to her knees as the wolf emerged.

"I can do this without your compliance, of course," he said, "but it will be . . . unpleasant."

Sera gritted her teeth as they became fangs. "Then you'll be doing it the hard way."

She pulled back her power, just like she would rein in an untamed horse she was seeking to break. Despite having just inherited the very power of creation, she found that her body was somehow attuned to it, like it was meant for it—for her.

. . . But just as she did, she felt the cold hand of the Holder fight against her. It was like the wind pushing against a redwood: tiny in comparison, but absolutely compelling. The difference in magnitude between her power and his was almost too much to comprehend—yet he had control over her by the link that they shared . . . a link to which she never agreed.

She felt the icy waters of the Holder's power as it crashed into her own, the sensation promulgating through her entire being. It was enough to make her flinch.

By now, she had fully transformed as the Holder manipulated her power; she could feel the Wolfblade inside her, at one with her. This was a battle that she could not win, but she would do everything she could to fight it. A sensation deep inside her—a voice nearly too faint to hear—kept tugging at her.

She listened, blocking out the pain from the Holder and all other distractions in the realm.

Give him time, it said.

And she meant to.

Chapter 90

Wastes of Khulakorum

Kuu

THE VERY MOMENT THAT BOTH of them blinked back into reality, Kuu spilled his guts. Unfortunately for him, it wasn't quite the way that he had hoped: all over the desert floor.

"I've never—" he began to say, cut off by a dry heave. He doubled over, putting out his hand to shoo off Jinda, who moved to help. "I didn't know Farsteppers could go that far," he said, eyes watering.

"Not many can," Jinda replied. "I'm the only one I know of, in fact." He dusted off his hands and looked around. "The air feels the same. This place feels the same."

"Well, you know the Wastes," Kuu said, standing upright again. The journey had forced him back into his human form, and he was certain that the trauma of changing back, plus the stress of the travel, was responsible for his current discomfort. "Always shifting, never changing."

Jinda chuckled. "It has been some time, yet it feels like I never left." He squinted, looking off into the distance. "I see the gates," he said, pointing toward the ruins of Do'baradai. "Come, I will—"

"Oh, no, you don't," Kuu said, recoiling as Jinda reached out for him. "I'll walk there, thank you very much."

"Suit yourself," Jinda said with a shrug. "The goatherd should be waiting for us up there. I'll scout ahead."

"You go do that."

A great rush of air preceded Jinda's disappearance, followed by the exact inverse of the sound from up ahead. Kuu knew without looking that Jinda had appeared somewhere just beyond the walls of the ancient city, and he was more than happy to follow—just on foot, the way the gods intended.

✦ ✦ ✦

As Kuu walked through the gates of Do'baradai, he saw Jinda waiting for him, leaning up against the stone wall.

"At least it's obvious where the tower came from," the Farstepper said, nodding toward a great open space in the middle of the desert floor. "But I'm not sure what that is beside it."

Kuu squinted to see a small, white tent set up by the chasm where the Tower of the Two Brothers had evidently come from. "Don't tell me it's been so long since you left the Wastes that you've forgotten what a tent is," he said.

Jinda looked down his nose at him. "No, Kuu. But what is it doing there?"

"Only one way to find out," he said, and took off in a run.

"Kuu, w—" Jinda started to say, but stopped when something emerged from the tent.

Kuu stopped dead in his tracks as he stared at the smiling face of a R'haqan man coming out from the tent and waving.

"You must be Jinda and Kuu," the man said. "I am Ulten. Please, come!" He said with a beckoning motion. "The Traveler told me to wait for you here. There is someone that he wished for you to see."

When the tent opened wider and Kuu saw inside, his heart nearly stopped in his chest. It was the last person he ever expected to see. "Jinda, are you seeing this?" he asked without looking away.

"I am, but I don't believe it."

Out from the tent, and onto the dunes, stepped Rathma Yhun—nearly the spitting image of the Traveler that they had just seen—twirling a blade in his hand that looked identical to the Wolfblade. "Took you long enough," he said with a grin. "Only ten years by my count."

"Eleven," Jinda countered, "and I still can't believe I'm back." Crossing his arms and smiling, he said, "Care to explain what you're doing?"

With a gleam in his eye, Rathma asked, "How would you like to help kill a god?"

Chapter 91

Kienar

Duna

TENNECH WAS SHOUTING ORDERS TO his Stoneborn behind them, and all Duna could do was watch the oncoming chovathi. They seemed to be driven by something . . . and whatever it was, it was more than just hunger.

She looked back at the makeshift army behind her and counted half a dozen—yes they were Stoneborn, but would they be enough? She turned her focus back to the advancing army, led from the front by something much larger than any chovathi she had ever faced, with the exception of the matriarch herself. She turned to the general.

"What is that? In the front of the pack?" she asked Tennech.

"I have my suspicions," he answered, "but I won't be sure until I get closer."

"What are your suspicions?"

"That it's someone I knew."

She paused. "I'm not sure I understand. You knew a chovathi?"

"Whatever that thing is," Tennech replied coldly, "it's no chovathi—but it's not human either. It's somehow both of those . . . and neither. It's something new."

"Well," she replied, and pulled out her sword. From a pouch on her hip she produced a sharpening stone, kneeling on the ground to put a better edge on the weapon. "Do you think it can bleed?"

"It's the one thing I hope for."

Stone slid over steel as Duna looked up with a smirk. "I guess we'll find out."

Tennech returned it. "I guess we will." He turned his head to his Stoneborn. "Who's ready to make some heads roll?"

The reverberating chorus of shouts served as answer enough.

Duna gave her sword a few more strokes with the sharpening stone, then stood back up, admiring the sharpened edge. She looked to Tennech.

"I'm not at full strength, I'm sad to admit, but I'm going to give you what I have."

Tennech placed a hand on her shoulder. "You have a warrior's heart," he said. "Sometimes that is what makes the difference between victory and defeat." Turning toward the advancing tide, he pulled his sword from its scabbard. "Let's give these bastards a taste of the afterlife!" he shouted.

The ringing in Duna's ear from the responding shout nearly drowned out the sounds of the coming chovathi. She readied her sword.

No matter what happened, she would be ready.

Chapter 92

The Otherworld

Thornton

GETTING INTO THE OTHERWORLD WITH the Traveler was much different than using one of the portals like Thornton previously had; it left him feeling queasy, and his body ached. It felt like he had been accelerated to a great speed, only to come to a violent, abrupt stop. Beside him, doubled over in pain, was Yasha, who was clearly going through the same thing.

"What did you do to us?" she demanded, fingers massaging her temples.

"Sorry about that," the Traveler replied. "It's a side effect of the far-stepping. Your body gets used to it after a while, but that could take years. We didn't have the time to sit around and wait," he said with a shrug.

Yasha frowned back at him and continued rubbing her head.

"Well," the god went on, "shall we do what we came here to do?"

Thornton could only grimace and nod.

"Then follow me."

+ + +

As they moved through the Otherworld, Thornton couldn't help but think that something felt off. He looked around. Everything seemed the same from the last time he'd been there—he didn't imagine this place changing much over the millennia anyway: the ground beneath them, craggy and broken, stretched into looming mountains of black that faded into the distance. Violent clouds formed above them, and the ethereal quality of the whole realm stretched on to infinity.

A dull hum worked its way into his ears—low enough that Thornton nearly missed it. Realizing what it was, he pulled out the Hammer of the Worldforge that was strapped across his back. It was glowing blue—just like it had been in the Temple of the Shaper in Annoch, where the Shaper's presence had been the strongest.

When the hammer had come home.

He placed it back in its holder, and the thought back in his mind.

+ + +

They covered miles. It took them years. Decades. Centuries . . . yet, as Thornton was constantly reminding himself, it took no time at all.

The Otherworld was outside of the very concept of time, and its non-passing felt like standing in the middle of a rushing river: the feeling of constant movement while standing perfectly still. Thornton had long ago learned to ignore the strange sensations that were at the very foundation of this place.

Yasha was not so lucky.

"I think I'm gonna . . ." was all she managed to get out before stumbling to her knees and vomiting.

She was definitely taking it hard. Thornton knelt down and put a hand on her back, doing his best to comfort her. He looked up at the Traveler. "Why couldn't you just have farstepped us where we need to be instead of making us walk all this way?"

The red-haired god looked at him incredulously. "And let this," he said, gesturing at Yasha, "happen when we confront the Holder? No, I think it's better that you both get accustomed to the Otherworld."

Thornton frowned and continued helping his sister. The god had a point.

+ + +

Thornton began to feel a slight shift in the air as they walked. Something changed.

He looked back at the hammer again; it was pulsing with a brighter blue than he had ever seen—so bright that he expected it to be hot to the touch. Yet, when he held it in his hands, it was the same as it had always been.

Yasha and the Traveler looked at it in awe.

"There is great power in that hammer," the Traveler said. "It is good that you have it."

Thornton looked it over, his old friend, and ran his hand over the smooth white ash of the handle. "It's exactly where it needs to be," he said, and put it back in its holder. When he did, he saw a great plume of crimson from up ahead.

"Look!" he said, pointing. "Are we too late?"

"No," the Traveler replied. "But we don't have long. I can already feel the essence of Khel-hârad bleeding into this world."

"Then what are we waiting for?" Yasha asked, crackling with power.

The Traveler didn't have an answer—and he didn't need one. He simply nodded and forged ahead.

✦ ✦ ✦

Sera

EVERY MOMENT WAS EXCRUCIATING, BUT Sera knew it was worth it—anything to hinder the Holder of the Dead in accomplishing his goal. The more time it took, the better the chances of help arriving. She gritted her teeth and fought the pull of the Holder's influence once again.

"Resist all you want," the Lord of the Dead said to her as he forced his will upon her. She felt the twin powers moving inside her—Breaking and Shaping—as they reached out to Khel-hârad, bonding with its energy. The Otherworld was changing, as was reality itself. "You're only making it harder on yourself and delaying inevitability."

The sky above them was a furious red, forming at the convergence between the two realms and spreading out into both. With every pulse of her power it grew as the energies merged. Violent thunder and lightning exploded where the two realms touched, like magma pouring into freezing water. She could feel the energy of Khel-hârad mixing with her own—and hers mixing with that of the Land of the Dead. If the Holder had his way, and the two powers merged, she knew that he would have no use for her anymore.

Yet another reason to fight it with everything that she had.

✦ ✦ ✦

Thornton

THE REDDENING SKY WAS GROWING more unnerving every step they took closer to the fracture between realms. Thornton looked to his two companions beside him and felt his own confidence surging along with them. In his hands was the Hammer of the Worldforge, at home here in the Otherworld where it was made. He could think of no other time that he'd been so grateful to have it at his disposal.

"I think I can see the Holder up ahead," Yasha said. "And it looks like there's . . . something beside him."

"The Godseed," the Traveler replied. "She is the source of—and conduit for—his power. In her lies the very essence of the Shaper of Ages, the Breaker of the Dawn, and the Ghost of the Morning. She is their avatar, the Holder's means for forging a new world where *he* sits upon the throne—and, currently," he said, turning to Thornton, "she is the most powerful being in existence."

Thornton's eyes went wide and he nearly stopped moving altogether. "Do you think we stand a chance?"

The Traveler looked at him, determination gleaming in his red eyes. "Just get me the Wolfblade. I'll take care of the rest."

✦ ✦ ✦

The three of them approached the swirling maelstrom, and the weight of power in the air was unlike anything Thornton had ever felt—even as a Vessel for one of the gods of creation. It was thunder, it was fire,

517

it was heat. He felt like a sword being thrust into a blazing furnace.

The Holder of the Dead was standing, arms raised, by the epicenter of the crack in the realms, directing the flow of energy coming from the creature beside him, the Godseed. The wolf-like creature looked to be steeped in concentration—and in pain.

The Traveler turned to Thornton and Yasha. "Listen well, for here we make our stand, he said." Meeting their gaze one by one, he went on. "You will both be pushed to the limits of your power, but I brought you here because I believe that you *can* be—and are willing to go to such lengths to do what must be done. Are you ready?"

Thornton nodded and saw Yasha do the same.

"As am I," he said, and turned back toward the Holder. "Now," he added, "I have some unfinished business with my brother."

Chapter 93

The Otherworld

Thornton

THORNTON COULD FEEL THE ESSENCES of the two realms merging. He had no idea how far along the Holder was, but it seemed like they had arrived not a moment too soon.

The power of Thornton's Breaking had always felt stronger here in the Otherworld, but as the power of Khel-hârad crept in, he sensed that it was unbalanced, like a knife whose edge had dulled. Beside him was the Traveler, whose power was rooted in the Land of the Dead, and who seemed to be growing stronger as the two realms merged. Thornton wondered if the Holder was experiencing the same energy surge—and then quickly realized that he didn't want to know the answer.

"With the power of the Godseed at his disposal," the Traveler said, "I have no doubt that this will be the hardest fight of our lives, but it is one that we must win." The Holder of the Dead was still a good distance beyond them, arms raised and crackling with power. "I will retrieve the Wolfblade," he went on. "Do you know your parts?"

Thornton pulled out the Hammer of the Worldforge and slapped the head into his open palm. He nodded to his sister, who nodded back. "We are with you."

"Good," the Traveler said. "Now here is where it gets fun." He turned his head toward the Holder of the Dead, and shouted, "Brother! Has it really come to this? Was one realm not enough; now you must have two?"

The Holder of the Dead did not so much as turn his head from the arcing power that surged from him and the Seed. "Ah, Lash'kun, you are so predictable. Come for your Asha, have you? I think you'll find that she is quite . . . absent." A low and rumbling laughter filled the space around them. "And you are too late."

The Otherworld shuddered as a new wave of power surged from the Seed. She cried out in agony as it happened.

The Holder turned his head to the trembling wolf beside him. "I told you that resisting will only bring pain."

"You don't have to do this, Ahmaan," the Traveler said. "You are already a god who reigns over a realm; must you truly keep taking until nothing remains?"

In response, the Holder clenched his fist, and another surge of energy arced from the Seed and through him, making its way toward the growing rift in the realms.

"You're killing her!" Yasha screamed out. Upon hearing her voice, the Holder turned. He looked at Yasha and tilted his head in curiosity.

"And what have we here? A servant of the Breaker?" he asked. "I killed your god, Khyth—do you wish to die as well?"

Thornton stepped forward. "We don't serve the Breaker—but at least he was a *real* god. You're nothing more than a pretender to his throne." He could see that last bit hit a nerve.

"Mind your tongue, mortal," the Holder said. "Lest I send your father's soul the way of the Breaker."

Thornton's vision went dim, and the air left his lungs. "What did he say?" were the only words he could muster.

"Don't listen to him," the Traveler cautioned. "He'll say anything right now to get what he wants—more time—and we're already giving it to him. We don't have long before the merging of the realms is complete."

But Thornton didn't hear any of it. He felt his anger rising. "What did you say about my father?" he barked. The hammer in his hands pulsed with a fierce blue hue.

The Holder of the Dead laughed. "It was truly a sight to watch him try to contact you when you and my brother went traipsing through my realm. I almost had half a mind to let him too, but you mortals are so fragile—so easily bent, broken, and swayed—and I knew it would be much more useful as a bargaining chip against someone who dared set foot in Khel-hârad without my permission."

"You lie!" Thornton shouted.

The Holder's deep laugh echoed through the realm. "Perhaps. But you know there is a part of you that whispers that what I say is true . . . and if you give me what I want, you can find out."

Thornton paused and narrowed his eyes. "And what do you want?"

The Holder sniggered. "Your allegiance."

"Don't you dare, Thornton Woods!" Yasha shouted at him.

Thornton felt the hammer pulsing in his hands as a million images of his father flashed in his head. Growing up, learning to work the forge, laughing, crying, mourning, bonding. He owed everything to the man that the rest of the world simply knew as Olson Woods, master blacksmith of Highglade—but Thornton knew him better than all of them. His father had been larger than life, once . . . and then, in this very realm, his flame had been snuffed out. Just like that.

And now this god, the Lord of the Dead himself, was hanging that over his head?

"What would you have me do?"

The Holder's eyes gleamed.

"Don't tell me you are seriously thinking about listening to him," Yasha said.

"Allow me to finish uniting these two realms," the Holder said, "and you shall rule by my side."

"And my father?"

The Holder flinched, like he didn't expect the words. "He will rule beside you."

Thornton took a deep breath and held up the hammer in his hand, inspecting the head. Breathing out, he said, "See, that's the problem. I don't believe you." He flicked his eyes to the Holder. "But it bought your brother just enough time."

The Holder of the Dead whirled around to the Godseed just in time to watch the Traveler blink her away, reappearing behind Thornton and Yasha.

Thornton, still holding the gaze of the Holder, asked, "How is she?"

"She'll live," said the Traveler, "but I don't know how much of her power he used—or how much he siphoned off for himself."

"The answer to that, dear brother," the Holder said in response, "lies before you. Behold." The massive tear between the two realms was now so large as to be near-incomprehensible. It was impossible for Thornton to tell where the realm of the gods began, and where Khel-hârad ended. "While you were busy buying time, I was fulfilling my destiny: uniting the two realms under my command."

A great tremor shook the Otherworld, like a volcano about to erupt, and the swirling red of the sky shot out in all directions.

Thornton looked down to see the Seed beginning to transform. She was becoming . . . human!

"It's . . . too late," she said weakly. "The joining . . . is . . . complete."

The Traveler cursed. He looked down at her. "It's not too late," he said. "Where is the Wolfblade?"

The Seed groaned in pain as she continued to transform. Her fangs receded into teeth, her paws, hands and feet. "It is . . . a part of me . . ." she said.

"If we have any hope of saving what's left of the mortal realm, it lies with the Wolfblade. We need it—now!"

The Godseed looked up at the Traveler, eyes barely able to focus. "Then I will give it to you."

Thornton watched as the Seed put a hand to her rib cage . . . and pushed. To his horror, her hand went through the skin—and came back out, clutching a dagger coated in blood.

Before the Traveler could reach for the blade, an impossibly bright explosion of light came from all around, and all of existence trembled as Thornton looked off in the distance, where the rift used to be. What he saw looked like a black dot on the horizon . . . a black dot that seemed to be growing.

"Are you seeing that?" Thornton asked.

"I am," Yasha replied. What is it?"

"You don't want to know," the Traveler said.

Another shockwave came again, knocking them all to the ground, as a rift like the one in Khel-hârad began to open, revealing the bone-white forest of Kienar, and Naknamu dead ahead.

Thornton swallowed hard and began to mentally beseech every god he knew. If they didn't stop the Holder here and now—nothing would.

Chapter 94

Kienar

Duna

THE HORDE WAS NEARLY UPON them.

Duna's pulse pounded in her head as she did her best to focus her thoughts. She was never a warrior, she had to admit, but she knew how to swing a sword. Her gift had always been tactics and strategy—not brute force. She would use that to her advantage. Looking around, she tried to find the best place to mount an assault. She would be at a severe disadvantage on the front lines—especially if she were to be surrounded—but she was certain that she would be able to take on one chovathi warrior at a time in single combat. It was a small part, but it was still a part, and something was better than nothing.

The entrance to Kienar, where the chovathi were headed, was preceded by a wide open meadow surrounded by trees that distinguished it from the larger Talvin forest. Twilight rays shone down like a beacon through the leaves, illuminating the path to the forest of the Kienari. In her mind, Duna envisioned the white wave of chovathi coming in and conforming to the contours of the forest, grouping together like liquid pouring out of a bottle, converging as they reached the neck where the trees were thickest. She thought this to be her best point of attack, so she dragged herself over there and set up. The less walking she had to do, the better. She could still swing her sword if she used both hands—and fully intended to go down swinging.

Tennech shouted to his troops as the horde thundered toward them. They were nearly upon them; Duna's heart pounded like the hooves of a thoroughbred. Her adrenaline surged, clearing her mind of all other thoughts.

When the horde was close enough, she looked again to the creature that was leading them and was struck by the strangest notion of familiarity. The lumbering white abomination was covered in orange and black burn marks, ravaging its entire body. It reminded her of—

Khyth!

The thought was both unexpected and unwelcome as she looked closer at the creature's face. A wave of awful recognition spread inside her as she realized exactly what— or who—this creature was; nothing could disguise the dark, swirling eyes of a Khyth of the Breaking:

Kunas.

Even though he was missing the signature black robe which the Master Khyth of Ghal Thurái always wore, it was unmistakable, even in his current condition. Whatever had happened to him beneath the Mouth of the Deep had changed him forever. Tennech was right: this was something much worse.

✦ ✦ ✦

When the first of the Stoneborn swords sliced into chovathi flesh, Duna felt alive. She readied herself, palms sweating, to do what must be done. The thundering of thousands of legs marching over the ground of Kienar felt like an earthquake. She had no idea exactly how many of them there were, but it was too many to count.

A thought in the back of her mind told her that they were hopelessly outnumbered, but she was too busy picking out her first kill to listen.

She saw her opportunity: a lumbering chovathi warrior on the outskirts of the pack. He would be easy to pick off if she kept herself hidden. Making sure to hide her form completely behind one of the trees at the edge of the forest, she watched him walk closer. She waited. As he drew near, she saw the perfect opportunity to strike, and she took it, leaping out from the forest and swinging her sword in a beautiful, perfect arc that sliced right through the creature's neck. She looked at the edge on her sword, admiring her handiwork. The sharpening stone paid off.

"This is our oldest enemy—and our last!" shouted Tennech. "Go for the head and show them no mercy!"

The small collection of Stoneborn rushed into the advancing tide like ships on the waves, swords arcing through the air with deadly precision. Each of them knew where to strike, and none of them held back.

Yet the chovathi kept advancing.

Duna watched as the walkers of white poured past the tower, encircling it and flowing by like a river. Their numbers were great, yes, but it was almost like they didn't even care that the Stoneborn were cutting through their numbers.

In fact, they seemed to not even notice they were there—almost like they were focused on something else entirely. Several huge chovathi walked right past Duna—so close that she could smell their breath—and just kept on walking.

Something was wrong.

Tennech must have noticed it too. He looked around, finding Duna. With a panicked look in his eye, he shouted, "They're not coming for us!"

Duna traced the advancing line with her eyes, following it all the way to the front. When she saw Kunas, her eyes went down the path that he was following . . . right toward the heart of the forest.

"Naknamu!" she shouted. "They're heading for Naknamu!"

Tennech nodded, and jumped into the fray, swallowed up by a field of white. Duna knew where he was headed—and for whom.

Looking up at the tower, her thoughts immediately went to Alysana. Would she find the Heart in time? Would it even matter, if Kunas and his horde overran Naknamu? Sweat formed on her brow as dozens of thoughts flitted through her head.

All of them were cut off, though, as a great and sudden tremor shook the earth, and a tearing sound pierced the air. Duna looked back to where the chovathi were marching and, to her horror, saw what looked to be a tear in reality that was growing larger by the second—and, pouring out of it in countless numbers, was a sight that chilled Duna to the bone, even more than the sight of the chovathi. Whatever the Holder had done after he had crossed into the Otherworld was now of no consequence, for he had broken through into the mortal realm, followed by the souls of the dead—all under his command.

Duna let the sword drop from her hands as the terror took over. She knew she wouldn't need it; she dropped to her knees, and prayed for something that she would.

She had always wondered what the end of the world would look like.

She never imagined that she would witness it herself.

+ + +

Thornton

THORNTON WATCHED THE SOULS OF the dead pouring out of the Otherworld, commanded by the Holder, who now wielded power over two realms—and, from the looks of things, a third was not far off.

He turned to the Traveler. "Whatever you have to do to stop him, do it now."

The red-haired god looked at the Godseed beside him, still weak from most of her power being drained. "I need the Wolfblade," he said. Looking out of the ever-widening portal to the still-standing Tower of the Two Brothers, he added, "And Alysana needs the Heart." He looked back at Thornton. "The pieces are nearly assembled. There is still time— but not much."

Thornton stood up and grabbed his hammer. Turning to Yasha, he said, "Then we will do our best to slow him down. Are you with me?" Yasha nodded, her green eyes flickering with a fire that Thornton had only seen once before, during her fight with D'kane—immediately before her Breaking. Behind them, a quiet boom told Thornton that the Traveler had farstepped elsewhere.

"I am," Yasha answered.

"Then follow me."

The two of them charged forward, Thornton's blue hammer shining in the darkening dusk. All around him them, the souls of the dead were landing, striking the ground like falling stars—only to burst back up in bodies of decayed flesh and bone. They looked and moved nothing like the mortal bodies that they clearly once were—and Thornton had no qualms about sending them back to Khel-hârad where they belonged. Calling upon his Breaking, he split the earth in two, swallowing up a half-dozen or so of the shambling corpses, crashing the chasm back together in a surge that sent debris flying. Yasha broke off boulders from below, whirling them around her head like a flail, and striking out where she could. A few swings of Thornton's hammer dealt with more of the dead around him, but he felt like their numbers were too great—and the Holder was too strong.

He turned his head to call to Yasha—when a bright, blinding explosion of light filled the air. He shielded his eyes with his hands to try and see where it came from.

What he saw nearly made him drop his hammer.

There, emerging from Naknamu and dwarfing it in size, was the largest chovathi that Thornton had ever seen, clutching daggers of pure light. Thornton watched in awe as the creature moved toward the Holder.

"Ahmaan Ka," the creature called, and Thornton recognized the voice; it was Kethras! "You are neither welcome in this forest nor wanted in this realm. Your very presence profanes the earth you stand upon. Leave now in peace, and I—the remaining god of creation—will grant you mercy."

The Holder of the Dead turned toward Kethras and rose up into the air. His skeletal face was awash with an unholy orange glow that reminded Thornton of the power of the Breaker—when he had the chilling realization that it *was* in fact his power that was flowing through him.

"Your offer of mercy is as shortsighted and empty as the Vessel of the Breaker of the Dawn," the Holder said with a laugh. "If you think that I will leave now, on the precipice of merging all three realms under my control, then you are just as naive as he."

"Then mercy is too good for you," the Binder replied, and he raised his arms up, palms pointed toward the sky. "Be gone."

At the Binder's command, the forest shook . . . and a wave of white came crashing in, flooding into Kienar and swallowing up the dead. At first, Thornton couldn't even wrap his head around what was happening, but when he looked closer, he realized what it was.

Chovathi! He thought, almost out loud. *But how?*

Thornton looked around, too shocked to even move upon the chilling recognition that every chovathi in existence must have been here, in this very forest . . . under the command of the Binder of Worlds? He was puzzled, but the "how," he quickly realized, was nowhere near as important as the "what"—and the "what" was currently swarming, relentlessly, over the Holder's army.

A strong swing of his hammer took out another dead soldier as he hoped that, wherever the Traveler had gone off to, there was still time.

✦ ✦ ✦

Alysana

GASPING FOR BREATH, ALYSANA TUMBLED into the room and collapsed on the floor. Her legs had long passed the point of burning and were now numb from the exertion. Far beneath her were the sounds of battle, and she knew that her friends didn't have long; no one could withstand a chovathi army of that size. No one.

She forced herself up off the floor and looked around the throne room of the tower.

It must be here somewhere, she thought. A dull boom sounded from somewhere nearby. When she turned around to investigate, she almost leapt out of her skin to see the Traveler standing beside her.

"Just me," he said softly, almost morose.

"What are you doing here?" Alysana asked, trying to steady her heartbeat. "Shouldn't you be in the Otherworld, trying to stop the Holder?"

"Unfortunately we are past that," he replied. "He merged the two realms before we could stop him, and now he is at our door trying to do it again. I came up here to see if you've had any luck."

"Well," she said, gesturing at the empty room, "two pairs of eyes will make quicker work, I suppose." With an afterthought she turned to him and said, "Unless you know where to look."

The Traveler gave her a weak smile. "I do," he said—but something about the way he said it made Alysana curious.

"Is . . . is something wrong? You almost sound like you don't want to find it."

The Traveler gave her a long, contemplative look. He took a breath. "There is something I need to tell you . . ." he began, "about the Heart of the Two Brothers."

✦ ✦ ✦

Thornton

THORNTON WAS CALLING DOWN FIRE on a group of the Holder's dead when Alysana and the Traveler appeared next to him out of nowhere.

"Did you get it?" Thornton asked. "The Heart?"

Alysana and the Traveler exchanged glances, and the G'henni girl pointed to the dagger on her hip. "We have what we need," she said. Then she looked around at the swarms of chovathi clashing with the souls of the dead, and confusion swept across her face like a windstorm.

Thornton, seeing it, said, "Kethras controls the chovathi."

"I see," said Alysana. She scoured the battlefield. "And the Holder?"

"Up ahead," Thornton said with a nod. "He's walled himself in at the base of Naknamu and is working to merge the realms."

She looked at the Traveler. "I'm ready," she said. "Can you get me close?"

The red-haired god steeled himself. "I can."

"Wait," Thornton interjected. "What about his Vessel?"

"I've taken care of it," the Traveler answered. "All we need to do is get Alysana close enough to use the Wolfblade. She and I will handle the rest."

Thornton's hammer glowed intensely as he struck another skeletal warrior, sending pieces of it flying. "Then let's clear a path."

Thornton and Yasha set about cleaving their way through the swarms of the Holder's creatures, mercilessly unleashing the height of their power. Calling down lightning and fire, Thornton used it to scorch his way through, and Yasha took the fire that he called, whirling it around them like a shield of flame. A few mindless chovathi warriors were caught in the crossfire, but Thornton was far beyond worrying about collateral damage; nearly everyone he cared for was enveloped in Yasha's fire.

+ + +

Approaching Naknamu, Thornton saw the skeletal face of the Holder — and the overwhelming power that was flowing from him. With the might of two realms behind him, the Holder of the Dead was now more powerful than any one single god of creation ever was.

No one, though, told Kethras.

"You are in my forest," the Binder of Worlds bellowed, "and my realm." The titanic Kienari rose and thrust his hands forward, sending wave after wave of chovathi after the resurrected souls of the dead. "I will not see it fall to a greedy, selfish half-god like you."

Thornton had never witnessed chaos on this scale before. The Holder was channeling a great deal of power in two directions: in one direction, with Naknamu as the epicenter, he was unweaving the fabric that separated the two realms and merging them into one; in another direction, he was commanding the unending army of souls that he had called from Khel-hârad. Under any other circumstances the blossoming colors and rippling waves of force would have been a sight to behold—but Thornton knew that they were nothing more than precursors to destruction.

All around them the wind picked up, sending dirt and debris flying. Each of them covered their faces just to see through the growing cloud.

"Do not speak to me of half-gods," the Holder shouted. "You began this day as a mortal; I have been a god for longer than you can dream, *Binder*." With a flick of his wrist, the Holder upturned the forest floor in a burst of energy and light. "I would sooner destroy this realm than have it kept from me. Would you throw away their tiny, insignificant lives for your cause?"

"I would give my life, my very existence, if it meant that all of creation was safe from you," the Binder replied. "And so will those under my control."

As he said this, a massive chovathi emerged from the forest. Thornton saw that it was different from the rest—not only was it larger, but its body was scorched with orange and black . . . almost like it had been through the Breaking.

"I answer the call of my matriarch," the creature said, and his eyes glowed red. From his hands shot out white-hot flames whose heat was so great that the Kienari trees didn't even catch fire—they began to melt. Great tremors ripped the forest apart as trees were uprooted and chasms swallowed hundreds of soldiers from both sides. The energy enveloped the Holder, but it looked like it was taking every ounce of strength that the chovathi had as well.

Yasha grunted under the strain of holding the shield that protected them. "They're going to rip this whole place apart!" she shouted.

Thornton looked at the Traveler next to him. "What do we do?" he asked.

"What we came to do. Our time is now," he said, looking at each of them. "Never forget: we are here because of your willingness to fight for each other, and to die for each other. This is where the road ends," he said, and stood up. "Forward."

Three of them—Thornton, Yasha, and the Traveler—marched

through the flames toward the Holder, who looked to be doing everything he could to fight off the chovathi's onslaught.

The red-haired god stepped to the edge of the shield. Shouting above the roaring flames, he said "Ahmaan," and the Holder turned his gaze to them. "It's time to end this."

The swirling winds of chaos whirled around them. Ashes from the dying Kienari trees choked the air.

Steeped in concentration, the Lord of the Dead looked at his brother. "You've said all you have to say, Lash'kun. You've plead your case. I will hear no more of it." He pulsed with power and strain.

"I do not come with a plea, Ahmaan—just a longing for what once was." The Traveler took a step forward. "You and I share the same soul, the same heart," he said, "but somewhere along the way you were lost."

"I was never *lost*," the Holder said angrily—and his power bulged out with it. "I knew exactly where I was going."

"But that's the problem, Ahmaan: you didn't. You were so distracted by your pursuit of power," the Traveler said, lowering the shemagh from his mouth, "that you didn't even recognize your own Vessel, did you?"

The Holder stared in disbelief as the Traveler unwrapped the shemagh completely and let it fall to the floor. The red eyes of the Traveler—the hallmark of every man born a Farstepper—shone defiantly through the maelstrom.

The Holder's eyes grew wide. "You wouldn't . . ." he stammered. "You . . . you can't!"

"I would, and I can," said the Traveler, and there was a flash by the Holder. Materializing behind him was Rathma—wielding a blade identical to the Wolfblade. "And thinking it would never happen will be the last mistake you ever make."

Thornton saw movement to his left and looked over to see Alysana draw a dagger of her own and raise it up in the air.

"For Miera," she said. Confusion struck Thornton dumb. He couldn't comprehend what he was seeing. Before he could even think, instinct took in. He tried to shout at her—"No!"—to try and get her to stop . . . but it was too late.

Alysana thrust the Wolfblade, hilt deep, into the still-beating heart of the Traveler, Lash'kun Yho.

Chapter 95

Kienar, The Tower of the Two Brothers

Alysana

THE TRAVELER CROSSED THE ROOM to a mural, painted on the rear wall, of three figures: twin brothers, and a silver-haired woman between them—the Traveler, the Ghost, and the Holder. Alysana walked over and joined him at the mural.

"It wasn't always like this, you know," the god said as he looked it up and down. "Although I suppose all sad endings once started out as happy beginnings."

The words cut her straight to the core. She felt them too deeply, too real; she knew all too well about things not working out the way she intended.

She looked back up at the mural, hoping to distract herself from the thoughts.

Seeing it from this close, she saw for the first time the sheer scale of the thing: it was huge, spanning the height of the wall, and nearly half of the length. It was clear that the artist had meant to convey the shifting sands from beyond the Wastes and had done so perfectly. Despite its apparent age, it held up—and, although the paint was fading, the message was still clear: the whole world would one day know the names of the Three.

One detail drew her attention—or rather, two: Each of the twin gods held a dagger that resembled the Wolfblade to a tee. Pointing to the one in the Traveler's hand, she asked, "Is that it?"

"The Wolfblade? It is," he said, and pointed to the one in the Holder's. "And that is its twin." After a pause, he said, "It was his idea, of course." A weak smile showed on his face. "Twins are a rather special thing, after all. No other person in existence knows you better than your own. You think the same, speak the same, look the same . . . everyone around you and everything in you tells you that you'll be the same for your whole lives." He looked away again and was silent.

Alysana looked from him to the mural, and back. When she did, a thought slowly dawned on her.

"The Holder's anchor," she began slowly, " . . . it was never here in this tower, was it?"

The Traveler gave a breathless chuckle and shook his head. "No," he replied.

"His anchor," she went on, "the Heart of the Two Brothers," she said, "is you."

The red-haired god took a deep breath and let it out with a sigh, holding out his arms in weak surrender. "I am indeed," he replied. "And he is mine."

"He is—" Alysana began, letting that last bit sink in. "He is *your* anchor?"

A nod.

A cold wave of realization washed over her. "So defeating the Holder," she said slowly, " . . . means destroying you?"

He looked down and unsnapped the sheath on his belt. "That," he said, and he pulled out the Wolfblade, "is correct." His face was awash with sorrow.

Alysana was dizzy, too shocked to speak, and braced herself against the wall. "No," she choked, as she took a knee. "No, I need . . . I need time to think."

"There is no time," the Traveler said, kneeling to meet her eyes. "We both know that."

She tore her gaze away, unable to look at him . . . but she knew he was right: time, their unrelenting enemy, was running out. "You can't just . . . ask me to do something like that."

"But I can, Alysana," he countered. "And I do, because deep down, you know the truth: sometimes, to save a life, you have to take one in exchange."

Alysana looked back to see that his eyes were filled with sadness— yet, beyond the redness and tears, she recognized the thing that had gotten them this far.

Hope.

Reluctantly she put out her hand, and the Traveler clasped it, pressing the ornate, golden dagger into her palm. Wrapping her fingers around the hilt, she held it up and eyed the blade. *The fate of a god—and everything we know—lies somewhere here, between the handle and the point,* she mused. Her stomach sank, but she did her best to not think about why.

"Thank you," the Traveler said softly, placing his hand on her arm.

"Don't thank me," she said, standing up and tucking the Woflblade into her belt. "I'd rather not think about it."

"You and I both," he replied. "Are you ready?"

"No," she confessed. "But are we ever, when fate calls?"

A smile cracked the plaster of the Traveler's grim visage. "Your confidence is inspiring, Alysana. It is a gift. Take it with you—please—until the end."

"Until the end," she repeated. She gave him a nod, closed her eyes, and held her breath.

In the blink of an eye, the two of them were gone.

Chapter 96

Kienar

Thornton

THORNTON WAS TORN BETWEEN ANGER and confusion as he watched the Traveler slump to the ground. He shouted at Alysana, who was still clutching the Wolfblade.

"Have you lost your mind?"

"No," she said, and she let it fall to the ground. "It was his wish." She pointed past him, to where the Holder of the Dead had been standing. "Look."

Thornton turned, and the surprise that he had just felt now seemed like nothing more than a shadow. The Holder of the Dead was standing clutching his chest—and in front of him, with a hand on the blade in the god's chest, was Rathma Yhun. Beside him was his brother, Jinda, who crossed his arms and smiled. "I had hoped we would not be too late."

The Holder fell to his knees, eyes focused on the Traveler. "How . . . could you," the Lord of the Dead choked. "My own . . . flesh . . . and blood."

The Traveler broke his gaze, locking eyes instead with Rathma. "No, brother. That," he said as he pointed to the young Farstepper, "is my flesh and blood." As he spoke, a placid smile worked its way across his lips.

Thornton then watched in strained confusion as wisps of smoke began floating off the edges of the Traveler's fingers, working its way to his palms. As he watched the "smoke" move, he suddenly realized that it wasn't smoke at all—he was watching a god slip away. The Traveler's body—solidified, statuesque—began to crumble away, piece by fragmented piece, like the ashes of a fire floating to the sky.

Across from him on the forest floor, the Holder of the Dead was meeting a similar fate as his own ashes intermingled with that of his brother's, the Traveler.

Even in death, Thornton mused, the twins would not be separated. As he watched the ashes ascend, Thornton noted that, oddly, there was no breeze.

+ + +

Soon, nothing more remained of either god but scattered dust—and, in the midst, a pair of onyx-black daggers. Thornton knelt to pick up the one closest to him and found it warm to the touch. The Wolfblade, once-mighty godkiller, was now nothing more than a burnt-out shell, like someone had taken a piece of coal and molded it into a dagger. Whatever power was pulsing in it before had now disintegrated along with the Traveler.

Thornton set down the blade and walked over to where Rathma was standing. The Farstepper reached down to pick up the Wolfblade's twin, holding it up to examine it.

"He didn't mention that it would destroy the blades too," Rathma said with more than a hint of disappointment.

"Wait a second," Thornton said. "You knew what he was planning?"

"Of course. Why do you think I'm standing here, and not a pile of ashes as his Vessel?" he said with a smirk. "He gave me back my body when he took his brother's Vessel in Do'baradai, then filled me in on what he wanted me to do. Although," he said, looking where the Traveler was moments before, "he didn't tell me it would involve . . . this." The last word was said softly, barely more than a whisper.

"He didn't tell any of us," Thornton said. Catching himself and looking back to Alysana, he added, "Well, almost any of us." He walked back over to find her kneeling beside the remnants of the Traveler. When he approached, Alysana looked up with tears in her eyes.

"It hurts," she said. "When I would look at him, all I could see was Jinda . . . and when he put the Wolfblade in my hand, he showed me why I needed to do what I did—but not without showing me what kind of soul he was as well."

Thornton put a hand on her shoulder. "He was selfless," he said

543

quietly. Looking over to Rathma, he added, "and that selflessness lives on."

When he turned and looked back, she was smiling through the tears. "My life would be so different today if it weren't for him and his blood-line," she said. "I owe him a lot."

"After today," Thornton said, standing up, "we all do."

He looked at the ground. The creeping corruption that had spread from Naknamu onward, turning the forest a dismal bone-white, had be-gun to recede. "Yasha, look," he said, pointing at the ground. The white that had stained the ground was melting away like a frost, unveiling the browns and greens of the forest that had been hidden away by Zhala.

"I think it has something to do with him," she said.

Thornton looked up to see what she was talking about, only to see the gargantuan chovathi lumbering toward them.

"Kethras," he said, craning his neck to look at the towering creature. "You look . . . different."

Kethras knelt down, his shoulders still above the trees, and looked at Thornton. "I had to take this Vessel when I left my own," he said. "My sister gave me no choice."

"Sister?" Thornton asked.

Kethras turned away and looked at Naknamu. "It is a long, tragic sto-ry I'm afraid." Looking back with a sad smile, he said, "Such is the history of the Kienari, I suppose."

Behind him, Yasha approached.

"Is Kienar going to be alright?" she asked.

Kethras stood back up, surveying the ground. The corruption that had once covered the forest was now in rapid decline, revealing the grass and flowers that it once threatened to suffocate. "It will, thanks to your help, and the help of the Traveler. And of course," he said, looking past them, "the Godseed."

Thornton turned to see the Godseed walking toward them, a radi-ant, godly glow about her. He felt the overwhelming urge to kneel. So, he did.

"Please," she said, "none of that. Duna would lose her mind if she saw you do that." Looking around at their faces and not seeing the queen's, she asked, "Where is she anyway?"

"Over here," came a voice from the distance. Thornton strained his eyes to see as, dragging a sword behind her and clutching an arm, Queen Duna Cullain emerged from the trees in the direction of the tower. She was clearly in pain, but otherwise looked alright save for a few bruises and scratches.

When she got closer, she walked right up to the Godseed, dropped her sword and smiled. "I definitely didn't think I'd see you again after those chovathi started swarming us," she said and leaned in to give her a kiss on the cheek. "Hi, Sera."

"Hi, Duna," the Godseed smiled back.

"Well," the queen said, holding her arms out and looking around. "What are we all standing around for? Don't tell me I missed the end of the world?"

"Nearly," Sera replied. "Though something tells me that you'd find a way to be there for it one way or another." She turned and looked up at Kethras. A distant look came over her, and she cocked her head to one side, ever so slightly. Her eyes clouded over, and the entirety of the forest was deathly still.

Then, from deep within her, a soft blue glow began to emanate.

Kethras, she said, with a voice that seemed to come from all around. *Our hopes lie here, now. You must teach this one about who she is—what she is—so she can set the world right again, for at last, the Great Uniter has come. Long may she reign.*

A whooshing sound came like air leaving a room, and Sera snapped back to reality. "What . . . what was that?" she asked. "I felt like I was watching the world from somewhere else."

Thornton looked at her and could barely manage to overcome the aching in his heart. A warmth went through him as goosebumps formed on his arms. "That . . . that was Miera's voice," he said. "She spoke through you."

Sera looked at him, then closed her eyes. When she opened them again, she was smiling. "My sister's power lives on in me, as it was always meant to: two souls, once separated, now rejoined."

Thornton's jaw dropped. "Wait, what? Sister?"

"I am the Shaper of Ages," was Sera's reply. "And the Breaker of the Dawn. I am the Ghost of the Morning." She turned to Kethras, who had taken a knee before her. "I am the Godseed, and I will see this world restored. Rise, Binder. There is much to be done."

Kethras stood and bowed his head. "As you say."

Rathma had made his way to Sera, taking knee before her. "The Traveler said you would ask something of me when this was all over," he said. "What would you ask?"

Sera looked at him and to his brother, Jinda, behind him. "Though the Traveler and the Holder are gone," she said, "the roles that they filled are not. There is much to be set right with this world, and much that was undone must be made whole." She looked back at Rathma, effulgent power behind her eyes. "Would you, Rathma Yhun, blood of the Traveler—and you, Jinda Yhun, blood of the Ghost—take up the mantles these two brothers left behind?"

Rathma looked up at Jinda with uncertainty in his eyes.

The elder Farstepper came forward, kneeling by his younger brother. "We would be honored, Godseed." He turned to Rathma. "Never again will I try to shirk my destiny," he said. "And never again will I let those I love pay for my mistakes." He stood up and offered Rathma his hand. Rathma took it, and Jinda pulled him in, embracing him as both a brother and an equal. "I am so proud of the man you've become."

"All I ever wanted was to be like you," Rathma said with a small quiver in his voice. "When the Traveler asked me to be his Vessel, it was like a puzzle piece sliding in. I was honored to do it."

Both of them turned and faced Sera.

"We are ready," Jinda said.

"You have always been," Sera replied. She closed her eyes and lifted her hands. The two black daggers amidst the ashes rose up, coming to life with color and light. Out from her hands came soft, radiant light that flowed into the daggers, and each dagger came closer to the two brothers, hovering inches before them. "Just as the Holder was Anchor for the Traveler, and the Traveler for the Holder, so shall it be for you, Jinda and Rathma. So long as you keep your brother's heart, you shall be gods."

There was an explosion of light as each dagger flew apart, forming a fragmented shield around each brother—and then, just as quickly as they came apart, they converged, one in each brother, becoming part of them like the power that was now imbued in each. Both brothers' red eyes now glowed with an unearthly light as they each seemed to have changed in ways that Thornton could not even begin to comprehend.

Sera looked at Rathma. "I have need of your skills, Traveler," she said.

"Of course. What is it?"

She put up a finger, as if to say, *wait*. As she did, another voice came from the trees.

"I. . . never seen more chovathi in my life, and I've seen a lot. You did great out there, son. Your mother would hardly even have recognized you."

Thornton turned to see General Aldis Tennech approaching with a young boy—both of them Stoneborn by the looks of it. As Tennech approached the gathering of people, he slowed down, then came to a stop.

"What, exactly," he said haltingly, "is going on here?"

Duna extended her thumb sideways at Sera. "This one is a god now. Kind of a big deal. I think she even outranks *me*."

Tennech looked at Sera, his face as hard as the stone he was made from. "Sera, what is she talking about?"

"It's true," she said. "I was set on a path long ago, before I was even born, that led me here. The Ghost of the Morning saw it when we first met in Khadje Kholam, and the Holder revealed the truth to me in the same."

Tennech nodded with admiration. "I always knew there was something special about you," he said. He looked at the faces of those around him. "Where's Venn? I want to be the one to tell him."

Sera was silent, as were the others.

Tennech noticed and looked immediately to Sera. "Where is he? What aren't you telling me?"

"I am sorry, General," she said, "but his purpose was fulfilled."

Tennech took a long breath in, and his body rocked back like he'd taken a kick to the chest. "So he's . . . gone," he said.

"He is."

"And that means . . ." he said, more softly this time. "I probably don't have much longer."

"There are some things even gods cannot undo," she replied. "When the Holder was destroyed, his power over me was broken—but so was his power over you."

"I know. I can feel it," Tennech said as he turned away. "How much time have I got?"

Sera let out a breath. "Sunset, tomorrow."

Tennech let out a joyless chuckle. "So this is it, then."

Sera walked over to him and spread her arms, putting her head into his chest without saying a word.

The general looked down, almost like he was surprised to see her. He put his arms around her, leaning his cheek against the top of her head, and closed his eyes. "Thank you," he said softly, "for everything."

"I wouldn't have it any other way."

Tennech stepped back and wiped his eyes. "I've had a long life, Sera—full of battles and glory—but do you know what I'm most proud of? What I'll leave this life knowing I gave everything for?"

"Tell me."

"You," he said. "It's always been you."

+ + +

Thornton watched as Tennech and the Traveler disappeared into the night. Duna and Sera were off somewhere talking quietly with occasional loud bursts of laughter, and Yasha was sitting on a rock nearby, looking up at the stars. He walked over to his sister and sat down. She didn't take her eyes off the sky.

"You never did let me show you how to use your Breaking," she said. The faintest hint of a smirk showed on her face.

"And you," he said, nudging her with his elbow, "are never going to let me live that down, are you?"

"Probably not," she said, and grinned. She leaned over and put her head on his shoulder. She was quiet for a moment, then asked, "Do you miss her?"

Before Thornton could ask *Who?* he stopped himself.

"Miera? I do. A lot." He looked over to Sera, who had just thrown her head back in laughter at something Duna had said. "But, for some reason, I don't feel like she's really gone. Does that make sense?"

"It does," Yasha said, and picked her head back up. "It's a lot like the stars," she went on. "Even in the daylight, you can't see them, but you know they're always there." She turned to Thornton. "That's how I think about her too."

"I like that," he said. "And I think it's true. Besides," he added, looking over at Sera, "I think a part of her is always going to live on—and as long as we keep her memory alive, she'll always be with us."

Thornton heard footsteps approaching and looked up to see Alysana.

"Can I sit?" she asked.

"Be my guest," Thornton said, and moved over to make room between him and Yasha. Sitting down, Alysana put her arms around both of them.

"So . . . to say that I am not exactly welcome in G'hen would be an understatement," she said. "And now that all this business with the Holder is over, I feel a bit like a ship without a rudder."

Thornton leaned forward and looked at his sister. Then, turning to Alysana, he asked, "How much do you know about blacksmithing?"

Chapter 97

Haidan Shar

Duna

IT HAD BEEN A LONG few days, but Duna finally felt like she was rested. After returning from Kienar, she had put it off long enough, but today, she had to resume her duties as queen.

Walking through the hall toward the empty throne room, she could hear the gulls near the bay as they fished for their meals. She was happy to be back, but mostly because it meant things would finally settle down—hopefully. She walked past a pair of guards who opened the door for her, rendering salutes as she passed by. Returning them, she entered the hall to see Captain Jahaz patiently waiting by her throne. He smiled as she approached.

"I believe you'll be needing this," he said, holding out her golden crown.

Duna groaned. "I suppose you're right," she said, and bowed her head for him to place it. "I might as well look the part."

"Honestly," Jahaz said as he looked at her, "you could receive your subjects wearing a blanket and wielding a corn stalk and you'd still have their respect after what you've done."

"Don't give me any ideas," she said as she took her seat in the granite throne. "What do we have on the docket this morning?"

Jahaz pulled out a scroll and cleared his throat. "A pair of merchants were having a dispute that they hoped you could settle."

"What about?"

"Territory, mostly. One of them claims he should be allowed to sell his wares in a stand closest to the castle, while the other one says that it should be his because his family was there first."

Duna sighed. "After that?"

"A representative of the blacksmith guild wishes to speak to you about increasing their allotment."

"Sounds simple enough. What next?"

"A woman from the Flats requests an audience with you."

Duna's ears perked up. "What is her name?"

"It doesn't say—it just lists a reference: 'Aldis Tennech.'"

She sat up. "Send her in first."

"As you wish," Jahaz said. He turned to the guards at the door to throne room and said, "Send in the one from the Flats."

The guards nodded and opened the door. One of them pointed to a tall brunette in little more than rags. "You," he said, "the queen requests your presence." The woman nodded and began to walk toward the door. "You'll have to surrender your weapon," he said, pointing to a sword hanging in a sheath around her waist.

"It's fine," Duna called out. The guard stepped aside and let the woman pass. She approached the throne and knelt.

"Thank you for seeing me, Your Majesty. Aldis insisted I wait until he was . . . gone," she said, as her voice trailed off.

"Any friend of the great Aldis Tennech is a friend of mine," Duna said. "Rise and tell me your name."

"Nessa, Your Majesty," she said, standing. "I believe you know my son, Benj, as well."

"I do," she said with a smile. "He's an incredible young man. You should be very proud of raising such a fine young warrior. I foresee great things in his future."

Nessa smiled and bowed her head. "You're too kind, Your Highness."

"What can I do for you, Nessa? I owe you and your family a great debt after what they've done for this realm."

"I actually didn't come here to ask anything," she said. She looked at the sword in her sheath. "May I?"

Duna nodded.

Nessa reached over and pulled out the sword with all the grace of a practiced swordsman; Duna noted that she knew her way around a blade. "This was the last request of Aldis Tennech," she said, unclasping the sheath. She held both items in her open hands and bowed low, offering them up to Duna. "He wanted you to have this. He named it *Dharak'unum.*"

Duna was dumbstruck. She knew she should say something, but all she could do was look at the blade, the one that she had given him at their last meeting. She stood up, walking down the steps toward Nessa, and took the blade by the handle. "Please," she said in a near-whisper, "rise. I've done nothing to earn such graciousness."

Nessa stood up straight, but kept her head bowed. "You brought us back together—not intentionally, perhaps," she said, looking up, "but it was because of you and the people around you that we were able to find each other again."

Duna held up the sword and admired the edge—just as sharp as when she'd given it to him. "Something tells me that fate would have conspired to bring you back together with or without me. And speaking of fate," she said as she took the sheath, clasping it around her waist and putting away the sword, "you may be aware that there was a power vacancy when I ascended the throne."

"Y-yes, Queen Duna," Nessa replied.

"Then I only wish you'd come to me sooner," she said with a grin. "I heard you served in the Thurian army. Is that correct?"

"It . . . it is, my queen, but that was a long—"

"Perfect. Have you ever led troops?"

Nessa looked stunned. "Just a platoon."

"Great. Being a general is a lot like leading a platoon—just on a much larger scale."

" . . . General . . ." Nessa whispered, like she was trying out the word.

"Of course, it comes with pay commensurate with your rank," Duna said as she turned and ascended the throne. "And a few perks as well." Sitting down, she looked at Nessa. "Like being able to choose your own commanders and captains, for one. I hear there is a young armiger who studied under Tennech and Venn that would one day make a fine general, once you retire."

Nessa's jaw hung open. "I . . . I couldn't possibly," she stammered.

"Couldn't possibly say no? That's great news," Duna said, leaning back in the throne. "Jahaz," she said, turning her head to address the captain, "will you show her to the General's quarters? I want her to get a feel for the place before she and her son move in."

"Of course, Majesty," he said, and gave a slight bow of his head. Turning to Nessa, he said, "If you'll just follow me," and took a few steps for the door.

Nessa, still apparently in shock, just stared.

Duna smiled to herself. She stood up and walked down toward Nessa. Placing a hand on her shoulder, she spoke softly so only Nessa could hear. "Loss is a difficult thing to bear, and you have my condolences—especially for a man as great as Tennech. The world grieves with you, truly. No one will ever know the pain that you bear."

Duna could see the tears in Nessa's eyes as the woman brushed them away. "Thank you."

"Of course," she said, and she withdrew her hand. "Take all the time you want." With a smile, she added, "General." Nessa had a look in her eyes like a stallion let out in an open pasture. She snapped to attention and rendered the crispest salute that Duna had ever seen. Duna returned it. "Now go; Captain Jahaz will help you with whatever you should need. Don't hesitate to ask."

"Of course, Your Majesty," she said, and spun on her heels to head toward the waiting captain.

As she retreated, Duna called after her. "The name that Tennech gave his sword," she began. "What does it mean?"

With a look normally reserved for co-conspirators in a great secret, Duna turned her head and said, "'Holder's Bane,'" and continued on past the door.

The last parting gift of Aldis Tennech.

And what a gift it was.

The End

Epilogue

Highglade

Thornton

NIGHT BREATHED OUT AS THE dawn breathed in, and Thornton awoke to Alysana's hand shaking him awake. He swatted it away, asking groggily, "What is it?"

"It's ready!" she said in an excited whisper. "They're about to unveil it."

"This early?" he asked, incredulous.

"Apparently it couldn't wait."

"Alright, just give me a minute," he said, and rolled out of bed and rubbed his eyes. He listened to his wife's footsteps retreating from the room and heading down the stairs.

As he put his feet on the cold, wooden floor, his mind went back to that day, all those years ago, when he woke up to make chains with his father . . . the last time the two of them would ever work together.

The air today reminded him of how it felt back then; he could still hear his father's laugh, see his eyes, feel his calloused hands. He pulled his shoes on and went downstairs.

Walking outside, Thornton glanced out back to the forge—still warm from his previous day's work—and looked at the anvil beside it. Resting on top, as it had since he was a boy, was the hammer. His hammer. His father's hammer.

He smiled and walked off toward the square.

✦ ✦ ✦

As he approached, Thornton counted nearly three dozen people gathered around the center of the square, where a great cloth was draped over an object standing nearly twenty feet high. He looked up and waved at his old friend, Kethras—who still wore the chovathi Vessel, as well as great, flowing robes of black that reminded Thornton of how the Kienari used to look.

Thornton walked through the crowd to find his wife, who was already there waiting for him.

"Did the whole village come out?" he asked.

"Looks that way," Alysana said, turning to him. "Would you try holding her? She's been fussy with me all morning." She held out her arms, and a pair of brown eyes looked up at him.

Thornton smiled a big, toothy grin at his daughter, and her eyes lit up. "I think she just misses her daddy. Isn't that right, baby girl?" He took her in his arms and rocked her a bit, making her giggle as he rubbed his beard against her.

"I swear she loves you more," Alysana said as she nudged him in the ribs. "Do you, Miera? Do you love your father more than me?"

The baby girl looked at her mother and squealed as Thornton tickled her again.

"That's a yes if I've ever heard it," he said with a grin.

Alysana rolled her eyes at him so hard that he thought she might fall over.

Just then, the village's reeve took the stage on a platform that had been built for the day's ceremony.

"The village of Highglade," the reeve began, "will be forever etched in the history of this world as it brought forth not one, not two, but three heroic figures who fought to keep the balance of creation intact. Of course I speak of Miera, Olson, and Thornton."

The crowd applauded again when the reeve said Thornton's name, and Thornton waved and smiled politely right on back.

"It is for that reason," the reeve went on, "that, in this place, their heroic deeds will always be remembered, and a symbol of their struggle shall be set for eternity." He turned and motioned for two people, standing on either side of the cloth, to come forward. "I present to you," he said, raising his arms, "the latest addition to our humble village." He nodded to the two helpers, who slid off the cloth. When it fell to the ground, an enormous stone sculpture was revealed: the uncanny likeness of the

Heroes of Highglade, Miera, Olson, and Thornton.

Applause thundered through the village with much more power than three dozen people should have been able to muster.

"And," the reeve went on, "to christen the statue, it is my honor to present to you the Binder of Worlds."

The applause continued as Kethras stepped next to the statue. From the sleeve of his robe he produced a branch, which he held above his head.

"This was taken from The Old One, Naknamu," he said, to the awe of the crowd. "A branch from the very heart of the forest of Kienar." He held it high in the air, and as he spoke, roots burst forth from the soil behind the statue. "Here it shall be planted to grow anew; a symbol of rebirth, and of the continuity of life."

From the roots in the ground came a great groaning of wood that began to twist its way up, weaving, snaking, and growing—a rapidly rising sapling which continued its upward movement until it was five, ten, fifteen feet high. Just when Thornton thought it might not stop until it was the size of Naknamu itself, the groaning suddenly ceased—and when it did, a fully formed oak tree stood in the center of the village.

The people of Highglade burst into applause. Thornton, however, was only slightly impressed; he had spent a lot of time with his old friend these past few years, and it would take a lot more than planting a tree to grab his attention.

The reeve took the podium again.

"This concludes the ceremony, everyone. Thank you for coming out, and don't forget to thank our guests."

The murmur of the dispersing crowd was followed by a few people coming over to congratulate Thornton, talk about memories of Miera and Olson, and to thank him for what he did. More than a few mothers wanted to say hello to the baby too.

After a great deal of stories, handshakes and smiles, nearly everyone had cleared out; only Kethras and Alysana remained, with baby Miera being rocked back to sleep by her mother.

"It was good to see you again, Thornton," Kethras said as he towered over the oak tree.

"You, too, old friend," Thornton said with a smile.

"I must now return to Kienar where the rebuilding effort continues. We are making good progress, but there is still much to be done." He turned his gaze to Alysana. "If you don't mind, I would like very much if you would accompany me to the edge of the village."

Alysana gave him a lighthearted but graceful curtsy. "It would be my honor."

✦ ✦ ✦

Thornton watched the two of them walk away. When they had disappeared from view, he took a seat at a bench by the statue and looked up in silent contemplation. Behind him, distant thunder boomed, quiet and low. He let a smile spread across his face.

He knew that sound.

"It's not bad," came a voice, "but the beard is wrong."

Thornton didn't turn; he just kept looking up at the statue. "I told them they should have made it bigger, but they wouldn't listen." After he said this, he craned his neck back, still smiling. "Can you stay longer this time? Maybe say hi to your granddaughter before she takes her afternoon nap?"

The flickering, ghostly form of Olson Woods walked around the bench and sat down next to Thornton. "You know I can't, son. I'm lucky the Holder is even letting me spend time at all." He looked up at the carved stone. "After all, it's not every day that a statue of yourself is unveiled," he said, "even if the beard is off."

Thornton looked over at the spirit of his father. He was just as he remembered him in life: sturdy and strong, with a gentle face. "Make sure to thank him for me. How is he, anyway? Jinda. How is he doing with the mantle of Holder?"

"He's a lot better than the last one, that's for sure—and he took to it rather well, I'd say. He and his brother make quite the pair—though I suppose that's what the Godseed intended. It's in their blood, after all."

"Good," Thornton said. He looked back at the statue, reflecting on everything that the three of them had gone through together—all the growing, the fighting, the chasing ... and the losses that they felt as well. "I missed you when you were gone, you know."

"I know."

"It's hard to get over, even though I can still see you. It's just . . . it's just not the same."

"When we lose someone we love," his father began, "a part of us dies with them—but the part of us that remains is what matters; that is how we celebrate their life: talking with others about their memory, treasuring the things they once treasured, and living our lives in a way that would make them proud." He put a ghostly hand on Thornton's shoulder. "And you are doing all those things, son. You make me proud."

Thornton looked at him and smiled, then dropped his head. Looking back up at the statue, he replied, "That's all I ever wanted out of life."

The words hung in the air, met with silence. Thornton didn't have to look up to know that the Traveler had taken Olson back to Khel-hârad. Giving one final glance to the statue in front of him, he stood up and turned back toward his house, still standing after countless generations. Behind it, he would feed the forge, and do what his father raised him to do.

✦ ✦ ✦

The sound of a hammer striking an anvil again rang out in the small village of Highglade; here, where men and women once walked among the gods . . . and the gods, of all things, listened.

Glossary

Ahmaan Ka: twin brother to **Lash'kun Yho**, he is also called "the Holder of the Dead," or simply "the Holder." His domain is the night.

Aldis Tennech: a human general of Khala Val'ur, he once commanded all the armies of Gal'dorok until he fled to the Wastes with his second-in-command, **Sera**. He was killed by a Wolfwalker, **Sivulu**, during the siege of Khadje Kholam.

Aldryd: an aged Athrani and brother of **Yetz**, he lives in the Temple of the Shaper in Annoch where he holds the title of Keeper.

Alysana: a G'henni woman, younger sister to the second-in-command of the Guard of Annoch, **Mordha**. She was ordered by Annoch's keeper, **Aldryd**, to watch after the traitorous half-eye **Dailus**.

Annoch: The capital city of Derenar, it is also called "the City of the Forge" and is home to Athrani and humans alike. Inside its walls lies the Temple of the Shaper. A person from Annoch is called an Annochian, and their army's colors are scarlet and gray.

Anvil of the Worldforge: used by the Shaper of Ages, along with the Hammer of the Worldforge, to create the world. It can be found in the Temple of the Shaper in Annoch.

Asha Imha-khet: a woman who long ago captured the attention of the Traveler and the Holder, she was cursed with immortality through her banishment from Khel-hârad, Land of the Dead. She currently inhabits the body of **Kuu**, one of her descendants.

Athrani: a people who worship the Shaper of Ages and are known for their power to transmute matter, called Shaping. Their distinctive multicolored eyes allow them to be easily distinguished from humans.

Aurin LaVince: a captain in the Valurian army, he serves under **Queen Duna**.

Benjin: a young Stoneborn from Haidan Shar, he is armiger to **Captain Jahaz**. His nickname is **Benj**, and he wields the sword called Glamrhys.

Binder of Worlds: one of the creators of the world, along with the Shaper of Ages and the Breaker of the Dawn. She is the guardian of the two worlds and helped to imprison the Breaker in his chains. After dying at the hands of **D'kane**, her spirit now inhabits the body of **Ynara**, one of her children.

Breaker of the Dawn: One of the creators of the world, along with the Shaper of Ages and the Binder of Worlds, he was seemingly destroyed by **D'kane**, only to have been found to have transferred his spirit instead. He now inhabits the body of **Thornton**.

Breaking (power): Gifted by the Breaker and wielded by Khyth, it allows the user to move or reshape matter, but not to change its essence. It can be learned by anyone and is not limited to those born of Khyth blood. (See also **the Breaking**.)

the Breaking: a ritual undergone by Khyth apprentices that serves to increase their ability to wield the power of the Otherworld. The ritual is often fatal, scarring the Khyth for life and leaving their skin looking burnt and cracked.

Cavan Hullis: a captain from Ghal Thurái known for his gift for strategy. He followed **Aldis Tennech** to Khadje Kholam along with **Sera** and **Farryn Dhrostain.**

Chovathi: a race of subsurface-dwelling creatures who formerly inhabited Ghal Thurái. They are pale and carnivorous and can only be killed by removing the head.

Cortus Venn: commander of the Lonely Guard of Lash'Kargá, he is a Stoneborn who was called upon to aid **Duna** in her attempted recapture of Ghal Thurái.

Dailus: an Athrani half-eye from Ellenos. He betrayed **Thornton** and stole the Hammer of the Worldforge, intending to surrender it to Khala Val'ur. He was sold to **Djozen Yelto** in a slave auction in Théas, who used his body as a Vessel for the Holder of the Dead, **Ahmaan Ka.**

Derenar: a large region encompassing many human and Athrani cities. It is bordered to the east by the region of Gal'dorok and to the south by the Wastes of Khulakorum.

Djozen: the title for the ruler of a number of tribes.

Djozen Yelto: a Khôl who leads two of the three tribes and seeks to unite all three under his rule.

Do'baradai: an ancient city far to the south of Khadje Kholam, it is said to be the resting place of **the Three**. Its name means "the Two Brothers" in Khôl.

Duna Cullain: former second-in-command of the Fist of Ghal Thurái and subordinate to Commander **Caladan Durakas**, she assumed the rank of general when her commander was killed and **Aldis Tennech** fled. During the siege of Ghal Thurái, her sister, **Queen Lena** of Haidan Shar, was killed, leaving Duna as the sole heir to the throne.

Ellenos: also called "the First City," it is home to the Athrani and is their capital city and the seat of their government. A person from Ellenos is called an Ellenian, and their army's colors are purple and gold.

Elyasha: called **Yasha** by her friends, she is a Khyth of the Breaking who is the daughter of **Olson Woods** and sister to **Thornton**. She was a former apprentice to **D'kane**.

Endar: an Athrani half-eye who ascended to the rank of commander of the Athrani Legion.

Farryn Dhrostain: a short, fierce captain from Ghal Thurái who followed **Aldis Tennech** to Khadje Kholam along with **Sera** and **Cavan Hullis**.

Farstepper: a rare breed of humans possessing the ability to move from one point to another by traveling through the Otherworld. They are descended from the bloodline of the Traveler, **Lash'kun Yho**, and come from beyond the Wastes of Khulakorum.

Fist of Ghal Thurái: a greatly feared and respected army out of Ghal Thurái, it was led by Caladan Durakas until his death, where it passed to **Duna Cullain**. Alternatively referred to as "the Fist of Thurái," or simply "the Fist."

Gal'behem: the mountain range that surrounds Khala Val'ur in Gal'dorok. Its name means "the Great Serpent."

Gal'dorok: A large region encompassing many human and Khyth cities. It is bordered on the east by the Tashkar Sea, to the west by the region of Derenar, and to the south by the Wastes of Khulakorum. Its name means "Great Pinnacle."

Ghaja Rus: a G'henni magistrate of Théas who made his fortune from the slave trade. He had former dealings with Khala Val'ur through **Aldis**

Tennech. His men were responsible for the attempted selling of **Mordha** and **Alysana** when the two were little girls.

Ghal Thurái: also called "the Mouth of the Deep," it is a Khyth city built into a mountain. A person from Ghal Thurái is called a Thurian, and their army's colors are copper and white.

G'hen: A city that borders the Wastes of Khulakorum. Its people are known for their dark skin. A person from G'hen is called a G'henni.

Ghost of the Morning: see **Asha Imha-khet**.

Gwarái: An ancient beast created by the Breaker of the Dawn in order to hunt down Athrani. They feed on the blood of Shapers and can be used to absorb their powers. They were believed to be hunted to extinction during the Shaping War, but methods to bring them back were discovered by High Khyth **Yetz**.

Haidan Shar: A city east of Ghal Thurái, also called "the Gem of the East," it is a prosperous city that has grown from a once-simple fishing village. A person from Haidan Shar is called a Sharian, and their army's colors are blue and white.

Haldir: Lieutenant commander of the army of Khala Val'ur under **Aurin LaVince**, and commander of the artillery.

Half-eye: A derogatory title given to one born to an Athrani father and a human mother. One of their eyes appears human, while the other appears Athrani (with a second ring of color behind the first). They are capable of Shaping.

Hammer of the Worldforge: an ancient artifact that the Shaper of Ages used to create the world, along with the Anvil of the Worldforge. Collectively they are referred to as the Pieces of the Worldforge.

Hand of the Black Dawn: The name of those who serve the Breaker of the Dawn and seek to free Him. They are led by Khyth, but humans are drawn to them as well. They operate primarily out of Khala Val'ur.

Hedjetti: the title for the ruler of one tribe. The singular form is *Hedjetten*.

Highglade: a village to the east of Lusk whose claim to fame is **Olson Woods**, a blacksmith of great renown. A person from Highglade is called a Highglader.

the Holder: see **Ahmaan Ka**.

Jahaz: a captain in the Sharian army, now advisor to Queen **Duna**.

Jinda Yhun: Captain of the Guard of Annoch. He is a Farstepper from beyond the Wastes, and brother to **Rathma Yhun**.

Keeper: A title given to an Athrani who is charged with the protection of the Temple of the Shaper found in their city. There is one Keeper for every temple, and there is typically one temple in any given city where Athrani are found.

Kethras: a Kienari male, brother to **Ynara** and son of **the Mother**.

Khadje Kholam: a city situated near the northern end of the Wastes of Khulakorum, it is a large tribal city and the current seat of the ruler of several tribes, **Djozen Yelto**. To its west is K'har, and to its east is Menat.

Khala Val'ur: also called "the Sunken City," it is the capital city of the Khyth, as well as the capital city of Gal'dorok. A person from Khala Val'ur is called a Valurian, and their army's colors are black and white.

K'har: a tribal city to the west of Khadje Kholam. One of the tribes in the area is the Ohmati.

Khel-hârad: the Land of the Dead, whose keeper is the Holder of the Dead.

Khôl: the language spoken in Khadje Kholam and some of the tribal cities nearby. It is also used as a term for someone from Khadje Kholam.

Khyth (title): one who has undergone the ritual of the Breaking in order to gain access to the power of the Otherworld. Above this title exist Master Khyth and High Khyth.

Khyth (people): a people who worship the Breaker of the Dawn and are known for their power to move and manipulate matter, called Breaking. Their eyes resemble smoke and are inherited by their offspring.

Kienar: a small forest near the Talvin Forest that is home to the **Kienari**.

Kienari: Creatures of stealth and mystery, much taller than humans, who call the forest of Kienar home. They are often described as cat-like, with fine black fur and tails. Their night vision is exceptional and uses heat rather than light to locate their prey. They are master marksmen and feel at home in the trees.

Kunas: Master Khyth of Ghal Thurái, he was sent to the city shortly after his Breaking. He was next in line after **Yetz** and **D'kane** to ascend to the position of High Khyth, but was used by **Zhala** to serve her will. His fate was unknown following the siege of Ghal Thurái.

Kuu: the youngest of four brothers, he is a Wolfwalker who is still mastering his power. He is able to transform into a gray desert fox. His body is currently inhabited by **Asha Imha-khet**.

Lash'Kargá: a southeastern city of Gal'dorok that sits on the edge of the Wastes of Khulakorum. It is nicknamed "Death's Edge."

Lash'kun Yho: twin brother to Ahmaan Ka, he is also called the **Traveler**. His domain is the day.

Lena Cullain: the former ruler of Haidan Shar, she ascended to the throne over her older sister, **Duna**, by rule of might. She was killed, along with most of her army, in the siege of Ghal Thurâi, thus leaving the throne to her sister.

Lilyana Coros: a young Athrani girl from Ellenos who fled the city with her mother and was placed in the care of **Aldis Tennech,** to whom she is loyal. To protect her origins and identity, her name was changed to **Seralith Edos.**

Lusk: a human town on the edge of the Talvin and a hub of trade in Derenar.

Menat: a tribal city to the east of Khadje Kholam. A few tribes inhabiting the area are the Qozhen, Khuufi, and Elteri.

Miera Mi'an: a young woman from Highglade who has known **Thornton** since they were young, she was revealed to be, unbeknownst to her, the reincarnation of the goddess the Shaper of Ages.

Mordha: a G'henni woman who is part of the city guard of Annoch. She is second-in-command to **Jinda Yhun** and older sister to **Alysana.**

the Mother: often called the First Kienari, and the Binder of Worlds, she was one of the three gods of creation, and mother to **Kethras** and **Ynara** (see **Kienari**). She was killed by **D'kane** in the Battle for the Tree and was replaced as Binder of Worlds by her daughter, **Ynara.**

Olson Woods: a highly skilled blacksmith from Highglade and father to **Thornton Woods** and **Elyasha**. He was killed by **D'kane** in the Otherworld.

the Otherworld: an ethereal place of power that exists parallel to—and beyond—this world. It is where the Breaker of the Dawn was imprisoned and from where the Athrani and Khyth draw their power.

Pieces of the Worldforge: the Hammer of the Worldforge and the Anvil of the Worldforge. Both were used by the Shaper of Ages when creating the world.

Rathma: a Farstepper from Khadje Kholam and younger brother of **Jinda Yhun**. His body is currently the Vessel for the **Traveler**.

R'haqa: a tribal city usually found south of Khadje Kholam and north of Do'baradai. Its nickname is "the Roaming City," due to the transient nature of its inhabitants.

Seralith "Sera" Edos: an Athrani woman serving under **General Aldis Tennech** who fled the Athrani city of Ellenos for Khala Val'ur. Her birth name was **Lilyana Coros**.

Shaper of Ages: one of the creators of the world, along with the Breaker of the Dawn and the Binder of Worlds. She gave up her power to the Athrani so they might defend themselves against the Khyth, who were empowered by the Breaker. Her most recent reincarnation was the Highglader **Miera Mi'an**.

Shaping: gifted by the Shaper and wielded by the Athrani, it is the ability to transmute matter into any form imaginable. Only those who are of Athrani blood can Shape.

Shaping War: a long-finished but not forgotten war between the Athrani and Khyth, which served to drive a permanent wedge between the two races. It has been a continuing source of hatred for both of them.

Sh'thanna: the female Athrani Keeper of the Temple of the Shaper in Ellenos. She is friends with **Aldryd**.

Sivulu: the oldest brother of **Kuu.** He killed **Aldis Tennech** in Khadje Kholam before himself being killed by **Seralith.**

the Spears: a mountainous region in the east of the Wastes of Khulakorum. Its peaks run north–northeast into the mountains of Gal'behem, the Great Serpent.

Théas: also called "the City of a Thousand Towers," it is situated halfway between Ellenos and G'hen and is a hub for the slave trade. A person from Théas is called a Théan, and their army's colors are forest green and black.

Thornton Woods: a young blacksmith from Highglade, son of **Olson Woods** and brother to **Elyasha.** His body was forcefully inhabited by the **Breaker of the Dawn.**

the Three: the collective name for the Traveler, the Holder of the Dead, and the Ghost of the Morning. Their original bodies remain in Do'baradai though their spirits are elsewhere.

Thuma: former second-in-command of the Athrani Legion, he was killed by **Thornton** after attempting to stop him from waking **the Three.**

Thuremond: Lieutenant commander of the army of Khala Val'ur under **Aurin LaVince,** and commander of the cavalry.

the Traveler: see **Lash'kun Yho.**

the Wastes of Khulakorum: a desert region far to the south known for producing Farsteppers. Most of the region is referred to by outsiders as "beyond the Wastes."

Wolfblade: an ancient weapon infused with the blood of the Ghost and the Holder, and that binds them together. **Djozen Yelto** has it in his possession.

Wolfwalker: a human who is able to transform into a wolf by the use of an ancient power, descended from **Asha Imha-khet**. Stronger Wolfwalkers are able to transform into larger, monstrous wolves; less powerful Wolfwalkers like **Kuu** can only muster the form of smaller canine animals, such as foxes.

Ynara: a Kienari female, sister to **Kethras** and daughter of **the Mother**. She ascended to the role of Binder of Worlds when her mother was killed.

Yetz: brother to **Aldryd** and longtime advisor ("Tallister") to the High Keeper of Ellenos, he is a born Athrani who defected to Khala Val'ur for reasons known only to him and the High Keeper. He currently serves as High Khyth.